LIVE NOW
PAY LATER

Also by Jack Trevor Story and published by Allison & Busby:

THE TROUBLE WITH HARRY

Jack Trevor Story

LIVE NOW
PAY LATER

a trilogy comprising

**LIVE NOW PAY LATER
SOMETHING FOR NOTHING
THE URBAN DISTRICT LOVER**

Allison & Busby
Published by W.H. Allen & Co. Plc

An Allison & Busby book
Published in 1989 by
W.H. Allen & Co. Plc
Sekforde House
175/9 St John St
London EC1V 4LL

Live Now Pay Later copyright © Jack Trevor Story 1963

Something for Nothing copyright © Jack Trevor Story 1963

The Urban District Lover copyright © Jack Trevor Story 1964

All three titles were first published in Great Britain by Secker & Warburg

Printed in Great Britain by
Courier International Ltd, Tiptree, Essex

ISBN 0 85031 994 3 (PB)
ISBN 0 85031 815 7 (HB)

LIVE NOW
PAY LATER

For Bill Johnson

PART ONE

Jam Today

1

ALBERT was late.

This was a feeling in his stomach rather than a matter of fact. There was nowhere he had to be this morning by any particular time; the tyranny of school had decided him into a career which made no demands of punctuality or personal convenience. He had purposely flopped the eleven-plus because he had heard that the local grammar school had a Saturday-morning attendance.

'There are two sorts of people in the world,' he used to tell his mother; 'slaves and masters.'

His mother, by the time he was fifteen, was already aware of this fact.

Now twenty-four and living in a bed-sitting-room, Albert was ironing yesterday's shirt by heating a table spoon in the gas-ring and rubbing it over his chest. Orphaned and alone, he had discovered most of the short cuts which make women unnecessary. He could cook a three-course meal on a gas ring in fifteen minutes flat, putting all the vegetables into one saucepan and sharing the flame with a frying-pan and then washing up in the potato water. The woman's confidence trick lay in creating a three-act drama out of their place in the kitchen.

'Feel my chin,' he would say to his girl-friends if he detected the possessive instinct. Then he would say: 'I have shaved for years in boiled-egg water without getting a single wart.' It always defeated them.

Albert struck two matches, blew them out, scraped off

9

the carbon with his finger-nail and inserted the sticks into his collar slots. In selecting a tie to go with the continental-cut grey tweed suit Albert looked out of the window at the weather and decided it was probably spring; people were beginning to go to work without their coats. He whistled a passing girl and hailed her when she looked up at him; it was a pale, early-morning stranger's face, still inanimate and with the make-up predominating; but it lifted as she came alive a little and walked on, encouraged.

Albert smiled and selected the green-spotted bow tie; to the man who sold charm the early-morning whistle was the full extent of his early-morning exercises; everything was still working. He was big and blond and handsome and he had a way with him again today. He would do a lot of selling and a lot of collecting and somehow he would put back the ten pounds he had borrowed from the kitty.

The feeling of lateness came from being broke again. Like most men who dispense with authority and discipline and insist on being their own master, Albert's most pressing and urgent appointments were with himself. If you're broke, you're late; if you've been slacking, you're late; the self-employed man is either asleep or running.

Albert was not entirely self-employed – though this would be news to Mr Callendar, his boss; his card, gold-embossed, would prove that he was senior sales representative for Callendar's Warehouse who sold everything from vacuum cleaners to shoes, cocktail cabinets to transistor radios on a weekly door-to-door basis. He earned twelve pounds a week basic, plus commission on all he sold. And he spent rather more than this, whatever it was; thirty or forty pounds he could accurately predict and overspend.

'The most important thing if you want to be a success,' he used to tell his mother, 'is to keep up appearances.'

His mother, dragging herself off to work with her varicose veins and ulcer, was too tired to argue the point.

Ready now, Albert had a quick think for things forgotten. It was Wednesday, a neither here nor there day. He opened the flap of a cocktail cabinet and wardrobe combined – a strong Callendar line in a bed-sitter community. With a six-inch rule he measured the level of whisky in one bottle and gin in another, noting the figures on a card and initialling them with the date. This one solitary attention to a meticulous economy started him off into the day with the feeling that he was a methodical man. The man who doesn't know where forty pounds a week goes can live with himself if he knows definitely where five shillings of it goes.

And in fact the reason Albert had chosen the spirits to be meticulous about was that for one thing it was easy to do, once he had remembered it, and for another he didn't like people like Jeff and Arnold drinking his spirits for nothing and not replacing. Considering that he was doing them a favour by letting them bring birds in; they paid him for it, but it was still an inconvenience. More than once he had had to stand out in the rain while one of them finished, and there was always the risk that it would get talked about and he would lose the room.

In the beginning it was agreed between the three of them that they would stick to vintage cider which was getting almost one hundred per cent results back in nineteen fifty-eight and fifty-nine; but either the girls had become immunized to the apple or else they had got wise to it and now straight scotch or gin-and-tonic was the usual request. And some of the girls Jeff and Arnold found weren't worth either.

11

Albert clattered down the stairs and across the second-floor landing feeling like a polished diamond in a pig-iron setting. In the big old Victorian house the bed-sitting-rooms were kept according to their occupants' tastes, but the stairs and passages were a no-man's-land of bare boards, peeling wallpaper, and brown paint; nobody's responsibility.

Through a partly-open door he saw a black man shaving.

'Moh'n baas!' Albert called.

'Hi, white man!' came the reply.

Albert ran on down to the ground floor, feeling pleased; he had never seen the Negro before, yet his cheerful crack had been accepted in the right spirit. There was a secret in getting on with people, with strangers, and Albert felt that he knew it. It was a skilled business, a stock-in-trade. He would never starve; if you could sell yourself you could sell anything. He lost no opportunity in giving people gratuitous samples of himself and thus reinforcing his ego and his belief in himself.

Checking himself, checking the effect he had upon people, checking their reactions to what he was selling – the smile, the word, the package – was a continuous process with Albert. As he often looked into a mirror to rehearse his smile, a new wry or waggish facial expression or a new wisecrack, so he looked often at his personality as reflected in other people's reactions.

His ability to manipulate people gave him a sense of power – the first essential in salesmanship. Or acting, or statesmanship, come to that. He also felt that he had all the other essentials; charm, honesty, humility, sincerity. Sincerity above all. Sincerity really paid off; with selling, with girls, with getting out of a scrape.

With the equipment, physical and mental, that Albert

now had he felt like a master puppeteer; for instance, housewives' psychology he had down to a fine art. In the affluent society of today the tally-boy was the new messiah, bible-punching the full-colour brochures which carried the cleansing needs of humanity. You get automatic temperature control, you get automatic time control, you get double penetration supersonic washrays. . . . Everybody was getting and the tally-boy was giving.

Albert was sufficiently cynical to know all this and sufficiently susceptible to believe it. He was trapped in hire-purchase debt as deeply as any of his customers. He would refuse to admit that this was a weakness – it was yet another facet of his technique. If you sell on easy terms you've got to live on easy terms: otherwise where's your sincerity? Where's your consumer identification? This he had explained to Mr Callendar the last time he had been caught raising a personal loan out of his takings to avert a judgement summons.

'Git the goods in the 'ouse, boy,' Mr Callendar had told him. 'That's all you have to do – this stuff sells itself.'

No wonder Albert despised his boss for his crude, unsubtle, unappreciative approach to the applied science of selling. But Albert felt that he also had power over Mr Callendar; if he left tomorrow and took his clients to another firm – or started up on his own, given the capital – he could put Callendar's Warehouse out of business.

Unknown to Albert Mr Callendar knew this and did not lose any sleep. Albert was a good tally-boy because he was like every other tally-boy; and Mr Callendar knew tally-boys. You give them a small basic wage, a Mini-Minor van, easy hours, and a lot of rope. You allow them ten per cent commission on sales and another ten per cent fiddle on sales and expenses and you give them the sack or send them to prison when they go over this mark. Or you wait for them to get their sales up so high they ask for a partnership, then sack them.

Albert was the most brilliant door-to-door salesman Mr Callendar had ever had; this meant, by the same token, that he was a super show-off, a super-womanizer, a super-fiddler and confidence trickster – the last man to have in any business except as a tally-boy.

Unknown to Albert, all the power that he thought he had and all the power the other tally-boys thought they had was harnessed to Mr Callendar and his simple creed of gitting the goods in the 'ouse, boy. Tally-boys to Mr Callendar were just a means of getting the goods in the house. They were a necessary evil in the distribution of consumer goods. Tally-boys had no power of any kind because they had no money. Nobody with money would become a tally-boy. Nobody with any self-respect would become a tally-boy. No man with an ounce of real ability or even with any ordinary sensibility or human feeling could stand on a doorstep in his best suit and pretend that he was doing working people a favour.

The good tally-boy was the man who enjoyed the smart suit and the van and a pocketful of other people's money, the handling of new shiny goods and the vicarious pleasure – not always vicarious – of chatting up other men's wives while the children were at school. The good tally-boy possessed elements of delinquency, amorality and furtive adventure; showmanship, self-delusion, and self-aggrandizement. The good tally-boy was perennially and incurably improvident; when he bullied a woman for her arrears he really needed the money.

Mr Callendar therefore had the greatest respect for Albert as a tally-boy – and would never allow him within

14

miles of an executive position in the firm. He knew by Albert's increasing sales and growing arrogance that such an application was nearly due, but happily he did not even have to waste time considering it. Albert was a brilliant salesman but he could go tomorrow. What Albert didn't know, and what few salesmen knew, was that it was not the selling that made a business, but the buying. The executive brains of any business was in the buying. A bad salesman could lose you profits, but a bad buyer could bankrupt you.

Mr Callendar did his own buying. He bought wisely and well from those companies who backed every selling campaign and every new domestic appliance with a million pounds' worth of advertising. He bought the goods which were already sold by a system of mass-hypnosis through the mediums of television, newspapers, periodicals, films, and direct-mail. He dealt, not with that section of the buying public who sleep-walked their way into the shops as willing victims, but with those equally hypnotized people who were waiting to have the goods thrust into their homes. The tally-boy had no real selling to do, it had already been accomplished; his job was to insinuate the merchandise across the doorstep as painlessly as possible with no mention of money. Then, calling a week later when the customer had had time to become irrevocably addicted to spin drying or stereophonic sound, he started collecting the small, unmissable tally.

The good tally-boy, in the name of a higher standard of living, could trap half a family's income every week. If there was any difficulty in collecting the money, the good tally-boy could bully and threaten the length of a garden path and bring out the neighbours – the most effective system of blackmail; or if that failed he was backed, because of the agreement which no hypnotized person remembered signing, with all the terrifying paraphernalia of the law from solicitors' letters to county court summonses and even prison. The good tally-boy, in Mr Callendar's opinion, was a low but essential form of life and Albert was the best tally-boy he had ever had.

Albert, starting his day and checking his charm and his power, was totally unaware of this view of himself – and his brother tally-boys Jeff and Arnold – held by their boss. If he had any knowledge of any part of the truth about himself and his job he successfully submerged it in the remotest regions of his subconscious. He was cynical about the people he trapped into high living on easy terms but was ignorant and blind to the fact that he was equally trapped by the same glossy snares. To keep up appearances, Albert was in debt up to his ears.

Besides such small things as electric razors, transistor radios, tape recorders, typewriters, radiograms, suits, shirts, coats, and shoes, there was a car which he was now running and another which had been reclaimed by the HP company but on which he still had a two-hundred pound liability. Had Albert kept up all his payments – an impossibility since he no longer knew what they were – his total weekly outgoings of easy payments would have totalled twenty-two pounds a week; ten pounds a week more than his basic wage.

And on top of all this, after two years he still owed ten pounds for his mother's funeral.

Albert was very late indeed and it was getting later.

CALLENDAR'S Warehouse was a shabby double-fronted shop with its windows partly painted out and partly smashed in. It stood in a smoke-blackened street of terraced houses and small shops opposite a large, grim prison-like building which had once been a cardboard box factory. This was one of the few remaining depressed areas due for eventual demolition and development; a criss-cross of ugly streets lying between the modern, sodium-lighted shopping centre and the main railway line to the north. There were old, disused factories, empty blocks of Victorian offices, silent workshops, and sprawling yards behind high rotting gates, crowded with builders' supplies.

From Victorian years up to the late nineteen-thirties the area had constituted the busy heart of a town once devoted to and famed for its gay straw hats and frou frou millinery. A long history in ribbon and felt, boxes and blocks, steam presses and lace was written on the gravestones of green brass door plates and isinglass lettering on black-screened windows. Callendar's Warehouse stood like a traitor in the graveyard, dispensing the mass-produced luxuries which had put the fine arts out of business.

Callendar's shop window had been smashed by an angry girl who had thrown a bicycle through it. It was now boarded up and the timber slats bore the commemorative legend in white chalk:

TREASURE WAS HERE

17

A reminder obscure to the passers-by but clear, indelible, and painful to Albert Argyle, who knew what it meant.

Jeff and Arnold were in the showroom selecting wares for the day and at the same time listening to Mr Callendar who stood at the counter chatting up a new customer. The young woman, pretty, nicely-shaped, was plainly ill at ease and had not yet been indoctrinated into credit buying. The state of strain which resulted from this was composed of many subtle elements. Many contributory facts of which they were all aware, but which could not be allowed to emerge baldly. She wanted some things and she hadn't the money to pay for them. She couldn't admit this outright. If she had had the money she would not have come to Callendar's at all but would have gone to one of the many shops in the town which offered a wider choice and lower prices. Mr Callendar couldn't admit this. She had been recommended to Callendar's by a similarly hard-up friend who consistently defaulted on her payments. Neither of them could mention this.

'I heard your stuff was very good,' Coral Wentworth was saying.

'The best, madam,' Mr Callendar assured her. 'We only have the best. You pay a little more for quality and it's worth it in the long run. . . .'

Coral began to relax; Marjorie was right, it was quite a nice firm to deal with once you got inside. Mr Callendar began to relax; he fully appreciated that the few customers who began by visiting his blind-fronted shop looked both ways before entering. Credit buying was the accepted thing these days, but so was prompt treatment for venereal disease and nobody liked to be seen going in.

'I'd like to see some children's clothing,' Coral told

him. 'School blazers, trousers, dresses, and so forth – some shoes.'

'Yes, of course – you can't afford inferior quality there. The youngsters go through clothes like a tank, these days – of course you realize,' Mr Callendar added, apologetically, 'we don't deal in cash, here, Mrs Wentworth – you don't object to weekly payments, do you? The usual shilling in the pound – most people do it these days and it's not missed. You can have twenty pounds worth of stuff for one pound a week – after all, who wants to save up for things these days? By the time you get it you may not be here with things as they are – and incidentally if anybody drops an atom bomb before you've finished paying we automatically cancel the account.'

'I see,' Coral said. Then, at the look of strain on Mr Callendar's face, she realized that he had made a joke. She laughed. 'Oh yes, I see!'

Mr Callendar laughed also and so did Jeff and Arnold and Hetty behind the cash desk who, until now, had kept a discreet silence and made an elaborate pretence of not noticing there was a customer in the shop.

Now that the ice was broken, Mr Callendar was happy to include his staff in the transaction. It was not really a counter trade, most of their customers were prepared to shop from catalogues or samples taken to their door; but the few who came to the warehouse he liked to attend to himself and try to preserve some kind of normality.

The door-to-door salesman had a technique unsuited to counter service. It was not that he wasn't at home in a shop, he was at home anywhere – that was the trouble. The tally-boy technique was essentially theatrical and familiar; it was related to the technique of the variety uncle, the quiz-master, the phoney let's-get-together man. 'Good morning, darling, I've brought you some black undies that'll drive your husband raving mad,' was often acceptable in the intimacy of the home between a tally-boy and an otherwise bored housewife, but over the counter with other people present it could lose customers.

Women like Mrs Wentworth had to be inaugurated into the system and Mr Callendar was happy to get the process over and done with. He didn't like the selling side of his business; he preferred the buying and the book-keeping. The tally-boys who sold on easy terms and the people who bought on easy terms he thoroughly despised, even though they made him rich.

'Besides getting the best goods money can buy,' Mr Callendar went on, 'you'll have the added pleasure of one of our charming young men calling on you every week.'

He introduced Mr Jefferies, an ageing tally-boy who looked and acted like the old Zube caricature of the villain Jasper Gadd whose throat just like his heart was bad. A polished, bald dome of a head, a fair moustache, and a long chin which dropped in a smirk as his hooded eyes possessed Mrs Wentworth for a moment with a calculating passion which had sold a hundred washing machines.

'Charmed,' he murmured, wrinkling his nose.

And Arnold, Mr Baxter, a large, rubicund, countrified young man with a big, honest, ingenuous grin and an apparently simple mind who said 'Pleased to meet you' shyly enough, but whom Mr Callendar knew to be as crudely sexed as a stud bull once the gate was opened. Arnold, a recently joined trainee, was taking the place of Max who had gone to prison after getting into a tight spot and trying to get out of it by holding a private auction of three hundred pounds' worth of Callendar's domestic appliances in a disused church hall. Arnold was not likely

20

to get into that kind of trouble; indeed he was not obvious tally-boy material at all except to someone who knew the type as thoroughly as did Mr Callendar. He had come in for the interview clean, smart, and bringing a refreshing air of dairy herds and green pastures. He couldn't talk, his thinking was slow, he knew nothing about their wares, he seemed shy of strangers and Mr Callendar was about to dismiss him when he noticed Arnold absently picking his nose.

From this Mr Callendar had reasoned there was more to Arnold than appeared on the surface; men who picked their nose in public were often underprivileged in some ghastly, unwholesome way. Later his faith was justified when he had learned that Arnold had once worked for a shady second-hand car dealer who had been handling stolen cars when the police caught up with him; it was to Arnold's immense credit, in Mr Callendar's opinion, that the car dealer and all his staff had gone to prison with the single exception of Arnold, against whom, apparently, there had been no evidence. Or at least, no believable evidence in the face of Arnold's steadfast denials.

Nobody could look at Arnold and say 'Guilty'; this was Arnold's personal gimmick and but for that one obnoxious personal habit, he could have fooled even Mr Callendar.

Arnold was already proving his worth in the territory carefully selected for him which covered, since Mr Callendar knew more about consumer identification than Albert would have given him credit for, those far-flung red brick slums, the council-house estates, which festered on the once green hills outside the town. He understood the problems of the new-rich working classes and spoke their language fluently, since he also had graduated from one of their glacial secondary-modern palaces; he also

21

wrote their language in his occasional sales memos to
Mr Callendar:

Somefink up the spout on Mrs Fishers washing machine can
we service same soon as poss? Customer flaming. Second time
in a month, init? Can we send bod up there instead of hafting
to hump machine down here?

                    Signed: A. Baxter – Junior Sales Rep.

Of course, Arnold would never do for the residential
districts of the town. The middle and upper class terri-
tories were covered by Jeff and Albert; at least, that was
the theory. In practice, as Mr Callendar well knew, the
tally-boys swapped clients between themselves as if the
housewives were slave girls – not that any of them suspected what went on. Jeff would give Albert two blondes
for one redhead, even if it meant making a three-mile
journey out of his territory. There were other and finer
considerations in their bartering; whether the customers
were 'easy' or not came into it, if they were prompt with
payment; whether they were married, single, widowed or
divorced, twenty-five or forty.

One of the many chaotic results of such a haphazard
exchange of accounts from one muddled book to another
muddled book was that none of the tally-boys knew
exactly where he stood financially and neither did the
firm. There were machines and clothing going out in vast
quantities and money coming in and it was Hetty's job
to give the accounts some semblance of sanity and
balance. In order to do this she had long ago discarded
all the garbled explanations from the three tally-boys
and resorted to equating stock and money by a simple
algebraic system all her own which bore no resemblance
to the facts but gave a healthy end column.

'We'll say that Mrs Granger has paid for the vacuum

cleaner but not for the refrigerator, then when Mrs
Bockett clears her spin dryer we can put that as clearing
Mrs Granger's refrigerator – and vice-versa,' Hetty would
tell Jeff on a Friday night, which, again theoretically,
was supposed to be the night for tally statements.

'That's all right,' Jeff would say, 'except that Mrs
Granger hasn't got that refrigerator – if you remember
I swapped it for a radiogram with Albert.'

'I thought he still owed you a washing machine –
remember that demonstration model? Or did that come
in?'

'No, we wrote that off – it burst into flames, remember? Albert owes Arnold three transistor radios off his
dem stock – '

'Oh, leave it to me!' Hetty would say, and get busy
with a rubber and pencil; she found it necessary to keep
the accounts in pencil up until auditing time, then after
final adjustments she would ink them over. Hetty was a
plump, blonde, placid, happy-go-lucky mum of fifty who
didn't give a damn about the job beyond keeping the books
'tidy' as she called it. To this end she had taken care of
serious deficits by inventing temporary arrears, and large
incomprehensible surpluses by inventing new clients
complete with addresses and account numbers. Some she
copied from gravestones.

'Well, it seems to work,' she would tell her family
when recounting the day's activities. 'Nobody's said
nothing.'

After three years of Hetty's book-keeping nobody
short of Einstein himself could possibly have made any
coherent remark about the Callendar's Warehouse
accounts. Mr Callendar, who knew more about tally
selling than Einstein, made perfect sense of it; he knew
that complete disorder of the tally-boys' kind needed

complete disorder of Hetty's kind to produce something that was approximately order. While pretending to keep his eye on the daily transactions and weekly accounts he in fact concentrated only on the major situation of money in, money out, and stock.

The overall unsoundness of the people who lived on a hire-purchase economy of jam today and the dubiety and furtiveness of the tally-boys who gave it to them was reflected on a larger scale right through the business. With every credit squeeze or raising of the bank rate Mr Callendar creamed off his capital and profits to a Swiss bank; with each lightening of the situation he creamed it back. And ever since the possibility that Britain might join the European Common Market Mr Callendar had kept a case ready packed in anticipation of the kind of calamitous national prosperity which would demand higher quality and competitive prices for exportable goods, wages in accordance with work done – regardless of tea breaks – and unemployment for those who disliked hard work – regardless of their hire-purchase commitments.

Such a state of affairs could leave Callendar's Warehouse with a load of bad debts, a pile of frozen stock and the prospect of those smaller manufacturers who were geared to small-quantity shoddy production for the home market either closing down or frantically calling in all credit. The dark possibility of a population living according to its means on an orderly cash basis was terrifying to Mr Callendar and he had made his plans to get out.

His pretence of being *au fait* at all times with the trivial everyday tangle of the business was necessary in order to keep his staff on their toes. Tally-boys were vulnerable through their sheer inefficiency; Mr Callendar had only to be specifically critical from time to time to create the impression that he knew everything that was going on – a horrifying thought for Albert, Arnold, and Jeff.

'These expenses,' he would say to Albert. 'They're two pounds five over the top – you're forty miles up on your mileage meter, you've charged three lunches too many, and you've duplicated stationery and printing expenses. Watch it, will you?'

Albert would watch it for weeks after that and so would the others, even though the whole list had come straight out of Mr Callendar's imagination. Since expenses also came out of the tally-boys' imagination there was no core of hard fact to fight criticism.

With Hetty's book-keeping, Mr Callendar would interfere only when it was glaringly necessary.

'These infra-red cookers, Hetty – where did you get 'em? They haven't been put on the market yet – and you've got three sold and one coming back for repair.'

'Sorry, Mr Callendar – I must have seen it in a magazine or on the telly. Sorry, Mr Callendar I'm sure.'

'That's all right, Hetty, love. You'd better change it to Crosby's Mark Four cooker – then the prices might come out about right.'

'All right then.' Hetty would scan her books with an appearance of high efficiency, then add: 'Or should I make it Mark Two? We've got ever such a lot of them . . .'

And she would get busy with pencil and rubber and make it tidy; it was like doing an immensely complicated jig-saw puzzle in which the picture didn't matter as long as the pieces roughly fitted together.

Coral Wentworth, opening her first account with Callendar's, was, of course, unaware of all this, but she could detect that it was not any ordinary shop. Marjorie had hinted as much when she told her about the tussle she had had with the young man who called for the payments; she had not said how she got into the fight nor how she came out of it but she hadn't appeared to be complaining. It was just one of Marjorie's amusing anecdotes. Lately, when Coral had grown envious of all the marvellous clothes and furnishings Marjorie seemed able to afford on the weekly payment system and had inquired about Callendar's she had become quite reticent; almost as though she didn't want Coral to be in on it. Or else – and Coral had heard it was true up and down the street – Marjorie had got into difficulties with the payments and didn't want her name mentioned.

'It's fifteen Cavendish Street, is it?' Mr Callendar was saying now. He produced a printed form. 'Just a formality, Mrs Wentworth – all you need do is sign it.' His tone said he wanted to make everything easy for her, rather than: 'For God's sake don't read it.'

To cover the moment as she signed he made a little friendly conversation. They had several good customers in Cavendish Street – was it Mrs Mason the schoolteacher's wife who recommended her there? And at her hesitation he added that Mrs Mason was one of their best and most valued customers, making no mention of the odd state of her account and the fight the tally-boys had had for the privilege of calling on her. Marjorie Mason was a dish, apparently.

'Well yes, it was,' Coral admitted now.

Mr Callendar looked regretfully across the shop at his tally-boys who were still busy selecting their goods for the day. 'Sorry, boys – I'm afraid this is Mr Argyle's territory – '

'Would that be Albert?' Coral asked, adding, at the

26

little man's fleeting anxiety: 'I believe that's what Marjorie calls him.'

'That's Albert – he's very popular with the ladies. Charming, of course, a real gentleman, never a word out of place.'

Coral smiled her pleasure; but that isn't what Marjorie said about him; not that she didn't want you to think every man went wild about her, because she did; it wasn't difficult to guess who made the first overtures; no man attacked you without a little encouragement; and it was hard to see how she had surrounded herself with so many beautiful things on a schoolteacher's salary; although Cedric had to do several part-time jobs to keep up with her; or was it just to keep him out of the way?

'Mr Jefferies . . .' Mr Callendar had noticed Jeff's sulky reaction to the news that she was going to be in Albert's book instead of his and offered him consolation. 'Take Mrs Wentworth up to Boy's Wear to start with, will you?'

'Lovely!' Jeff said, extending his arm in a corny old-world gesture and moving towards the stairs.

Mr Callendar inwardly groaned; no shop assistant did or said things like that. He added to the new customer as a by-the-way: 'Does your husband work locally, Mrs Wentworth?'

'Yes, he's a foreman at the tractor works – he doesn't have to sign, does he?'

Mr Callendar shook his head and smiled his satisfaction; she was trying to make the housekeeping stretch a little farther without her husband knowing; the best kind of customer. He called Jeff back and muttered: 'Take her through electrical goods.'

When Albert breezed into the shop half an hour later Mrs Wentworth was stooping behind the counter with Jeff looking at children's shoes.

'Ah, Albert!' Mr Callendar exclaimed, realizing a little too late that Albert would start the day as always with a rehearsal of his doorstep wit. 'I've got a new client for you – '

'And I have something for you, Mr Callendar – a new domestic appliance!' He could have been on a stage, rubbing his hands and sharing the patter between Callendar, Arnold, and Hetty. 'Economical, labour-saving, well-styled – it's called a wife!'

Mr Callendar laughed, swiftly, but Albert went for the payoff.

'Simple to operate, few moving parts – you simply screw it on the bed and it does the housework!'

There was a moment's silence, but only the time Hetty took to work it out. In the silence, keeping below counter level, Mrs Wentworth met Jeff's probing eyes.

'I think these will do,' she said, with a dry throat.

'Good, good,' Mr Callendar shouted, slightly demented.

Albert now saw the customer and fell silent.

It was then that Hetty roared with vulgar laughter. 'That's a good one! Oh dear, oh dear! I must tell my old man that one!' She looked at Mrs Wentworth with streaming eyes. 'Did you hear that one?'

Mr Callendar hurried to the office: 'You must excuse me, madam – I have to go. I leave you in good hands – business meeting . . .'

The young woman watched the little man hurry out of the shop clutching a bag of golf clubs.

'Social climber,' Albert explained, smiling at his new customer, and regaining his good spirits and his confidence. 'There are no heights these days, you know – you climb sideways along the golf course!'

Coral Wentworth laughed with the others. Getting rid

28

of Mr Callendar was like getting rid of the sober guest at the drunken party. Inhibition, never heavier than gossamer in this establishment, had blown away.

'Well, introduce me, Jeff,' Albert demanded. And in a theatrical aside to Arnold: 'Another of your washing machines is coming in, Arnold – do me a favour, don't sell washing machines to people who want to keep their coal in them – sell 'em refrigerators, there's no moving parts!'

Hetty was smiling proudly at the customer: 'He's a real card!'

Outside Mr Callendar sat for a moment in his car, knowing that everything would be all right now that he wasn't there; they were really all of a kind. He looked across the street at the empty windows of the old box factory and his spirits lightened. A broad white-painted wooden arrow had been erected all around the building to bracket it from the others; a big notice bore the announcement of this valuable commercial site for sale under the banner of Chas. Arthur Ltd, auctioneers and estate agents.

Mr Callendar had vaguely formed and nebulously held ambitions about that site. If the government didn't sabotage the credit business and if he didn't crash, then the chances were he would be able to interest enough local capital to demolish and build on the box-factory site; it would be nice to have a real retail business with real shop assistants and a valuable office block above as a property investment.

When Mr Callendar said he was going to a business meeting he was telling the truth. The kind of men who could afford the time to play golf during the working week were the kind of men who could raise capital; they were sometimes also the kind of men who could afford time out for influential things like local government and the magisterial benches. Mr Callendar's target for today was a certain Reginald Corby who happened to be a junior partner in the estate agents firm of Chas. Arthur; although Corby had no financial resources as yet – something that made him that much more manipulatable – he did have the building site in his pocket and as a strong member of the Labour Party and club he was also angling for a place on the local council. And Mr Callendar was an expert in the art of wooing with a bad game of golf.

Mr Callendar's inner image of the new Callendar Building, all glass and satin-walnut, was rudely shattered by the sound of Hetty's loud cackle of laughter coming from the showroom; the palace of the future vanished and he was jerked back to the necessary now and present. Mr Callendar started his motor and drove away, as though trying to escape.

They were a vulgar lot; Hetty, the tally-boys, everybody in the business. No doubt when she was sufficiently warmed up the shy Mrs Wentworth would soon be regaled with their favourite record on the tape recorder. He had come in one day to find the three tally-boys – it had been in Max's day, and even worse – having what they called a farting contest in the textile department, putting the vile and noisy triumphs on magnetic tape. Max's last gesture before the police came for him was to substitute the tape on the demonstration model in the showroom and Mr Callendar, demonstrating to a new customer, had been subjected to the most embarrassing experience of his life.

Mr Callendar had outgrown those kind of people and this kind of business. He was a common man and he knew it; he had more than once overheard Albert mimicking the 'Git the goods in the 'ouse' slogan. But you could rise above a lack of education and your environment – if you had money. It was already becoming less of a strain to remember his aitches and to modulate his voice in the company of decent people. And it might be a good idea to change his Cresta for a second-hand Bentley like Corby's – he swerved and braked sharply as a lorry came out of a side turning.

'C—t!' Mr Callendar screamed.

3

'I THINK I'll have one of those white nylon-fur fireside rugs,' Coral Wentworth was saying. 'Marjorie's got one of those, hasn't she?'

'And she uses it,' Jeff said, smirking. 'I know it well!'

Albert ignored him and said: 'Oh, you know Mrs Mason?'

'We all know Mrs Mason, don't we?' Jeff put in.

'She's rather sweet,' Coral said. 'In her way.'

Jeff clicked his tongue and said: 'Any time!'

'All right, Jeff – stop kidding and don't insult the customers,' Albert told him. Jeff hadn't the wit or the halfwit to know that if you spoke like that about one customer then it would be taken for granted that you were the same about all of them; it was not the best way to encourage a relationship.

Coral had already appreciated this point and her feelings were towards Albert. 'I thought *you* called on Mrs Mason?'

'She's changed hands four times since she was first registered,' Jeff said.

Arnold, who had been listening with bull-red face and watering eyes, said: 'Is that the one Max measured for jeans when she was wearing a shortie nightie?'

Hetty cackled her delight and looked at the new customer: 'They're a lot of sex maniacs, you know!'

'You speak for yourself,' Albert said. 'I think you're all going a bit too far – especially in front of a customer. I'm sorry about this,' he said, sincerely, to Mrs Wentworth. 'Can I show you anything else?'

'Famous last words,' Jeff said. But at the look on Albert's face he drifted away to sort over his own stock.

'What does it all come to?' Coral asked. She was suddenly apprehensive at the mounting pile of goods on the counter. She laughed, ruefully: 'This place is like an Aladdin's cave.'

'Mind what you rub, madam,' Jeff called across.

'Come into the office and we'll tot it up,' Albert told her.

They went into the office, leaving Jeff, Arnold and Hetty sniggering together.

'What an awful man!' Coral exclaimed, softly.

Albert registered his own disgust. 'They're like dirty-minded school kids, some of them . . .'

Their mutual disgust drew them together; there was a silent communion of common feeling as Albert totted up the cost of the goods. Coral liked Albert very much and had completely forgotten his opening joke; a tribute to his technique and it explained why he was senior salesman.

'Thirty-three pounds seven and ninepence – we'll knock off the odd shillings and pence, shall we?'

'Thank you – but it's more than I intended spending, to tell you the truth.'

'It's only thirty-three bob a week – say it quickly,' Albert said.

'How much does Marjorie – Mrs Mason – pay a week? Or shouldn't I ask?'

'You shouldn't, but I'll tell you . . .'. Albert put his arm around her shoulders and whispered, his face in her hair: 'Five pounds a week – when she pays it!'

Coral's thoughts were racing; it was probably true what she had heard and suspected. 'However does she do it?'

Albert met her eyes, man to woman. 'Oh, you know – it's a bit of a struggle sometimes . . .'

Coral suppressed a smile, but let him know that she appreciated the joke; it was quite different with just the two of them, in private.

'Well,' she said, 'if she can do it, I can do it.'

'Eh!' Albert said, waggishly.

They laughed together. It was the beginning of a weekly relationship which could last longer than a marriage.

Mrs Wentworth was in Callendar's Warehouse something less than an hour, but in that time she had been subjected to the full tally treatment – the familiarity, the vulgarity, the intimacy, the nudging lifyness, the sheer filth, veiled and unveiled, the inauguration, the indoctrination – so that on leaving she experienced a sense of shock when Albert said decorously:

'Good morning, madam.'

'Good morning,' she said, blushing – half-betrayed as though at sudden coldness from a lover; half-embarrassed because she had in a curious involuntary way gone along with the familiarities and was therefore rebuked; half – for there were more than two halves to her mixed feelings – stunned at the things which had been said; half frightened at the amount of housekeeping money she had mortgaged – also involuntarily – on things which were not really essential and which she had not set out to buy. And then she stopped in the doorway; she had forgotten the most important items – Timothy's pants and vests. But she couldn't go back now.

Jeff was peering over the painted window, watching her rear as she walked away. He turned back to Albert: 'Talking of moving parts – how about transferring her to my account? I'll give you fourteen Devon Road for her?' Albert was not interested. Jeff quickly thumbed through his book: 'Eighty-four Hillary Crescent? She's a widow – you can spend nights there. You know I can never spend nights out.'

'Do you mind?' Albert said. 'I like to get finished by six too you know – besides, I can't stand women who only operate after dark. Anyway, I've broken the ice there – I'm sticking.'

'The breakfulness and the stickingfulness, if I may say so, old chappie, is terrific – as Huree Jamset Ram Singh might put it – what!' Jeff laughed at Albert's lack of response. 'But there, you wouldn't know about that – no education!'

Jeff Jefferies's education had come almost entirely from the *Magnet* and the *Gem* of the thirties; in common with many of his contemporaries who went from elementary schools to errand-boy jobs he had assimilated an entire public school world complete with majors and minors, shells, removes and upper fifths, tuck shops, boot boys, heads and matrons, halves and hols, prep and rugger. It had shaped his attitude, his choice of friends, his vocabulary, his diction, his facial expressions, and the way he held his head. His ties and scarves, obscurely striped, obscurely coloured, never quite challengeable, had their origins in the misty ancient piles of Greyfriars, St Franks, and St Jims while the only boyhood friends he cared to remember were Harry Wharton, Bob Cherry, D'Arcy, Ram Singh, the only enemies those rotters in the sixth. This not discreditable veneer was, however, only eggshell . thick and lacked the strengthening qualities of the real thing of creed and code, heredity and tradition; Jeff Jefferies – the yolk, that is – remained a soft gooey amalgam of errand-boy smut and workaday vulgarity; the fictitious boy had never matured into a fictitious man. Jeff had grown slowly and naturally, dirty joke by sexual malpractice, into the tally-boy slot; he could still quote in dog Latin, still maintain a 'varsity accent, but he could also speak freely of what he did to his wife and where he had suddenly discovered spots.

Albert didn't like Jeff Jefferies. They were different. They were both tally-boys, they were motivated and activated by the same desires, the same urges and the same shapes – it was the only thing that would keep a tally-boy busy – yet with Albert it was different. Albert could fall in love several times a week, twice in a day; but Jeff Jefferies didn't know what it was. On the interpolated line between masculine and feminine, Jeff Jefferies was masculine; he had no woman in him; he had never felt the thrill of a touch of hands or a gaze of eyes, never sensed the woman's need for tenderness or fulfilment or protection. Love as he understood it was soppy, un-English and embarrassing – as any decent, full-blooded, rugger-playing boy knew. Jeff Jefferies could cut into one of Albert's many soliloquies about a pretty girl he had seen walking in the sun with: 'But did you get there old chappy, that's the point!'

. But it wasn't the point and there was the difference between them.

'Tell you what. Tell you what I'll do,' Jeff persisted,

following Albert, who was now parcelling up Mrs Wentworth's purchases and stacking them on the shelves for eventual delivery. 'I'll part exchange you Mrs O'Connell and that spin dryer I've got that needs a bit of attention – Hetty's cleared it as paid on the books.'

'No thanks – forget it, will you?'

'How about the girls in the basement flat behind the technical school – there's five of them, all students.'

'I've finished with single girls who don't know how to take care of themselves,' Albert said.

Jeff laughed and looked across at Hetty and Arnold, who was now trying to make an old vacuum cleaner work. 'Now we're back to Treasure again,' he said.

Albert stopped what he was doing and glared at Jeff. 'Don't talk about Treasure, if you don't mind.'

'Who's Treasure?' Arnold said, looking up.

'Mind your own f—g business,' Albert said. 'And stop yapping – I'm late.' He walked away.

'They were shacked up together,' Jeff told Arnold. 'Something nasty happened – you can guess what. Albert walked out on her.'

'Is that the one who came down here and smashed the place up? I heard about that.'

He could hardly have avoided hearing about it. Besides the broken window, the scars of Treasure's visit were everywhere in the shop – a cracked counter glass, a hole in the ceiling, an electric chandelier still festooned with broken globes.

Jeff laughed again. 'You should have heard her smashing the place up.' He talked across to Hetty, who was also smiling at the memory. 'How much damage did she do?'

'Hundred pounds' worth,' Hetty said. 'We're still stopping it out of Albert's wages – ' she broke off and frowned through her ledger. 'At least, we should be . . .'

She was remedying her neglect with pencil and rubber when Albert came back and found out what had happened. He swore at Jeff for mentioning Treasure just when everybody had forgotten her. 'I'm buggered if you'll have Mrs Wentworth now – not that she'd look at you.' He wheedled Hetty from her duty. 'Turn it in, sweetheart – I paid off forty quid and the old man's forgotten all about it.'

'Don't you believe it! She threw a toaster at him.'

'He doesn't know I'm not paying it off – another pound a week'll cripple me, honest!'

'Well . . .' Hetty pondered over the books. 'If you get that washing machine back from Mrs Mason I'll call it quits – it's been on the dem list for three months and we've got the auditor in again next week.'

The three tally-boys became attentive and worried. It was the second time in a month.

'I know,' Hetty said. 'I don't know why he bothers – the auditor hasn't got a clue. Night and day for a week he worked – I ask you! A firm this size. I can do these books in me sleep. He doesn't seem to grasp this business any more than the last one did – and look where *he's* landed, in a loony bin!'

'I know what's in old Cally's mind,' Jeff said. 'He's got his eye on that place across the street – and you can't raise capital without audited accounts . . .'

Before they left on their daily rounds the talk got briefly away from sex and on to business. From their relative knowledge of the two subjects any sane auditor listening would have recommended a swift return to sex.

'I've got a switch job,' Arnold told Albert. 'Which cleaner do I take?'

'The one that's been noised-up of course – it's got red paint on the handle.' He switched on the old vacuum cleaner and shouted above the resultant din: 'For God's sake don't let them buy it – it cost fifty quid to get this racket without any suction. . . .'

The noised-up vacuum cleaner was the key appliance in the switch racket. Callendar's advertised reconditioned cleaners at seven-pounds-ten and followed up inquiries with a demonstration of this specially wrecked model. The housewives' understandable horror was then quickly alleviated by producing one of the new expensive machines on a no-deposit system. Switching the new for the old was a specialist piece of psychological selling and Arnold had not yet mastered the art.

'You'd better go along with him,' Albert told Jeff when the din had died away.

'We're getting bossy, aren't we?' Jeff muttered.

Arnold gestured him to silence. 'The key!' he whispered.

This was humorous patter which Albert was meant to overhear.

'Oh yes, of course,' Jeff said. 'Anything else you'd like me to do, old chappy? How about letting me reclaim that electric guitar? I know how sensitive you are about taking possession – sex apart, I mean.'

'Get stuffed,' Albert told him.

'.That's what we were coming to,' Jeff said. 'The key, old chappy? It's Wednesday, y'know – early closing. Lots of little shop girls in the coffee bars with nothing else to do with their fannies except sit on them. Or had you forgotten?'

'You owe me ten bob each,' Albert told him. And when he had collected it: 'The key's under the mat. Go easy on the liquor and don't make too much noise – there's some new tenants underneath.'

'Are they any good?' Jeff asked.

'Niggers,' Albert said.

'Ugh!' Jeff said. 'How frightful! You'll have to move, old chappy. This town's getting loused out with them – it's no place for decent people. . . .'

Hetty at her desk was singing Beulah Land Sweet Beulah Land as Albert went out to load up his van. There was one good thing about Jeff and Arnold – they gave him a feeling of superiority which, in this business, you sometimes needed. Also mention of Treasure's name had given him a twinge of conscience and with it a sense of responsibility which might last for an hour or two. With this feeling still upon him he conscientiously checked his petrol and mileage readings before driving the heavily loaded Mini-Minor out of the yard.

As he turned into the dingy street Albert set himself a mental target of at least twenty calls, collecting and selling. He had done the same yesterday but had been sidetracked by a beautiful red-haired girl in a green swagger coat he had seen getting on a bus; he had followed the bus for miles, picked up the girl, taken her to lunch and afterwards spent five pounds on her in a shopping spree, finishing the day by taking her to a cinema, to dinner, and on an expensive pub crawl which had ended at Paul's drinking club. After all that he had failed to get her back to his room, struggled on the front seat for an hour without success and got home tired, frustrated, and ten pounds short in the kitty.

This was not going to be one of those days. He was going to be efficient and things were going to click. The people who were still dithering were going to buy; the people in arrears were going to pay up. He could be tough; when Jeff said he was afraid to re-possess goods from people who thought they could get away with

39

paying when they felt like it he was being sarcastic. Albert was not afraid of anything except time, Monday and Tuesday had gone, but he still had the rest of the week. It was always a job getting started, but once he had he made up for it . . .

A fair-haired girl with a slim figure was walking in the shopping crowds along the main street. Albert looked round at her as he drove, then adjusted his mirror to see where she turned in. Well, there was no harm in starting the day with a coffee.

He parked in the first available space, checked his bow tie in the mirror, and combed his hair. When he entered the coffee bar the girl was sitting alone at a table.

'Is this chair taken, miss?' he asked.

'No – nor are those,' she said, pointing to the vacant tables.

Albert laughed. 'That's what I like – a sense of humour. Haven't I seen you on the stage – are you at the theatre this week? You don't mind me sitting here, do you – I haven't got long. God, what a day – it's all go, isn't it?'

An hour later Albert ran back to his van, jumped in, stopped long enough to jot another name and telephone number into his book, then roared away. There were still four or five hours of the working day left. In fact, this was really the best time of the day to start if you wanted to find 'em at home. Albert could always justify whichever hour of the day he started as being the best hour, whichever day as the best day; whatever kind of a mess he got into he could, by torturing all the various alternatives, convince himself that it was a well thought out plan.

Besides, by this time Marjorie would've got the kids back to school. The twinge of conscience had gone and with it the sense of responsibility, the conscientiousness, the panic feeling in his stomach of being late; while the target for today had unified, simplified, and crystallized into one desirable bull's eye – Marjorie Mason and her fluctuating account.

4

IN the beginning there were two green hills outside the town; one steep and craggy with its back to the sun and its face to the smoke of the town and the winds of the north; the other gentle, undulating, prettily wooded and facing south. Of the two, from the point of view of human amenities and congeniality when it came to planning the vast council estate in the post-war slum clearance plan, the choice of hills should never have been in doubt.

It never was; the battlements of red brick houses were built upon the ugly hill with its view of smoke and chimneys, its coldness on a summer's day, its Siberian bleakness on a winter's day; its one-in-ten gradient which gave the old men coronaries and the young wives dropped wombs as they struggled against it with their heavy prams.

The gentle slopes of the other hill, green, bosky, and warm, were preserved; not by the town-and-country-planning-act or the green-belt or the fact of being a national monument or a national park, but simply because it was a Labour-council golf course.

Towards lunch-time Mr Callendar brought Reginald Corby into the clubhouse for a drink he had won. They seated themselves in wicker armchairs by the club windows overlooking the course, a large whisky apiece.

'I enjoyed that, Reggie,' Mr Callendar said.

'A nice round old man,' Mr Corby said, gratefully. He looked at his watch; he did not want to be stuck with Mr Callendar for lunch, quite apart from the cost. 'Haven't got time for more than one, though – business this afternoon.'

'And me,' said Mr Callendar. And after a moment: 'About that other business – I've got me feelers out.'

'Well you'll have to look sharpish,' Corby said. 'There's somebody trying for an option.'

Mr Callendar put down his drink and his hand trembled a little. 'You don't mean it!'

Corby smiled ruefully. 'Sorry, old man – nothing but the truth. Can't tell you who it is of course – ethics and all that.'

'Not a chain store, is it?' Mr Callendar asked, fearfully. 'I can't compete against those bloody crooks.'

'No – not a chain store. A local interest, I can tell you that – they're willing to go up to a hundred thousand pounds for the site if the deal goes through. Of course, it depends on planning permission and all that malarky.'

'And they want an option?' Mr Callendar said.

'Don't worry, it hasn't been granted yet – as a matter of fact I'm not advising it at present. An option can tie you up and stop competition.'

'Of course it can!' Mr Callendar exclaimed. 'You'd be stupid to grant an option on a site like that just when people are getting interested in it.' Trust my bloody luck, he thought, that people should be getting interested just as I make a start. The old factory had stood empty, uncared for and unwanted for ten years.

'Is it anyone I could join forces with?' he asked. 'I mean, if they're short of capital I might just be able to swing it – I wouldn't object to a partnership if they're the right sort of people.'

42

Corby shook his head and lowered his voice. 'It's not just a financial interest, old boy – it's commercial.'

'You mean they've got their own line?' Mr Callendar was depressed.

'I really can't tell you – sorry, old man. Like to, of course. Friends and all that. Could lose my place.'

'Is it radio and television?' Mr Callendar asked.

'No.'

'Is it furniture?'

'No – not furniture.'

'Have another whisky.'

'Thanks – no thanks. No. I'd better not – busy afternoon you know.'

'Too late,' Mr Callendar told him for he had ordered by signs. 'Tell me this then, Reggie – is it something they're likely to get planning permission on?'

Reggie Corby gave him a sorrowful, reproving glance. 'Now how would I know that, Cally old boy? I'm not on the council yet, you know' – he broke off to wave to a passing golfer just going out – 'he is, old Rogers. Got in on the swimming-pool ticket – luck, that's all, happened to be a hot spring.'

'You'll get in, Reggie – it's a Labour community and they're short of good candidates. You know I'll help wherever I can – you can put your bills all over my vans and I'll help you with door-to-door canvassing.'

Reggie Corby sighed. 'It takes more than canvassing. Besides, Independent's the only thing – that's a clean word for Conservative in a town like this. The working class don't want the hard-hitting Labour candidate any more, old boy. Old boy.' He rubbed it in, self-mocking.

Corby was thirty-four, grey, full of self-interest, without any particular ability except the ability to impress an urbane personality on his clients. His ambitions lay

43

beyond the limited horizons of a provincial estate-agents'
office. His mother's ambitions for him were even greater
– she saw him as at least a member of parliament. A
great-uncle of hers had once been member for Hull and
his brother Mayor of Cambridge before it was a city. In
an effort to live up to their ancestors she had given Reggie
a good education, sent him to riding lessons, and pushed
him through his professional exams in the property
business – which was as much as you could do unless
you had direct county connexions. He had repaid her by
chaining himself to oblivion in marrying a common little
working-class girl who happened to win a beauty contest
which Reggie was helping to organize for the Labour club.

'Well, of course you're right, Reggie,' Mr Callendar
told him. 'It's the working class that wield all the power
today – what with their high wages and their unions and
their strikes.'

'Second-hand aristocracy, old boy, that's what they
are. Biggest snobs in the country today, the working class.
They don't want that "Living wage for the working man"
stuff any more. Call anybody a working man today and
he's insulted. He surrounds himself with the left-offs of
his betters – second-hand Jaguars made for somebody
else, big houses built for gentlemen, refrigerators, washing
machines – well, you know better than I do. Half the
riding schools are full of snotty-nosed gorblimey kids
from the council houses – you don't know where you are
these days. No quality any more, Cally.'

The remark about the second-hand cars had pricked
Mr Callendar. 'Well, you'll never get in with a speech like
that, Reggie.'

'You see who comes up here golfing at weekends –
ruddy shopkeepers, factory foremen, cloth-cap oafs who
don't know one end of a club from the other. Never

have done before the war, you know. Nothing sacred now.'

'How about keeping the blacks out?' Mr Callendar said suddenly.

'What?' Reggie Corby was at sea for a moment.

'If you're looking for a ticket to get in on, I mean? There's a lot of anti-colour feeling. You've got to have a policy that'll appeal to a majority.'

'I dare say. Phew! That's the last thing. You try being anti-colour in print or on a platform – they'd stone you! You can think it but you mustn't say it – otherwise you're a black-shirt. No – nothing controversial, old boy. Good heavens, no! What?'

'There must be something,' Mr Callendar urged, anxious to be helpful in view of what Corby had told him about the pending option.

'All the best things have been used,' Corby said ruefully. 'Free school milk, open spaces, swimming pool – of course it has to be something that benefits their pockets, that's the only way to get a vote these days. But my God, you try to think of something they haven't got already – it's impossible.'

'How about touching their hearts?' Mr Callendar suggested.

Reggie Corby laughed at the little man. 'We're being idealistic, aren't we?' He finished his drink and wiped his mouth. 'Well, have to go – '

'No, wait a minute – I mean it,' Mr Callendar said. 'I was thinking of animals.' Corby waited, frowning. 'You see it really boils down to salesmanship,' Mr Callendar said, 'so it's not completely out of my line. You've got to sell yourself to the electorate with some kind of gimmick – right?'

'Yes, I suppose so.'

'Well, animal-loving in this country is like black-hating – if you see what I mean. People pretend they're not anti-colour – and people pretend they love animals. You've got to appeal to their pretence. Take dogs, for instance. We're all supposed to be dog lovers – I hate 'em, so do most people, but you can't afford to say so. I mean, they shit everywhere.'

Corby glanced around the club-house, nervously: 'What can I promise for dogs?'

Mr Callendar racked his brains. 'I don't know. There must be something. How about dog-drinking troughs on all the street corners?'

Corby thought about this for a moment and Mr Callendar watched him.

Reggie called for another drink and Mr Callendar smiled.

'I must say,' Reggie Corby said, slowly, 'it does show a bit of imagination, Cally old boy.'

Mr Callendar shrugged, modestly. 'It's not completely original, Reggie. Look at His Master's Voice – EMI, HMV. Where would they be without that little dog trademark? Look at Kosset Carpets and their cats – Baby Cham, British Lion, Kitty-Kat – '

'White Horse,' interjected Mr Corby, tipping his glass.

'Bunnyrugs!' said Mr Callendar, quoting a new line.

'Elephant and Castle!' Corby exclaimed.

They laughed together, finished their drinks and got up.

'I tell you what, Cally, old boy,' Corby said with a new warmth. 'Why don't you drop in for cocktails about sixish? I'm having a few bods round – Major Simpkins, he's sponsoring me as candidate, you know old Simmy? I mean this might be what we're looking for. At least it does give us something to bite on – that reminds me, I must ring Joyce. About six, then?'

46

Reginald Corby was about to drive away in his big Bentley when Mr Callendar leaned in at the window.

'Is it a supermarket?'

'Eh?' Corby looked at him, blankly, for a moment, then smiled, chastisingly. 'Oh, the corner site – no, sorry old boy, can't say. It really isn't done, you know – ethics. Must preserve them. . . .'

Must preserve them! Mr Callendar thought, bitterly, watching Corby's car bumping down the hill towards the road. Cocktail parties! Bentleys! And his wife, to Mr Callendar's certain knowledge, heavily in debt. They hadn't even paid for their cocktail cabinet. Ethics! He knew the kind of ethics Reggie was waiting for – LSD. Otherwise why tell him about the option offer and then say that he had advised against it? He hadn't that much influence with Chas. Arthur Ltd, or his wife wouldn't be buying things out of a tally club. No, Reggie was waiting for Mr Callendar to do a spot of palm oiling. Well, it was a good job Mr Callendar had his ethics or he might – he just might – take out a summons against Joyce Corby before she had time to pay up her arrears. The threat of a county court action just before the council elections would be more effective than a bribe.

But Mr Callendar turned away from the suggestion with a certain amount of pride and arrogance. And he wouldn't go in for a second-hand Bentley, either. He might be in the tally business now, but one day. . . .

5

Jeff Jefferies stopped his van outside one of the few
detached houses in Archibald Road. He checked the
number against the list in his book, then went round to
the back of the van and pulled out a large carton bearing
the blazoned name Wondersew. He was in the mood to
sell something.

Luckily, tallying was the kind of job which catered for
several moods; you could canvass, if you felt like it,
knocking on strange doors and making new contacts,
getting them interested in the whole range of goods; or
you could spend the whole day collecting money if you
felt belligerent; or you could, if you were in a technical
mood, spend the day on dems – demonstrating this and
that; or if it was an adventurous day you might pick one
of the sure-selling gimmicks which demanded all your
nerve and personality and come away with the customer
signed up and another commission to be added to the
week's harvest.

That morning's brush with the delightful Mrs Wentworth had whetted Jeff's appetite and sharpened his
personality; he was ready for adventure.

On second thoughts the carton was too heavy to carry
the length of a garden path and back again if there was
nobody in; besides, it was psychologically good to break
the news and then leave them waiting long enough to get
them excited and anticipative. This was actually a third
thought and untrue; it was just too heavy to waste time

on. He walked up the garden path and rang the bell. He was relieved to find the housewife was young and attractive – it made his job easier. It made his smile easier; he glowed at her.

'Mrs Galletty? My name's Jefferies of Callendar's Warehouse – I've got good news for you. . . .'

Mrs Galletty was not so young that she did not know a salesman when she saw one; without actually drawing back or closing the door or even losing her polite interest, she nevertheless stiffened, imperceptibly, summoning her sales resistance. She was twenty-four, well proportioned, two years married and her deceptively sleepy eyes were headlamps on an intelligent brain and a cynical sense of humour. She was a unilateralist from way back and had sat down tenaciously with the best of them in all kinds of uncomfortable places. Jeff couldn't possibly know it at this stage – that was the challenge of the job – but he had come to exactly the wrong person to try out the Wondersew lark. For one thing she knew all about it.

'Do you remember the Wondersew slogan contest we ran a few weeks ago, madam?' Jeff asked her. 'Well, I have to congratulate you – you've been very lucky!'

'Oh?' Her face slowly lightened and brightened with a thrill of sheer pleasure. Her husband, or any of the friends she had made in the old B-the-B campaign would have run at this stage. Jeff relaxed; the sale was as good as made.

'I've got the new Wondersew machine in the van now – you may care to be looking at the leaflet while I get it.' And producing the leaflet: 'You see it's an all-electric machine – straight sewing, embroidery, crochet, pleating, smocking – '

'You liked my slogan, then?' Mrs Galletty said. 'I

49

hoped you would. You get the machine, I'll get the table ready – is it a three-pin plug or a two-pin?'

'I'll see to that, dear – just leave the door open. . . .'

When Jeff had gone back to his van, Mrs Galletty flew through her house and picked up the telephone.

'Daisy! He's here! Hurry up. . . .'

When Jeff came in with the machine the young woman was perched on the end of a settee with her legs crossed. 'You will have a cigarette, won't you? Coffee? I'll fix it while you're setting it up – ' she gazed at the machine as he withdrew it from the carton, enraptured: 'It's really what I always wanted! Do you know I've never won anything before – fancy getting first prize!'

'Ah, well, your slogan was very good – brilliant, one of our directors said – but it didn't quite win first prize, darling. Very nearly, but not quite.'

Mrs Galletty looked puzzled. 'But I thought this was my prize?'

'Well, in a way it is, angel – you don't have to be disappointed. You are on ordinary mains, I suppose – two-thirty volts, fifty cycles. There, let's plug it in. . . .'

She waited. He plugged in the lead, turned a switch, got the machine humming. 'What do you think of that? Like a Rolls Bentley, isn't it? No interference with radio or television, either.'

'Well, is it mine or isn't it?' Mrs Galletty asked.

'Now a piece of material – any old panties? Give 'em to me and I'll embroider your initials on 'em – or mine!' He wrinkled his nose at her. 'No offence, I hope?'

'Tell me what I've won and I'll let you know!'

Jeff laughed at her, lit up cigarettes for both of them. 'That's the spirit!' He became confidential, generous, secretive. 'Now, look, sweetheart – I'll tell you the score. This machine as you know – look on the leaflet – costs fifty pounds. And very good value I might say! Why you could earn as much in six weeks with it – '

'I haven't got fifty pounds!' the young woman exclaimed.

'Of course you haven't – that's where your prize comes in. My firm is giving a ten pounds bonus to every runner-up in the slogan contest – this machine is yours for forty pounds! What do you say to that?'

'Just parcel it up and take it away, Mr Jefferies – '

'Ah-ah – wait for it! Not so fast!' Jeff got to the stage of putting his hand on her arm. 'Of course you haven't got forty pounds – who has, these days? You can spread it over two years at ten bob a week or nine months, if you want to clear it up quickly at, let me see – '

'No, thank you,' Mrs Galletty said, firmly. 'I wouldn't dream of getting into debt for a sewing machine – my husband would kill me!'

'Oh? He's like that, is he?' His grip tightened on her arm and he smirked. 'But perhaps you like 'em rough, eh?'

Mrs Galletty smiled. 'I can be rough, too.'

Jeff laughed, delighted. 'I like that! Nothing like a fight, I always say – did you know you've got wicked come-to-bed eyes?'

'Not green, I hope?'

'What?' Jeff detected wit and got back to business. 'Look, I'll tell you what I'll do – I like you. A nice sense of humour. Mind you I shouldn't do this – come over here.'

The young woman obediently followed him to the machine and he pointed to the sewing head. 'Look closely – you see those scratches? You can hardly see

51

them, can you? But it is a little scratched – it's a demonstration model, you see. Quite as good as new – tried and tested of course. There's no fear of it ever giving you trouble now. But I can make a reduction for you.'

'How much?'

'Shall we say – five pounds?'

'Oh!' She turned away.

Jeff slipped an arm around her waist. 'Ten pounds?'

'It's too much still.'

He stood close behind her and ran both hands around her waist. 'I'll take off fifteen pounds – that means you get a fifty-pound Wondersew machine for half price. What d'you say?'

She was standing very still in his arms. 'Perhaps.'

The word seemed to have little to do with the transaction. Jeff tightened his hold on her. She strained away from him and he pulled her back. She turned swiftly and smacked his face with all the strength she could muster.

Jeff fell back, badly hurt, rubbing his face. 'Hey! What's the matter?'

'You assaulted me – I'm going to call the police.'

Jeff felt the ice in his stomach, suddenly knowing the score. The real score. 'Don't try that on me, dear – I've had some.' His voice trembled very slightly; the prospect of the *News of the World* could do this even to strong men who weren't married. 'Forget it,' he said. 'I'm going.' He started packing away the machine.

'Leave it where it is,' Mrs Galletty said.

Now he stared at her, his face still burning from the slap. This was new.

'Sign a receipt for twenty-five pounds and put my name on it.' She spoke calmly, watching him with her sleepy eyes.

Jeff laughed, harshly. 'What's this – a try-on?'

'No – just technique. You assaulted me – just touching me is assault. I shall make a complaint to the police unless you do as I say.'

'Don't be bloody silly – you've got no witnesses.'

'I only have to scream to get witnesses.'

Jeff turned white and the red finger-marks showed up vividly on his cheeks. 'Don't start screaming! That's a dirty trick!'

Mrs Galletty laughed. 'You think *that's* a dirty trick, do you, Mr Jefferies?'

'I'm going. . . .' He had started packing the machine away again when she screamed, ripped her blouse open with one hand, tousled her hair with the other.

'You bitch!'

The door opened and a woman came in; she had been waiting for the scream. Jeff stared at her, dismayed. He knew her.

'Hello, Daisy,' Mrs Galletty welcomed her friend. 'This man assaulted me.'

'I know – I heard you scream. Dirty tyke – he tried it on me.'

'What are you doing here?' Jeff said.

But he already knew what she was doing there. He didn't know how it had been worked, but it had been worked. He had walked right into it.

'Now you listen to me, Mr Jefferies,' Mrs Galletty said. 'Daisy's husband went to prison because her little boy sent in one of your precious Wondersew slogans – oh yes he did! Summonses, judgement summonses, commitment – the lot. He went on short time and couldn't keep up the payments. Now you just sign the receipt.' She smiled at her friend. 'We'll flog it for what it's worth and share the proceeds – okay?'

'You could go to prison for this!' Jeff told them.

'But you've got no witnesses, darling, angel, sweet-heart – lover boy!' Mrs Galletty told him.

Jeff opened his receipt book.

Crumbs! he thought.

The two women looked at each other across his bent bald head as he wrote. It would be something to giggle about at the next pacifist demonstration.

6

THE din and the debris, the roadworks and the demolitions taking place where the condemned roads of the town met the new developments all combined to give the noise, the appearance, and the activity of a grisly, barbarous battlefield where some bloody last stand was taking place.

A pioneer corps was busy with picks and shovels, a trench-digging machine lumbered back and forth like a blinded tank, heads in steel white helmets were moving to and fro in slit trenches while incongruously neat and natty gents were manipulating theodolites, aiming and sighting them like new slim-line machine guns at other young men who stood, unoffended, holding red-and-white striped poles and waiting, it seemed, to be shot.

On the fringe of this holocaust six terraced cottages stood in a row awaiting execution. Arnold Baxter stood at the door of one of these; he was holding the noised-up vacuum cleaner and banging a brightly-shone brass knocker. Behind him the god-awful row was punctuated by the staccato bursts of pneumatic-drills; banging the door seemed somehow superfluous – he couldn't even hear it himself.

It was some tortured moments before he noticed the neatly-printed card in the letter-box:

'Gone to the Garden of Rest – Miss Riley.'

Arnold thought about this for a moment; it conjured up various understandable possibilities; but then, remembering, he turned and scanned the square. On the far side of the raging battle an oasis of trees could be seen, shrouded at the moment in dust and smoke like a bizarre detail from the *Four Horsemen of the Apocalypse*.

Arnold replaced the cleaner in his van, then picked his way across the battlefield towards the garden.

The elderly and infirm inhabitants of the square sat in troupes in a rustic shelter in the garden, placidly chatting.

'Surely you remember Ada?' Miss Riley was saying to a woman companion. 'She was the wild one of the Frisbys. Always gadding off to funerals and such like. I don't believe she even had arthritis.'

'Was that the one who finally married that retired policeman with one kidney and a huge pension and went off to live at Worthing?'

'Now you've got her!' Miss Riley exclaimed. Then: 'What was I saying about her?'

'Look out!' her friend explained. 'Here comes old hot-rod!'

The two old ladies watched the approach of a motorized invalid carriage which came snorting across the square towards them, its driver leaning forward over the wheel, his beard, scarf, and hair flying in the breeze.

'Pretend you haven't seen him,' Miss Riley muttered. 'or we'll get bored to death with Villiers's engines and two-stroke three-wheelers . . .'

But hot-rod's target was the group of fellow motorized invalids at the far end of the shelter.

'They've condemned the tree!' he quavered, before cutting his engine. 'They're going to chop it down!'

'Nonsense!'

'Poppycock, my dear fellow – they're just trying to demoralize you – '

'That's what it is – the Turks used the same tactics.'

'Then why have they painted a white cross on it?' hot-rod demanded. 'Don't take my word for it. Come and see for yourselves . . .'

The invalid carriages, pedalled, hand-driven, and motorized, all started into motion across the square, followed by a vanguard of bath-chairs pushed by faithful friends glad of the support.

'Did you hear that?' Miss Riley said. 'They're going to chop down the tree!'

'Come!' her friend pleaded. 'We must stop them!'

'Miss Riley!' Arnold called, meeting the group of elderly men and women as they hurried away from the shelter.

'I'm Miss Riley, young man?'

'I've got your vacuum cleaner – '

'It will have to wait, young man – ' her words came back to him as she trotted after the rest. 'They're going to chop down the tree . . .'

'Lot of bloody kids!' Arnold muttered, sauntering after them.

The approach of the elderly army, male and female, mechanized and foot, gradually, like a developing storm, stopped all work in the square. All eyes focused towards the big sycamore tree which a ranging theodolite had found to be standing in the direct path of a line of digging.

'Leave this to me,' said a sturdy foreman.

Others willingly fell back, including the workman who had painted the condemning cross on the tree and still held the whitewash brush, dripping guilty as blood into the bucket.

'Now, sir – what's all the fuss?' asked the foreman of hot-rod.

'You can't chop down that tree!' the old gentleman said. And turning to the others: 'Can he?'

They all shook their heads.

'Why not, sir – if it's in the way?'

The old people looked at each other, speechless. If he didn't know, how could they tell him?

The sycamore tree had stood there longer than even the oldest of them could remember. It had been tall when the square was still green fields, the only traffic the passing of the seasons. Houses, shops, factories, streets, and paths had been built around it, deferentially and politely; sewers and mains had been laid a respectful distance from its roots. As children its bark had carried their sweetheart messages, as newly-weds its branches had tapped their bedroom windows; it was more than a tree, it was a totem, a family album, a familiar – and for some a monument and a memorial.

'You just can't, that's all,' hot-rod said, short of a reason.

'Where will all the birds go?' Miss Riley put in, helpfully.

'You'd better write to the council about it,' a surveyor suggested.

'We'll start a petition!' Miss Riley exclaimed.

'You do that,' said the foreman. 'Only you'll have to be quick. . . .'

Arnold cornered Miss Riley and led her back to the cottage, collecting the vacuum cleaner on the way.

'Of course, at seven-pounds-ten it's quite old, y'know, madam – not like a new one.'

'I prefer old things,' she said, letting him in. 'They'll never get away with it.'

'Just chuck a bit of dirt on the carpet,' Arnold said, as he plugged in. 'Then I'll give you a demonstration – only don't expect too much.'

'I haven't any carpets,' Miss Riley told him. 'You see it's not worth buying a carpet until they put me in the council flat – that's what they want to do. And I thought a bargain like this was too good to miss – you can try it on the lino.'

Arnold frowned; his training had been on carpet, not lino. Anything would pick up dirt from lino – even this old thing. He sprinkled sawdust on the floor of her parlour and she sat down to watch.

'You will clear it up afterwards, won't you?'

'Well, that's what this is supposed to do,' Arnold said.

'Switch it on, then,' she said. 'They'll just have to build round it – that's what they did before.'

The one way of getting her full attention, Arnold felt, was to switch it on. This he did – then screwed up his face at the noise. On the polished lino the old noised-up cleaner sounded like a squadron of aeroplanes. He looked round at her – and frowned again. Miss Riley sat watching and listening with a happy, but, at the same time, militant gleam in her eyes. She said something which he didn't catch and he was glad to switch off the machine.

'Blimey!' he said. 'This one's a bit noisy, isn't it?'

'I like it!' Miss Riley said.

'I beg your pardon?' He had a sudden awful thought: 'Can you hear all right? You're not deaf, are you?'

'Goodness me, no! The doctor said I have grade one acuity – I can hear every word they say next door if I press a tumbler to the wall and put my ear to it.'

'But you can't use a noisy machine like this, madam – it'd drive you nuts. I'll get on to them at the workshop when I take it back – '

'But you're not taking it back – I like it! I want it – and just look at the floor, all the sawdust has gone. I must try to get some sawdust.'

'There's a little still there,' Arnold said, lamely. 'Look, why don't you let me show you our newest machine and see the difference – I happen to have one in the van. Quiet as a kiss it is – '

'But it's the noise I like! Switch it on!'

Arnold switched the machine on again and the room was filled with the grinding of broken bearings and the clatter of asymmetric wheels.

'Listen!' Miss Riley cried.

From outside, as though competing with it, came the roar of the tank and the clatter of the drills.

Miss Riley's eyes shone as brightly as her door-knocker; 'It's like fighting back!' she said.

Going out, having lost the firm's expensive dem model and with it his commission, Arnold met Miss Riley's friend coming in with a bundle of foolscap sheets.

'You must visit a lot of people,' she told Arnold. 'Will you collect as many signatures as you can and return it to me – you'll be helping to save the tree.'

'I'm sorry, but – '

Behind him Miss Riley had switched on the machine again. Arnold nodded, grabbed the papers and rushed away. The lady smiled gratefully after him, then popped

her head into what could have been a high-pressure ball-
bearing grinder.

'Are you there, Agatha?' she inquired.

Outside in the road a man operating a pneumatic drill
was looking thoughtful; slowly he lowered his ear
towards his machine to see if it was working. Even he
knew Agatha was there.

7

ON the other hand Albert, more efficient, a better salesman, and justifying Mr Callendar's belief in him as a
brilliant tally-boy, had had more success than either Jeff
or Arnold. Having by-passed the carpet he had already
been on the bed with Marjorie Mason and was now
getting off.

'Oh, good God,' she cried, 'look at the time – it's
three o'clock!'

'School doesn't come out till half past four,' Albert
said, 'and Sir won't leave till five.'

She spared him a glance from the mirror as she remade
her face. 'I'm not talking about my husband, petal – I'm
expecting the carpet man. Do you know fitted carpets
cost the earth – I seem to have been paying for ten years!
Do hurry, Albert – did you have to take your shoes off?'

'When I make love,' Albert said, 'I like to feel it means
something. . . .'

She smiled at his reflection, tenderly: 'You are a petal,
Albert. You're different from any of the others – do you
believe that?'

'I rely on it,' Albert said, tying his laces.

Of his target of twenty calls he had made only one; he had made no sales and collected no money, but he felt better. Besides, Thursday was really the best day to start. People had more money on a Thursday, unless they had more money on a Friday.

'Can I take your washing machine in?' Albert asked when he was ready to leave.

She gave him a swift farewell kiss and straightened the bed. 'You marked it paid.' She thought for a moment. 'Or was that Sam?'

'It hasn't gone through the books yet – I just want to borrow it for stocktaking. Let you have it back in a few days.'

'Take it as you go out, then.'

'I don't think I can manage it by myself – not now.'

'But I don't want to get dressed!' She was wearing nothing.

'Slip your mac on,' Albert said, giving her a slap. 'Come on, hurry up!'

Together, hugging the washing machine, they went out of the house, down the garden path, across to the van, Marjorie trying to hold down the blowing mac with one hand.

'You could have put some shoes on,' Albert said, catching the movement of a curtain nearby. 'The neighbours are all at home.'

'There's not one of them got a home like mine, petal ...'

Albert drove away, laughing.

At three o'clock that afternoon Reginald Corby was telephoning his home.

'Joyce? I'm having a few friends in for cocktails this evening – now don't panic! There's plenty of drink.

61

Rustle up a few canapés and we – that's right, canapés, snacks – won't you ever learn? All right, I'm not grumbling – but you've got to get used to this sort of thing – well, get mother over to put you right – all right. No, I can't get home early; I've got to go out – oh, and put on a decent dress – nothing common, beads no. Let's have a little class, shall we?'

He hung up and said, 'Christ!' then went to a hook festooned with keys and bearing the overall label: 'Furnished flats to let.' He selected a key with care.

A moment later he passed through the outer office of the Chas. Arthur establishment and threw a word to the receptionist.

'Back in about an hour, Shirley.'

'Yes, Mr Corby.'

'Shirl . . .' the girl on the switchboard, sitting back to back with the receptionist, spoke without turning. 'Has he tried you, yet?'

'What d'you think – he's tried everybody.'

'One or two have never admitted it.'

'Don't be daft – they're the ones he succeeds with.'

Shirley looked to heaven. 'I shall never understand married men. I'd rather live with a bachelor.'

'She idolizes him,' the telephonist said. 'Hello, yes – Chas. Arthur estate office, putting you through. But he treats her like something the cat brought in. Of course, his mother doesn't help – Lady Muck.'

'I shall marry an orphan.'

'She's terrified of upsetting him. Just a moment, Mr Arthur, I'm ringing them for you. You should hear her when she rings him – you'd think she was asking for royalty instead of her own husband. "Don't disturb him if he's busy, I'll call later" . . . I'm putting you through now, Mr Arthur.'

'I wonder what she'd do if she knew what he was really like?'

'She'd never believe it. That kind never do – they build their whole existence round their heroes. She daren't even ask him for money. She thinks he's a saint and she's got to live up to him.'

'I'd like to tell her the truth.'

'That wouldn't be any good – she'd have to have her nose rubbed in it. Chas. Arthur estate office . . .'

It was almost as much as anybody could ever hope to know about the private life of the Corbys.

Joyce Corby was counting the remains of her house-keeping money when Albert arrived at the door. Had she known who it was she would not have answered the bell, but it was mid afternoon and she was not expecting any more callers after money. She opened the door, still holding her solitary pound note and wondering how she was going to make it provide snacks – canapés, rather – and also stretch to the end of the week.

'You owe more than a pound, Mrs Corby,' Albert told her. 'It's four weeks now.'

She screwed the pound note up, protectively: 'Oh, this isn't for you, Mr Argyle – I mean, it's all the change I've got and I've got to do some shopping with it.' Got, got, got, Reggie would say. The word got is only permissible in certain contexts, otherwise it's vulgar. 'I'm terribly sorry – would you mind waiting one more week till I get some change?' Never say you haven't any money – especially to tradespeople; say you haven't any change at the moment.

'Can't let it go another week, dear – madam. Sorry. I'd get the sack!' Albert felt sorry for Mrs Corby and always wanted to call her dear; not that he wanted to make her, she wasn't the kind. Sex wasn't by any means the usual thing on the tally-boy round; they were always looking for it, ready for it, but there weren't more than half a dozen Marjorie Masons in his whole territory. Most married women weren't interested in it any more; either it bored them or they loved their husbands or they looked down on tally-boys. The sort that were going to play you could tell from the first glance, the first half-dozen words; as for the rest all the charm in the world wouldn't soften them, it would only bore them.

Of course there were all sorts of other relationships; there was the chummy relationship or the gossipy one or the cup of tea and cake one. But this one had always been Mrs Corby and Mr Argyle, even though they were much of an age and came from the same background. Albert had always felt a bit sorry for her; she was pretty, but she seemed lonely and out of her depth in this luxury flat, like a cat in a lion cage. She tried to put on airs, but she was tense and worried and couldn't quite pull it off. Also, not having the weekly instalment embarrassed her; had she been in the same class as the flat she would carry her debts with a fine careless flourish of unconcern. Albert knew that type and could deal with them with a few careless flourishes of his own. But Mrs Corby, while calling him Mr Argyle and keeping her distance, at the same time appealed to him in a mute way. Her grammar, her speech, her uncertainty and lack of self-confidence brought her as close as the girl in the tobacco kiosk; the flat and her feeble pretences, which she seemed unable to believe in herself, held them apart.

'Who's that for then?' Albert said, indicating the pound note. He would never have asked such a question of the class of woman she was trying to be.

'I got to get some stuff in for a party,' she said. She

would never have told him if she had really been the educated woman Reggie should have married. 'Canapés,' she added, carelessly. 'And that.'

'Well, what's most important?' Albert said.

'I'm ever so sorry,' she said, wretchedly. 'Only he's – my husband's holding a cocktail party for some friends. It's business.' She bit her lip, returning to the other problem for a moment. 'Dunno what I'm going to give them.'

'You want to get somebody in to help – a cook or something.' Albert often found himself worrying for her, in spite of her attempt to be stand-offish.

'Are you kidding!' she said.

Then she broke off and smiled artificially over his shoulder. A lady from the flat above was going across the carpeted landing. 'Good afternoon, Mrs Jenkins – lovely now!' she called, in an artificial voice to match the smile. And then to Albert: ''ere – you better come in. He don't like – my husband objects to washing the dirty – discussing private affairs where the neighbours can hear. Their ears are always flapping.'

'There's no point my coming in if you haven't got the money.' The sentence rang strangely in Albert's own ears; he couldn't think of many pretty blonde girls he would have said it to.

'Supposing I can get some change tomorrow – would that be all right – ' Joyce Corby stopped speaking again as the neighbour walked back. Albert, by silent mutual agreement, went into the flat with her.

She looked at the clock. 'I dunno though – half past three. It's a bit late.'

'The banks are shut,' Albert said. 'But I'll take a cheque if you like.'

'What?' she said. 'Oh, well, I don't think I've got a

cheque. He keeps – my husband has the cheque book.'

'Get him to write a cheque out tonight and I'll call – '

'He wouldn't do that! I mean, I couldn't ask him. Not very well. You see, I manage all the weekly accounts and so on.'

'Does he know about them?' Albert asked, baldly.

'Oh, well, not the details. He gives me ten pounds a week and I have to manage – of course, it's ample, really. Only I'm not very good at it. Money seems to run away – d'you know I went into the supermarket this morning and got through twenty-five shillings without seeing a thing for it! Just a packet of soap flakes, tin of salmon, tea, coffee, shampoo, and chocolates – nothing you could really make a meal out of!'

She had forgotten the distant relationship and was immersed in the awful morass of her own misery. She was glad of somebody to talk to and Albert sat on the arm of a chair to listen, sympathetically; it was a story he knew well.

'You want to get a system,' he said, earnestly. He felt methodical again. 'What are your weekly payments – tally clubs and so on?'

'About four pounds altogether – including the bedroom suite in his – in my husband's room. He's got this quilted plastic headboard – it's really lovely.'

'You don't have to pay for all that, do you?'

'I do now. But of course he started most of the things off with a deposit – he's very good really. Only now he's got the Bentley – he had to have it when they made him junior partner – '

'Blow that,' Albert exclaimed, indignantly. 'Why don't you ask for a rise! You're stupid, you are, madam,' he added, remembering himself momentarily.

He was infected by the odd way she had of talking

66

about her husband as though he were a V.I.P. employer; they might easily have been two dissatisfied members of the staff.

'Now they're talking about taking his bed back. I don't know where he's going to sleep! I believe he thinks it's paid for.'

'How long have you had it?' Albert asked her.

'About nine months – '

'How much have you paid off it – if it's more than half they can't touch it without a court order. Let me have a look at your card, dear.'

As she went to a writing-bureau Albert went on: 'You should've got it from us, you know.' It didn't occur to him that he was encouraging a bad account in his own books. She came and sat in the chair with him and together they added up the payments.

'There you are, you see – they can't touch it! You write them a stinking letter – in fact if you wait till to-morrow I'll dictate it for you. Then every time they threaten court proceedings, send 'em the odd five bob – you can stall 'em off for years if you know what you're doing.'

'It's very good of you!' she said. 'What with that and the distraint warrant I didn't know – '

'Which distraint warrant?'

'Well, it hasn't come yet – it's about a suit he had – my husband got. A long time ago. They're coming to distrain on the furniture for it – I don't know what he'll say if he finds out!'

'Whose name was the suit in?' Albert asked.

'Mine. It was a present, you see.'

'Whose name is the furniture in?' Albert asked, businesslike. 'I mean have you got anything in your husband's name – anything at all?'

'Only this three-piece his mother give him,' she said. 'Why?'

'Do you know if she's got the receipt?'

'Yes – it's in the bureau.'

'You're all right then, dear – when the bums come to mark the stuff up, tell them to distrain on the three-piece and give them the receipt to cover it. They can't touch it! You won't hear another word about distraint after that – they won't even pursue it to court, it'd cost 'em money.'

Joyce Corby laughed up at him in sheer relief. 'It's not so bad when you know all the ropes, is it?'

'They can still hang you!' Albert said. He stood up. 'Okay tomorrow, then?'

Worry flitted across her face again. 'I'll try – I'll see what I can do if I hurry. I've got this part-time job – '

'Part-time job!' Albert exclaimed. 'If you ask me you've got a full-time job here – and I thought you had a cocktail party tonight?'

'Well, I can't promise about the money,' she said. 'Will you be angry if you come tomorrow and I haven't got it?'

Albert laughed at her, touched. 'I don't know how anybody could be angry with you – you're just a kid and you're right in it, aren't you? You don't want a husband, you want a father. You shouldn't let chaps like me frighten you, y'know.'

'I'm always frightened,' she admitted. 'I hide in the bathroom sometimes when the bell goes.'

'I know you do, dear,' Albert said. 'And you're not the only one.'

'Would you do me a favour, Mr Argyle?' she asked, suddenly. And at his nod: 'Would you tell me which dress to wear tonight?' And before he could respond: 'Just wait here a minute.'

68

He watched her go into a bedroom. 'Blimey,' he muttered. 'What's the matter with me?'

Joyce came out of the bedroom with two dresses, holding them up. 'I like this one, but I'm not sure.'

'Slip it on,' Albert said.

'Look the other way, then.' She unzipped her skirt and stepped out of it.

Albert turned away, obediently, lighting a cigarette and one for her. The next moment she was twirling in a flowered, flared dress in front of him.

'Not that one,' he said. 'Too much frilly petticoat – it's pretty, mind you – I'd go a bomb for you. But it's not a cocktail party with him and his pals. More the palais or the pictures or a quick snog in the woods. Haven't you got something straight – black, say?'

'Just a minute.'

Albert dressed her in a simple straight-cut black dress with a straight top shoulderless bodice and strings.

'Marvellous!' he said. 'When you've got curves always wear straight dresses. Of course you want dark stockings, high heels and your hair up – '

'I was going to have it down –

'No no – come here. . . .'

He sat her down, got busy with a comb.

'Where did you learn to back-comb?' she asked.

'I used to do this for Treasure,' he said.

'Is that your girl?'

'She was till she found out about me – she hates me now.'

'I bet she doesn't really.'

Albert dwelt on the thought as he worked at her hair.

'Treasure's a nice name,' she said.

'It's only what I call her. Her name's Teresa Hunter –

Treasure Hunter, get it? She's the give-away girl at the Bingo Hall. Well built too – plenty of superstructure. Treasure chest!'

Joyce Corby laughed. Then sympathetically she said: 'Was it another chap?'

'No – abortion. You know, usual sordid mess. And she's very sensitive.'

'Poor thing.'

'Oh, I dunno.' Albert said. 'That's the trouble with women – you always get involved and then you're stuck.'

Joyce Corby sighed, turning her head this way and that as he shaped her hair. That's what had happened to poor Reggie; she should never have married him. She was only a drag on him. She had mucked up his whole life. He couldn't stand her friends and his friends seemed to stay away from her. And if his mother came she always made her feel like sixpence.

'There you are, Mrs Corby – you look lovely and don't let anybody tell you you don't!' Albert stood admiring his handiwork.

Joyce looked at herself in the mirror, just to turn the tears of self-pity away from him.

Albert came behind her. 'What are you crying for?'

The tears came faster at his gentle tone. 'I always blub if people are kind to me. . . .'

Albert gave her his breast-pocket handkerchief and she blew her nose, noisily.

Albert was touched; uncomfortably touched. The only time Treasure had cried was when she lost the baby – and after months of trying to lose it. It wasn't even a baby. It hadn't affected him much at the time; but each time he had thought about it since it had affected him a little

70

more. Now, seeing Joyce Corby cry it was as though it had all happened again only this time it was digging into him.

'Don't cry. You'll be all right, love.'

'Sorry, Mr Argyle.'

'Call me Albert – Maison Albeeerr, coiffures for mesdames!'

'I'd better not,' she said, but smiling now and tucking the handkerchief back into his pocket. 'I might let it slip out – he doesn't like me – my husband doesn't like me making new friends. Outside his – ring – circle. You know.'

'You don't sound very happy with him – '

'Oh, no,' she broke in, quickly, 'he's a wonderful husband – it's just me, that's all. I mean, I'm not educated or anything – he went to a good school – mind you he never talks about it, he's not a snob or anything. But he likes things proper – properly done, I mean. He's trying to get on, you see. He's putting up for the council. He brings all sorts of people here. That's why I have to keep the place nice. Of course, it costs a lot. Glasses, silver, serviettes – I mean napkins. Men don't realize, do they? It all has to be paid for – and Reggie – that's his name – my husband – don't I mean doesn't believe in debts. He's got very high principles – ethics. No, principles. Is that right?'

'Don't ask me! Jesus – if he gets you mixed up like that what's he going to do with the council?'

'It's me, not him! It's I, I mean. Oh dear. I always wanted to better myself – he's only trying to help me. I don't mind. I mean, I want to be a credit to him. If a man's going to get on in local government and all that a wife's very important to him. That's what his mother always says.'

Albert's heart went out to her. 'And what does your mother always say?'

'They're dead – I've only got a sister. She lives up on the council estate. He doesn't – my husband doesn't like me visiting her. She's married to a bus driver.'

'He sounds delightful!'

'Who – oh, George?' Her face brightened with enthusiasm. 'Oh, he is – he's a scream. Ever so kind to the kids – or do you mean – '

'Skip it,' Albert said. He reset a piece of hair which had fallen on to her forehead and said: 'Can I ask you a personal question? Why do you have separate bedrooms?'

She didn't mind answering; she could have been gossiping with an old schoolgirl chum. 'His mother doesn't think we should have any children until he's properly established. You see, we had one or two near squeaks in the beginning.'

Albert smiled at her, appraisingly, mock-wicked: 'I can believe it!'

'Don't be cheeky!' She was enjoying the compliment.

'He's not playing the field, is he?' Albert asked.

'What, Reggie?' There was a small element of scorn in her voice and she was shocked by it. 'Certainly not! You don't know him. He's very strong-minded about that sort of thing.'

'I don't know how you live up to him,' Albert said.

'It's because he's worth it,' she said, simply. 'I'd do anything for him.'

Albert sighed, ruefully: 'Some fellows get all the luck.' He looked at the time and groaned. 'See you tomorrow, then?'

'Are you going, then?'

''Fraid so. Running late. It's all go, isn't it?'

'Thanks for doing me hair and that,' she said. 'It was nice to have somebody to talk to – I don't feel half so worried as what I did. Will you write that letter to them people for me tomorrow about the bed?'

'Sure,' Albert told her. She looked lonely now that he was going and he smiled at her, reassuringly. 'Cor! You look terrific – is it right you were a beauty queen?'

She blushed with pleasure. 'Who told you that, then?'

'My spies, of course – why do you think I come canvassing in the first place?'

Joyce laughed at him. 'You're a tonic, Mr Argyle! Fancy you knowing that. I was Miss Agricultural Tractors two years running – that's how I met him – my husband. He was the host at the Labour club where they give us dinner – I drank half a bottle of champagne!'

'He knew what he was doing!' Albert said. 'Still,' he added as a serious bit of advice from kind to kind, 'you want some real friends, too, y'know. I mean, these toffy noses are all right, I suppose, but they're all the same – estate agents, solicitors, bank clerks, all on the grind, all in each other's pockets in a town like this. I mean, 'you go in the lounge of the Marquis and listen to 'em – "haw haw with their little caps and old school blazers, what".'

Joyce laughed aloud; it was not a modulated or cultured sound. It was a laugh. She was not sufficiently self-analytical to know that she was laughing the tension out of three years with Reginald; it did not occur to her that they were both talking about Reginald.

'You're too good for them, you are. We're flesh and blood, we are. They wouldn't know what to do with a real woman. You don't go for tea and a chinwag in Mary's Pantry, do you? 'Course you don't! My Christ, what a lot of horse-faced hockey-stick horrors they are!'

73

Joyce laughed again; she was laughing at Reginald's mother without realizing it.

'Of course, they're all as phoney as arse-oles,' Albert said, 'if you'll forgive *le mot juste*. I mean, they're as lady-like as hell on sherry, but you get a few vintage ciders into them when the old man's not around and see 'em get their finger-nails in your back!'

'Oooo! Mr Argyle! They don't! Do they?'

Albert put his finger to his lips: 'No tales out of school! But I tell you this – you want to watch yourself at that cocktail party tonight. You're the kind of dish they think about when they're in bed with their missis!'

'I don't have to worry,' Joyce said. 'He'll be there – my husband. Else I wouldn't trust meself alone with that horrible Major Simpkins – he keeps patting my hand!'

'That's what I mean,' Albert said. 'Bloody insult! If he was half a man at all he'd pat your bottom, wouldn't he? They haven't got the courage of their convictions.'

Joyce was still laughing immoderately when she saw Albert out of the flat. It always gave Albert a feeling of success to leave them laughing; whether he had sold anything or not, whether he'd collected long-standing arrears or not, whatever the dismal state of his personal finances or whatever catastrophe threatened, some deep theatrical instinct, deeper than care, was satisfied if he could leave them laughing. It was perhaps the applause that he badly needed, a measure of his charm and likeability. It was what hurt him most about the affair with Treasure; that in the end, after all the laughs they had had, he had left her hating him.

'Well, you know what they say,' he told her as a parting shot on the landing, unaware that Mrs Jenkins was again – with furtive purpose – going or coming. 'We put up with the same thing day after day for the sake of the same thing night after night!'

'Ooooo!' Joyce cried, with a laughing pretence at being outraged.

'Ta ta, love!' Albert called as he ran down the stairs.

'Toodle-oo!' Joyce Corby cried, adding, as she saw her neighbour's shocked face, 'Mr Argyle!'

'Good afternoon, Mrs Corby!' Mrs Jenkins made it sound like an accusation and a reminder as she passed by the door.

Horse-face, Joyce thought. She went back into the flat and crossed to the window. She was not in the mood to be intimidated now. Why should she better herself? Albert had made her feel that she was already the right kind of person and, what's more, in the majority. She looked down as Albert was opening the door of his van; he looked up and waved and she waved back. A young police constable was proceeding along the opposite side of the road and she heard their shouted greetings.

'Up your pipe, Albert!' called the policeman.

'And you, Sid!' Albert replied, sticking up two fingers.

It warmed Joyce to hear the friendly exchange. Mr Argyle was right; from the eleven-plus onwards there were two kinds of people in the world – her sort and his sort. Her husband's. Reginald's. And she was beginning to feel – first prize or no first prize – that inter-marriage was wrong.

When Joyce had watched Callendar's little van speed away, she closed the window and sat down to review her problems. Now that he had gone she felt completely cut off again. It was a lovely flat, tastefully decorated and furnished with fitted carpet, Regency chairs and settee, scraps of wrought iron holding flower vases and lamps,

75

delicate bits of china and pottery, the latest coalglow electric fire and a pair of good reproduction paintings of horses each side of the mantelpiece; in fact the room had come straight out of a *Homes and Gardens* photograph and it was just the kind of place she had dreamed of having while she was working in the Agricultural Tractors factory office. But the part of it not in the dream was that she would be alone in it most of the time and worrying about paying for it. What was the good of a house of cake if there was nobody to share it with and if you had to pay for it?

'I'll have to give him something,' she told herself, looking at the paltry pound note which wouldn't go anywhere. She was thinking of Mr Argyle and his kindness and patience. 'And I'll have to give them something,' she added, remembering the cocktail party.

She looked at the clock, then went to the telephone, driven to an inescapable solution which she would never have dreamt of if it hadn't been available and convenient in the town.

'Is that the Confidential Secretarial Service? Miss Alcott? This is Joyce – have you got a part-time job I could do before five o'clock?' she asked.

'As a matter of fact I think I have,' came Miss Alcott's voice. 'Pamela's let me down – but you'll have to get cracking right away!'

'I'm coming now,' Joyce told her.

She slipped on her nylon-fur coat and as an afterthought cleaned her teeth. 'When it comes to helping her husband,' Joyce liked to remember Reginald's mother saying at this particular stage of what had become her life, 'it's a wife's job to do everything she's capable of, no matter how little that may be.'

And she rushed out to do it.

8

MISS ALCOTT'S flourishing call-girl service was the
result of a happy chance. Elizabeth Alcott was the
daughter who stayed at home to look after her parents
until either they died or she did. This left her forty-eight,
straight as a board, Victorian in her conversation and
outlook, completely inexperienced with men but with a
rudimentary knowledge of cats. During the last ten years
as nurse and companion to her surviving parent, her father,
she had learned touch-typing to provide for the future.
She had gone twice a week to night classes at the technical
school, sitting with a class of young girls, her hands
hidden by a cover while she memorized the home keys.

Alone at last to earn a living in a town whose material-
istic values were far removed from Queen Victoria's, she
had spent her small legacy on a good reconditioned typewriter, a second-hand electric duplicating machine and
the lease of one of the little dingy derelict offices which had
once been part of a ribbon factor's establishment. It was
an appropriate place; the Victorian office and the Victorian lady were in business.

Miss Alcott ventured a small advertisement in the local
press and distributed cards around the newsagents'
boards then sat back and waited. The first week brought
her one boy scout who offered ten shillings to have a
jumble-sale circular typed and duplicated. After this she
typed a few letters for people who wanted to impress or
were writing for jobs or in debt and hoping to convince

their creditors that they were not poor and helpless. The first month brought her a gross of three pounds five and a net loss of ten pounds sixteen – she had ample time to do her books meticulously.

Oddly enough it was at this time that she had got into trouble with the police for the most, she considered, obscure reason. They had arrived at her office in two squad cars – a detective superintendent, an inspector, and four or five other ranks. They had with them a copy of what up until then had been her most lucrative job – a twenty-page booklet which she had been paid ten pounds for by some nice young man. She had set it out neatly, typed it most accurately and artistically with both margins straight-edged right down the pages. She had run off fifty copies from the stencils and bound them in blue covers with pretty gold-tinselled string to hold them together. The young man had been very pleased and had promised to recommend her to all his friends; especially as she had been diplomatic enough to tell him how much she had enjoyed reading it when in fact, apart from some pleasant jingles which were reminiscent of nursery rhymes, she had not understood a word of it.

'Did you print this, madam?' the superintendent had asked her. Then, at a second glance: 'Or did you allow somebody to use your machine?'

'I did it myself,' Miss Alcott said, proudly. 'Is anything wrong?'

It was pornography of the crudest kind. The sex act put to rhyme in a dozen different ways; new positions set to old rhythms, organs put to music, anecdotes in biological detail, exploits legendary and apocryphal in which pelvic cavity rhymed with depravity in a saga of filth and four-letter words unknown in Miss Alcott's vocabulary.

'It's a little anthology,' she told the C.I.D. man. 'Most

78

of it rather over my head, though I do appreciate its merit. I'm not much of a one for modern verse, though of course I know what I like.' And then, seeing the glances the policemen were exchanging, she said, nervously: 'It's not political, is it?'

'No madam,' the superintendent told her. 'But if that young chap ever comes in again, ring the police station and then lock yourself in the back room.'

Miss Alcott was never certain what exactly was wrong with the booklet, but to be on the safe side she had taken the sample copy out of her specimens book; when she came to think of it it might explain why the Vicar of Little St Paul's had changed his mind about giving her the parish magazine to duplicate.

After this she had become over-cautious about accepting manuscripts from authors and refused to type them unless she fully understood the context; as it sometimes took weeks of reading and research for her to understand the simplest stories and as authors objected to being cross-examined about their work, the business gradually fell off, from being almost nothing, to nothing.

It was then that Miss Alcott discovered a small but steady demand for the services of a typist who could attend at under-staffed offices. She took to doing morning work here and there, filling in during summer vacations and generally obliging local business people. Sometimes she found that she was wanted in two places at once and by advertising she was able to contact other women who could help out and who were willing to pay her ten per cent of what they earned for the convenience of having their part-time work organized for them.

As this business began to build up, so more typing came in, for she had made some personal contacts and was ready to accept office overflow work. To increase this work so that she could spend as much time as possible in her own office – the dingy place suited her and she liked it – she expanded the agency to include domestic workers, locals and continentals *au pair*; she took on the tedious business of addressing thousands of envelopes for direct mail advertising for people like Callendar's Warehouse with an extra fee for folding leaflets, putting them in, stamping, and posting. From all this, if she worked a twelve-hour day, never looking up, she found that she could average, from commissions and direct earnings, about ten pounds a week gross, five pounds net. Just enough to live on and keep the cats.

Then, quite fortuitously, she had been put on to what seemed like – to Miss Alcott – a good thing. She was always looking for a good thing; the part-time office work was a good thing, so was the direct-mail envelope addressing. Anything for which she could see a steady demand until she was old enough for a pension looked like a good thing. This good thing had come about when one afternoon one of her married women part-time typists had come into the office crying and deeply distressed. That morning Miss Alcott had sent her to work for a local historian, a nice old gentleman who was compiling a history of the town and borough with particular reference, Miss Alcott gathered during her usual screening, to the town's past association with the textile industry.

'He attacked me,' the woman said, between her sobs.

'Mr Weatherhead? I can't believe it! Do you mean he tried to kill you?'

'He tried to get my clothes off!'

'Whatever for?' Miss Alcott exclaimed.

'What do you think?' the woman said angrily.

Miss Alcott had no idea; the woman, with a family and a considerable hire-purchase commitment, was badly in need of the work and impatient with Miss Alcott's simplicity.

'Don't you know anything about – life? He wanted me. He wanted to – to cuddle me.'

'Perhaps he's grown fond of you?' Miss Alcott suggested. The romantic stories in *Christian Girl* were her only vaguely remembered authority on such matters.

'I've never been there before!'

'But you've been there all day, dear,' Miss Alcott said. 'Besides, he's quite well-known locally.'

'Then I think you might have warned me!' the woman said, bitterly. 'If I told my husband he'd get six months!'

'Don't bring the police into it!' Miss Alcott cried, with the fear of one who, although completely innocent and unaware, already has a record.

The next day she had happy occasion to telephone the woman. 'Have you told your husband about Mr Weatherhead?'

'No – he wouldn't believe nothing happened if I told him.'

'Well as long as nothing happened I shouldn't tell him, dear – Mr Weatherhead has just called in and left five pounds for you! He wants you to go again!'

'When?' the woman asked.

That's how it had started. The word had spread, at first between Mr Weatherhead's close circle of friends and later to a wider clientele. Because of her innocence Miss Alcott was able to build up the business into a good thing much faster than somebody who knew exactly what she was doing.

'Is it private and confidential work at your home?' she would ask, coyly. 'Then you want somebody attractive – I know!'

She knew nothing. Until Mrs Christie told her a few

81

things. Mrs Christie was one of Miss Alcott's busiest part-time workers and she had been sitting in the office one day when a telephone conversation was taking place.

'I can't make it less than two pounds for half an hour – plus her bus fare of course. . . .'

'You take a few risks, don't you – talking like that over the telephone?' Mrs Christie had said, afterwards. 'If anybody gave you away you'd get five years!'

'I don't understand!' Miss Alcott said.

Mrs Christie, once she believed Miss Alcott didn't understand, explained at length. It took a great deal of explanation, for she had to cover in half an hour or so what should have been covered over the past forty years.

'You mean – like cats?' Miss Alcott whispered, as the light began to gleam.

It said much for Miss Alcott's determination, strength of character, and Victorian stoicism, that once she learned the gravity of the crime she was committing in running business premises for an illegal purpose she did not panic or faint, but took all her records and burnt them.

A few months later she moved into a suite of new offices over a bank in the main street and resumed the typing and duplicating business as a necessary front. Financially it was unnecessary, for the call-girl business was bringing in a clear eighty pounds a week profit; there were so many men like Mr Weatherhead and so many young wives who needed the money.

Besides – and this was Miss Alcott's secret – because of the way she had started she had the knack of making prostitution seem a respectable and necessary amenity in the Welfare State. No matter what had been explained to her, it would always be part-time work. The men seemed to like it, the women seemed to need it, so there couldn't be anything very wrong in it.

'Here's the key, dear,' she told Joyce Corby when she came in this afternoon. 'It's fourteen Grosvenor Court – he's been on before and he sounds rather distinguished, but don't forget to pick up the fee before you let him stroke you. . . .'

Miss Alcott still had only the vaguest idea what actually went on and she wasn't terribly interested now.

Joyce Corby's first qualm of fear came when she saw the well-known board outside the block of flats at Grosvenor Court: 'Furnished Flat to let: Apply Chas. Arthur, Auctioneers and Estate Agents.'

She hesitated in the forecourt. If it was to let, why was somebody apparently living there? And if somebody had moved in recently, did they know him – Reginald, her husband? It was unlikely. And even if they did it was more unlikely that they would know her. She was the last person he would introduce prospective clients to. She had never met one of Reginald's clients. On this thought Joyce went to the lift and pressed the button. Why shouldn't she meet one of his clients? It would just serve him right meeting them like this and he not knowing! They were always lords or ladies, sheriffs or millionaires, according to him – Reginald. He was a great name dropper – it went with the business. She wasn't criticizing him for it. It was just aggravating that he never brought the famous ones home for cocktails so that she could have a bit of excitement in a dull life.

As she went up in the lift, she saw a possible small scene taking place at the breakfast table.

'Yes, I showed Sir Arthur over the Grosvenor Court flat – he was quite taken with it. Nice chap, asked me to play a round of golf sometime.'

'Well, why don't you, dear? I slept with him yesterday and we got on very well together.'

No need to say it was only for half an hour and that he'd paid her three guineas. She could just imagine his face!

On the third floor Joyce walked along to number fourteen and hesitated outside the cream-painted door. It was a very expensive flat. She tapped, then listened at the door for a moment. She could hear the sound of running water. It was the bath routine. Well, it was always nice to know they were clean. There was one thing – apart from a baby – which she would never be able to explain away.

Using the key, she let herself into the flat.

The scene was set as for a play. Dim lights, the curtains drawn to keep out daylight, a fire glowing. A table against a big divan, lush with cushions. Drinks on the table. Through a green glass partition the sound of running water and the silhouette of a man taking a shower. Joyce went to the settee, kicked off her shoes, flung off her coat, settled down on the settee. She studied the bottles for a moment – whisky, gin, vermouth sweet and dry. The three pound notes were tucked under the gin bottle, the three shillings alongside. Joyce picked up the money and put it into her handbag, gratefully. It would provide Mr Argyle with his arrears and the cocktail party with its snacks. Canapés.

Joyce helped herself to a gin and French, drank it quickly, then filled up again before calling:

'I'm here!'

The water stopped running.

'Hello?' said a man's voice. 'Is that you, darling? With you in a minute!'

Joyce jumped to her feet, spilling the drink. She picked

up her coat and then looked for her shoes. One she found and put on.

'Make yourself comfortable, darling!' came the voice again. The familiar voice, though not in any familiar tone; a voice that had criticized her, picked her up on a million points of etiquette and grammar; a voice cultured, mannered, sophisticated. The voice of him. He. Reginald. Her husband.

'Honest to God!' Joyce exclaimed, petrified.

'Are you all right?' came the voice again.

'I can't find my bloody shoe!' Joyce muttered. She started groping round on her knees in the gloom.

'Come and join me if you like!' He had half-opened the door.

This was Reginald who had told her off for opening the bathroom door when he was there. It was un-ethical. Or un-something. Now she found the shoe and hurried towards the outer door.

'Is that Pamela?' came the voice. 'Or Joan? Strip off, darling – we haven't much time, have we?'

Joyce closed the door behind her and ran.

'Coming soon! . . .' Her husband's voice followed her, fruity with passion.

9

BY half past five Albert was driving back towards the warehouse, the day's work nearly done. He had not met the brave target he had set himself; he had sold nothing beyond a bit of counter business with Mrs Wentworth that morning, he had demonstrated nothing except his skill as a lady's hairdresser, he had canvassed no new customers, collected no money and another day had gone.

As he drove through the main street, buses were disgorging workers from the factory estate. They crowded in their hundreds and thousands through the steel barrier poles at the bus stops.

'Bloody sheep!' Albert muttered as he drove. 'Sheep in the pens waiting for the chopper! What have they done today?' Talking to himself gave him a feeling of superiority; utterance gave authenticity to a man's philosophy. You could agree with yourself and it sounded like two of you. 'Still,' he continued – slowing down for a mob on a pedestrian crossing – 'you can shear sheep. Big deal! That's right, mate, stare – you do the work, I get the lolly!' Tomorrow he would really get stuck in. . . .

'Albert!'

Albert heard the call, caught a glimpse of Cedric Mason standing by the gate of the playground at the school. Oh Christ! Albert thought. But he stopped and the schoolteacher came running up; a middle-aged man in a dirty macintosh holding a bulging shabby suitcase full of homework.

'Give us a lift, Albert?' he asked, stooping to the low window of the van.

'Yes, sir – Cedric – sure. Hop in! Welcome!'

'Sold my wife anything today?' the teacher asked when Albert had started up. 'One of your best clients I should think – our house is like a palace. It's a marvel how she manages, isn't it? Still, she's the organizer in our family. Nothing like a good marriage, Albert! Catch 'em while they're young and train 'em up. We all need organizing.'

86

'That's your washing machine in the back – taking it back for service,' Albert told him.

'What's the matter with it?' Cedric Mason asked, looking back into the van.

'Acid got into the bearings,' Albert said. 'That's all the sweat out of your shirts, sir – Cedric.'

The schoolteacher laughed. 'You can't work too hard. Keeps your mind off the state of the world. Besides, if you work hard you haven't got time to be ill. Remember what I used to tell you in standard six?'

'Long time ago, sir.'

'I expect it seems like it to you. There you are, you see – you've got older but I haven't, have I? Do I look forty-five?'

'Forty-five! No, sir!'

Cedric beamed at him. 'It surprises everybody – born nineteen-seventeen – '

'I remember, sir – same year as the Russian revolution, Ingrid Bergman, and Nancy Spain!'

They laughed together as they had in standard six.

'You've got to keep going, that's the secret, Albert.'

'Yes, sir – it's all go.'

'You take Marjorie – full of energy! Pops like a breakfast cereal all day long! Mind you, she's only twenty-seven.'

'She's always at it,' Albert said, his eyes on the road ahead.

'You're wasting your time there, you know, Albert.'

'Eh?' Albert exclaimed. He dare hardly look at his passenger who was staring at him, seriously concerned.

'On this job,' Cedric said.

'Oh,' Albert said.

'You shouldn't be a tally-boy. Tally-boys are ten a penny. There's no future in it. It's a transitory occupation.

87

You're living on the sickness of the times – people living outside their income in a fool's paradise of plenty. They don't know it but they're going through the worst period of inflation in the history of the country.'

'Is that right?' Albert said.

'It won't last, thank God,' the schoolteacher said. 'The generation coming through school now will have different values – that's our job. It's the only place to start. I drum it into them. Work for what you get, pay for what you have – you ask Marjorie. Doesn't owe you anything now, does she?'

'She's clear up to date,' Albert said evasively.

'I educated her to start with,' the schoolteacher said. 'Of course, it's not easy. We all have to work it out in our own way. Pride of possession, that's what people don't have any more; I tell my class – the boy with an unbeatable conker in his pocket has got more to be proud of than the boy with an unpaid-for transistor radio.'

'I know what you mean,' Albert said.

And for the first time in their whole long acquaintance-ship as pupil and master, husband and wife's lover, Albert did know what he meant. Albert's greatest achievement in school was in having an undefeated conker. Albert had impregnated it with shellac, baked it, impregnated it again, and repeated the process over days and weeks – it was his greatest sustained effort and one which he would never surpass. The conker had finally become a dreadful thing; shellac, skin, and pith had merged and fused and polymerized until it was unnatured and harder and black-er and more uncrushable than granite.

Albert's conker had shattered hundreds of lesser conkers; it had subdued bullies, got him a place in the football team, won him a schoolboy's fortune in sweets and kind. The fearsome reputation of Albert's conker had spread to every school in the town and Albert had become a celebrity.

Moreover, it was Albert's conker which had given Albert a permanent taste for fame and acclaim and left him crippled by dissatisfaction and restlessness. Pride of possession! That's what was missing all right. You get this and you get that and you get the other – but it's never really yours.

Albert drove up a ramp into the petrol station and cut his motor. 'So long, then, sir.'

'Of course, it won't happen at once,' Cedric told him.

'What's that, sir?'

'Once we get right into the Common Market we're going to have to compete again. This country was always at its best with good strong competition – take the Spanish Main, take Hitler. War is competition, you know. We can work when we have to – once we can see the field!'

'That's true,' Albert said.

'Your dad was killed in France, wasn't he? I remember you used to do a job out of school hours helping to keep your mother – '

'I used to spend it all!' Albert said, growing red at this tribute. 'I never helped her much.'

'There'll be hard times again before they're good,' Cedric said. 'That's what I tell them. There'll be unemployment and poverty before we get any prosperity. But when it comes it'll be real prosperity. Not what we've got now, Albert – an artificial standard of living with everybody doing three jobs to keep up with it. That's not a healthy nation.'

'You're right,' Albert said.

'How old are you, Albert – twenty-two?'

'Twenty-four,' Albert said.

'There's still time,' his old master told him.

Albert looked at him.

'You were a bright scholar – good at English and maths when you put your mind to it. I didn't have any better start than you, Albert. I went to night school and studied through correspondence – you don't remember the old Bennett College? Let me be your father? I got an external B.Sc. with honours and won a grant to teachers' training college. You could do the same.'

'What me? A teacher?'

'Or an engineer or a scientist – they're the producers, Albert. They're what this country needs. Not tally-boys!'

'I thought I might have a go at the stage when I get the time – I've done a bit of singing.'

'Is that why you changed your name, Albert? Silly thing to do – insult to your father. Argyle isn't even spelt properly with an "e" – it's really a Scottish name. A place, a regiment, a football team!'

'I took it from Argyle Street – it was the closest I could get to the Palladium.'

'Silly chap,' Cedric told him. 'You're envying the wrong people. Actors, crooners, entertainers, strip-comic writers – they're not real, Albert, any more than tally-boys are. They're not giving anything, they're not achieving anything. At the end of a whole lifetime they haven't moved the clock forward by one minute. They live in the cracks and miss life altogether.'

'I couldn't be a scientist,' Albert said. 'I don't feel like a scientist.'

'You used to get top marks – remember how we measured the moisture content of grain?'

'What, the capacitive method in an oscillatory circuit?' Albert asked.

'There you are, you see – you haven't forgotten. Do you remember the dielectric constants of solids?'

'Not the figures,' Albert said.

'What's a pH unit?' the schoolmaster asked.

Albert thought for a moment, then said: 'It's a measure of acidity and alkalinity directly proportional to ten times the logarithm of the ratio of disassociated hydrogen ions in an aqueous solution – '

'In grams per litre,' Cedric gave him.

Albert felt strangely proud. 'I didn't know I could remember that!'

'Well, it just shows. You could go on. It takes years of hard grind and doing without, but it's the only way if you really want to do something worth while with your life – '

'Cedric – get your finger out, mate!'

The schoolteacher scrambled out of the van, took an oil-stained overall off a peg and started getting into it. 'Filthy expression!' he said. Then he said: 'You bear it in mind, Albert!'

There came the blaring of a motor horn, 'Coming sir!' Cedric cried, running to fill the tank.

Albert watched him, shaking his head. 'I will,' he said. And as he drove away, he added, to himself: 'I dunno – you are a shit, Albert.' And a moment later he added again, comfortingly: 'But at least you know it. . . .'

'There's a man been here after you, Mr Argyle,' Hetty told him as Albert came into the shop.

'What another one?'

'This was a different one. I never seen him before. He wanted your private address but I told him, I said: "I am not allowed to divulge information about the staff!" – you know, like you told me to tell that girl and she began to break the place up. Any road up, he went away without another word.'

She whispered then, bending over the cash desk to him and pointing towards the back room: 'I was afraid he might bump into Jeff and he might tell him where you lived – I wouldn't put it past him!' Jeff came through and she raised her head, talking loudly: 'So if you'll just give me your figures for the day I can get totted up and toddle off home to me dear ones!'

'Wait a minute!' Albert had a disturbing thought about the visitor and dashed out of the shop.

'Where's he gone?' Jeff asked.

'Have you got anything to declare, Mr Jeffries?' Hetty asked.

'One Wondersew machine,' Jeff told her; he was still smarting. 'I left it on dem – chalk it up, will you, Hetty?'

Albert came back. 'It's still there.'

'What is?' Jeff asked him.

'My car. I've got an idea the H P bods are after it.'

'Haven't you had a letter terminating the agreement?' Jeff asked. 'They always send a letter once you go over three months without paying.'

'You don't have to tell me. I'm still paying off on the last car – if they take this one I'll be paying for two cars I haven't got. Have we got any of those polyvinyl car covers left?'

Hetty scanned her books: 'Twenty-four,' she said.

'Three,' Jeff told him. 'Over there.'

Hetty shrugged it off, got busy with pencil and rubber.

Albert found a cover and took it out to cover up his car and hide the number plate.

'Why didn't you get a letter?' Jeff asked him when he came back in. 'They always send a letter. If they haven't sent a letter they're not after it. Why go to all that trouble of covering it up? You can't put a plastic cover right over the bloody car every time you stop for ten minutes. If they haven't sent you a letter you're all right.'

'They don't know where I live,' Albert said. 'Why do you think I moved out of my last place?'

'I thought you run out on Treasure because she was expecting – '

'Why don't you knock it off?' Albert told him. 'I left to get away from letters and bailiffs and court orders – now you know. And if anybody wants to know where I live, you don't know. Okay? Christ, of course they've sent a letter by this time. The place was roof-high with bloody letters when I left – what d'you think?'

'I don't know all your bloody business,' Jeff said. 'You can't be in it any deeper than I am.' He drew Albert away from the cash desk. 'I got something to tell you – '

'Talking about Treasure, Mr Argyle,' Hetty called, 'did you get that washing machine from the Masons'?'

'In the van – tell Arnold to get it in, will you? I'm not going to strain my gut any more today.'

'There was this bloody cow of a woman,' Jeff told him. 'She was ugly. I swear she was really ugly – I wouldn't've touched her with yours let alone mine. . . .'

Mr Callendar came from his office wearing a navy-blue double-breasted suit. 'Lock up tonight, Hetty, will you – I've been invited to a cocktail party – '

'My, my, we're coming up, aren't we?' Hetty said.

'I don't know why you should say that. I often go to cocktail parties – I hold them meself. A man in my position is bound to get invited to cocktail parties. Where else do you think we business men talk business – ' He glanced round, then said: 'See that the boys all get away before you lock up. Good night, Hetty.'

'I've got a petition for you to sign,' Arnold told Hetty, coming down from the upper floor. 'Woodman spare that tree! What a day's work! Four orders and twenty-five signatures for a tree – did you tell Mr Callendar I lost the dem cleaner?'

'No. He was in a good mood. I didn't want to spoil his evening.' She looked at the tree petition. 'What's this then?'

'Ah, never mind – I'm going to tear it up. Waste my time on a lot of old fogies – I should say so.'

'Let's have a look,' Albert said, coming back with Jeff trailing behind.

'It was a real confidence trick,' Jeff was saying.

'What d'you want to tear it up for?' Albert said to Arnold, reading the petition. 'It might be the only useful thing you ever get the chance to do in your whole mucky life.'

'You take it round, then,' Arnold said. And in case he was under any sort of misapprehension: 'They're all old dears – there's no crumpet, y'know.'

'I tell you what.' Albert turned to Hetty. 'Make out two more sheets.' He gave her the one to copy, then said to his colleagues: 'I'll lay a quid I get more signatures than you by six o'clock Friday night?'

'That's on,' Arnold said.

'I've got a good mind to report 'em to the police – they could get five years for a trick like that,' Jeff said broodingly.

Albert picked up the telephone receiver, dialled a number. 'Hello, darling – oh, can I speak to Miss Doris Masters, please ... Doris? Remember me? Coffee bar this morning? ... I know – you've been on my mind all day, dear. Wondered if you'd like a little drink somewhere this evening. ... Wherever you like, I'll pick you up. ...'

94

Jeff and Arnold exchanged a glance behind his back. Jeff put his thumb up.

Hetty was typing a heading on sheets of lined foolscap paper, using two fingers, laboriously:

We, the undersigned, do hereby register our strong disapproval at the intended destruction of the old sycamore tree in Cheveley Square. This tree has great sentimental value to the elderly residents and we petition the council to reconsider its decision, save the tree and earn the heartfelt gratitude of the community.

Having written, read, and inwardly digested this, Hetty looked up at the tally-boys in sheer disbelief, suspecting a joke.

10

'AND what's the little lady drinking? What are you having, my dear?' Major Simpkins was patting Joyce Corby's hand in a corner of the room. 'They don't look after you, do they? If you were mine, I'd look after you – by golly, yes! Wish I was six months younger, what?'

Joyce was staring across the room at her husband, who was talking to Mr Callendar, Mr Wisbech, a bank manager, Mr Solly Cowells who owned the biggest department store in town, and a woman he had brought with him but had not introduced. Joyce's eyes had not left her husband since he had arrived home. She was trying, quite simply, to reconcile him – Reggie, the husband she thought she knew – with the voice from that bathroom.

'What?' she said to the elderly military strategist.

'You look lovely,' he said. 'Ravishing, my dear.'

'Thank you.'

'And what's the rest of this delightful flat like, eh?' said the major, opening a bedroom door and easing her through. 'We shan't be missed, shall we? Keep talking. Rhubarb, rhubarb, rhubarb. Oh yes, lovely room. Lovely. Looks south.'

'Reggie!' Joyce called, from behind the gentleman's bulk as he bulldozed her into the bedroom.

The woman who had arrived with Mr Cowells came across, talking to the bank manager but with one interested eye on the open bedroom door.

'Mind you,' she was saying, 'I always know what kind of people are living in any house, just by looking at it. They may take big houses, but they remain vulgarly working-class – did you call, Mrs Corby?'

'Just taking a look round – lovely place, don't you think so, Mrs – er – um?' said the Major.

'I was just saying to Mr Wisbech, so many of our best houses and flats are falling into the hands of the working class – such a pity!'

The rest of the party eased across the threshold of the bedroom, which was Reggie's.

'And look at that divine headboard,' said Mr Cowell's lady friend. 'It's a work of art! It really is.'

'And why not?' Major Simkins said. 'Reggie's going to be chairman of the council before long, you see.'

Reggie laughed, modestly. 'I have to get elected first.'

'I'll get you there,' said the major. 'Tactics, old boy!' He smiled down at Joyce. 'I'm a master of tactics. A bit of money, a bit of influence – when you haven't got party funds then you need a few good friends, eh?'

'And another thing that always gives them away is

their windows,' said the woman to Mr Wisbech. 'You don't have to meet the people, just look at the bedroom windows. The working class, no matter what kind of mansion they may be in, always block out their windows with the ugly back of a dressing-table – '

'That's right,' Mr Wisbech said. 'That's perfectly true.'

'They prefer themselves to the view or the daylight,' the woman said. 'Complete lack of aesthetic feeling, you see – no amount of money will give them that.'

'And they always vote Conservative,' said Mr Wisbech. 'It's a kind of defence, I suppose. Not that class bothers me, mind you – it's a completely classless society these days.'

'Completely!' his companion echoed. Then she cleared her throat. Everybody was staring at the Corby dressing-table which Joyce had arranged with its back to the window, blocking the view.

'Yes, well, how about letting me fill you up?' Reggie said. He had darted a disgusted look at his wife who had turned scarlet.

'That's the idea!' exclaimed Major Simpkins. 'Back to the pump!'

But he stood his ground, holding his hostess's arm until the others had gone back into the lounge. Then he went over and closed the door.

'Lot of nincompoops, you know, my dear. My dressing-table's got its back to the window – wouldn't have it any other way.'

'It never occurred to me before,' Joyce said. 'I'll move it tomorrow.'

'You don't want to do that – be an individualist. A beautiful gal like you can have anything the way she wants it.' He took her glass and placed it beside his own on the offending dressing-table. 'Now let's look at you!'

He squeezed her close. 'My word, what a stunner you are!'

'Major Simpkins!' she exclaimed.

In the mirror, as she stood thus embraced, unable to move, she saw the door open and Reggie look in.

'Ooooops!' he said. 'So sorry, Major – don't let me interrupt.' And he closed the door firmly on them.

'Splendid chap, your husband,' muttered the Major, thickly, kissing her all over her face as she tried to avoid him. 'Knows how to make his signals!'

'What are you doing!' Joyce exclaimed.

'Let's get over to the bed, eh – too old for knee tremblers these days – '

Joyce Corby brought her knee up, sharply. The major collapsed back on to the bed, holding himself, blue in the face, gasping and groaning.

'Can I get you a drink?' she asked, going to the door and flinging it open. 'I think Major Simpkins has had a bit of an attack,' she said to the lounge at large.

They all turned towards her, Reggie's face white as a daisy in a bed of poppies. Instinctively he knew that she had let him down again.

In a house in Cavendish Street, Mr and Mrs Wentworth were in bed together.

'And what sort of a day have you had?' he asked.

Coral wriggled closer to him, feeling a little conscience-stricken. 'I did a bit of shopping. What sort of day have you had, dear?'

'Lot of trouble with the management.'

'Oh, never mind. Don't worry about it,' Coral told him.

'I'm not at the moment,' he said.

'You do your job and don't get mixed up in it,' she

advised. 'We don't want any strikes – not now we're getting straight.'

'There won't be any strikes, darling.'

'I'm glad,' she said.

'We're going to work to rule,' he said.

'Oh. What does that mean?'

'Just cut out overtime for a bit – what's the matter, darling?'

'But we've budgeted on overtime!'

'Well, don't let's worry about it now. Darling ... Darling. Coral.' There was no reply. 'Have you lost interest? Darling? Never mind,' he said. 'Just keep still.'

Outside the house where he lived Albert was fed up. It had been another of those evenings. It had again cost him money that wasn't his, but this time he had managed to get the girl back with him – only to find that the light in his room was on, the curtains drawn. Jeff or Arnold was in possession.

'We had this funny old schoolmistress, Miss Thanet,' the girl was saying. 'She had these stuffed birds. They used to give me the creeps! She tried to make us wear shorts for gym, but I wouldn't and she didn't half go on. That was where I met Hilda – I told you about Hilda – who married John, you remember, the parson's son who worked on the roads? I saw John's friend Ken only last week – he was very keen on me, I don't know why – but he didn't see me. I was coming down Butterhall Street – you know where Cranby's is? Well, I saw him looking into this shop window and I crossed over, see? Well, when I got to the end of the street – I didn't turn back, mind you – he must have seen me because as I turned up to the office he came hurrying along. I pretended I hadn't seen him and went in. The girls were killing themselves –

they were looking out of the window and they told me afterwards – where are you going?'

'I'm driving you home,' Albert said.

It was never, never worth it.

At one o'clock he let himself into his bed-sitting-room. There were dirty cups and saucers, bottles and glasses still out, the divan cover half off showing a patched mattress. Albert lay down on the divan, lit a cigarette, stared at the ceiling. Bloody tally-boys; they had no respect for anything or anybody. On the ceiling little silver paper egg-cups had been tossed up and gobstuck. God knows what he would find in the lavatory.

Albert turned on his side, suddenly, as though to hide his face from the empty, smoke-soured room, and pulled a cushion towards him.

'Treasure,' he said, 'why do you hate me?'

PART TWO

Never Jam Tomorrow

11

As Albert ran down the stairs the next morning the black man came out of his room.

'Mr Argyle?'

'That's me, Sambo.' Albert's friendly grin took away the impertinence. He noticed a Negro woman just inside the door and a child sitting at a breakfast table, staring and listening.

'Could I have a word with you?' the Negro asked. 'My name is Russel – Joe Russel. It's about last night.'

'Oh. You got some noise from my place?'

'I don't want you to think I'm the complaining kind of neighbour as I've just moved in, but – '

'I can guess – it wasn't me, you know,' Albert said. 'What were they up to?'

Joe Russel shook his head in wonderment. 'Man! There was some kind of I-don't-know-what going on – shrieking and banging and girls and fellows on the stairs undressed – well, I don't want to complain, but – '

'It won't happen again, Mr Russel! I give you my word.'

'You see, I've got a family to consider and my kid – he was in and out of bed – well, somebody swore at him – mind you, I think they were drunk, but you know – well, we can't afford trouble and if anybody's going to complain I've got to get my complaint in first – do you understand that, Mr Argyle?'

'Sure, sure – it won't happen again.'

'That's the position we're in – but mind you, we like it here, only last night my wife was frightened we'd got into the wrong house – we have to be careful – and she wanted me to go and see the landlord this morning but I'd rather have a word with you first – do you understand?'

'It won't happen again,' Albert told him. 'I'd already decided that when I saw the mess they left – you do somebody a favour and that's what happens. They're not coming here any more. I'd already decided – as a matter of fact I'm getting married myself pretty soon.'

'Well, congratulations!' Joe Russel said. His wife was smiling now round the door, the black child was eating again.

Albert said: 'Thanks.'

'Perhaps you'd like the wife to clear up for you?' Joe Russel said. 'She'd be happy to clean the place up for you.'

'Well that's good of you – ' Albert was feeling in his pocket.

'No money!' the Negro exclaimed. 'I didn't mean that – you just leave the key.'

'Well thanks,' Albert said. 'The key's under the carpet outside my door – it's very good of you. Much obliged. See you!'

Albert was glad to get away. When people started behaving like human beings he ran out of patter. Besides – who was getting married? You could take consumer identification too far. And however he felt last night, Albert was his own man again this morning. No targets today. Just get stuck in. If he didn't make any appointments with himself then he didn't fail to keep them; if he didn't make any promises to himself, he didn't break them.

He had parked the car two streets away to be on the

safe side, and it was shrouded in the polyvinyl cover. He took a quick look round before taking it off. He didn't want to lose this one. What else did he get out of life for all the work he did and the running around and worrying? The car, cigarettes, the occasional girl.

He drove quickly away, feeling like a thief.

The Corbys were having breakfast.

'You could have played him along a little,' Reggie said. 'He doesn't mean any harm.'

'I got frightened,' Joyce said. 'You don't know what he did. He touched me – you know where.'

'Don't be vulgar!' her husband said.

'Perhaps you wouldn't mind if I went with him,' Joyce said, 'as long as he got you on the council.'

'That hardly needs an answer,' Reggie said, coldly. 'You have a typically working-class view of that sort of thing.'

'You mean I think it's wrong when you're not married?' Joyce said.

'I mean it's something one doesn't discuss at the breakfast table.'

Joyce picked at her bacon. 'Would you go with anybody else?'

'Certainly not. Not if it meant anything.'

'Oh, I see. It's all right if it doesn't mean anything?'

'It's all right for men, I suppose. Not really important. For women it's different.' He looked at her. 'Shall we talk about something else?'

Joyce said: 'That's a typically universal view – amongst men!'

He said: 'Have you got a spare pound out of the housekeeping, dear? I ran out yesterday – had an expensive client to entertain. I'll get it back out of petty cash.'

'Who was she?' Joyce asked.

'Who said it was a she? Anyway, have you or haven't you?'

'Did you take her out to lunch?' Joyce asked.

'No. Drinks – and so on. I'll give it to you back tonight.'

'How much did it cost you?'

'About three pounds.'

'Was it successful?' Joyce asked.

'What d'you mean?'

'Well, did she do whatever you wanted her to do?'

'She didn't take the flat, if that's what you mean. Too small for her – Lady Renwick, you've heard me speak of her. President of the Dog Club. She's interested in my proposal for dog-troughs in the town. It may help me to get in. She thought it was an excellent idea to offer the voters something that would appeal to the heart rather than the pocket. She said I was an idealist.'

Joyce waited for more, interestedly. 'What did she look like? I mean, what is she like? Pretty?'

'Good heavens no – raddled old thing. Stinks of dogs.'

'I haven't got a pound to spare,' Joyce said. 'Not even ten bob.' If he could invent the conversation, why not a less revolting woman?

'Ten shillings!' Her husband corrected. 'I don't know what you do with it.'

'Funny you should say that,' Joyce said. 'I've got a list made out.'

Reggie stopped eating. 'I've got to go,' he said.

'If you go now,' Joyce said, 'I shan't be here when you come back!'

It was their first quarrel and it was a big one, though for the first time Reggie took the minor role of listener. He learned what he did with his money and what she had

106

to do to get it back. He discovered how many things in their home were still unpaid for. He found out what she thought of his mother. She spoke steadily for a quarter of an hour and although she was not always grammatically correct she was graphic, fluent, and frighteningly articulate. He could either go, leaving her the flat and its contents, most of which she was paying for, and making her a suitable allowance; or he could stay on her terms.

'What terms?' he asked, nervously.

'I want a baby and one of those new thirty-guinea prams to take in the park,' she said. 'I don't care if it's your baby or Major Simpkins's, if that's of any help to you, but – '

'I'll stay,' Reggie said. 'But don't tell mother!' Now that the cards were on the table he tried to get his money back.

'No,' Joyce told him. 'I've promised it to Mr Argyle.'

Reggie went. Joyce collapsed, laughing, on the Regency settee. He's not the only one who knows how to make his signals, she was thinking. And if you can't fight 'em, join 'em. On this thought she went into the bedroom and started moving the dressing-table away from the window. It was heavy and she had to struggle with it, one end at a time. Whatever else we are, she thought, let us not be working-class. With the dressing-table out of the way she opened the big window and gazed at the unaccustomed view. Perhaps Mr Argyle would give her a baby? Reggie would never know and never care. She started singing. Honest to God – what she had been missing! Ethics could be fun once you knew what they were.

She took a dartboard from under her bed and hanging it on the wall she started playing. That was another thing he didn't know about.

On a mischievous impulse she took one of the darts into the lounge and aimed it at the painting of the horse.

In a semi-detached house at Fenton Park, one of the middle-bracket owner-occupier estates, a plump, homely girl was making porridge when Albert came in the back door. She held the saucepan at arm's length while he cuddled and kissed her.

'You've got nothing underneath again, you naughty mother!'

'I haven't had time!'

'Mummy!' came a cry from the next room.

'Go and keep 'em quiet, love,' she told him. 'There's some tea poured out.'

'You smell warm and clean and milky,' Albert told her.

He went through into the living-room. Four young children were round the table, one in a baby's high chair. There was a clamour of welcome from them. Albert gave them a sweet each to spoil their breakfast, then looked at the tea tray.

'Where's mine, Grace?' he called.

'He's on the pottie,' came the reply.

A moment later she came in with the porridge and the small boy who was a little older than the washing machine.

'How long have you worn that shirt?' Grace asked as they sat with the children, Albert feeding his son, drinking tea. 'You'd better let me have it – you can have a clean one of Fred's.'

'I think this is Fred's,' Albert said. 'How is he?'

'He's fine,' Grace told him. 'Did I tell you he's just had another rise? They think a lot of him at Oggles.'

'They should. He's a good mechanic.'

'He misses you,' Grace told Albert. 'He keeps asking when you're going to bring Treasure round for a game of Monopoly again. I thought it best not to tell him you weren't with her any more. Have you seen her? I wonder how she's getting on?'

'What about another cup?' Albert said.

She poured him a second cup. 'Fred liked Treasure. You know what he always said? She is just right for Albert! Just what he needs! Somebody to keep his feet on the ground! I wish you'd make it up, Albert. I mean, she must've got over it by this time. That stuff worked, didn't it? In the end.'

'Everything worked at once,' Albert said.

Grace sighed her sympathy. 'I know – you've got to be careful when you're single. Still, you looked a lot better then – are you eating enough?' Then she said: 'Did she know about – him?' She nodded to the child on Albert's lap.

'What d'you think? She knew about everything. She knew what I was thinking before I thought it.'

Grace laughed. 'Well, I suppose that's what Fred meant. It's nice to have somebody you don't have to fool – then you don't have to fool yourself, do you?'

'It's like having an affair with your own conscience,' Albert said.

'What's an affair, mummy?' asked a boy of five.

'Wait till you start school, matey,' Albert told him.

Grace laughed with him. Later he changed his shirt in the kitchen and she gave him a clean ironed handkerchief for his top pocket. He cuddled her again.

'What's the matter, Albert?'

'Nothing. I just need cuddling.'

'I wish you weren't always wracking around, Albert. I think about you. I wish you were settled.'

109

'You haven't changed your mind, have you, Grace?'

'No, dear. It wouldn't be right. It was right once. It wouldn't be right any more. I don't need it now. I've got all I want. You don't know what that's like, do you?'

'I'm only twenty-four, Grace.'

'You seem older. You seem a lot older, sometimes.'

'I feel it,' Albert said. 'Time I got a partnership and told other people what to do.'

'You'll never get a partnership, Albert. You'll never do any more than talk about getting on. You don't want to get on. You don't want responsibility.'

'You sound like Treasure,' he said. Then he said: 'I've got my hand on your navel.'

'Feel better now?' she said. 'Come on – let me give you some money.'

'Could you pay a few weeks in advance, Grace – I'm a bit short?'

'Yes, of course – you can have five pounds and finish off the carpet shampooer.'

'Would you like something else?' he asked. 'I've got the catalogue outside.'

'If I start looking at that I'll never get any work done – leave it with me, I'll see if there's anything Fred wants. . . .'

He kissed her again, fondly, took the money, called a farewell to the children. Grace followed him out into the garden path, looking at the sky.

'What's it going to do?'

'Take care of yourself,' Albert said.

'You take care of yourself, Albert.'

'I nearly forgot,' he said. 'Will you sign this petition to save an old tree?'

She read it, then put the sheet of paper against the doorpost and signed it with his biro.

'You're getting soft-hearted, aren't you?' she asked.

'Don't be daft – I've got a quid on who'll get the most signatures. Treasure would've known that!'

She smiled after him as he got in the van, then remembered the catalogue. 'Albert!' She waved. 'What about the catalogue?'

Albert waved back, putting the money into his pocket as he drove away.

Grace smiled to herself as she went in; Albert got all he wanted and went. Treasure would know that too. He couldn't help it. That's the way he was. But he still loved you in his own selfish way. Of course, it would never do to marry him. No doubt that's what had finished Treasure. In the end a woman always wanted marriage.

12

GRACE had relaxed Albert and lightened his spirits; to get the essence of a woman you didn't have to make love to her always. The love between them was implicit and unfiery, like ever-warm ashes from an old blaze. There was mother, mistress, and wife in what she gave him without going to bed – though he was still ready, for she had a climax in every touch.

Grace, surrounded by her children, seemed always warm and clean and naked underneath as though recently bathed and glowing with the milky vapours of clean warm flesh, and ready for another confinement. What she gave birth to in his heart and loins flowed in through his hands each time he touched her. 'I've got my hand on your navel,' he had told her. It was natural and elemental; somehow she seemed to expect it and accept it. She was calm, soothing, and good for him. She wanted him to have all that he could get from her, to make the best, moistest, and most sensuous contact he could, without breaking any more rules or hurting any more people.

Grace was contented within herself and she cared for him and for the child and she was happy to release him from all responsibility except that of taking care of himself. Take care of yourself was a polite cliché to all except those who loved and then it was a sacred responsibility. Albert was happy because he was loved; it wasn't Treasure, but it was something.

By eleven o'clock he had made fifteen calls and collected thirty-three pounds ten shillings. It wasn't his money, but it bulked in his inside breast-pocket and he was rich. Now he could set himself a target; he would make it, say, fifty pounds.

'You shouldn't have done that,' he told himself as he drove across town. 'You said no targets. You silly old bugger.'

And supposing the child in Grace's home was what Treasure had seen when she pulled the chain in the cinema lavatory. Wouldn't that make her hate him forever? The picture was getting more horrifyingly clear each time he thought about it. He was seeing it through Treasure's eyes.

'Let's celebrate!' he'd said when she crawled back into the balcony seat and whispered it to him.

'You bastard,' she had said, quietly, her eyes on the screen. 'You wicked bastard.'

Even then she had not cried.

To re-establish his self-confidence he decided to tackle

some of the tough ones, get a few of the arrears in. At twenty-three Latimer Road he banged on the front door, then ran quietly around to the back just as the lady of the house was creeping out with a shopping basket.

'Hello!' she said. 'I wondered if I heard somebody knocking or if it was the pipes – could you leave it this week?'

'I left it last week and the week before,' Albert said, scanning his book. 'Can't let it go on any longer. Sorry, Mrs Kelly.'

The woman took her purse out of her shopping basket and gave him a pound note which he recorded. 'Ta very much, dear – can I give you a lift down to the shops?'

'Not now,' she said, throwing the empty purse back into the basket.

Farther along the road the opposition was stiffer. Albert had to get tough.

'Either you give me something or I'll have to take back the cleaner – suit yourself.'

'You wait a week and like it,' the woman said.

She closed the door on him. Albert didn't go.

'Mrs Fordyce!' he called. 'Mrs Fordyce!' He banged the door. 'Are you going to give me that cleaner or do I have to fetch a policeman?'

The door opened again and the woman glared at him, livid with anger, looking first one way then the other. 'Do you want the whole street to hear?'

'Yes, dear,' Albert said.

'I can give you ten shillings – and that's all!'

'A pound,' Albert said.

She gave him the money; he put it into his book.

'You can be really nasty, can't you, Mr Argyle?' she said.

'I'm in a nasty mood,' Albert told her.

I'll re-possess something today, he promised himself; he re-possessed more things than either of the other tally-boys. It took moral courage, and physical courage, sometimes. Callendar depended on Albert to deal with awkward customers.

'If they won't pay, git the goods out of the 'ouse!' was his alternative war-cry.

'I always know when you're hating yourself,' Treasure would tell him. 'You take it out on other people.'

'Balls!' Albert said, getting back into his van, slamming the door.

Outside a house in The Avenue, Albert opened the back doors of his van and cleared a space. He felt sure they wouldn't have the money; he didn't want the money.

'I've called for the guitar,' he told the woman who answered the door.

'Peter's guitar?' she said.

'No, our guitar, Mrs Barnwell. He's had it two months without making a payment – '

'I'm afraid you can't take it – '

'Has he left the four pounds?' Albert asked.

'No, but – '

'Then I'm taking it,' Albert said. 'If he likes to come down to the warehouse with the money he can have it back.'

'It's not here,' she said.

'Has he sold it? He'll go to prison if he's sold it.'

'Of course he hasn't sold it – he's learned to play it. He's very good!'

'I'm glad,' Albert said. 'But we're not the musicians' benevolent society – will you get it for me, please?'

'He took it with him, this morning – on his scooter.'

'To work?' Albert said.

'All right, if you don't believe me – come in. Come and

114

look for it! I'm not going to stand here and be insulted –
I shall tell my husband about this. You're very rude. I
know your sort – go around bullying women when their
husbands are at work. It's you that ought to go to prison!'

'Well let me come in, then,' Albert said. 'I'm at work
too, you know.'

He went in.

'This is his room,' the woman said. 'That's where he
keeps it.'

Albert looked around the bedroom without finding a
guitar.

'What about the other rooms?'

She took him all over the house. He looked into everything big enough to hide a guitar, including the gas oven,
which wasn't.

'All right – where is it?' Albert said when they were
back in the front hall.

'He took it to work with him. He's going straight on
to a jazz party tonight in Beachfield Road.'

'Then why didn't you say that in the beginning?'

'I just wanted to see how objectionable you could be,'
the woman said.

'What number Beachfield Road?'

'I don't know and I don't care – now do you mind
going?'

'You could do with some new stair carpet,' Albert
said. 'Would you like our catalogue?'

'What!' she exclaimed.

'And that television's about a hundred years old,'
Albert told her. 'You want a new slim-line, madam.'

'It works perfectly!'

'I know – those old sets do.' Albert said. 'It's those old
sets that are putting the manufacturers out of business.'

The woman suddenly laughed.

'You think about it,' Albert said, and he produced the petition. 'Would you like to sign this for me?'

She read it. 'You've got a nerve!'

'It's not just a tree,' he told her as she signed. 'They're chopping down all the old people.'

He slammed the back doors of his van on a lighter note – he had insulted her, searched her house, got her signature and left her laughing – he would probably get an order from her before very long.

'It's a gift, Albert,' he congratulated himself as he drove away.

By one o'clock he had collected forty-seven pounds; could he make his target of fifty before lunch and break all records? He sat in his van in a side-street, smoking a well-earned cigarette and scanning the list of customers. A girl walked past and he only whistled her. He could be strong. Especially when they scowled at him. But automatically his eyes searched for names which would smile at him and cancel out the scowl. Mrs Corby! If she hadn't any money she might give him lunch. Anyway, he would cheer her up if she needed it.

He started the motor, drove away.

Money? Lunch? Cheer her up? Who was he fooling? Write a letter for her – ah, there's an excuse he'd forgotten because it involved doing something. He was going to see Mrs Corby again from the moment she had stood there in that slim black dress with her hair high and looking tearful.

'Then why didn't I do it yesterday?' he asked himself.

That was the groundwork, Albert. We know that, don't we?

He was talking to Treasure again.

Joyce Corby was in the bathroom rinsing a shampoo out of her hair when the doorbell sounded.

'Coming!' she called.

She groped around for the towel and remembered that she had left it on the dressing table. She went out of the bathroom with her eyes closed, crossed the bedroom to where the dressing-table used to be. As she groped in front of her the bell sounded again.

'Coming!' she called.

Her knees struck the wall and she fell headlong across the windowsill; she opened her eyes and as they smarted with the soap she clutched for a hold with her wet hands. Most of her weight was out of the window.

'Oh my gawd! God!'

They were her last words.

There was a moment when she was holding and a moment when her fingers were slipping. As she fell out of the window, she screamed.

Albert, outside the flat door, heard the scream and the thump of her body on the ground without knowing what it was or where it came from. He rang the bell again, then tried the door handle; the door opened and he went into the flat.

'Mrs Corby? Are you there? It's me.'

He crossed the lounge and went through the open bedroom door. He looked from the open window to the open bathroom door and then to the towel lying on the dressing-table. That's a funny place to put a dressing-table, he thought. He went back into the lounge, then looked in the other bedroom. She was out, but she couldn't be far away. On the other hand she was sufficiently disorganized to have left the place open. He then saw her handbag lying on one of the Regency chairs.

Albert picked up the handbag. She had said that she

might have his money today. He opened it and took out three pound notes. He put them in his pocket with the rest and marked up the book. While he was doing this he heard a woman's frightened voice calling.

'Mrs Corby! Are you all right?'

The voice seemed to be coming from the bedroom and he went in. The calling drew him to the window and he looked out.

'Young man!' the voice came again. 'What's happened to Mrs Corby?'

He looked up and found Mrs Jenkins' frightened face gazing down at him from a window above.

'Did she fall?'

Now Albert looked down and saw the figure motionless and spreadeagled on the paved terrace below. He stared down blankly for a moment, not understanding. Then the sounds he had heard came back to him. He shouted up to the woman above: 'Don't be bloody silly – phone the ambulance!'

He rushed out of the room. It was her calling – Mrs Corby – when he rang the bell. It suddenly fitted into a terrifying pattern; the calls, the scream, the thump. It had hardly registered at the time, it could have been a radio or noises from another flat.

Albert jumped most of the stairs, raced across the vestibule and out round the side of the block. He was hoping somebody would get to her before he did. He knew nothing about first-aid. Accidents frightened him.

There was no blood. He went down on his knees beside her. She was lying half on her side, her face up, eyes closed. He listened for signs of breathing. She was all wet.

'Mrs Corby!' he said.

He pulled the bathrobe away from her throat – she

was naked. Must have been having a bath, he thought.

'I've telephoned – they're coming!' The voice came from above and he looked up. 'The police as well!' Mrs Jenkins called.

'Bring some water!' Albert called. 'Bring some brandy!'

Mrs Jenkins was staring at him with frightened eyes. She withdrew from the window, crossed the room and locked her door, drawing both bolts.

When the ambulance men arrived with a doctor Albert was blowing into the girl's mouth; he had read about it somewhere and it was all he could think of. He watched the doctor take over. People from near by had been drawn by the arrival of the ambulance; an old lady with a small dog, a boy on a tricycle, two window cleaners. At-home-in-the-middle-of-the-day people; incidents like this dropped like a bomb into their unbusy world.

'I'm afraid she's dead,' the doctor told Albert. 'I'm sorry. Is she your . . . ?'

'Mrs Corby,' Albert said. 'One of my customers. She fell. She must have fallen. I don't know.'

'You'd better sit down,' the doctor said.

Albert sat on the front steps of the block of flats, watching the draped body being carried into the ambulance. A police car stopped and several policemen alighted from it. Mrs Jenkins now appeared out of the flats and ran past Albert towards the policemen.

'I heard her scream!' he heard her exclaim.

Albert felt weak, sick, empty. He had liked her. He had felt sorry for her. He really had. Yesterday he had combed her hair, now she was dead; a stranger again. He had not even known her first name.

'Is this the gentleman, madam?' A policeman was bringing Mrs Jenkins back to the flats. She nodded, staring at Albert without speaking, still with that shocked, frightened look.

'Will you come inside, sir?' the man said.

'Yes, sure.' Albert stood up.

'Hello, Albert,' one of the policemen said.

Albert was grateful to see a constable he knew. 'Hello, Sid – this is a rotten business, isn't it – ' Suddenly, without warning, he was sick. He had tasted toothpaste from the unbreathing mouth.

'Put you head down there, mate,' the constable said, holding Albert's shoulders.

As he retched by the door into the shrubbery he heard the voices as if a great crowd was gathering.

'He did his best for her,' came the doctor's voice. 'But it was too late.'

'Did you know her well?' a police sergeant asked.

Albert felt the question was directed at him. 'No. She was a customer.'

'What's her full name?'

'I don't know,' Albert said. 'Mrs Corby. That's all I know.'

'Well I only said what I thought,' came Mrs Jenkins' voice from a great distance. 'And if it isn't blood it must be lipstick!'

'You should be careful,' came the sergeant's voice.

'Better, mate?' asked the constable.

Albert stood up, wiping his mouth. 'Thanks, Sid.'

They went inside, leaving a group on the pavement.

'I'm sure I'm wrong, superintendent. I'm sorry I mentioned it. I wouldn't like him to get to hear.'

Mrs Jenkins was in her sitting-room talking to Detective Superintendent Collins of the county C.I.D.

'It was just the way it looked to me. I saw him go into

120

the flat with her yesterday afternoon and when she saw
him off wearing a different dress – and their conversation
was very familiar. Well, that was yesterday. Then today
I heard her scream and when I looked out of the window
she was lying on the terrace. The next moment he put his
head out of the window and looked up at me. He seemed
very frightened and he spoke to me roughly – but of
course I can see now that he could be perfectly innocent.
I'm sure he is. You won't say I saw anything, will you,
superintendent? Once he knew my life wouldn't be worth
twopence!'

'Did you like Mrs Corby?' the detective asked.

'Well, I never had much to do with her – none of us
did in the block. She was very working-class for our
neighbourhood.'

'I see.'

'Not that that means anything these days, of course.'

'Well that'll be all, thank you, madam. We shall want
you to give evidence at the inquest.'

'Oh dear – shall I have to tell them everything? I mean
– will *he* be there? I suppose I can have police protection?'

'It's people like us who want protecting from people
like them,' the superintendent told his subordinate officer
as they drove back to the police station. There wasn't a
man on the force in the town who had passed his eleven-
plus or its equivalent.

'It's not fair on Argyle,' the sergeant said. 'He ought
to have her up for libel.'

'I don't think she'll say any more. I let her see it wasn't
popular. Anyway, she's too scared.'

Later Albert made a statement to the superintendent
at the police station. In the statement room, besides the
superintendent, there was the sergeant, two constables,
including the one called Sid whom Albert knew, and a

woman police constable. Sid had provided Albert with tea, biscuits, and cigarettes.

'It's quite true,' Albert said. 'I was there nearly an hour, yesterday. I helped her choose a dress for this party.'

'That was decent of you,' the superintendent said.

The woman police constable, who was busy writing, now looked round at the men.

'Then I gave her a new hair-style,' Albert said.

'I bet she was pleased,' the sergeant said.

'And then I helped her with her accounts – she was very worried about some debts.'

'Was she now?' the superintendent said. 'That's interesting. Wait a bit and we'll take that down.' He turned to the sergeant. 'Write that bit down, it might be pertinent. Very worried about debts. That's a good bit.' He turned to Albert. 'Would you like some more tea?'

Albert accepted another cup of tea and told them what he had learned and what he had, since Mrs Corby's death, conjectured about the marriage.

'He kept her short of money,' Albert said.

'I'm not surprised,' the superintendent said. 'We'll get that down. Anything else?'

'He kept pulling her up about the way she spoke and so on,' Albert said. 'I think he made her feel inferior.'

'Isn't it marvellous!' the superintendent said. 'And yet that old bitch liked him all right. He's the right class. Him and his Bentley.'

A young constable looked in. 'Mr Corby's here, sir.'

'Is he? Is he now?' the superintendent said. 'Has he done the identification?'

'Yes, super.'

'Well now he can wait till I've finished with Mr Argyle, can't he?' the superintendent said. 'Inferior!' He turned to Albert: 'And you say that lipstick was on

122

your shirt before you called at the dead woman's flat?'

'Yes, I got that at an earlier call,' Albert said.

'Yes, well, we'll scrub round that, shall we? Miss that bit out, Sergeant. That's not pertinent.'

The woman police constable sighed and continued with her work.

As Albert went out of the superintendent's office, Reginald Corby got up from a chair and intercepted him. They had met briefly in the police station entrance as Albert was coming in and Reggie was going to the mortuary.

'Mr Argyle – could I have a private word with you?' Reggie asked.

'What about?' Albert asked.

'Did she say anything before she died? My wife?'

'What sort of thing?'

'Anything? Did she speak?' He broke off as the constable beckoned him. 'Just a minute, officer!' Then softly to Albert: 'Did she?'

The slight interruption had given Albert time to hate Corby. 'As a matter of fact she did,' Albert said.

'What did she say?' Reggie whispered. 'Was it about me?'

Albert said: 'She said: "He drove me to it!" They were her last words, "He drove me to it!"'

Reggie turned pale. 'Have you told the police?'

'No,' Albert said. 'It slipped my mind till you mentioned it.'

'Don't tell them, will you? I mean, it can only make it worse. After all, it was an accident. Must have been. You won't tell them, will you, Mr Argyle?'

'Not unless they ask me,' Albert said.

'The coroner will ask you. Bound to.'

'Well, I can't falsify evidence, can I?' Albert said.

123

'You work for Teddy Callendar, don't you?' Reggie said. 'He's a great friend of mine. I'm negotiating a big deal for him.'

'What's that got to do with it?' Albert said.

'Come along, sir,' the constable called.

Reggie watched Albert go out of the police station. He drove me to it! My God, that's just the sort of cliché she would go out on. He could see it in the papers.

The early edition of the local evening paper carried a full-length picture of Joyce Corby wearing a bikini bathing suit, a crown, and the 'Miss Agricultural Tractors 1959' sash across her middle. 'Ex-Beauty Queen dies in fall from bedroom – local man's heroic life-saving attempt' was the heading. And opposite was a head-and-shoulders photograph of Albert taken on the steps of the police station alongside a picture of Corby.

'Oh, brother – what a figure!' Jeff was saying as they all looked at the paper spread on the counter. 'Look at those child-bearing hips. Don't tell me you weren't knocking it, Albert!'

'Oh, Mr Jefferies!' Hetty exclaimed.

Arnold said: 'You could've had half my territory for that, Albert.'

Albert looked at his colleagues in disgust. 'If you rotted I wouldn't use you for manure,' he told them. 'No bloody feelings. You're lower than animals, you are. She's dead, in case you've forgotten.'

Arnold said: 'She looks alive there.'

'The lifefulness is terrific!' Jeff said.

'And I don't want you picking your nose over my carpet any more,' Albert said to Arnold. He looked at Jeff: 'I've had complaints about your orgy last night – it's all over, finished. You owe me a quid each.'

124

'You go and fart for it,' Jeff told him.

Arnold said: 'You're going to owe me a quid each this time tomorrow – how many signatures have you got?'

The three of them buried their animosities while they compared the petitions for the tree. Hetty took the newspaper back to her desk.

'You lousy bugger, Jeff! You've been forging those signatures! Two hundred and fifty my arse! That's your left-handed writing you use to bump up your sales contracts!'

'Pssst!' Hetty called. She pointed to Mr Callendar's office.

In his office Mr Callendar was also studying the front page of the paper. 'Heroes! ! Such heroes!' he muttered.

'Albert!' he called.

'Now see what you've done!' Jeff said.

Albert went into the office.

'Close the door, Albert. Sit down. Can you spare a moment? It's been a very 'arrowing day for you, my boy.'

Albert noticed the Sunday-best voice usually reserved for customers and put it down to the newspaper item. 'It was very upsetting,' he admitted.

'But shall I tell you something?' Mr Callendar said. 'I'm glad it was you and not the others. I wouldn't trust them with a naked woman, even if she was dead.'

'They've got no feelings,' Albert agreed.

'That's the point. You've got feelings, Albert. You've got depth. It's the people like us who suffer.'

What's this? Albert was thinking.

'You get away early tonight – have a restful evening.'

'I haven't done me money yet – '

'Never mind that, my boy. Spend the morning with Hetty tomorrow. Or the day after – take a day off if you feel like it. We'll manage somehow. At a time like this

when tragedy strikes at one of our good friends, we have
to show a little human feeling, don't we?'

'I feel all right now,' Albert said.

'I mean my old friend Reggie Corby,' Mr Callendar
said.

Aye aye, Albert thought.

'This is a great shock to him,' Mr Callendar said.

'I don't know why,' Albert said. 'If you treat a woman
like that you should expect it, shouldn't you?' My God!
said Treasure, inside his head.

'We all make mistakes,' Mr Callendar told him,
fervently. 'We got to be generous, Albert. He's a broken
man.'

'You mean he will be if I tell the coroner his wife's
last words,' Albert said.

'Yes, Albert, that's the truth. And I know how you
feel about it. How we all feel. It's a matter of conscience
and I've thought about it very deeply. You see, you've
got to think about the living as well as the dead. I ask
myself, what good will it do if Reggie loses public support and fails to get elected on to the council?'

'Between ourselves,' Albert said, 'what good will it do
if he gets elected – I mean, what's in it for you, Cally?'

Mr Callendar looked at Albert in a stricken way for a
moment. Then, cheerfully changing tactics, he said:
'Have a cigar, Albert – I'll tell you about my plans. . . .'

Albert put his feet up on the desk and lit a cigar.

Mr Callendar was not the most adept at turning his
dream into words, but he did manage to convey to
Albert a picture of the Callendar Emporium which could
take shape on the factory site across the street. Mr
Callendar had thought about it so much and he saw it so
clearly that he had the habit of talking about the proble-
matical future as though it were already a halcyon past.

'In those days all of this area will be a paved shopping centre,' he said. 'Instead of a catalogue we shall hāve big shop windows and arcades – get the people in the shop.'

'I should've thought you were doing all right now,' Albert said.

'All right, yes. I am very successful. But this business ...!' He showed his distaste. 'You know what Solly Cowell said to me last night at the cocktail party? He told me the tally business is a furtive business – you know? Like having a stall on the market. We ain't even represented on the local trades council. Oh, it's all right, but it's got no prestige, Albert. These days you got to have prestige. Besides, look at the types I have to employ!'

There was a small silence between them; Mr Callendar then extricated himself.

'You and me want something better, eh? Imagine a big shop – two, three floors. Real classy goods. Why not? Marks and Spencer started with a street stall. Gordon Selfridge used to have one crummy little shop.' He tapped his chest. 'I can do it. Better than Solly Cowell. You got to think big. You got to have vision. Imagine it, Albert, fifty pretty girls in green overalls with Callendar embroidered on their collars.'

'Where do I come into it?' Albert asked.

'What?' Mr Callendar, carried away, had forgotten that Albert did not come into it; but he had to persuade him to forget Mrs Corby's last words.

'I have great plans for you, Albert,' he said, to gain time. 'How old are you?'

'Twenty-four,' Albert told him. Why did people have to keep asking him his age?

'You could be a departmental manager – in charge of ten or twelve girls,' he added, knowing Albert.

'That might be years,' Albert said.

127

'And in the meantime,' Mr Callendar told him, 'if I can get Reggie's cooperation and secure an option on the site, you can take over here as manager.'

'What are you going to do?'

This was a new bit of the dream and Mr Callendar was making it up as he went along. 'Once I get the option I shall be busy organizing the Callendar Property Trust and Investments Co. Ltd. Have I mentioned this to you before? Its job will be to raise capital for the store – that's easy once you've got the site. Do you know a site like that is worth a hundred thousand pounds as security these days? I won't have time for this place. You can have this office, Albert – this desk. Any questions?'

'Can I have my name on the door?' Albert asked.

It drew them together; it was something they had in common. However big the dream, however vague and mist-enshrouded the loftier spires of the castle, what they saw were the small bricks of personal aggrandizement; Callendar's name on the shop-girls' collars, Albert's name on the door.

'Of course, Albert. A. Argyle, Manager. And you can have it printed on the next batch of stationery.'

'When do I start?' Albert asked.

'The sooner you give me your assurance that you won't mention what Mrs Corby said, the sooner I can get on to Reggie and make a deal.'

You two bastards! Treasure said in Albert's head.

'Let me sleep on it,' Albert said.

This hesitation was inexplicable to Mr Callendar. Then he remembered something. 'Of course, your money will go up. I'll increase your basic salary and you can take a bonus as a percentage on total sales – a nice steady figure, Albert.'

In the cigar smoke Albert could see a small white face

128

beneath a high bouffant hair style and a pair of brown eyes waiting, cynically. It was Treasure.

'I'd like to think about it,' Albert said.

Mr Callendar looked at him, puzzled. 'Were you having an affair with Mrs Corby?'

'No,' Albert told him. 'But I liked her. I felt sorry for her. I was trying to help her. I wouldn't like to let her down.'

'A hundred pounds cash,' Mr Callendar said.

Albert said: 'There are some things more important than money, Cally.'

When Albert left the office, Mr Callendar sat staring into space for a long time. Albert wouldn't like to let somebody down for a hundred pounds cash? There's your tally-boy! You couldn't even rely on them being unreliable.

He checked the time then rang Chas. Arthur Ltd. Mr Corby was not expected back. Before he could ring his home number the telephone buzzed and Reggie Corby was on the line, angry and threatening.

'Have you talked to your salesman yet?'

'Yes, don't worry, Reggie. He's going to think it over –'

'Well, let him think this over,' Reggie said. 'If he goes blabbing to the police I'm going to ask them to ask him what happened to three pounds my wife had in her hand-bag – it could look very ugly for him.'

'Hold on a minute, Reggie. That might be useful.' Mr Callendar cupped the receiver and called: 'Albert!'

Arnold put his head in at the door. 'He's just having a slash – anything I can do?'

Albert appeared, pushing Arnold out and closing the door after him.

'Albert – did you take three pounds from Mrs Corby's handbag today?'

'Yes,' Albert said. 'She promised it to me – I thought she'd gone out and forgotten. I've marked it up in her account – you can see the book if you like.'

Mr Callendar motioned him to stand by and spoke again to the telephone: 'Reggie – are you there? Yes, he took it – she had promised it to him. He's marked it up to her account – yes, I realize that, but – '

Albert took the receiver out of Mr Callendar's hand.

'Mr Corby – you tell the police I took the money and I'll tell them where she got it from. Okay?' Albert gave the receiver back to his boss. 'He's not talking.'

'I hope you haven't upset him!' Mr Callendar spoke again to the telephone: 'Reggie? Are you there, Reggie?' He looked at Albert, distraught. 'It sounds as if he's crying!'

Albert shrugged. 'I don't expect he wants everyone to know his wife had to go out to work.'

Mr Callendar's eyes widened with interest. 'Is that what it is? That's useful.' And to the phone. 'Hello, Reggie? Don't worry. Nobody's going to say anything. You stick by me, I'll stick by you. . . .'

Albert sneered as he went out. What a pair. They even made him feel superior.

13

AT the police station the detective superintendent was in conference with the chief constable considering the statements so far received from Albert, Mrs Jenkins, and the dead woman's husband.

'The lady upstairs seems to think she jumped out of the window to get away from him,' the chief constable remarked. 'Is there anything in that, superintendent?'

'I shouldn't think so, sir – not unless she moved the dressing-table to do it.' He laughed. 'Perhaps he helped her?'

The woman police constable was still sitting at the desk, writing. Her pen hesitated for a moment at the laughter, but she did not look up.

'When there's a naked woman involved,' the superintendent said, 'there's always somebody ready with perverted ideas.'

'Do you think it was an accident, then? If she had moved the dressing-table and forgot about it – that would account for it. According to the doctor's report there was soapy water on her face. And a towel on the dressing-table. It looks as though she heard the bell, rushed straight out of the bathroom and through the window – terrible shock for her.'

'Still,' the superintendent said, 'she was dead on impact. Didn't know much about it.'

'On the other hand,' the chief constable said, 'she might have heard the bell, realized it was another creditor, and jumped out of the window. It's happened before – I mean, there have been several suicides. Housewives in debt – all this hire-purchase they seem to go in for.'

'Have to let the coroner sort that one out,' the superintendent said. 'I don't think it was that, somehow – not if she knew who it was. They got on very well.'

'What sort of chap is he – this Argyle?' the chief constable asked. 'Seemed to have great presence of mind – not many people would have had the courage to try mouth-to-mouth respiration.'

'Oh, he's all right. Sid knows him.' The superintendent

shouted: 'Sid! Got a minute?' And when the constable
looked in, he said: 'You know Mr Argyle – what's he
like?'

'Who, Albert? Oh, he's all right, he is. I knew him at
school – when he was there! None of the girls were safe,
y'know! Great boy, Albert!'

'Was that grammar school?' the chief constable asked.

'Grammar school?' the superintendent exclaimed,
scornfully. 'I should think not! He's a sound lad, he is.'

'One of the boys!' said Sid.

'Thanks, Sid.' The constable went and the superintendent continued: 'Now Corby – he's different.
There's your grammar school man. All side! The courts
are full of 'em. If it's not fraudulent conversion it's drunk
in charge. What? I wouldn't give one house room!
And we've had a few on the force – but they never stay.
You know why, don't you? Prejudice! They hate the
working classes. All prejudice.' He noticed that the
chief constable had fallen silent and checked himself:
'Still, that's not pertinent, is it? Let's get back to the
facts.'

While they were engaged with the facts, Miss Alcott
was shown into the office; she was holding a copy of the
evening paper and a small booklet. The chief constable
sat aside while the superintendent interviewed her.

'I understand you know something about this case,
Miss Alcott – is that right?'

'I don't know whether it has any bearing or not,' Miss
Alcott said, 'but it seems to me it might have. Perhaps
you remember this booklet? You told me to get in touch
with the police and lock myself in the back room if
that man ever came in again – well, that's him in the
paper!'

'Corby?' the superintendent said.

'No – Mr Argyle. That's the young man who wrote these dreadful poems – not that I knew what they were at the time.'

The superintendent scanned the duplicated book. 'But that was two years ago, Miss Alcott – you can't start bringing charges against him now, y'know.'

'I'm not bringing a charge,' the lady said. 'It was you that wanted him. Don't you remember?'

'Oh, was it? Well, there was a purge on against this kind of thing at the time, I suppose. Harmless stuff, really. Still, thanks for letting me know. You can leave it with us.' He handed the book to the woman police constable. 'File this, will you?'

Miss Alcott was shown out. The woman police constable scanned the contents of the book, blushed, and quickly laid it aside.

'Can I see that?' the chief constable asked.

As he read the obscene poems, the superintendent came and looked over his shoulder. 'Clever stuff in its way, y'know.'

The chief constable looked up at him, stunned: 'What kind of mind invented all this?'

'Oh, I doubt whether he made it up,' the superintendent said. 'He's not the type. Probably got it off lavatory walls – he's one of the boys, he is. Anything for a laugh!'

The woman police constable had not yet been able to resume work when another visitor was announced.

'Another twisted mind,' the superintendent said. 'We're really getting them this time.'

'A Miss Teresa Hunter,' the desk sergeant said.

Treasure came into the room holding the evening paper. Pretty, slim, neatly dressed, and burning with a quiet, angry flame.

'This man is a murderer,' she said. 'And he's not going to get away with it this time!'

'Who's this – Mr Corby?' the superintendent asked.

'Albert Argyle,' Treasure said. 'And that's not even his right name. His real name is Albert Harris. When you've conducted an autopsy you'll find that poor woman was pregnant. That's why he pushed her out of the window.'

'Sit down, will you, miss?' the superintendent asked. 'Now then – how do you know all this?'

'Because he pushed me down two flights of stairs for the same reason!' Treasure said.

The superintendent looked at the girl more closely. 'Haven't I seen you working at the bingo hall?'

'Yes.'

'Ah – I thought so.' He glanced at the chief constable with understanding. 'Very well, miss. We'll look into it.'

'I don't want you to look into it! I want you to arrest him.'

'Well, that's for us to say, miss. Meanwhile I shouldn't go saying things like that – you might get yourself into serious trouble.'

It looked for a moment as though the girl was about to launch herself at the detective. The chief constable intervened, gently.

'I think you should bring Mr Argyle in, superintendent, to answer these charges personally.'

'Do you, sir? It's a bit of an imposition on him, isn't it? I mean, he's had a very harrowing day – ' then at a sudden whitening of Treasure's knuckles on the arm of her chair, he called: 'Dick!' And when a sergeant came in: 'Go down to Callendar's and ask Mr Argyle if he'd mind calling here when it's convenient for him – try not to upset him. Tell him it's nothing very important – '

'You tell him he's a murderer!' Treasure interrupted, rudely. 'And watch him run!'

Over her head the superintendent motioned the sergeant to ignore this direction.

Then he said: 'Would you mind waiting outside, miss? He may be some time.'

When she had gone the superintendent shook his head and sighed. 'Poor devil!' he exclaimed, softly.

The woman police constable looked round at him. 'Who?'

'Him,' said the superintendent. 'Fancy having that round your neck!'

'Good grief!' the woman police constable exclaimed.

She got on with her work.

When Albert came out of Callendar's Warehouse a police car was waiting by the kerbside and the sergeant beckoned him over.

'The super would like to see you at the station. I thought it best not to come inside – only cause a lot of talk.'

'What is it, then? I gave him my statement.'

At this moment Albert's attention was taken by something that was happening a little way up the street. Idiot! He had forgotten to put the cover on his car and now a man was trying keys in the lock!

'Some girl came in,' the sergeant said. 'Bit of a nut case if you ask me. There you are, it's never safe to get your face in the papers. It happened to my chum when he won the third dividend – he got stuck to two years back maintenance. Lost the lot!'

The hire-purchase agent was now going back to his own car, having failed to open Albert's door.

'This one's raving,' the sergeant said. 'She reckons you murdered that Corby piece – '

He broke off, for Albert had suddenly dashed away.

'Mr Argyle!' the sergeant called.

But Albert got into his car and drove away.

'That's funny!' the sergeant said.

'Should we follow him?' asked the constable at his side.

'I don't think so. The super didn't say anything about bringing him in. Get on the blower.'

The hire-purchase man had also jumped into his car and was setting off in hot pursuit of Albert.

'Bloody civilians!' the sergeant grumbled. 'Always trying to get the limelight. Hello, super? He's made a run for it!'

'Who's that – Corby?'

'No – Mr Argyle.'

'Oh, that's all right. He'll be back.'

'It's all right,' the sergeant said to the constable.

They drove away.

The town was not designed for a car chase. Through the main street there was a set of traffic lights every fifty yards. At the first of these Albert's pursuer stopped behind him at the red, jumped out of his car and ran forward to Albert.

'Mr Argyle – I have a warrant for the re-possession of this – '

The lights changed, Albert went into gear, the hire-purchase man dashed back to his own car and started up again. At the second set of lights the same thing happened.

'Mr Argyle!' the man said, breathlessly, holding Albert's arm through the window. 'I have a warrant for the re-possession – '

Again came the yellow and Albert drove on; the hire-purchase man raced back to his car and got away with hooters blowing behind him. It happened again at the next set of lights, but the time was decreasing.

'Mr Argyle – I have a warrant – '

The lights changed and Albert put his foot down. This time the man was in trouble with the following drivers, several of whom overtook him, swearing, before he could get away. At the next lights the hire-purchase man had more of a run and arrived just as the lights were changing. He managed to get his hand on Albert's arm.

'Mr Argyle!'

'Evening,' Albert said, driving away.

He left the main street and took the road out towards the ring-road. He was now enjoying the chase. Poor sod, he thought. He hasn't a clue. If I did my re-possessions like that I'd expect to lose my job. If that'd been me I'd be sitting on the bonnet now. 'Get off, you stupid clot!' he called, as though it had really happened. Then he glanced into his mirror and found the following car. 'Let's see who's best at geography,' he said.

Albert took the next turning on the right, the first on the right again, one on the left, then straight ahead to a T-junction. He had to wait an irritating moment to get on to the main road; in that moment the following car came into view behind him.

'Local man,' Albert said.

He concentrated. He overtook everything he came to, taking chances and getting hooted at. Five minutes later he struck the twin-track ring-road and got up to top speed. He had now lost the pursuing car and he lit a cigarette. Manager, eh? His name on the door? And on the stationery. It would look good. He would be able to pay off all his debts. This car would be his! Not before time – it was bloody nearly worn out.

137

He came to an island, circled it and travelled back on the opposite track of the same road towards town. Suddenly he saw the hire-purchase man rooting towards him in the opposite direction. Albert eased over to the grass dividing verge, put his finger on the hooter button and kept it there. He glimpsed the poor chap's anguished face as they flashed past each other in opposite directions at a combined hundred-and-twenty miles an hour.

'That's how fast you have to be to catch Albert,' he said, unfairly taking all the credit.

And then he said: 'Murdered who!' Worried, he drove on. The bitch! She wouldn't! But he knew she would. She still hated him, then? Well, at least it meant that she hadn't grown indifferent.

14

WHEN Albert walked into the reception room at the police station, Treasure sprang to her feet and threw a small brown suitcase at his head.

'You're going to hang!' she said.

The superintendent had witnessed this scene as he came out of his office. 'Would I be right in saying,' he said, 'that the witness is biased?'

Albert was staring down at the floor. The suitcase had broken open and from it had come a shoal of letters.

'Yes, they're all yours,' Treasure told him. 'Summonses, writs, last demands, distraints, do you know I've been sleeping on the floor without a bed for the past two months?' And to the superintendent she added: 'There's even a judgement for ten pounds he owes on his mother's funeral – and she's been dead two years.'

'Not quite two years,' Albert said.

'Is your mother dead?' the superintendent said. 'I'm very sorry.'

Baffled, Treasure stared from Albert to justice. The woman police constable came out on her way home; she gripped the girl's arm in passing. 'You're wasting your time, dear – he's one of the boys.'

'Now let's be fair,' the superintendent said. 'Even if this is just a lovers' tiff – I don't mind listening.'

'She hates me!' Albert said, quickly, at Treasure's swift reaction to this mistake.

With this fact established, she said: 'I advertised for a room-mate – this was nearly two years ago. He turned up!'

'That wasn't an advertisement, darling – that was a message!' Albert said.

'Bad jokes,' she said, 'get worse when they're repeated.'

'You laughed at the time,' Albert told her.

'I didn't know you.'

'We were together eighteen months,' Albert told the superintendent, mistily.

'One month getting to know you,' Treasure said, 'the other seventeen trying to get my own back!'

'You weren't happy together?' the superintendent hazarded.

'I was happy!' said Albert.

'And why not?' Treasure said. 'Eating my food, using my furniture, my gas, electricity!'

'Sleeping in your bed,' Albert reminded her, gently.

'And when I got pregnant he pushed me downstairs!'

'It was your suggestion,' Albert told her.

'All I said was it happened to a friend of mine – and that was a pure accident!'

'Well there you are then,' Albert said. 'I knew it wouldn't work if you were expecting it.'

'It didn't work anyway,' she said.

'What happened?' the superintendent asked.

'I was on crutches for a fortnight!' Treasure said.

'I mean about the baby?' asked the detective.

'I lost him when we were at the pictures one night,' Treasure said. 'Just when I didn't want to lose him.'

'Him!' Albert exclaimed.

'A woman knows,' Treasure said. She looked at the superintendent. 'I was half dead with pain and misery and he said "let's celebrate!" I shall never forgive him for that.'

'I thought that's what it was,' Albert said.

'You're still very sensitive, I see!'

The superintendent said: 'It might have been worse, miss. Supposing you had had the baby? I mean, if you hate him so much – you might have been married to him now.'

'Marry!' Treasure exclaimed. 'Albert marry? He would only marry himself!' Then she said, 'Besides, I wouldn't have hated him if I'd had the baby.'

'You wanted my baby?' Albert said, softly.

'Well, let's face it,' she said, 'you never gave me anything else in the whole time we were together!'

'They were difficult times,' Albert said. 'I was missing my mother.'

'You mean I failed you?' Treasure said. 'I can't think in what tiny way. Of course, I wasn't quite as soft as your mother – I didn't work myself to death.'

'That's unkind,' the superintendent said.

'I feel unkind,' Treasure told him. 'I want you to hang

140

him. Even apart from this latest murder he deserves it –
he killed his mother, he killed my son, he almost killed
me – and I can't think of one exonerating circumstance
except that he's Albert. Is there a separate law for the
Alberts of this world?'

'She doesn't mean it,' Albert told the superintendent.
'It's just her extravagant way of talking.' He looked at
Treasure. 'I don't hate you, Treasure.'

'Try to think of one reason why you should!'

'You came down to Callendar's and broke the place
up – I'm still paying for that.'

'Are you?' she said. 'Well, that's a comfort – I wish
I'd known.' And to the detective she explained: 'You can
only hurt Albert if you hit him in his pocket.'

'I'm afraid a lot of us are like that these days, miss,'
the superintendent told her.

The girl looked at the detective superintendent in
sudden weariness. 'You're not going to believe that
Albert killed this woman, are you?'

'I know he didn't,' the superintendent said.

'You believe he was in a flat with a naked woman and
that was a coincidence?' Treasure said.

'I was not in the flat,' Albert said. 'I was ringing the
doorbell when she fell. I thought I heard her scream and
I went in. At first I didn't know where she was. Then I
heard somebody calling and I looked out of the window.
I saw this woman upstairs – and then I saw Mrs Corby
under the window. Do you believe me?'

'Yes, of course,' said the detective.

'Do you?' Albert was talking to Treasure and looking
her straight in the eye.

She refused to admit that she believed him; instead she
said: 'Why were you ringing the doorbell?'

'I was collecting,' Albert said.

141

'That's his job,' the superintendent said.

'Why were you there?' Treasure said.

'I told you – '

'That's not the truth, Albert.'

'Look, miss,' the detective said, 'if it's his job to – '

'No, it's not the truth,' Albert admitted, wearily. 'I was hoping to make her – it was as good as in the bag.'

'That's better,' Treasure said.

'It's not really pertinent,' the superintendent said.

'Her husband might think so,' Treasure said.

'Are you trying to make trouble for me?' Albert asked her.

'Yes. If I can't see you hanged I'd like to see you beaten up. Just once would do.'

Albert said: 'You're going to hurt Mr Corby more than you hurt me, Treasure.'

'He's right,' the superintendent said.

Treasure looked to heaven. 'You see what I mean?' she said. She went out of the police station, walking over the debris of Albert's old bills.

Albert and the detective superintendent looked at each other for a moment.

'Phew – mate,' said the superintendent.

Albert gave him a brave smile before scooping the documents into the case and leaving.

Albert hurried out of the police station, clutching the unfastened case and searching for Treasure. She was about to step off the pavement and cross the road when he spotted her.

'Treasure! Treasure, don't go!'

She did not even turn her head. She had heard him, Albert knew that; it was just that it diminished a man to have to run. Albert ran, catching up with her as she

142

reached the far side of the road. He fell into step with her.

'Can I give you a lift?'

Treasure just kept walking. She had a nice, easy stride; she had nice long legs, it reminded him, if he needed any reminder. Sideview, from his height, her face gave the impression that she had forgotten him; that she was not unaware of his presence, but slightly irritated that some stranger should be presuming an acquaintance.

'Come on, Treasure,' he said, 'I know you're there.'

Caught unaware her lips quivered like a ventriloquist trying to prevent mouth movement.

'That's better. No hard feelings, eh?' She quickened her pace and he skipped to get into step. 'What do you think of the political situation in Transcaucasia?' he asked. She stopped walking suddenly and he made a pretence of over-shooting, then shunted back to her like an engine. 'You should have an air-brakes warning on your back!'

She had waited long enough for him to see that she was not amused, then said: 'I don't know where you're going, but I'm going home.'

'That's funny,' he said. 'You used to know where I was going.'

'I don't even think you're funny any more.'

'Well, it's an old picture – stick around, I've got new stuff.'

'You are annoying me,' she said.

'Annoying you! But darling, don't you see? This is a fantastic improvement – you used to hate my guts!'

'You haven't got any guts.'

Albert laughed, delightedly. 'Now who's being nostalgic?'

'You are a self-centred, ego-maniacal crumb!'

'These foolish things remind me of you, too,' Albert

said. 'Remember? The night I sleep-walked and you opened the window? The lighted cigarette you put in my shoe? Those hours I spent nailed in the lavatory? Don't they mean anything to you?'

'Get out of my way,' Treasure said. 'I don't want to know you.'

'Now you know it's too late for that, darling.' She was walking and he fell into step with her again. 'That's what I really miss. Nobody knows me the way you know me.'

'Don't bank on it,' she said. 'I'm hoping there's a God.'

'You can say that? You just tried to get me hanged!'

'That was just a silly, wishful impulse,' she said.

And then all at once she laughed; but bit it off, quickly.

'Oh my God,' Albert said. 'You haven't changed, have you – you still only laugh at your own jokes.'

'Then why bother?'

'Shall I tell you? It's because you're my only failure. Everybody else I've fooled. After all we went through together – '

'After all *I* went through together.'

'After all you went through together I don't like being strangers. I miss you, Treasure. I want to make it up to you.'

'You want to take me to bed tonight.'

'I want to take you to bed tonight – ' he pretended to remember himself. 'I mean . . .'

'You decided to try and take me to bed from the moment I threw that case at you in the police station,' she told him.

'You see? I knew you were only flirting!' Albert said. He offered the case. 'Here, do it again!'

'You'll never make love to me again,' Treasure said.

'Oh yes I will!'

'Oh no you won't!'

'Oh yes I will – and I won't use a contraceptive!'

'Oh yes you will!' she said.

They both laughed. They had stopped on a street corner. It was growing dark, the street lights were on.

'You see?' Albert said. 'We still laugh at the old jokes.'

She looked at him, soberly. 'You always thought a laugh took the place of everything. It doesn't, Albert. You think I haven't changed, but I have. Being a mother changed me – but you don't even know you were a father. That's something you're too selfish to know. You're a tally-boy. A wife to you is a bit of crumpet. You've got no respect for other people's marriages and you'd have none for your own.'

'I respect you, Treasure,' Albert said.

'Well,' she said, 'you did wait until I'd gone into hospital to get over my miscarriage before walking out on me – I suppose that's a kind of respect.'

Albert said: 'I didn't walk out on you – I walked out on the postman and the bailiff and the police. Everybody was catching up on me at once. I couldn't leave an address. I meant to come and see you – then you came down to the shop. Well, I didn't think it was any use, then. But I've felt worse about it every time I've thought about it. I've started talking to you when I'm alone. I mean it.'

Treasure stared at him. 'This is new,' she said. 'I should have to have time to figure this one out.'

'I miss you like hell,' he said.

'No,' she said. 'It's not that.'

'You're like a conscience – I told Grace that this morning. You see, I was talking about you this morning.'

She said: 'How's your eldest? The youngest is dead.'

'Isn't that a bond between us?' Albert said, earnestly.

145

'No,' she said. 'Not a bond, Albert. Whatever the opposite of a bond is, that's what's between us.'

'A gulf?'

'That'll do,' she said.

'Well, what do you think it is? My talking to you when I'm alone, I mean?'

'Well, I don't know. But I suppose the feeling of being with somebody who knows what a swine you are could give you a sense of peace or something.'

'I think that's it,' Albert said. 'That's what I miss. When I'm with you I don't have to put on an act or make conversation – '

'Or be civil or polite or thoughtful, or spend money,' she added.

Albert laughed. 'Look, while we're chatting here I could be driving you home. Just to the door. I wouldn't get out of the car. And you can sit on the back seat – by yourself, I mean – as we're going. It's no trouble, Treasure. It'd be a privilege.'

'Are you trying to tell me you've changed, Albert?'

'No. We never change, darling – but you can feel worse about the way you are.'

It took her by surprise and she stared at him again, as though for something missed. 'Did you read that in a book? But I forgot, you don't read books.'

'I thought about it when I found that girl dead this afternoon. She was a good type – a real sweetie. I felt awful, Treasure. I was sick.'

'Death does something to you,' Treasure said. Then she said: 'All right, Albert – you can drive me home.'

He took hold of her arm and looked at her, tenderly: 'Do you still hate me?'

'Yes – I shall always hate you,' she said, softly.

'Even when I'm old and grey?'

146

'Even more then,' she said.

She took his hand off her arm and they walked back separate and apart, but also together.

They came back towards the police station, chatting like old friends.

'You haven't ridden in the new car yet, have you?' Albert said.

'No, but I've had all the demand notes. They've been trying to find it for weeks. Quite a nice man – he put up some bookshelves for me.'

'Well that's all taken care of now – Cally's making me manager. Did I tell you? More money, a bonus, no more tallying – ' .

'You're talking to me – did you forget?'

'It's true, Treasure!'

'Then you must have got something on him at last.'

'In a way, yes.' He told her about Reggie Corby and Callendar's anxiety to make a property deal. 'He's worried sick I'll bring it out at the inquest.'

'But you'll have to – why should he get away with it if he drove her to suicide?'

'But didn't I tell you? She didn't say it. I made it up. You know how I make things up. She was dead when I found her – how could she say anything? But I knew what he was afraid of when he asked me. "Have you told the police?" he said. Why, he made her life a misery.'

'So you're going to cash in on it?'

'I didn't say I would. I said I might.'

'You said he was going to make you manager.'

'Well, I don't see why not. I mean, I'm not lying or breaking the law if I forget something that was never said – it's just his bad conscience that's paying dividends.'

'It's also blackmail,' Treasure said.

'How is it blackmail? I didn't go to them – they came
to me. I wouldn't even have thought of saying what she
said if he hadn't asked me. Besides, it's time I got a
responsible job and more money. I've earned it. I've
pushed the sales higher than anybody he's ever had.'

'You'll never settle in an office,' Treasure told him.
'You're a tally-boy. It's not just a job, it's a state of mind.
Wayward, irresponsible, fly-by-night, immoral – you've
got all the qualifications, Albert.'

'Not me, darling. Not any more. You're talking about
Jeff and Arnold. I want something with a bit of prestige
to it. These days you've got to have prestige.'

'Are you still giving Marjorie her weekly tumble?'
Treasure asked, politely.

'What a disgusting thing to say! You've never met her
husband. I like Cedric. He talks a lot of cock but I respect
him. After all, he was my schoolmaster.'

'That means you are,' Treasure said. 'You'd never
settle in a humdrum office, even if it did have your name
on the door.'

Albert made no reply to this; he knew she was there
even while Callendar was making the offer. They came to
the car and the hire-purchase man was sitting behind the
wheel.

'Hello, Mr Drake!' Treasure said. 'You've caught up
with him, then?'

'Good evening, Miss Hunter.' And then to Albert:
'I think you know the rules, sir. When we've sold the
car you'll be held responsible for the liability.'

'You know the big end's gone, do you?' Albert said.
'I just came back to cover it up for the night – the garage
were collecting it in the morning.'

'The big end?' Mr Drake said. 'That's an eighty pound
job on this model!'

148

'I know,' Albert told him. 'You'll have to have it seen to before you sell it. Oh, and it's not insured for any other driver – you'll need special cover before you can take it away, anyway.'

'My insurance covers that,' Mr Drake said.

'Oh. Well, just the big end, then.'

'Of course,' Mr Drake said, 'if you brought your payments up to date now you could keep it.'

'It's hardly worth it, really,' Albert said. 'How much do I owe in arrears?'

'Fifty pounds,' Mr Drake said. 'I shouldn't really accept it at this late stage, but in view of what you've told me . . .'

'Okay – jump out,' Albert said.

He took the wad of notes from his inside pocket and nonchalantly counted them. Treasure and Mr Drake watched. Only Drake was impressed.

'There you are, old man.' Albert gave the notes to Mr Drake, who carefully recounted them before making out a receipt.

Mr Drake was half-way back to his own car when he heard Albert start up. Looking rather sick he watched the car move smoothly away.

15

'THAT was Callendar's money,' Treasure said, as Albert drove her across town.

'I can make my own terms with Cally in the morning.'

'You're getting a power complex,' Treasure told him.

Albert grinned at her; the little brush with the hire-purchase man and having Treasure there made him feel suddenly in command. And he knew that he could get Treasure home to bed. He was not certain where this was going to lead, but it was what he wanted now. But she would need a drink or two; Treasure had always got helpless on cider.

'How would you like to come to a party?' he asked her.

'You're driving me home,' she reminded him. Don't do it, the inner voice told her. You shouldn't even be in the car. You shouldn't have dawdled when you came out of the police station.

'All right – just as you like. I shan't go. I'm not very keen on parties these days. Don't know many people.'

'Why do you say things like that to me?' she said. 'This car stinks of cheap scent.'

'Well, I've been out with one or two girls,' he admitted. 'But they bore me to death – talk talk talk!'

'I talk talk talk,' Treasure said.

'That's different,' he said. 'You talk about me.'

She laughed spontaneously. 'What sort of party?' she asked.

'A jazz party in Beachfield Road – a rock group and so on. I suppose there'll be some food. They wanted me to get along to ginger things up if I could. But I don't know, I suppose it'll be crowded with kids.'

'You mean you know where there's a party going on which you might be able to gatecrash,' Treasure said.

'That's right.'

They drove on in silence for a minute, then she said: 'I've got nothing to wear, anyway. Not for parties.'

'I can soon fix that!' Albert said.

He took the next turning towards Callendar's Warehouse. Stop him! Treasure's inner voice exclaimed. She wasn't listening.

The women's clothing department at Callendar's Warehouse was well stocked with mass-produced model dresses in the enormous range of fittings necessary for an off-the-peg business.

'Does Mr Callendar know you've got a key?' Treasure asked.

She was holding a pretty green sleeveless number up to herself and judging its effect in a long mirror.

'Not yet,' Albert said. 'But it'll soon be official – '

'Keep your hands off me!' Treasure said.

Albert had been draping the dress around her hips; he now stood back, obediently.

Treasure looked at him in the mirror: 'No obligation, you know – I'm just borrowing it.'

'No obligation, madam,' Albert confirmed.

He left her to browse amongst the dresses and petticoats and lingerie and went himself to the men's wear department. She heard him singing and her heart sang too; in a big warehouse filled with gay modern styles they felt like children in a toy factory with no one to supervise them. She chose shoes, stockings, panties, bra, petticoat, and a bright crimson dress.

'Albert!' she called.

Don't do it, said the voice.

'I'm not doing anything!' she replied.

Albert came through a curtain of coats dressed in a dinner-jacket suit with bow-tie and black suède shoes.

'You look marvellous!' he said.

'So do you!' she told him. Then, dubiously, 'Shall we be all right for a jazz party?'

'Will they be all right for us?' Albert said.

151

'You're having them all back,' Treasure told him at the look in his eye.

'On the stroke of midnight!'

'I don't know about that.'

'Come on,' Albert said. 'Let's see what happens.'

'Just keep your hands off me,' she said.

He tucked his hands inside the breast of his jacket and followed her out with a comic, cringing walk.

She felt him close behind her and shivered in the old way. 'Don't put the lights out till I'm outside!' she said.

They found the party in Beachfield Road by the number of scooters and motor-cycles parked outside. It was a semi-detached house full of teenagers and parents away. The lights were low, the hall, stairs, passages were clogged with motionless snogging shapes. Three young men were wedged into the front bay window playing an electric guitar, drums and bass. Four or five couples jived desperately in the middle of the room. Albert burst straight in:

'Carry on, folks!' he exclaimed. 'As if I were just an ordinary person!'

'Who the hell are you, then?' asked a literal-minded boy in charge of drinks by the door.

'Friend of Peter's,' Albert said. 'Peter Barnwell – he's here, isn't he?'

'Bloody cheek!' the boy said. Then he called: 'Pete!'

Peter laid aside his guitar and came over.

'This chap says he knows you. You might ask before inviting people!'

Peter stared hard at Albert, then at Treasure. 'I don't know you!'

'Either you know me,' Albert said, 'or I'm taking that guitar back!'

'I know him,' Peter said. 'Anyway, we can do with more girls.' He took Treasure's hand. 'You come upstairs; I'll show you where to put your coat – you can look after the drinks,' he said to Albert.

'Here, just a minute!' Albert said, as Treasure allowed herself to be led away.

'Share and share alike, mate – we're always short on birds,' the other boy said. 'Haven't bought any drink, have you?'

'Whose party is this?' Albert asked. 'Yours or mine?'

Without the uncertain melody of the guitar the drums and bass went on producing a thumping rhythm. Albert poured himself half a tumbler of whisky.

'Any vintage cider?' he asked the boy.

During the next two hours Albert and Treasure caught sight of each other through the crowd now and then; she stepped over him snogging on the stairs, he stepped over her similarly engaged.

'How about a dance?' Albert had pulled a young man's head aside to ask her the question.

'Don't do it!' she said. Then she hiccuped. 'I wasn't supposed to say that – sorry. Not on top of that cider – where's it keep coming from?'

'There's another glass just by your hand,' Albert said, passing on.

By midnight Albert had run his technique over every girl in the house, drunk half a bottle of whisky, jived, played the drums and was now raiding the kitchen.

'Albert!'

He stopped cutting cheese to listen, his mouth full. Treasure's voice came distantly above the sound of the music, talking, and dancing. It didn't come again and he went on listening for a moment. He popped another piece of cheese into the mouth of a girl sitting on the table.

'Have you ever kissed while you're eating?' she asked.

'You kids!' Albert said. 'Always looking for some perversion!'

He stopped kissing her and listened again. 'Stay there!' he said. 'Don't move. . . .'

He went slowly out of the kitchen and through the dark passage, stepping over shapes. The trouble was, in his head she was always calling him.

'You can't go up there, mate – they're busy!' A large youth blocked his way on the stairs.

Albert hooked his arm around the youth's neck and yanked him down the stairs. He went to the only bedroom with a closed door, burst in. In the half-darkness he found two youths holding Treasure on the bed; all he could see of her was bare legs. Albert swung them off one at a time, crashing his big fist into their faces. Treasure scrambled off the bed, pulling her clothes together.

'Get out to the car!' Albert told her.

She rushed out of the room and down the stairs, through the hall and out of the front door, up the garden path and into the car, slamming the door behind her. She was sitting in the front seat, her head on her lap, crying, when Albert came out.

'I've got the guitar,' he said. He put it on the back seat, started the motor and drove away. 'Have they mucked that dress up?' he asked.

Treasure's crying turned into hysterical laughter. With one hand on the wheel he turned and slapped her face, hard. She slapped his, harder.

'You're not supposed to do that!' Albert said.

'You bastard!' she said. 'You nearly had me fooled again!'

Albert looked at her. 'I don't get it! I did my best! I should've thought you might have thanked me!'

154

'What for?' Treasure said.

He stared at her in astonished disbelief that slowly turned to appalled belief. She lowered her head and covered her face with her hands.

'I'll kill them!' he muttered.

'Just take me home,' she said. 'And don't get out of the car. . . .'

'Mr Callendar wants to see you, Mr Argyle,' Hetty said as Albert came in the next morning.

Jeff and Arnold were sorting the day's merchandise.

'What've you been up to, old chappie?' Jeff asked.

'You want to watch yourself,' Albert told him. 'There's going to be a few changes around here.'

'So I understand,' Jeff said.

Albert looked from smirking face to smirking face.

'You want to clear up after yourself when you bring birds in at night,' Arnold said. 'I always do.'

Puzzled, Albert tapped the office door and entered. Mr Callendar did not immediately look up from his paperwork; this was a depressing sign.

'I've decided not to say anything,' Albert said, kicking off on an optimistic note.

Mr Callendar looked at him. 'That's very good of you, Albert – considering she was dead on hitting the ground.'

'She couldn't have been!'

'Two doctors say so – I wouldn't go against them if I were you.'

'I didn't actually tell the police,' Albert said.

'Now we know why, don't we? Mr Corby is not very pleased.'

'What's he doing about the site?'

'This is not your business, Albert. Sit down. I want you to explain one or two things. . . .'

It was one of Mr Callendar's specific criticisms and this time he had a lot to go on. A pair of girl's panties found in the showroom, signs of clothes having been taken – though what kind and how many Hetty's book-keeping had failed to reveal. The washing-machine returned from Mrs Mason had never been purchased at Callendar's at all – it was the wrong make and five years old.

'I also took the liberty of going through the suit you left here last night – since you had taken the liberty of wearing one of ours. Your accounts book shows fifty pounds collected yesterday – '

'You told me not to bother to pay it in until this morning,' Albert reminded him.

'So I did,' Mr Callendar agreed. 'Give it to me now.'

'Now?'

'Now,' Mr Callendar said.

'Okay – I'll give it to Hetty.'

'I asked you to give it to me,' Mr Callendar said.

'Don't you trust me or something?'

Mr Callendar picked up a slip of paper which he had also found in Albert's suit pocket. Albert stared at it; it was the receipt for fifty pounds from the hire-purchase man.

'Well, what else could I do?' Albert said. 'I'll pay you back – you know that.'

'That's the only reason I'm not ringing the police.' Mr Callendar said. 'You remember what happened to Max? I'm going to be lenient with you this time, Albert.'

'Stop it out of my money,' Albert said.

'I will – but don't depend on Hetty's book-keeping this time. I shall keep a separate account. With the damage your girl-friend did you owe me a hundred pounds, not counting what you took from here when you broke in last night.'

'I didn't break in – I've got a key! Yesterday I was going to be manager!'

'If that was your first night's work as manager I can only thank my lucky stars you lost the job – we'll say four pounds a week deducted from your salary, that makes – '

'I can't live on eight quid a week!' Albert exclaimed.

'You'll have to step up your sales, won't you – one more thing. What's this?'

Mr Callendar was holding the petition for the tree which he had also found in Albert's pocket. Albert explained what it was. Mr Callendar expressed his incredulity.

'You're helping the old folk save their tree and getting nothing in return?'

'You've got to help people sometimes,' Albert said.

'If you're going to start being eccentric, don't do it in my time, please, Albert.'

'We're all doing it!' Albert said. 'Why pick on me?'

'It's incredible!' Mr Callendar said. 'Loaded atom bombs all over the world, the Common Market only two steps away – and all these people signing a petition to save an old tree!'

'There's a lot of feeling in the town,' Albert said, righteously. 'Somebody's got to stick up for these old people!'

Mr Callendar suddenly had goose-pimples, but they didn't show. 'Get me those other petitions,' he said.

When the tally-boys had gone on their rounds Mr Callendar telephoned Reginald Corby at the Chas. Arthur offices.

'Reggie – have you parted with that option yet? Good – don't do it. I've got something to put you on the council

157

without fail – better than dogs, better than the swimming pool or playing fields. Something the whole town will support you on – I've already got seven hundred and twenty-three bona-fide signatures. Seven hundred and twenty-four,' he said, as he added his own.

When Coral Wentworth answered the door Albert stood there with all her parcels piled high in his arms.

'Father Christmas!' he said. 'Sorry I'm late delivering them, madam!'

'Well I don't know what to say!' she exclaimed. 'I'm afraid you'll have to take them back. My husband's gone on short time – at least, they're working to rule, that's the same thing. I can't honestly afford thirty-three shillings a week now – I'm terribly sorry.'

'It won't last forever, will it?'

'It might be weeks – they haven't got much consideration for us housewives.'

'Husbands are a dead loss,' Albert said. 'I could've told you that.'

She laughed. 'It's a bit late telling me now!'

'Let's talk about it inside,' Albert suggested. 'I dare say we can manage something between us, darling.'

Coral giggled. 'I don't like the sound of that!' And as she let him in and closed the door: 'You'll have to excuse me – I'm afraid I'm in the middle of dressing.'

Albert followed her through to the sitting-room, appraising her figure wrapped in a flimsy housecoat. He was glad he hadn't swapped her for those girls of Jeff's. Single girls placed too much importance on it. No sense of values.

He helped her unpack the nylon-fur rug, the curb and curb-set, a chiming clock, a parcel of clothes and shoes, a bedside lamp.

158

'Where does this go?' he asked, holding the lamp.

'As if you didn't know!' Coral said. 'Hasn't Marjorie got one?'

'Oh yes – I remember.'

He followed her upstairs, waiting while she drew the curtains on the landing. He looked at his watch.

Albert was going to be late again.

SOMETHING FOR NOTHING

For Bill Howard Baker

1

'It's ucky. That's what it is. It's ucky,' the barber said.

Albert, his chin tucked tightly into his chest as the bits of hair fell down his back, grunted. The barber didn't know what ucky meant, but it was ucky. Albert's tongue was ucky, his liver was ucky, his eyes with the sand in them were ucky. Saturday was ucky. Weddings and haircuts. All ucky. A new word for the old miseries. The world was ucky. All he wanted to do was to sick it up. But the barber only meant the weather.

'Think they'll play?'

Saturdays, weddings, haircuts and football. Amputations. Albert was having an amputation this morning instead of a shampoo. The amputation was going on at the church around the corner.

'Of course they'll play, Charlie. Why shouldn't they play? They like a bit of mud.'

Voices over scene.

'You're right. They play better with a bit of mud.'

Sat-upon newspapers, tobacco smoke, body-odours, cosmetics.

'Not too bad for an old gentleman,' said the barber.

Mustn't grumble. None of us getting any younger. You've got to take the rough with the smooth. It could be worse, couldn't it?

Albert gripped the chair tightly. It was worse than having a tooth out. All this stupidity. They had to talk in little slogans or they didn't know what was being said. The conversation had to be predictable or they would gape at you with their dead eyes.

'Another week gone.'

'Soon rolls round.'

'Tomorrow's Sunday.'

'Here comes Sam.'

'Lucky old Sam.'

'Hello mate.' Sam looked along the line of waiting men, then at the two engaged chairs. 'Somebody called Argyle?'

Albert looked up.

Sam gave him a sly grin. 'That your bird outside?'

Albert's heart jumped; he looked at the door and saw half a head of yellow hair. He didn't know it. She was not in bridal gown.

'She's asking for you.'

'Go on, mate.'

'You can't keep 'em waiting.'

Albert sank back, his chin hard on the ucky white sheet. 'Tell her I'm not here.'

Laughter all round. The door opening, Sam's lying voice, a girl's reply; more laughter, Sam's voice again.

'She would've come in only Charlie's got his rubber goods in the window.'

More laughter, more slogans, more ucky, more sick, more amputation. What happened when you lost bits of yourself? Take a finger that you'd used for twenty-six years before finally getting it caught in a machine. Was it still you? It seemed to Albert, ignoring the chatter around the barber shop, that anything that grew on you was always yours. The hair dropping into his lap would always be a part of him, whether it finished up burnt or stuffing a cushion. He had never burned his finger-nail clippings but instead treated them with a bit of reverence. And this morning he was having his heart out. That's what it amounted to. Like a tooth.

Treasure had grown on him and now she was getting married.

'Don't forget your stamps,' the barber said when Albert was leaving.

164

Albert took the six pink stamps. It was the only reason he came to this particular hairdresser's which was a mile across town from his digs. When he had a car things like that didn't matter. Not having a car was part of the way he was feeling. It was humiliating. Like having one leg or a hump on your back. No car and no money and no job. And now no Treasure.

The girl with the yellow hair was waiting for him. Albert smiled at her.

'I'm glad you waited,' he said. 'Long time, darling.'

'You've never seen me before,' she said.

Albert laughed again and gave a quick look round, mock-scared for the proprieties. 'Well, let's keep it a secret.'

She gave no sign of appreciation but just looked at him as if she was busy. 'Are you Mr Albert Argyle of number five Railway Street?'

'That's only half the story. Let's take it somewhere – how about a drink?'

'Are you or aren't you?'

'I can't deny it.'

'Then will you take this?'

What happened next was swift and ridiculous on a wet Saturday morning town street. She gave him a document. Albert swiftly looked at it and then dropped it on the path and walked away.

The girl picked it up and ran after him.

'They're getting sneaky, aren't they?' Albert said, still walking. She had to hurry to keep up with him. He said: 'Lady bums yet?'

'I'm not from the County Court,' she told him. 'I'm from the Inland Revenue. It's a High Court summons.'

Albert stopped walking and looked at her; all of her. She blushed and fidgeted. 'Income tax?' he said. 'Bloody renegade.'

She was getting angry now. 'You'd better take it. Here you are – '

165

She thrust the summons at Albert who quickly put his hands behind his back. She tried to tuck the document under his arm but he closed them tightly to his side again.

'Leave me alone!' he cried in a shrill falsetto.

The girl, red-faced, stepped away from him. People were beginning to stare.

'Tell you what I'll do,' Albert said, rationally. 'You have a drink with me, then I'll take it.'

'No.'

Albert shrugged, walked away from her. The girl followed him.

'Let him go, dear,' a passing woman told the girl. 'They're not worth it.'

The girl hurried to catch up with Albert. He grinned at her. They walked along in silence for a moment. Albert felt grateful towards the girl. He was feeling better.

'What happened to old Finbow, then?' he asked. 'This was his job.'

'Mr Finbow's dead,' she said.

Albert looked at her and saw that it was true. It saddened him. 'I'm not surprised,' he said. Then he said earnestly: 'You're on the wrong side, darling.'

'Will you please take it?' It was a plea now. She had detected a softening.

Albert stopped walking again, looked at his watch. 'You do something for me, I'll do something for you.'

'No. I'm sorry, it's not allowed – it's in the rules.'

He gave her an innocent stare. 'What's in the rules? Dirty old lot! Look, just come with me.'

'I've got to get back to the office,' she said. 'I've got the keys – I have to leave them with the caretaker.'

Albert walked on. She kept up with him, fretful, embarrassed.

'Five minutes,' he said, 'that's all.'

'Why don't you take this summons, Mr Argyle? You'll have to take it in the end. Where're you going?'

They walked on, Albert keeping sufficiently apart from her

166

to forestall any attempt she might make to serve the summons on him. Neither was aware of the comedy.

Albert walked with fastidious care, avoiding the places fouled and soiled by humans and animals. He'd been using the roads, driving shiny cars, for so long that he'd forgotten there were still dirty pavements. Dirty, smoke-blacked houses and tatty shops, wet grey slate roofs, dirty dogs. dirty people, dirty kids. Dirty, filthy, muck-heap of a town. Dough-faces, Saturday-busy, laying out the wages on the same things as last week – as a thousand other weeks past and future. Stinking, depressing Saturday routine. The Agricultural Tractor Factory had gone on short time and half the town was out of work, half the tally houses closed, finished, Albert with them. But they were no worse off: they had nothing in work, nothing out of work. Just food, bed and the telly. And this filthy, stinking Victorian town which they inhabited like worms in an old corpse. Ucky. All ucky. . . .

Albert spat. 'Sorry,' he said.

'Where're we going?' the girl said. 'I mean, where're you going?'

'Christ knows. Where's anybody going? You tell me.'

Dear Sir . . . Albert was composing a letter to the local newspaper. *Why don't they pull this fucking town down?*

They came to the church. A knot of people, mostly women, outside the lych gate, waiting for the bride.

'Morbid lot,' Albert said.

The girl began to smile, then remembered the situation.

'Hold my arm,' Albert said.

'No.'

'Hold my arm and afterwards I'll take the summons – promise.'

The girl held his arm. He pulled her to the front of the waiting people. The wedding party stood amongst the graves having their photographs taken.

The bride was about to have her photograph taken when she saw Albert.

'Can I have that one again?' the photographer asked. 'Smile, dear,' he told Treasure.

As bride and groom got into the car Albert threw the contents of a box over them. Immediately there was an outcry:

'No confetti!'

'No confetti!'

The vicar came running out: 'Who threw that?' The crowd dispersed, guilty. 'We'll have trouble with the police,' the vicar said.

Albert drew the girl away, staring after the departing ribboned car. He smiled admiringly. 'White, yet!' he said. Then he looked over the churchyard wall.

'My mum's in there,' he said.

'Don't you want to wait for her?' the girl asked.

'She's waiting for me,' Albert said. 'She's one of those with a gravestone.'

The girl was embarrassed again. 'I'm sorry.'

She wanted to take her hand away from his arm but felt that it would hurt him even more. Even more than something – she didn't know what. He saw this and gave her an appreciative smile. He released her and held out his hand.

'I'll take it now.'

Giving him the summons now the girl felt inhuman. Instead she said, 'I'll come for a drink if you like.'

'That's all right, love. I'm not in the mood now. Got to get to the station.'

'Oh,' the girl said. She gave him the summons.

He put it into his pocket.

'Are you going away?' she asked.

Albert was staring into the graveyard.

'What time is your train?' she asked.

'Plenty of trains,' Albert said.

Suddenly she was frightened. 'Shouldn't you go home?'

He looked round at her, surprised. 'What for?'

She was shy and she didn't want to be presumptuous. 'What about the children?' she asked. Then she gave a nervous cough.

'What children?'

'Your children.'

His genuinely blank stare frightened her even more. She spoke kindly, gently, reminding him. 'You've got three – two girls and a boy.' He didn't seem to remember and she tried again. 'Janice, Coral and Peter. At least, they're the three you claim allowances for.'

Now Albert got the girl back into focus. The girl from the income tax office. And Treasure gone. And Saturday.

'You're right,' he said 'Let's go back to my place for a drink, darling.'

'Your place?'

'Don't you like kids?'

'Oh yes, of course.'

They walked along by the churchyard wall, waited for the last of the wedding cars to splash past before crossing the road. Albert, gentlemanly, held her arm till they reached the other side, then he let go of her. He glanced down at her. Her face was closed now as she wrestled with something, then she said :

'I can't stay very long, I'm afraid.'

'Okay, darling.'

She said : 'My name is Miss Finbow.'

Albert looked at her again, compassionately. 'Was he? . . .'

She nodded.

'Sorry about your dad, love,' Albert said. He sniffed, kicked a stone which rattled off ahead of them. 'Still, I don't know that he's any worse off.'

They walked on and she held his arm as though she had temporarily saved him.

The little terraced cottage in Railway Street was empty and cold and damp. There were four bed-sitters sharing bathroom and kitchen; one was vacant, the other two occupants were home for the week-end or somewhere for the week-end. The fourth was Albert's and he led Miss Finbow there.

She gave a nervous cough on the narrow staircase as she followed him up. 'They're very quiet,' she said.

'Who?'

'The children.'

'Oh, well,' Albert said, 'I expect the landlady's taken them to the pictures.'

He stood aside and the girl went into his room. He followed her in, closed the door, pulled a chair round for her, switched on the electric fire.

She sat on the edge of the chair, looking round. 'It's early for the pictures, isn't it?'

Albert opened a cupboard and surveyed the survivors of his last party; a few drops of wine, a bottle of scotch. 'They do the rounds first – you know, Woolworths, Marks, Home Stores, the market.' He was looking at her, unobserved, trying to classify her for drink.

Miss Finbow was not easy to classify. She was not one of Albert's girls. Given a dozen girls only half as pretty he would not have chosen Miss Finbow. Briefly, in Albert's language, she was the scrubbed type. The natural gold-yellow hair was misleading and wasted in a way.

'Have a whisky?' he asked her.

The thought of it made her jump. 'Oh, no thank you – lemonade would be nice.'

'I've got cider,' he said.

'Just a little, then,' she said. Then, anxiously: 'What are you going to have?'

'I think I'll join you – don't drink much myself. Have to keep something in for friends, though.'

'Yes.'

She settled farther back in the chair. Albert watched her from time to time as he mixed whisky into the cider bottle. No make-up, thick untouched eyebrows, a nice mouth. A mole with a fuzz of whiskers on it near her left ear. She sat with her knees tightly together, a tweed skirt smoothly covering them. Her legs were long and undisguisedly good.

'Here we are.' Albert brought a tray with the cider bottle

and two glasses. 'They say it's a kid's drink,' he said, 'but I like it.'

'Yes,' she said.

He filled both glasses, gave one to her, raised his; she smiled politely at him and started drinking. Her face straightened at the first taste – then the moment was past and she went on drinking.

'What do you do in your spare time then?' Albert asked. 'Hockey?'

'No!' For the first time Miss Finbow was animated. 'Sorry!'

She collected herself. 'Whatever made you say that?'

Albert shrugged and she said :

'I suppose I look the hockey type?'

'I like the hockey type,' Albert said. 'I can't stand these sex-pots.'

'Thank you very much,' she said. She finished her drink, glanced at her watch.

Albert looked at her wretchedly; he had blundered badly and doubted his ability to save the situation. 'I said the wrong thing, didn't I?'

'No, of course not – anyway, I've got to be going.'

'I said the wrong thing,' Albert said, gloomily. 'What do you do, then?' He thought of a few unlikely things. 'Dancing? Skating? Courting?'

She bent round to pick up her bag and Albert quickly filled her glass; she caught him half-way. 'No more, thank you.'

'Sorry,' Albert said. 'Still, it won't hurt you – or don't you drink?'

She gave him an angry stare. 'Yes, of course I drink – and smoke. You make me feel like some sort of freak. Are you always like this with people you meet? No wonder your girl friends get married and your wife leaves you.'

'Who the hell told you that?' Albert asked her.

She wished she had not said it and picked up her glass to cover the situation. 'Just gossip at the office.'

171

'Of course,' Albert said. 'A tax office knows everything about everybody. Highly confidential stuff.'

'I shouldn't have said that. I'm sorry, Mr Argyle.'

Albert said: 'Don't you know my first name, then?'

'Albert,' she said, scarlet and confused. And then she caught him laughing at her and she smiled.

'What's yours, then?'

'Alice,' she said.

'Right then, Alice,' Albert said, 'What do you do in your spare time?'

'Swimming in the summer.'

'I bet you look good in a two-piece.' She gave him a half-startled look and he added: 'What about the winter?'

'I belong to a literary circle – we talk about books.'

Albert made a comic pretence of warm interest. 'That's nice!'

Alice laughed; it was partly Albert, partly the laced cider. 'Well, it's not hockey!'

'Nothing wrong with books,' Albert said. 'I like books.'

The girl brightened. 'Who's your favourite author?'

'Who's yours?' Albert said.

'Oh, I don't know – anything I like. Daphne du Maurier, Dennis Wheatley, Nevil Shute.'

'Oh yes,' Albert said. 'You can't go wrong there. Got time for a cigarette?'

'No thank you – well, just one, then.'

He leaned forward and lit her a cigarette, then gave her a drink to go with it. 'Ever read Hank Jansen?' he asked.

She thought for a moment and then shook her head. 'I don't think so. What sort of books does he write?'

'All sorts. About life. He has these marvellous covers. There's some over there.'

She looked across the room, searching for a bookcase. The lurid covers were pinned to the wall over Albert's bed.

She smiled politely. 'Very nice.'

Albert felt that he had blundered again and it had to be put right. 'I do a bit of writing myself,' he said.

And suddenly he had said the right thing. Alice Finbow looked at him as though seeing him for the first time.

'You look like a writer,' she said.

Albert laughed, modestly. She looked around the room again with fresh eyes.

'Nudes on the wall,' she said, 'whisky in the cupboard, inviting girls into your bedroom and everything, insulting them.'

Albert began to expand; apparently everything she had deplored in some men was perfectly all right in a writer. Albert sprawled a little and unfastened his tie.

'What have you written?' she asked. She was smoking and drinking with new zest now.

'This and that,' Albert said.

'A novel?'

'Sort of,' Albert said.

'Short stories?'

'Fairly short,' Albert said.

'Have they been published?' Alice asked.

'Printed?' Albert said. 'Oh, yes.' And then seeing the inevitable question coming, he added: 'In France.'

She laughed at him. 'Well! You must be terribly good. What name do you write under – or do you use your own?'

'Harris,' Albert said. 'Albert Harris. It's my real name – I live under a pen name. Different, you see.'

She was sitting back in the chair, her knees crossed, relaxed and laughing. 'Tell me one of your stories – one that's been published.'

Albert gave her an exciting synopsis of *The Guns of Navarone,* changing names and places, giving it a French title and several awards.

'It sounds marvellous,' the girl said. 'How did you think of it?'

'It was a true story,' Albert said. 'That's how my father got killed.'

'I'm terribly sorry,' she said. It drew them together in sympathy for a quiet moment. Then she said: 'Didn't it make you any money? You ought to be rich.'

'Tax took the lot,' Albert said, adding quickly: 'French tax.'

'I'm sorry,' she said, and she was apologizing for herself. Then, to make up for it, she said: 'If Argyle isn't your right name then that summons is invalid – you don't have to take it.'

'Phew!' Albert exclaimed. 'We can't open that one, can we? I mean that'd get me into more trouble.'

She frowned over it. 'I suppose it would. Your whole file's in the name of Argyle – there's reams of it.'

'Yes, I know.'

'Shouldn't you get an accountant to sort it out?'

'Do me a favour,' Albert said. 'It was getting an accountant that got me into all this. Never paid any tax until I had an accountant. He dug into all my past earnings – showed 'em everything. You ask your father – oh, I'm sorry.'

'It's all right.'

'In the end I couldn't pay the accountant and he sued me – well, you know, success is a crime in this country. They send you to prison for it.'

Alice laughed at him again. 'I can see I shall have to lose your file.'

Albert didn't laugh at this. 'What would that do?'

'I was joking,' Alice said. 'One file got mislaid once and the man didn't pay any tax for ten years.' She caught his thoughtful expression and grew sober. 'That couldn't happen these days. We're more efficient now.'

Albert was looking into her eyes. Her nervous cough came back.

'It would get me the sack.'

Albert did not appear to be listening. He started blowing smoke rings, poured some more drinks. Somehow it didn't destroy the conversation; what she had said still hovered in the warm room with the smoke.

174

'I'm only a temporary Civil Servant at the moment. My exams are just coming up. I have to support my mother now.'

'I was just thinking about that wedding reception,' Albert said. 'I think we ought to go.'

Alice was so relieved she smiled again: 'That would be nice – cheer you up.' Then: 'Wouldn't she mind?'

Albert said: 'I'll take her a nice wedding present.' Then, looking at the girl: 'I'll get two nice buttonholes.'

'*I* can't come!' Alice said.

Albert leaned over and held her hand. 'Of course you can, Alice. We don't want her to think I'm left on the shelf, do we?'

'I've got to get back to the office with the keys.' Albert continued holding her hand, smiling into her eyes. 'Besides,' she went on desperately, 'it's Saturday. I do all the shopping for mother. It's a terribly busy day.'

'I know,' Albert said. 'So we'll take my car, pick up your mother, do the shopping, then go on to the reception – with any luck we'll get there just before the happy couple leave.'

'No, I'm sorry,' Alice said.

Albert left his chair and put his arms around her, pulled her up from her chair, trapping her arms. He kissed her with great warmth, then looked at her; she was staring at him in sheer terror.

'Does it have to be the same old Saturday? Are you frightened of not doing the same old thing, Miss Finbow?'

'Leave go of me!'

Albert released her immediately, now completely tuned in to her. 'I'm sorry,' he said, simply and forlornly. He picked up her gloves and bag and gave them to her. She turned away from him, putting on her gloves. It became a long process.

'I didn't know you had a car,' she said, aggrievedly. 'I thought you were broke.'

'I'm only broke when I haven't any ideas,' Albert said. 'I

175

just got an idea, that's all.' It was no more than the truth.

'I thought you were depressed,' she said. 'Suicidal. That's why I came here.'

'I was,' Albert said. 'I was.' And with dignity: 'Thank you.'

He sat down and studied his feet. She turned and looked down at him. He knew that she wanted to shift ground.

'You writers!' she said.

He looked up and met her eyes, hopefully. She smiled at him. Her face was flushed, there was a gleam in her eye. He had given her the chance to be in command of the situation; the chance to make sacrifices in the cause of art if she wanted to. If she felt like it.

'Come on, then,' she said, exasperated. 'We'll see ...'

He *was* broke, he had *not* got a car, he *had* felt suicidal – in a light-hearted way. It was the barber shop mostly, rather than the state of the world or Treasure getting married. But when he had told Miss Finbow – who at the time had seemed homely and not his type – that he was going to the station, it was not to put his neck on the line. Ever since he left school the only unpredictable thing you could do in this town on a Saturday was go to the railway station and pick yourself one of the country birds coming in to the hops and pictures and the coffee bars.

Unpredictable was whether he would find something special, whether he would get her back to his room, whether she would stay the night and perhaps cook for him on Sunday morning. It had been harder the past two Saturdays without a car. Now he had settled for Alice and an idea and Albert started to come alive, started to extend himself. He was always at his best acting a part, always depressed being himself.

Alice waited while he went to the bathroom to change his shirt and get the hairs off his back, then she waited again in a café while he went to collect the car. He knew she would go on waiting. He had kissed her just once and she would go on waiting until he kissed her again. He could play it cool, choose his time now; he had set it up, he had got it made.

At a car-hire firm in Butterhall Street he booked himself a new Ford for the rest of Saturday and through to Monday, paying a ten pounds deposit with a dud cheque.

'You're sure this is all right, old chappie?' the manager asked him, without any delicate evasions.

'You don't have to take it,' Albert told him.

'If business was any better I wouldn't,' the manager said. It was a man named Jackson and they knew each other quite well. They had worked together in the same tally shop. Jackson spoke as a friend. 'If this one bounces, you'll go inside,' he promised. Then he said: 'Got a job, Albert?'

'A few offers,' Albert said. 'Got to keep up appearances.'

Albert watched as the big new car was rolled out and dusted, the mileage checked.

'Don't beat it up,' Jackson pleaded as Albert got in. 'You pay the first ten pounds.'

Albert looked shocked at the thought, then said, carelessly: 'What's Cally doing now?'

Jackson laughed. 'You can forget him. He doesn't want any of us old boys around. We know too much about him.'

'That can work both ways,' Albert told him. 'Is he in the money?'

Jackson shrugged. 'Still playing golf. Still got his Bentley. So he says.'

Albert said: 'I heard he was on the road.'

'That's not the way he says it.' Jackson winked. 'Area manager for T.T. Trading Stamps. He'll be up at the golf club tomorrow.'

Albert said: 'Have you got any clubs, Jacko?'

Jackson stared at him for a moment. 'What have you got on, old boy?'

Albert put his finger to his lips. Jackson was getting increasingly curious.

'Are you going to let me in, Albert? I'd do the same for you.'

'I'm sure,' Albert said.

Jackson said: 'Do you know what I make here? Ten quid a week – that's the truth.'

'And what you can pick up,' Albert said.

Jackson said: 'There's good money in trading stamps. Salary, car, commission on every customer – it's our field, Albert.'

'My field,' Albert said.

'Have you got the in?' Jackson asked, his voice thin with anxiety. And as an afterthought: 'You can borrow my clubs tomorrow.'

'Tell you what I'll do,' Albert said. 'I'll think about it.'

Albert started the engine.

'Is that a promise?' Jackson asked. The car was moving slowly out towards the street, he was walking alongside.

'If you promise me a couple of things,' Albert said. 'Lend me your clubs and tear up that cheque.'

He drove out into the street, blaring the hooter. Jackson stared after him; mournfully he looked at the cheque in his hand. Slowly he tore it up.

The café was in the main street and there was no parking. Albert drew up outside and hooted several times. It was as much to attract general attention as bring the girl out. He caught several glances from half-familiar town faces and made an elaborate business of lighting a cigarette. A police-constable came over.

'You can't park here, sir –' His face changed to a welcoming smile. 'Hello, Albert!'

'Hello, Sid.'

'New bus, then?'

'Not mine, mate.'

'Didn't think it was,' the constable said. 'Knocked it off, have you?'

'Something like that,' Albert grinned. 'And questions?'

The constable laughed loudly. 'You couldn't tell the truth to your maker!' He was still laughing when Alice appeared

178

at the offside door. 'Aye, aye – I might've known!' said the policeman.

He watched Albert drive away with the girl. If Albert was in business again the town was looking up. People like Albert were walking barometers in a town like this. Give 'em a shake and you could tell what was coming. The constable strolled away whistling, but he didn't know why.

To an intelligent girl the half-truth was always better than the lie. Albert told Alice the car was not his.

'I've got an old Jag. They haven't finished tuning the engine. Lent me this one. It's a bit too respectable for me.'

'You needn't tell my mother that,' Alice said.

Albert registered this quite unconsciously. It opened the door a little wider. There was practically nothing you couldn't find a use for in the game of human relationships. If he could tell her mother one lie then he could tell her another.

'The reception will be going on a bit latish,' he told her mother. 'Unfortunately I've got to leave early – business appointment.'

'Perhaps you can get a taxi, Alice,' Mrs Finbow said.

Albert said: 'I'll arrange it.'

The girl looked puzzled. 'I won't want to stay there on my own. I don't know anybody.'

Albert said: 'My sister will be there. She'll look after you. In fact, if you wanted to she'd put you up at her place and I'll pick you up there in the morning.'

'I couldn't do that,' Alice said.

'She likes to get home at night now I'm alone,' Mrs Finbow said.

Albert said: 'Quite natural.'

He heard them holding a whispered conference as he went back to the car.

'It's quite all right dear if you want to stay – you don't get out much.'

'I'll see . . .'

When they joined him at the car Albert smiled at the mother. 'Why don't you come? Do you good!'

'Oh! No thank you. But it's very nice of you to ask.'

Albert drove away, Alice waving back. Then she turned back and looked at Albert's face; a little fond, a little worried. 'She likes you, Albert.'

'Good taste.'

They laughed together.

'I'm not sure about that,' she said. He glanced at her, pretending to be hurt. 'You're two people,' she said. He glanced each side as if looking for the other one. 'You're not the Mr Argyle who came out of the barber's this morning,' she said.

'Well now I've got you.' They smiled at each other, then he said: 'How did you know I was there?'

She looked evasive. 'It's a trade secret.'

'Go on, then.'

'When it comes to serving writs we know the habits of the regulars.'

'There are a lot of barbers in town.'

'Only three give pink stamps,' she said. 'You're a pink stamp man.'

'Something for nothing,' Albert said.

'Is that what you believe in?'

'It's not always what I get,' Albert said with feeling.

Alice waited again while Albert went into the Treasure Trove Trading Stamp gift shop and came out with a record player, gift wrapped, got in the car with her.

'What more could I give her? Twenty books of stamps that cost. Do you know how many haircuts that is? How many pounds of potatoes, eggs, pots of jam, gallons of petrol – how many hundreds of miles looking for the shop with the franchise? How much shoe-leather? Tyre wear? Oil, service, depreciation and wear and tear? How much licking of stamps and drinking afterwards? Live for free with TTT! That's a laugh to start with.'

'Then why do you do it –?' Alice said. 'My mother doesn't believe in them. Nor do I. Shops don't give them in Bentley Park.'

'I know. It's very select.'

Alice flushed. 'I didn't mean that.'

'I've heard them,' Albert said. 'If the women ask for trading stamps it's always for their kid. Angela's collecting them, silly child – still, I may as well take them and keep her happy.'

Alice laughed at this. 'That's true.'

'I know it's true.'

They laughed into each other's eyes for a moment with complete *rapport,* all inhibitions gone. Then she became aware of this moment and grew self-conscious about it, started reading the label on the gift. It said: 'From Albert and Alice.' She looked at him. 'You shouldn't have done that, Albert. She won't like it.'

'They were her stamps anyway,' Albert said. 'I was saving them towards our home.' Treasure would have seen the idiocy of this remark but Alice saw only the poignancy and Albert had to make do with it; any girl but Treasure was making do. Still, it was easier, too. Not so much of a fight, but not so much of a triumph. Alice was already in the palm of his hand though she didn't know it. 'Ned led the moke to the pond,' Albert thought. It was as far as he had gone with shorthand when he had decided to become a star crime reporter and changed his mind.

'Don't worry about it,' Alice said. She had mistaken his brooding for anxiety and sadness.

'All right,' Albert said. Then he said: 'Do me a big favour, Alice?'

She looked at him. He took her hand and slipped an engagement ring on her finger. She tried to get it off but he stopped her.

'Please,' he said.

'No, Albert. It isn't right. I know why you want to do it but it's not right.'

'She won't know.'

'It's not right for me,' Alice said. 'You don't know what it means to a girl.'

'Yes, I do,' Albert said, fervently.

'It's not right to use it as a trick.'

'You can keep it – I mean, put it on another finger afterwards.'

Alice looked at the ring. 'Are they real?'

'But old,' Albert said.

Her eyes were moist with sympathy when she looked at him. 'Oh, Albert – I'm sorry.'

He applied himself to the driving.

She said: 'But I thought you were already married? And separated or something? Or did she – die?'

He concentrated on the traffic.

'Don't tell me if you'd rather not.'

He looked at her, gratefully. 'Someday,' he said.

Saturday afternoons were football matches and wedding receptions. The biggest reception was at the Town Hall, lesser ones at various hotels throughout the town, smaller ones at church and chapel halls and tiny ones in private houses. Terese and Charles were holding a reception for seventy guests in the banqueting hall of The White Hart. Dressed in their going-away clothes they were posing for the last photograph when the bride saw Albert come in.

'Could I have that again?' the photographer said. 'I don't think you were smiling.'

'All right, carry on everybody!' Albert called, cheerily.

'As if I were just an ordinary person,' Terese muttered, forcing a smile for the duration of the flash and not a moment longer.

'As if I were just an ordinary person,' Albert finished.

He came up to the happy couple with the parcel. 'Sorry we're late, Treasure – where shall I put the loot?'

'It's very kind of you,' Treasure said.

Charles was smiling at the newcomer. 'This must be

Albert?' He shook hands with him. 'Terese's told me about you.'

'Not too much, I hope?' Albert said. Then, pulling Alice forward like an alibi. 'This is Alice – my fiancée.'

The bride looked at the ring on Alice's hand before shaking hands with her; then she looked at the girl with genuine pity.

'Well, open it,' Albert said.

'It's a spin dryer,' Treasure said, opening the parcel.

Albert said: 'Record player. I thought you'd want a bit of light relief.' Then to Charles: 'Got a house, have you?'

'Yes, thank you,' Treasure said.

'Up on the London Road estate,' Charles said. 'Marshall's Drive.'

'Not thirteen, I hope,' Albert said.

'Twenty-three,' Charles said.

Treasure was glaring at Albert over her husband's shoulder.

'Got to catch a train,' Charles was saying. 'Enjoy yourself – Ted!' He called over the best man and made introductions then escaped with his bride.

'He's not so bad,' Charles told Treasure as they went out. 'Help to liven them up a bit – only one family, you'd think they'd mix . . .'

'Anyone seen my sister?'

Treasure heard Albert's voice as she went out and she frowned. Albert hadn't got a sister.

Albert left Alice waiting again, this time with Ted, the best man, who turned out to be a bore, which was also useful. She was overjoyed to see Albert return to the reception at nine o'clock. She clung to him.

'I thought you wouldn't get back. I was terrified you wouldn't get back. He wanted to take me home.'

'You've got to watch them,' Albert said. 'Still, you're prettier than the bridesmaids.'

'You're more handsome than the groom,' she said.

He smiled at her. 'What've you been drinking?'

'Phew!' she said.

'Come back to my place for a quiet drink?'

'Will the children be up?'

'Eh? Oh, I shouldn't think so.'

'All right then.'

Tucking her into the car his hands lingered around the back of her neck, stroking under her soft yellow hair. She looked up at him.

'Albert. You said I was prettier than the bridesmaids – what about the bride?'

'You're prettier than the bride,' Albert said, softly.

He meant it. She was. The temporary Civil Servant clothes had been replaced by a simply cut red dress with a low neckline. There was something prim about the way it covered her figure that excited him.

'You're the prettiest, more exciting girl I've ever known,' Albert said.

She was waiting for the second kiss, but he turned away, closing the door and tucking her dress around her legs and at the same time slipping the Inland Revenue office keys back into the top of her bag. One idea had come off, the other idea was worth waiting for.

He drove across town with frustrating slowness, not putting an arm around her, but touching her occasionally. The feeling between them was of a fuse burning towards something quite explosive.

She said: 'I like your driving.'

'Speed is for emergencies.'

'Mother was quite impressed.'

'She's not expecting you home tonight.'

'I'll have to go now.'

'Yes.'

'Albert. Will your landlady mind me coming in?'

'She'll be asleep.'

'What about the children?'

'They'll be asleep.'

'We'll have to be very quiet,' Alice said.

'Yes.'

'And I mustn't stay long.'

'No.'

'Albert, I've never done this before – been to a man's room, I mean.'

'I know.'

'How do you know?'

'I just know.'

'Am I square?'

Albert looked at her; ran his hand lightly around the back of her neck. She shivered and drew in her breath, audibly, pushed herself against his arm like a kitten and was suddenly nestling tight into his chest. Albert dropped his arm around her shoulders, ran his hand into the armline of her dress, caressed her gently as he drove, slowly.

Albert parked the car quietly near the house, got out, steadied himself a moment against the wing before going round to help Alice out. He could no longer keep down to the slow pace. He took her by the hand and hurried across to the front door.

'Ssssh!' she said.

He remembered the house was not supposed to be empty. This is why she felt secure. Quietly he unlocked the front door and they entered, closing it behind them. In the hall she removed her shoes and he felt her trembling as she held on to him. Albert removed his own shoes. They crept up through the empty house and into his room.

'Darling ...' Once inside, he held her very tightly.

She put her face up to him. He brushed her mouth with his, but no more.

'We'll have to whisper,' she whispered.

'There's nothing to whisper,' he said.

He picked her up quite easily and took her to the bed, laid her upon it.

'No!' she whispered.

'You have a rest,' he said. 'I'll just have a bit of a wash up.'

'Albert,' she whispered from the bed.

But he left her waiting for him again, went out of the room. She heard the landing creak, the bathroom door open and close. She lay there in the darkness, her ears instant for every tiny sound.

'Oh my God!' she whispered.

It was never going to be like this. Not a man like this. His children probably in the next room. His landlady downstairs. But if she changed her mind, she thought, she only had to wake them up.

Then suddenly the dark quiet world of the strange house was split by Albert's scream of pain. Alice leapt off the bed and stood listening. It came again, a cry of agony. The girl wanted to run out, but knew she would meet everybody on the landing. She forced herself to open the bedroom door. Now she heard Albert moaning and groaning and using bad language. By some miracle nobody had woken up.

'Albert!' she called, softly.

She followed the sound to the bathroom door which was partly open, a crack of light showing through, Albert's shadow dancing grotesquely, his groans of pain louder.

'Albert!' She suddenly realized that he had cut his throat. He had been thinking about it all day. She started opening the door.

'Don't come in!' he screamed. 'Oh my God! Oh Jesus! Oh Christ! Get a doctor!'

'Albert, what's happening? You're frightening me!'

'I'm frightening myself!' Albert said. 'Oh my God! Look out. I'm coming out.'

He came out naked, holding his clothes, clutching himself.

'Hospital!' he muttered as he flew past.

She walked after him; she had not seen any blood. She did not enter his bedroom but listened to his curses and groans. Seconds later he came out, half-dressed.

'Sorry, hospital . . .'

She ran downstairs after him.

If speed was for emergencies, this was a priority call.
Albert drove across town this busy Saturday night in a
criminal fashion. Alice was holding the door handle all the
way.

Instinctively she had stopped asking him what had
happened.

Alice waited again, sitting in the car, as Albert ran ber-
serkly into the Out-patient and Casualties department of the
City hospital. He appeared to be limping; he was shirtless –
in fact he had nothing on except jacket and trousers, one
shoe without any socks.

Funny really, Alice thought. Something always seemed to
happen in time. She sighed.

The Night Sister, a nurse and Albert were all looking at
the damage.

'It'll be all right,' the Night Sister said. She looked old
enough and wise enough to know.

'Are you sure?' Albert said. But he was enormously
relieved.

'What kind of after-shave lotion?' the Night Sister asked.

'I dunno. The ordinary kind. I spilt half a bottle on it – I put
it straight under the tap but it didn't make any difference.'

'It's a very sensitive place,' the Night Sister said.

Fear came into Albert's eyes again. 'It's a nasty colour.'
He had had cancer, venereal disease and leprosy on less
evidence than this. 'Shouldn't I see the House Surgeon?'

'There's no need.'

'What about the swelling? It's still coming up!'

'Just keep calm. It's your imagination.' And to the nurse
she said: 'Put this cream on and bandage it up.' Then to
Albert: 'Go and see your own doctor on Monday.'

Albert lay tense and frightened as the nurse did the dress-
ings. 'Careful!' he kept on saying. Then he said: 'Bloody
stuff. It shouldn't be on the market.'

'It's practically pure alcohol,' the nurse said.

Albert looked down at the young woman and what she was doing. 'How long do I keep that on?'

'About a week I should think.'

'Christ!'

The nurse finished the bandaging, gave it a little pat and smiled at him. 'It's a rest for somebody.'

Albert grimaced with the pain. 'Very funny!'

Alice was asleep in the car when Albert came out. She woke up shivering.

'Cold, darling?'

'A bit – are you all right?'

'Yes, thanks. Sorry about all that. Got a bone out of place –'

'Oh I see! Must have been terribly painful.'

'Cor!' Albert said. He started the car and drove off the hospital forecourt. 'It's an old trouble. You see I used to be a long-distance runner and I got this multiple fracture of the tibia. I shouldn't do exercises really. Still, they've set it again now.' He smiled at her, bravely. 'Get you tucked up in bed now, eh?' He caught a flash of hope in her eyes and added: 'At home.'

Alice squeezed his arm. 'I knew I could trust you.'

They sat outside her house in the car and kissed for a little while without much enthusiasm.

'I can't understand why nobody woke up at your place,' Alice said.

'They've all gone off.' Albert said, forgetfully.

'They must sleep soundly,' Alice said.

Now Albert remembered. This was going to complicate their relationship if they ever got round to having one. A number of Albert's girl friends had had babies by him; some comfortably absorbed into happy family life; some without any status at all. Albert had put a sprinkling of them into his tax return to increase his allowances. It was not the sort of personal detail a girl would normally find out about. Now

188

the heat was off Alice was going to be curious again. She was not the kind of girl who would have an affair with a married man.

'They get used to the odd party,' Albert told her. 'A bit of noise doesn't worry them. Not since the divorce. You have to have a bit of fun to take your mind off things.'

'I can understand that.'

Albert kissed her again and she said: 'Did you get the custody, then?'

'It's only a temporary arrangement. Of course I'd like to have them full time, but it's not practical, is it? Not for a man.'

'That's what I was thinking.'

'Besides, I might want to marry again.'

'Yes. If you still believe in marriage.'

'Of course I do. We weren't suited, that's all. You know, mistakes on both sides. Still, she's happy now, Kathleen.'

'Nice name.'

'She's marrying this tycoon type – they're going to take the kids with them to the Bahamas. For good.'

'You'll miss them. And they'll miss you.'

Albert sighed, stroked her hair. 'Sometimes you have to start again.' It was going to be a week before he could start again.

Alice's mother was wearing a dressing gown when they went in. She was surprised to see them.

'I managed to get back so I brought her home,' Albert told her. 'Thought you might be worried.'

'That's very nice of you, Mr Argyle. Look, I'm just off to bed, you stay and have coffee with Alice –'

'No, no,' Albert said. 'I don't think that's quite right, Mrs Finbow. Don't think I'm old-fashioned or anything.' He smiled in a brotherly way at Alice. 'Ring you next –' then checked himself. 'Or it may be the week after – got a lot on next week. Ta ta, love. . . .'

'I like him,' Mrs Finbow said when Albert had gone.

Alice was looking into the mirror, running her fingers

around the back of her neck, gazing deeply into her own eyes.

'Not bad,' Albert told himself as he drove home. He was talking about the mother. 'You bugger,' he said. Then he said: 'Well, it's Treasure's wedding day. Somebody's got to celebrate.' He laughed, his thoughts in some distant hotel. 'You'll find it a bit different now you've got a licence, gal . . .'

He wriggled himself comfortable on the seat. Pity about that. Still, there was a nice Spring double waiting for somebody.

2

On Sunday morning Albert drove the hired car on to the gravelled forecourt of the golf club and parked it conspicuously in the 'No Parking' bay reserved for the Members' Trolleys. He cut the engine but remained behind the wheel, summing the place up. The sun shone, brittle and bright on a high, washed world. Behind him the mock-log-cabin one-storey building of the clubhouse, around him the sharp green hillocks, flats and bosky arroyos of the golf course; in front and below him spread the dirty town of dirty houses and chimneys, factories, roads, new estates, toy traffic, winking signals, church spires; the menacing squat cylinders of the gasometers bowing low to half a million Sunday dinners; in left foreground two ugly sisters, the cooling towers of the power-station smoke-black and thick-waisted looking like the smell of sulphur and poison.

'No confetti!' Albert said, contemptuously.

He closed the door window and took out a pipe he had bought for the purpose; the purpose of looking solid and respectable in a golf club. He had never tried one before and it was worth practising for five minutes. The sunshine was deceptive for it was quite a chilly morning. He was grateful for the smoke and sparks of the pipe and he started the car engine again to get the last of the heat fanned in. He gazed at the view without any kind of appreciation. Albert was a lover of the great indoors who felt naked and insecure without four walls and a roof over his bed. Grass seemed alien and fresh air made him feel faint.

In Albert's week there was only one day worse than Saturday and that was Sunday. In a hypocritical world it seemed to be the one day set aside for hypocrisy. 'Jesus lad and his supernatural dad,' Albert murmured. That had been his last day at Sunday School when he had drawn a strip-comic representation of Miracle Boy. 'I only have two loaves and a few sardines,' said the balloonage. 'Watch that Magic Knife!' said Dad from the clouds. Oddly enough, after he had been sacked the idea had caught on in a more respectful way. It was only logical for the Secondary Moderns were turning out people who could only read pictures.

The church spire marked the spot. From here he could see the landmarks of his life in this home town. The canal where they'd all swum naked at the age of ten. There had been none to see them but the swans and the golden carp, for the tow-path was flanked by the high wall of the gasworks and the waters were warmed from the effluent, sustaining the tropical fish. At a time when sex was being introduced into the school curriculum as something entirely new, they were already playing 'dicks and bums' with boisterous enjoyment. The secret world of kids and the secret world of grown-ups and the gasworks' wall in between.

You never seemed to get rid of the gasworks' wall either and there was no knowing, later on, quite which side you were on. Albert and his friends had joined the church choir for the seven-and-sixpence a quarter which they spent on Russian cigarettes; they were black and seemed wickeder somehow. They had all contrived to get put on probation because the probation officer's club was the best in town. But whatever they had got up to on their own there had always been something nastier about organized recreation on the grown-ups' side of the wall. Albert's cynicism had grown out of a choirmaster who tapped his genitals to see if his voice was in danger of breaking and the probation officer who had kept him behind as a punishment to clear up the mess and had suddenly grown affectionate.

'No confetti!' Albert said again, as church bells began to peal. He meant, no confetti in a town as ucky at this one. It was a laugh.

Albert turned his attention to the enemy. The people entering the golf club and coming away; chattering groups of well-dressed citizens, high, loud, county voices. To Albert they were the enemy; they were the choirmaster and the probation officer, the schoolboard man and the magistrates; they were the women he could never make, the girls he could not impress, the Janets and Janes, Hildegardes and Christines. And the Janices – or whatever her name was . . . Albert shifted slightly in his seat at the painful memory of last night; now the pain had gone but the swelling and tenderness were still there. And the humiliation. Not being capable was worse than not having a car or having a hump; he was going into battle without a weapon.

Luckily there was only Callendar to tackle this morning. Callendar was a push-over. Albert would have needed all his equipment to do battle with this golf-club mob, but not with Callendar. Albert knew his own limitations and Callendar was well within them. Callendar was as much out of place in the golf club as Albert himself. Callendar, in fact, was waging the same battle, fighting the same enemy. Them . . .

'Cor!' Albert murmured, watching a woman get out, legs first, from a Jaguar Mark 10. Then he said 'ooh!' as the consecutive reflex reminded him of his condition. Then he said: 'Oh my gawd!' as Mr Callendar alighted from the passenger door of the same car. Oh Cally no! You're out of your depth, man. Come 'ome. Albert stared across the forecourt with the kind of mock incredulity he would use to make people laugh. Even if there was nobody to watch the act Albert was always his own best audience. Not that, Cally! Danger, man! Look behind you!

'He'll never learn,' Albert said, with waggish tolerance. He went on watching with a wondering, speculative eye and making subtle changes to his plans.

Albert's plan had been simple and slightly lunatic. Most of his plans were. Brought up on a diet of slick movies and strip adventures Albert was a technicolour man in a black and white world. Sometimes he knew this and was sad for the world, sometimes sad for himself.

'I'm the only part of this town five hundred feet above sea level,' he used to tell his mother, who was supporting him at the time and therefore not very impressed.

Of the people Albert most respected and most despised, Mr Callendar was both. Albert recognized in Cally his own potential for gaining the world with a few masterly strokes before he was forty; he despised him because Cally was now well past forty and had nothing. Whatever he might have gained he had lost. Albert thought he knew why. What Albert didn't know was that at Albert's age Callendar also had thought he knew why. On the road to nowhere Callendar was twenty years in the lead. Without knowing it Albert sat in his car this Sunday morning watching himself at forty-five escort the leggy blonde woman into the Golf Clubhouse.

'Oh my gawd!' he said again, when Callendar stood by the door and gave a small olde worlde bow for the woman to precede him.

Albert checked his hair and tie in the driving mirror with the confident air of one who knows how things should really be done. He switched off the engine and heater and got out of his car. Still attending to his new pipe he strolled across to the woman's Jaguar and noted the number: 'ET 1.' He looked back at his own car, trespassing on the wrong side of the forecourt. He had done it to get himself publicly summoned in the bar and focus attention, but now it would have to be twisted to suit the new circumstances. Who would have expected Cally to be with somebody and particularly with an attractive wealthy woman and a Jag. Mark 10? Not Albert. It gave a new zest to the business in hand and Albert entered the Clubhouse with the springs of his idea in his heels.

'I say!'

It was one of Albert's favourite impersonations. An impersonation of what he might have been like if he had passed his eleven plus. 'Who's this?' he would ask his mother, sticking out his teeth and wrinkling his nose in a fatuous smile.

194

Or: 'Who am I?' adopting another idiotic pose and an idiotic accent. His mother would always stop for a smile no matter how busy she might be, cleaning her own house or cleaning other people's. But there was a certain sadness in it too. She knew who he was, Albert didn't. He was always trying to act a part that would fit into the social pattern and bring success. But he only saw the surface patterns, the grain of the wood; never the growth or the strength. He could never impersonate hard work. Or integrity or purpose or what it takes.

'Do you know the secret of Churchill's success?' he would say. 'That cigar.'

Albert had worn nothing but spotted bow ties since he was sixteen.

'Yes sir?' A uniformed man at the reception desk looked up at Albert.

'Look where some silly sod's parked his jalopy!' Albert said.

The man came round the desk and joined Albert, looking out on to the forecourt at Albert's own misparked car. The man tutted and tsked and started going out but Albert stopped him.

'ET 1,' Albert said. 'That's the number.'

'Oh, thank you, sir.'

Albert examined a glass case filled with silver golf trophies as the owner of 'ET 1' was called. He did not turn until she had come out of the bar lounge and was going towards the outer door. Albert could never resist the back view of this kind of woman.

'Sorry to trouble you, madam,' the attendant was saying as she went out. 'Just park it on the other side, if you don't mind.'

He did not stop to see which car she went to, but came back to his desk.

'Who is she?' Albert asked.

'Don't know, sir. Not a member. A guest. Nice, though.'

'We could do with a few more like that,' Albert said, with an air of long membership.

Elaine Townend stood for a moment studying the parking situation on the Clubhouse forecourt and looking puzzled. Her car was in line with eight or nine others. She looked round at Albert's car which stood alone. Another car came in and she called to the driver.

'We've got to park on the other side, apparently.'

'Are you sure?'

'I've just been called out.'

'I swear they're all mad . . .'

Albert stayed long enough at the Clubhouse door to savour the beginning of confusion and then he went into the lounge bar.

Mr Callendar saw Albert a shade too late to turn his back on him. Albert came straight up, noticed the two drinks on the bar, the handbag and gloves; he gave Cally an open, friendly smile and a warm handshake. Callendar just stared at him with his baggy, hostile face.

'Nice to see you, Cally old man – got company have we?' He looked across the bar: 'Large Scotch, please. Don't mind, do you, Cally – I can't buy, I'm not a member yet.'

'If you ever 'ave a coat of arms,' Cally said, bitterly, 'I should 'ave that as your motto – "I can't buy, I'm not a member yet." That's you, Albert!' He was talking softly and fiercely in the whiskied sub-tone he had cultivated behind his customers' backs, at the same time wearing the pleasant smile he had cultivated for their faces. He went on, earnestly: 'You take that drink in the other room and stay away from me. I've got an important business conference on.'

'Very nice too,' Albert said. 'I saw it as I came in. Don't tell me you're going to *marry* for money after all these years? That's defeatism, Cally.'

'I've got all the money I want,' Mr Callendar said, searching for the price of Albert's drink.

'I'm glad to hear you say that,' Albert told him, cheerfully. He raised his glass: 'Here's to us!'

'Get out of here,' Cally muttered, viciously smiling and raising his own glass to touch Albert's.

'Okay,' Albert said. 'I just want to tell you about this proposition –'

'I don't want to 'ear any of your propositions. You couldn't
start a flea circus if you were lousy.'

'Have a look at this, then,' Albert said. He took a folded
letter from his pocket and gave it to Callendar who scanned
it, suspiciously. His face darkened with anger and mystifica-
tion. The letter was addressed to 'T. Callendar Esqr.' and was
from the Tax Collector. It was a carbon copy of a follow-up
to a last demand and threatened to take immediate legal
proceedings for the payment of two thousand four hundred
pounds overdue tax. It was dated three days ago. Callendar
looked up into Albert's smiling eyes.

'Where did you get this? It's private correspondence!'

'I've got more than that,' Albert said. 'I've got your whole
bloody file complete with all your lying letters –' then with
genuine admiration; 'Oh, Cally – I didn't know you were an
author. Such romances! You could go to prison for it.'

Callendar had lost his smile. 'So could you! So could you,
Albert. How did you get hold of my tax file?'

'It's my job,' Albert told him. 'I work there. Temporary
civil servant.'

'My arse!' Mr Callendar exclaimed.

Then he turned cold. All conversation in the lounge had
temporarily stopped. The nearest group of Young Conser-
vatives were trying desperately to think of something to say.

Albert, seldom at a loss, grinned round at them: 'Comes
the revolution! Har har har!'

The satirical bray, instantly recognizable as such from
one telly show or another, turned twenty resentful faces
towards them.

'Have I got your attention?' Albert said, to the room at
large. And now that he had he laid aside his pipe and appeared to take a lighted cigarette from Callendar's burning
red ear, puffed it twice, waved his hands in the air and made
it vanish, rubbed his hands together and beamed at them.
'Now we come to the real purpose of my visit – The

Medicine!' He picked up his glass of whisky and raised it to the light. The watching faces were beginning to relax into uncertain smiles. 'Made from an old recipe whispered by Cally's grandmother with her dying breath – she was a Red Indian of course. It's called, wait for it, whisky – yes, whisky, folks.'

'All right, Albert,' Callendar muttered.

'Just covering up for you,' Albert said, protectively.

He turned his back on his audience and Callendar forced a curtain-dropping smile on the performance. 'What's your pitch?' he asked Albert. 'I'll give you ten seconds.'

Albert took the letter from Callendar with a gesture of grand resignation and sadness; he folded it, tucked it back into his pocket.

Mr Callendar was looking at him, half afraid now. 'What are you doing with that?'

'Has to go back in the file,' Albert said. Then, rationally, as he finished his drink: 'You know what these inland revenue offices are like. One file got mislaid and the feller didn't pay any tax for ten years.'

It took Callendar five seconds less than it had taken Albert to see the possibilities.

'Have another drink,' Callendar said.

'Never mind the drink,' Albert said. 'Fifty pounds cash and a job with your firm.'

'Fifty quid? You're mad.'

'That's less than two per cent of what you'd have to pay them.'

'How do I know I'll get out of it. Paying, I mean?'

'I'll fix that.'

'That's criminal, Albert.'

'Anybody can have an accident.'

'I want to see you burn it,' Mr Callendar said.

'Do I get the money and the job?'

'I'll give you the money. I can't guarantee the job. I'll put in a good word for you.'

Albert was looking at him, shrewdly. They always conducted their conversations as though waiting for the bell to end the round. A series of moves, feints, ducks and evasions but seldom a straight right.

'I thought you were the boss. Jacko said you were the boss. You can swing it, you know you can. Get me a contract. I won't let you down, Cally. You know me. There's no racket I wouldn't improve.'

'This is not a racket, Albert,' Mr Callendar said with some dignity. 'It's a genuine business method. Treasure Trove Trading Stamps. It's genuine sales promotion, Albert, a big organization.'

'Sure, sure. I know, Cally. I save 'em.'

Mr Callendar realized that Albert was taking it for granted that anything he was doing must be crooked. In Albert's company he felt slightly ashamed of the fact that it wasn't.

'It wouldn't suit you, Albert. No fiddles. No conning.'

Albert laughed. 'No scope, eh? I thought you didn't look very happy.'

'What's going on out there?' Mr Callendar had been darting occasional glances out of the french windows, apprehensive of his companion returning. Cars were shunting back and forth across the forecourt. He could see Mrs Townend talking to other drivers. Voices came on the breeze with revving engines.

'Who said we have to park here?'

'He did.'

'Somebody move that Cresta for me?'

Mr Callendar said: 'What the hell are they doing with their cars?'

'They're putting them all in the wrong place,' Albert said. 'A little satirical sketch called "The Lion and the Uniform". That's Britain and Bureaucracy, of course. The moral is: there shouldn't be right and wrong places or, get rid of the uniform and we have utopia. Wrote it myself.'

'xue 255!' somebody called.

People began to hurry out.

'So when do we clinch this deal?' Albert asked.

'I think we'd better forget it, Albert.' Mr Callendar had had time to come down to earth. Albert was always able to get people off the ground for a little while. 'I don't want to get mixed up in anything like that.'

'You and twenty others,' Albert told him.

'You're joking. They wouldn't take the risk. Who for instance?'

'Solly Cowell. Reggie Corby – Major Simpkins, over there –' Albert waved across the lounge to where a party of men were drinking and talking. 'Hi, Major!' he called. Major Simpkins acknowledged Albert's wave without knowing who he was. 'Seen my car, have you?' Albert then said, pointing through the french windows. By this time all the cars had been moved across the forecourt to join Albert's on the wrong side.

'The new Ford – not bad, eh?'

Cally stared in disbelief. 'You're a liar, Albert. Jacko told me you were out of work.'

Albert winked. 'To all intents and purposes.'

'What about this job at the tax place?'

'Part time – you know old Finbow's dead, do you? They're very short of staff. Imagine me serving writs! Dog eat dog.' Having frightened Cally with the picture he now smiled, tenderly: 'Been asking after me, have you? That's kind.'

Callendar gave him a sour look. 'I just like to know where you are, Albert.'

'Well, I'll be in the George tonight – eight o'clock, saloon bar.'

'I'll see,' Mr Callendar said. Then looking over Albert's shoulder: 'Will you excuse me?' He picked up the waiting Martini, his own drink, his cigarettes, the handbag and gloves and walked away dropping everything.

Watching Callendar light a cigarette for the woman a moment later, singeing her hair, Albert felt some misgiving. Callendar was getting out of his class. The woman was genuine; her beauty, her grace; she was a pearl you could bite without cracking it. This disturbed Albert. It meant that

Callendar was shaking off some of his old habits. It meant that Albert could not predict him any more. Not completely. He had had the hook in his mouth for a few minutes there, but that was all. A hearty laugh took his attention to the group by the fireplace. Albert went over to them.

'Major Simpkins? Could I have a word, please?'

The Major looked at Albert, distrustfully, excused himself to his friends, joined Albert nearby.

'Could I have your autograph?' Albert asked. 'I'm trying to get the whole council. It's for my boy. They're doing local politics at school.'

'Ah, I see . . .'

At the table Callendar was putting in a good word for Albert.

'There's someone I want to warn you against, Mrs Townend,' Callendar was telling his companion in an earnest undertone. 'He just tried to batten on me for a job. You'd better have a good look at him – he's bound to turn up at the office.' Cally looked round towards the bar. 'Albert Argyle is the name. An absolute crook. He took me in once before – I don't want it to happen again . . .'

At this moment, across the room, Major Simpkins was signing something which he gave to Albert who in return gave the Major a friendly pat as he shook hands. Cally frowned.

'That young man?' Mrs Townend said. 'He doesn't look like a crook.'

'That's his secret,' Callendar said, bitterly.

Albert turned, saw Callendar, gave him a cheery wave and went out.

'Crook, thief, womanizer, con-man,' Cally catalogued bitterly.

'In fact, a good salesman,' Mrs Townend said, brightly.

She laughed at Callendar's momentary disconcertment. 'Don't worry – he won't get past the receptionist.'

'I thought you ought to know,' Callendar said.

'Yes, of course, Mr Callendar. That's why a good local man is so valuable to us. There's already a strong bias against trading stamps and we have to overcome it. We sell the scheme on facts and figures, nothing else.'

'Yes, I know,' Callendar said. 'And they're very impressive facts and figures.'

'We don't need selling tricks and we don't want them,' Mrs Townend said. Her eye followed Albert out through the foyer and then she picked him up over Cally's shoulder through the window as he went to his car. 'We don't want slick talk or cheap charm. We are dealing with hard-headed executives and each one of our team must be a hard-headed executive. Treasure Trove Trading Stamps constitute a business advantage to the trader and a bonus to the customer.'

Cally said: 'Treasure Trove Trading Stamps give the ordinary man a chance to fight the cost of living.'

Mrs Townend looked round at him. 'That's *very* good.'

'Thank you,' Mr Callendar said. He lay awake at night grappling with slogans as other people grappled with their lives.

Albert's car started up outside and both Mrs Townend and Mr Callendar watched him back out.

'What's his name again?'

'Argyle. Albert Argyle.'

'I must warn Dorothy,' Mrs Townend said.

Albert sat in the saloon bar of the George that Sunday evening from eight o'clock until nine o'clock, hating every minute. He wished that he had brought a girl along. Anything was bearable with a girl along. But the only girl Albert could ever think of offhand was the last girl he had seen and that was Janice from the Inland Revenue. She would be incompatible with the job in hand. Perhaps she didn't go into pubs. He wouldn't blame her. Albert wouldn't go into pubs if he could help it. 'Men go into pubs to pick up birds who don't go into pubs because men go into pubs to pick up birds. This situation accounts for the rise, decline and fall of the

English public house,' Albert was thinking. 'It is now an all-male institution, than which nothing is more crapulous, sterile and.' He couldn't think of the word but he knew what he meant. You had only to look around any public house. Those pipe-smoking nits along the bar were what he meant.

'There were these three girls –'

'I've heard it –'

'Then wrap up. One married a barrister, one a parson and the other a commercial traveller –'

'Christ!' Albert said.

He, personally, had resigned from the club by throwing the pipe out of the car window on his way down the golf club drive. You had to pretend to go along with the male species occasionally, like having your hair cut, drinking in a pub, talking in a golf club, doing business, buying clothes. But that's where it stopped. Albert, listening to the bar talk, was glad to reflect that he had never had a male friend. Nor a dog which seemed to have some smelly connexion.

'It wasn't Janice,' he said, suddenly. Embarrassed as though she were actually with him. It was something else. It was a name like Janice. He couldn't think what it was. He started going through the alphabet in growing desperation like a stamp collector who has mislaid a prize specimen. 'Agnes, Beatrice, Caroline, Daisy, Evelyn, Freda, Georgina, Harriet – ugh!'

'Did you want something, sir?' The barman had come half-way from the group, hearing Albert's mutterings.

'Brown and mild,' Albert said. He hadn't enough money for anything but beer. A lot depended on Callendar turning up. He was suddenly confronted with a pint of the foul stuff and was intimidated into accepting it. You had to drink pints to prove that you were a man. What a thing to prove. You had to drink beer, leer at sexy calendars, laugh at dirty stories amateurishly told. Albert couldn't stand amateurs.

'Eunice,' he thought. No, it wasn't Eunice. Think of Finbow – 'Alice Finbow!' he exclaimed. He looked into the mirror behind the bottles and saw her sitting at his side and it gave him immense comfort. The joke along the bar had got to the big dirty-laugh stage. They were still schoolboys in a lavatory laughing the fear out of their ignorance of Woman. 'How do you stand it?' he asked the mirage with the yellow hair. Was there any other man in the world besides Albert, worth looking at twice? Soft-seeking, beautiful, heart-rending woman in her all delicate shades of emotion and love and need – and only stinking old man dog for her companion. Somewhere evolution had gone wrong. Woman deserved a special creature for her mate. Albert could well understand Lesbianism; the soft and the softer yet.

'Homosexuals should be hanged,' he said. That was what revolted Albert into the ground. The proof that man was dog. Then where is woman's mate? 'One half of the human race is missing,' was his final conclusion. Perhaps they would be found on the moon or on Mars or Venus? By nine o'clock he had imagined an invasion of Alberts from outer space who banished Man to eternal buggery in barbers shops, rugby teams, public schools, public houses, lavatories and the Royal Navy.

'Anybody's stool, old man?'

Albert looked round at a man who had just come in. A weedy, tweedy old boy with a chubby face and grubby eyes. 'Yes it is,' Albert said. Janice was still sitting there. Alice, he meant.

The man took the next stool to the ghost.

'Turned out nice?'

Albert grunted his approval of the weather and sipped his pint of man-wallop. Closely questioned at the end of a busy day Albert would be unable to give the slightest description of any man he had come into contact with; he could talk to them, laugh with them, even appear to be listening intently to what they said, but he could not look at them. To the man who loved women, looking into the eyes of man was obscene. Unknown to Albert there were men who thought he was shifty because of this. The straight look, the firm handshake

204

was the badge of their ethics. To Albert they constituted an immoral relationship.

'Live here?'

Albert had to admit that he did.

'I've just arrived. Think I'm going to like it.'

Albert glanced at him. 'You'll like it.'

'New Public Relations firm.'

'Oh, there's plenty of them,' Albert said. 'If you know where to look.'

'Ha ha. See what you mean. Large Scotch, please – care to join me?'

Albert declined.

'No, we're the first in the field in this area. Big town too. Ought to clean up. Could do with a bit more capital, of course. After all it's all front in my business.'

'That's what the actress said.' Albert knew how to make man noises.

'Ha ha. Yes.' The man gave Albert a brief appraising glance. 'You're not in advertising, are you? You could be. You're very much our type.'

'Treasure Trove Trading Stamps,' Albert said. 'I'm the area manager.'

The man moved closer, then became aware of the vacant stool and moved back. 'Now that's very interesting. We might be able to do some business some time. My card.'

Albert glanced at the card and felt for his own. He had a dozen, ranging from 'Ventriloquist, Vocalist and Juggler – Private Parties, Cabarets, etc.' to 'Business Consultant'. But nothing in trading stamps yet. 'Albert Argyle,' Albert said.

'I expect you're using local advertising? We can get you some very advantageous ad-rates – and tie in paper, cinema and direct mail if necessary. What's your appropriation – I mean in this area?'

'It varies,' Albert said.

'Ten thousand?'

'More,' Albert said.

'That's a lot for one campaign – or does that include a twelve-month follow up?'

'It depends,' Albert said.

'Well, I'm sure you'd find us very useful, promotion-wise. We've already got several big accounts–selling local industry to the local population, you know. That's what I like about this town. Compact. Self-contained. Self-supporting in a curious kind of way.'

'I know what you mean,' Albert said. 'They eat their own shit. Threepence off and man! They're living!'

'Ha ha. Yes.'

A short hiatus ensued. Albert tried to re-establish contact with the vision in the mirror but she had gone. He got bored.

'Have you seen this?' Albert puffed his cigarette and held it up, waved his hand and made it vanish.

'This, you mean?' said the other, who repeated precisely the same trick.

'Yes,' said Albert.

The other man pulled the holder and the elastic band from his sleeve and displayed it. 'Let's have a look at yours.'

'That's what the Bishop said.'

'Ha ha. Yes.'

They looked at each other's cigarette trick and then Albert took out a pack of cards, cut them three times, did a swift mock-shuffle and looked at the other man. 'Put a pound on that.'

'No, you put a pound on this.' His companion repeated the process exactly though not quite as efficiently.

Albert took out the piece of paper bearing Major Simpkins' autograph and handed it to the other man. 'Draw a circle, put a number in it and I'll read your mind.'

'Really?'

'Yes. Don't you know it?'

'No.'

'Well, go on then.'

The other man drew a small circle in the middle of the paper and then sat thinking, heavily.

'People can never think of a number,' Albert said.

'Isn't it ridiculous? I know any amount of numbers.'

Now Albert stared at him, detecting insanity of his own brand. 'What sort of business is it?'

'Public relations – you know, P.R.O. I used to be with B.O.U. till they amalgamated with U.T.C. Now I've started up on my J.J.'

'How much capital do you want – for a partnership, I mean?'

'Wait a minute, let me see if I can do this.'

'A telephone number will do,' Albert said. 'A good one of course. Something close to your heart – that helps me to read your mind.'

'Ha ha. Yes.' The man scribbled a number in the circle.

'Fold it in half without me seeing it,' Albert said.

The man did as he was told.

'Now again,' Albert said. 'Now give it to me.'

Albert took the folded paper and immediately tore it up, sprinkling the pieces into the ash tray on the bar. 'Now set fire to it.'

'Set fire to it?'

'Yes, go on. With a match.' He waited impatiently while the other man searched for a match. 'Your lighter will do.'

'Ha ha. Yes. Of course.'

Albert watched his companion setting the small heap of paper alight, watched it burning high. It was at this moment that Mr Callendar appeared in the doorway behind them. His eyes fixed on the burning paper with instant horror. He came across the saloon in three quick strides.

'Not here, Albert!'

'You're bloody late,' Albert said. 'I was just off.'

'Well, go on,' said the man. 'What was the number?'

'I got delayed,' Callendar said. 'Business meeting. Where are we going?'

'My place,' Albert said. 'Don't want a drink, do you?'

They were moving away from the bar. The other man

stared after them for a moment, then summoned the courage. 'I say – what about the number?'

Albert remembered him again and turned back: '60452–right?'

'Right!' said the other.

Mr Callendar was looking at them both, suspiciously. Albert suddenly noticed his interest and turned again to the man.

'I'll think about your offer.'

'Righty-ho, Mr Argyle. Do that. I think we can help you. Incidentally, I don't know whether you've considered the cut-price thing? Talking about threepence off.'

'Ah yes,' Albert said.

'I mean we could handle that for you. Take something with a fixed price – butter, cheese. Knock sixpence off and give each customer a book and a free page of stamps – I mean we could smother the town with a thing like that. Very reasonably, too.'

Mr Callendar thought for a moment that he himself was being addressed, a reasonable assumption since it seemed to be his business that was being discussed.

'We have tried that,' Albert said. 'I'll talk to you about it. Ta ta.'

'Who the hell was that?' Mr Callendar asked before they'd reached the door.

But Albert had stopped on the threshold to allow a girl to enter the saloon bar. Albert got in her way. She had bright red hair in a high style, pale smooth skin with a few freckles, a beauty spot under one of her beautifully painted eyes and a figure, tightly costumed, that Albert knew well and could categorize. She was Albert's type, feminine, brainless and, once she was tanked up, easy to the point of frenzy.

'You're late,' Albert told the unknown girl, emotionally. 'I'm nearly twenty-eight.'

The girl laughed.

'Lois!' called a voice from the bar.

The girl looked round and her smile faltered fractionally.

'Peter!' She realized that she sounded disappointed to see him and hurried across to make up for it.

'*And* a soft heart,' Albert thought.

Albert sat behind the wheel of the car and entered the number 60452 in his little book. He then wrote the name 'Lois' with a fair degree of certainty alongside it. Mr Callendar sat at his side barely containing his curiosity and fear.

'Who was it?'

'Never met her before.'

'I mean the feller. You know who I mean. What were you talking about?'

Albert switched on his engine, turned on the lights, moved out of the George car park into the main street. 'He's a PRO – Public Relations Officer.'

'What's he doing for you?'

'We're trying to popularize Income Tax.'

'Don't lie, Albert. He was talking about butter and cheese.'

'Well, butter and cheese then. It's good for you. People should eat more butter and cheese. Got that fifty quid?'

Mr Callendar said: 'You were discussing trading stamps. What's going on, Albert?'

'I'm just swotting up, that's all. For my new job. You don't want me to let you down?'

'Har,' Callendar said.

'Well, I mean, you want me to be knowledgeable when I get this interview. What's he like? Your boss?'

'You won't like him,' Mr Callendar said. 'Nobody does. One of those gutless bastards with a limp and a big Alsatian dog to make up for it. He keeps it in the room while he talks to you. Keeps practising his commands. You see this?' Mr Callendar pulled back his sleeve as they drove on, showed Albert red teeth marks in his wrist. 'Only my watch strap that stopped it breaking the skin. He thought it was funny.'

'I'd like to see him try it on me.'

'You won't like him, Albert. I'd forget this job if I were you. I'll get a few contacts if you want a job –'

'Oh no. I've set my heart on being with you again, Cally.'

'You're making a mistake, Albert. It's a straightforward, honest job. You won't fit in.'

'What about you?'

'I'm not happy there, I'll admit it. It's the best I could get. You saw what happened to my business.'

'Well, let's face it,' Albert said reasonably. 'You couldn't expect it to last long once I'd left.'

'It wasn't that, Albert. Old Solly got those bastards on the council to make a compulsory purchase order. Pennies, that's all I got for it – you've seen my tax position. I'll be paying that off for the next five years.'

'Well, you won't have to now, will you?'

'I'm not so sure. I don't like it.'

'You've got too many scruples, Cally – that was always your trouble.'

Mr Callendar looked at him, but Albert was concentrating seriously on his driving.

'You take Major Simpkins and the others,' Albert said. 'He's on the council and he's not worried.'

'You're lying, Albert. I don't believe it. You wouldn't have the nerve to make the approach.'

'You saw me with him this morning,' Albert said. 'I've got his cheque in my pocket.'

'Bloody crook, he is,' Callendar said.

They drove in silence across town towards Railway Street.

'What happened to your Bentley tonight, then?' Albert asked.

'Being repaired,' Mr Callendar said.

'Oh yes.'

'What about your car?' Callendar asked.

Albert looked at him; Cally was looking at the hire company's label on the inside of the windscreen.

'Same place as yours, probably,' Albert said.

'I'm getting a company car,' Callendar said, cheering up at the prospect. 'I'm having my initials on it.'

'That's nice. Shall I have one?'

'Eh?' Callendar said. 'Oh yes. The whole team has them.'

'When shall I start then?' Albert said.

'We'll talk about that when I see that file.'

'Good,' Albert said. 'That's the secret of our whole relationship, Cally. Mutual trust.'

They smiled at each other, a warm, friendly salesman smile.

Mr Callendar's tax file had a black cardboard cover and an aluminium spine with his name and code number engraved on it. He and Albert sat in Albert's little top bedsitter with the contents of the file spread over the bed coverlet like a lot of old sins. Nostalgically they browsed through assessments, returns, demands, claims, final notices and hot denials spread over five years of tally selling. Callendar laughed and then shivered, tossing a letter at Albert.

'Remember that one?'

It took them back to a time when Hetty, the confused and muddled clerk in the tally shop, had accidentally put the turnover in place of the annual profit in a tax return.

'Good old Hetty,' Albert said.

'I talked my way out of that one,' Callendar said.

'But you won't talk your way out of this,' Albert said, bringing his old boss up to date with recent correspondence.

'It's gone through the commissioners, that's the trouble,' Cally said. 'They won't shift once it's gone through the commissioners.'

'Let's get rid of it, then,' Albert said. 'You won't hear any more. It's like joining the Foreign Legion – you disappear without trace.'

''Ow do you know? 'Ow can you be sure? There must be other files. Ledgers, books, cross-references.'

Albert gave him a pained look, 'You know me, Cally. I've got it all organized. There's a follow-file system for defaulters. Every so often your card comes up automatically.

Well your card won't come up automatically any more because your card is here.' Albert showed him the card.

Mr Callendar gazed at Albert with reluctant admiration. 'I didn't know you knew anything about tax.'

'I'm adapable. Of course I had to have training. All one afternoon. Well, you've got to specialize these days.'

'How much are you making in the civil service?' Callendar asked him.

'It varies,' Albert said.

They started destroying the income tax file, working happily together again like a team.

'You'd be silly to give it up, Albert,' Mr Callendar told him, earnestly, at the same time beginning to tear up the contents of the file. They were stuffing forms and letters into the empty fire grate. 'You've got yourself a good steady career with a lot of responsibility.' They put the demands and returns down into the fireplace, screwing each big document up to facilitate the burning. 'There's a bit of status in a job like yours. A bit of integrity. There's a lot to be said for local government work. It's what you needed. Steady, secure and with a pension at the end.'

Albert found a box of matches and went to strike one, then on a thought appeared accidentally to drop the box into the hearth. 'Okay,' he said, 'you can do the honours.'

Mr Callendar put the last letter into the grate, picked up the matches and struck one, applied it to the papers. Then suddenly he tried to put it out, frightened. 'I'm not doing this! You do it!'

'It's all right — you've done it,' Albert told him. 'Don't worry.'

As the flames roared up, consuming his tax liabilities for the past few years, Mr Callendar was equally consumed with anxiety. 'It's destroying government property. You'd get two years for it.' He reflected for a moment. 'No, three years.'

'Why should I go to prison?' Albert said. 'I didn't burn them — you did.'

Mr Callendar stared at him, frightened. 'You're not going to start being funny, are you? I knew I shouldn't trust you. Well, don't forget, Albert – it's you that stole them. And you a trusted employee – a public servant. Fine thing if we can't trust inland revenue officials. It'd go hard with you, Albert. You'd better not try anything. You know how far you can push me.'

'Yeah, I remember,' Albert said, fondly. Then he clapped Callendar on the shoulder in a fatherly fashion. 'You stop worrying. I don't want to get you into trouble – I want to work for you. Why bite the hand that feeds me?'

Mr Callendar relaxed a little. 'That's all right, then.'

'Anyway,' Albert said, casually. 'I don't actually work there myself.'

Callendar looked at him, sharply. 'You don't work where?'

Albert laughed. 'I don't work at the bloody tax office – are you mad? I just wanted to give you a bit of confidence. I was thinking of you.'

Cally looked at Albert in horror for a moment, then dazedly at the flaming embers of the burning papers. 'How did you get this file?'

Albert laughed. 'It's all right. Nothing's changed. I've got a bird there.'

'Somebody *else* knows about this?'

'She knows more about it than I do. That's just the point. That's how I know you won't pay any tax for the next ten years. It's happening all the time. They've got their favourites.'

'What bird?' Mr Callendar said. 'How do I know we can trust her?'

'She's got herself to protect, hasn't she?'

'You mean you've got the screws on her.'

Albert winced, comically. 'Don't say things like that. I'm not a crook. I'm the innocent party. *She* stole the file, *you* burnt it – I'm just the middleman.'

Callendar glared at him. 'You mean you're in the clear

213

and I'm in the shit. Well I'm not falling for it. You get no fifty quid out of me. And no job, either.' He stood up to go.

'What about the girl?' Albert said. 'I've got to pay her off. She's got a widowed mother to support.'

'By selling inland revenue files?' Cally said, incredulously.

'They've got nothing else to sell,' Albert told him, rather pathetically. 'You've got to think of other people.'

Mr Callendar buttoned his coat. 'Well you let Major Simpkins pay her off.'

'Who?' Albert said.

And in that instant Mr Callendar realized that this was a lone attempt; that he was in it on his own. The glance they exchanged was enough to convey this.

Albert smiled at him. 'Well, *I* saw the possibilities so I knew you would. I can't think of anybody else with the same feeling for adventure.'

'That's not a compliment,' Mr Callendar said. Moving towards the door he looked back at the fireplace, went across to it, stirred the black remains with his toecap to destroy the last vestiges of evidence.

Albert had not moved. There was something about his calm air of friendliness that worried Callendar.

'I wouldn't say anything if I were you, Albert,' he said.

'Oh no. You know I wouldn't do that.'

'You'd get pulled into it if anything came out.'

'Yes, I know I would. Don't worry, it's safe with me.'

Callendar was worrying. 'I'll tell you what I'll do, Albert. If I don't hear anything from the tax people for the next twelve months I'll give you that money.'

'Twelve months? That's helpful.'

'It's your own fault. I won't be conned, Albert.'

'I wouldn't try,' Albert said kindly. Then as Cally got to the door he added: 'I'll tell you what's worrying me a bit, though.'

Mr Callendar swung round quickly to an inevitable pay-off. It had to be good. It was going to take a lot to get that bundle of banknotes out of his inside pocket. In those few seconds Cally ran over all the possibilities, putting himself in Albert's place. He never found it difficult. Albert was largely the result of Cally's training.

'What's that?' Mr Callendar asked.

'Remember that last threat you had from the tax office – what was it? Two thousand four hundred pounds?'

'You burnt it,' Callendar said. 'I saw you put it in.'

'I know you burnt it,' Albert said. 'That's not the point. The thing is, did you reply to it?'

'Yes, of course I did – straight away. I asked for time.'

'Well, that's just what you might get,' Albert said. 'That reply wasn't in the file, was it?'

Callendar looked at the blackened fireplace. 'No. No, it wasn't. Well, I don't suppose they've got it yet. I only posted it on Friday.'

'Ah,' said Albert. 'Pity.'

Callendar stared at him, just a little bit ahead now. Albert got up and went to his cupboard.

'Care for a drink?'

Callendar sat down again. 'Scotch if you've got it.' Then he said to Albert's back as he poured drinks, 'What'll happen?'

Albert looked round at him regretfully. 'Well, they'll read it and then try to file it – but the file won't be there, will it?'

'But that could have happened any time.'

'Only if you'd written to them – and you wouldn't, would you? I mean if they find your file's been lost a few years after it's happened they don't stand a chance. They just start another one. That gives you a clean sheet. But if it's missing during the next few days – there'll be a real old stink.' He gave Callendar the glass of whisky and drank some himself. 'I'd rather not think about it.'

Callendar sat wrapped in gloom and despair. 'Do you think they've read my letter?'

'Not yet,' Albert said. 'It'll be in the seven-day box.

They've got this big backlog.' Then he said, offhandedly, 'Of course I could get it for you.'

'I see,' Callendar said.

He finished his whisky as if for courage, then put his hand into his pocket and brought out the bundle of notes, handed them to Albert.

'Ta,' Albert said. 'What time shall I be at the office to-morrow?'

'What office?' Callendar said. Then 'Oh – any time.'

He got up and Albert saw him to the door.

'Toodle-oo, then,' Albert said.

Callendar looked at him, sourly. 'I'm losing my grip, Albert.'

'I shouldn't let it bother you, Cally – you've always got me . . .'

3

Albert came soaring into the doctor's waiting-room on the wings of his newest fantasy to find a crowd of National Health patients sitting in gloomy silent rows at ground level. On his list of hates Monday morning and doctors' waiting-rooms were also in the top ten but with fifty pounds in his pocket and a project in view Albert was carrying all before him.

'You don't have to worry,' he said to the room at large. 'It's all in the mind.'

The only person laughing was a man with his leg off up to the knee and his face scarred.

'Now who's going to give me a seat?' Albert asked an old lady sitting near the door.

The one-legged man moved up for Albert to sit down. The other people were either exchanging embarrassed glances or staring at the ends of their noses or at old copies of *Punch*.

'Why do I always have to make an exhibition of myself?' Albert once asked his mother. 'There must be some theatre blood in the family. Yet I've never seen you dancing, mum.'

With bunions, varicose veins, and several full-time jobs, his mother had never felt like dancing. She told him there was no history of public spectacle in the family other than his grandfather who had been a lay preacher. 'A *what* preacher?' Albert had asked. 'Cor, no wonder I'm what I am. The sins of the grandfathers.' But his mother had never been his best audience. Watching him grow through the original Teddy-boy phenomenon with his velvet collars and tight trousers, then safely out the other side into manhood and still continuing the search for the grail of fame and acclaim and riches, his mother had spent many sleepless nights searching for the explanation of Albert. Of all the Alberts. Was it Hitler or was it The Bomb or was it simply that Albert had his grandfather's blood in his veins? A rich mixture part religion part anarchy and part lust. The old man with his bony face, long hair and hot eyes had toured the sleepy villages of the county with a big brass-bound bible chained to the back of his tricycle, preaching on the village greens and getting invited home for supper and anything else that was going. In the Harris family the old preacher had been a legend, the one bit of colour in a long line of grey; he had comforted widows, prepared brides, thumped the bible, hidden the *News of the World* under the carpet and kept his wife permanently pregnant, all on four pounds a week. 'Thank God!' she'd said, on the day of his funeral.

'I'm a throwback, that's what I am,' Albert would say, once he knew the truth about his grandfather. 'Good job I'm a devout atheist.'

A little later on with the doctor Albert had to suffer the humiliation of showing his wounds.

'Don't hold it back, doc, have a good old laugh.'

'I'll give you some lotion,' the doctor said. 'Not painful, is it?'

'Keeps me awake,' Albert said. It was just the fury of it.

'I'll give you some tablets,' the doctor said.

'I had some aspirin last night,' Albert told him, adding nervously: 'They won't react with the aspirin, will they?'

'No, of course not. What are you afraid of?'

'I don't trust drugs.'

'I'm glad to hear it. Too many people of your age rely on them.'

Albert did not trust drugs or drink for the peculiar reason that they might impair his finely-tuned mind. Once launched from the pad of depression he guarded his physical and mental condition with neurotic concern, nursed the project through all the delicate booster stages and finally put the warhead of his idea safely into orbit. One pint of beer, one aspirin, one slight head cold might be sufficient to give somebody an advantage and bring the entire dream crashing down to earth. Or make it miss the moon.

It had been one careless whisky-soaked blinder that had lost him Treasure who, now in retrospect, he sometimes thought had been the biggest project of all.

'Do you think I could sue the manufacturers?' Albert asked the doctor.

'I shouldn't think so. Once you've lost all the skin there'll be no permanent scars. And anyway the stuff is meant to be put on the face, surely?'

'I was in a hurry,' Albert said. He had dressed again and was preparing to leave. 'How long do you think it's going to take?'

'Oh – a week I should think.'

'But that's what the sister said on Saturday! It's Monday now.'

'A day here or there doesn't make any difference, does it?'

'It does to me,' Albert said. 'How can I live a natural life? I mean, what can I tell the birds? It's all turnover and no profit.' He had a self-take on this and grinned. 'That's original by the way.'

'I'm sure it is,' the doctor said.

'Here.' Albert took the prescription. 'Ever thought of giving free gift stamps to your patients? They wouldn't half flock round. They'd do themselves an injury to get a free washing machine. Think about it and let me know . . .'

The doctor did not press the button for the next patient until several reflective minutes after Albert had gone out whistling.

The Treasure Trove Trading Stamp Company had established their county bridgehead in a suite of rented offices over their gift shop in an ancient, condemned building in the High Street. The tatty old house, paintless, slateless and dirty, had been tarted up with fluorescent orange-lettered billboards and banners.

'LIVE FOR FREE WITH TTT' was the slogan plastered across the shop window.

Albert had parked the hired car across the road where later he could be seen getting into it by anyone who cared to watch from the office windows. He stood looking into the gift shop window and trying to absorb as much as he could of the TTT gift stamp system. He was always prepared to spend time mastering a new job, though not much more than ten minutes. With the merest smattering in his head he found that things usually came to him as he went along.

'You have to play it by ear' had been one of his favourite slogans to his mother. In what he laughingly called his formative years Albert used to practise on her, but he might have been talking a foreign language for all she understood.

On a monstrous washing machine and spin dryer combined was stuck a big card:

'ONE BOOK ONLY OF TTT STAMPS GIVES
YOU THIS:'

But underneath in smaller print, it said:

'Fifteen shillings TTT gift value or: nylon
stockings, make-up box, undies for HER.
Socks, shirts, cigarettes for HIM.'

The washing machine itself was given away absolutely free in exchange for (small print) only sixty books of Treasure Trove Stamps.

'Christ Almighty!' Albert said. It was the only way he used religion. Already conversant with every twentieth-century philanthropy known to man, it did not take him long to do a rough conversion. On the basis of one stamp for sixpence spent the washing machine would involve the housewife in a spending spree of about twenty-five thousand pounds or, say, fifty years' steady work at the Agricultural Tractor Factory for her husband.

'LOOK FOR THE SHOP WITH THE TTT FRANCHISE' was another bold announcement.

'Failing that,' Albert said, 'pop along to your nearest lunatic asylum.'

Albert entered the door leading to the offices above on a warm surge of confidence that he had something to offer, something to give, a real contribution to make to the Treasure Trove Trading Stamp Company. Or any other organization that printed its own money.

At any other time Albert would have considered the girl receptionist alone sufficient justification for the visit. She was not pretty and she wore the rather hard expression which admits this without caring. It was something she had accepted and to combat her lack of facial beauty she had made the most of herself in other ways. Her hair was inky black and she wore it aggressively and unfashionably down her back so that in presenting an enchanting back view she could turn and watch a man's face change.

'Good morning,' Albert said. 'I have an appointment with your managing director.' He gave her his 'Chief Salesman' visiting card from his Callendars' Warehouse days. 'Argyle,' he said as she looked at it. 'Albert Argyle. I think he's probably expecting me.'

Now the girl looked up from the card and examined him, minutely, as one would look up from a travel brochure to compare it with the leaning tower of Pisa. '*Who's* expecting you?'

Albert knew immediately that Cally had not put in a good word for him. There was a fight ahead. 'Your area manager promised to have a word with him this morning.'

'We haven't got an area manager and the Managing Director is a woman.'

'Yes, well, let's start again. I'll come in, you look up and smile,' Albert said.

The girl laughed.

'You know what Callendar told me?' Albert said, in an injured tone. 'He said your boss was an ugly, sadistic, nasty bit of work with a dog for eating people.'

'That's her husband,' the girl said.

Albert began to like her very much. He had not struck these kind of sparks from a girl since Treasure. 'Haven't I seen you at the Town Hall hops? Or was it the coffee bar across the street?'

'Neither. I live ten miles out. I'm a scooter commuter.'

'What's your name?'

'Dorothy.'

'I like you, Dorothy. We'll have to date sometime.'

'Okay.'

It was terrible not being able to take things up immediately while the fire was alight. Dates put off never came to anything. You were strangers again. It could never occur to Albert to have a preliminary canter of a social, friendly nature. Love for Albert had always been now or never, rather than now and always.

'What are the chances of a job here, then?' Albert asked.

'For you – not a chance in hell.' She spoke matter-of-factly.

'How do you know?'

'Because you've had a big build-up. From your friend.'

'I see,' Albert said. 'He did put a word in for me then?'

'And how. He said you'd have me in bed within twenty-four hours.'

Albert grinned in spite of the impossibility. 'What other nice things did he say?'

'He said you were a crook and a con-man and out for number one. Oh yes, and he said you pushed your girl-friend downstairs once to get an abortion.'

'Bloody cheek!' Albert exclaimed, his voice cracking high on a note of injury. 'Fancy telling strangers personal things like that.'

'I don't think it worried Mrs Townend.'

'How is it she's the boss and he's only her husband?' Albert asked.

'He's a bankrupt,' she said. 'Treasure Trove is the Phoenix out of the ashes. Don't know how long it'll last.'

Albert said: 'I thought it was a good solid organization.'

'Oh no,' Dorothy said. 'It's a bandwagon.'

'Good,' said Albert. 'That's my favourite means of transport.'

What she had told him might have put off any ordinary person hoping to make a career for himself, but to Albert it was good news. His opinion of Treasure Trove Stamps had suddenly soared. It was not a bad firm after all. It was the 'Big Organization' thing that Cally had sold him that had been depressing Albert. Now it was as though he had found out that his bank manager was a sex maniac; vulnerable, weak, human. Likeable, perhaps was the word.

The Treasure Trove Trading Stamps Company was after all just about Albert's size; shady, fly-by-night, sharp. He looked around the reception hall now with a sense of belonging. Even Dorothy fitted in; her personality, her wit, her air of despising the whole set-up. In the firms Albert had graced all the staff without exception had despised the whole set-up. In fact, everybody despised everybody else. It was an accepted thing.

'Close your eyes and count ten.'

'It's no use,' Dorothy said. 'You can't go in. Mrs Townend's holding a reps.' conference. She won't see you anyway – Mr Clive has forbidden it. That's His Nibs.'

'Is he in?'

'You don't think he'd leave her alone with all these men, do you?'

'What about the dog?'

'Lying at his feet, ready to pounce.'

'What's the best time to see her alone?' Albert asked.

'I don't know,' she said. 'I'm sorry.'

'For instance, when does she take a bath?' Albert said.

The girl laughed. 'That's about it.'

'Have lunch with me?' Albert said.

'Sorry. I've got no relief today. Got to whistle and work.' She remembered something. 'Incidentally there was a call for you this morning –'

'For me?' Albert exclaimed.

'Mr Argyle – Area Manager – that's who he asked for. Some public relations firm.'

'Oh him. I suppose you told him?'

'No. I put it through to Mrs Townend.'

Albert looked at her, mock-bleak; he got off the desk and pulled a sad-sack face. 'It's not my day.'

'Sorry.'

Albert smiled at her. 'I'll be in touch.'

'I'm sure.'

The switchboard buzzed behind her and she swung round on her stool to attend to it. He stopped on his way out to savour the gleaming black hair down her back and the akimbo legs under the desk with one very high-heeled shoe lying on its side.

It was as good as in the bag. He could get his cards printed. Getting his cards printed was always the most exciting thing about a new job. For Albert, the receptionist had made his day, since the available perks were more important than the job; the news that the boss of TTT was a woman had sewn the whole thing up definitely and indisputably, husband or no husband, dog or no dog; the fact that the firm was shaky meant that he would be at home there and would therefore be in control of the situation. He sat in his car sketching a new card layout on the back of an old one.

ALBERT ARGYLE ESQ.

He crossed out the ESQ.

ALBERT ARGYLE,
Area Manager,
Treasure Trove Trading Stamps Ltd

224

On second thoughts he decided to put the firm's name in one corner in small gothic. Albert knew all the type-faces by this time, Bodoni, Times, Playbill. He used a lot of Playbill.

When Elaine Townend came out of the old building across the street Albert was truly surprised. It seemed immediately logical that this was the woman he had to win, but it had not occurred to him until now that Callendar's companion of yesterday and the Managing Director of TTT were one.

'Cor!' he said. 'On a plate!'

He had roughed out a possible means of effective introduction and he started his car in readiness. He watched the woman drive the Jag. out of a service road into the High Street, then brought his own car out in front of her as she came along. He judged it nicely so that only their bumpers crashed together. At least, that was the plan.

Elaine Townend got out of her car and came round to meet Albert. They both inspected the embedded conjunction. The Jaguar with its big over-riders had suffered not at all; the hired Ford on the other hand had a smashed spotlight and a crumpled radiator.

'Oh dear,' Albert said. 'That was careless. Of me,' he added.

'You just came out in front of me, Mr Argyle,' she said.

Albert was smiling at her. 'You've got my name, have you? Well that saves a bit of time. We may as well observe the formalities.' He took out a pen. 'You know? Exchange names, addresses, telephone numbers, opinions about the last film we saw and when we're going to meet again.'

'*And* insurance companies,' Elaine Townend said.

'Look, I tell you what,' Albert said, looking round at the gathering crowd. 'We don't want to stand here like the Band of Hope. Let's take it somewhere – we can do it all over lunch. Have a little aperitif first at the White Hart? Do you know the White Hart?'

'Then I take it that this accident was arranged?' she said.

'Oh well, you know – fate. Kismet. It's all in the stars.'

She said: 'Mr Callendar told me most things about you but he didn't mention that you were a comedian.'

'Ah well,' Albert said. 'I'm that rare thing, a legend in my own time. One has to live up to it.'

'I should think it must mean living alone,' Elaine Townend hazarded. 'Now do you mind backing up so that I can get away?'

'But I want to talk to you,' Albert said. 'That was the whole idea.' He had felt that she was playing along very nicely but now she seemed to take a sudden dislike to him.

She said: 'Please move your car before I call the police.'

'Don't be like that, Mrs Townend,' Albert said. 'I'm sorry.'

Albert knew when to cut the act. He had discovered that he was not irresistibly funny to everybody; not everybody found him endearing or charming. There had been housewives on his tally round to whom he had never said more than 'Good morning, madam'. They had never discovered his wit or his lovability. But usually he could tell these people in the first five seconds. By their first word. Even by the look of them from a distance or the shape of their head. He had not been able to judge that Elaine Townend was amongst that unhappy number who did not know what they were missing. She had not looked black and white; she had not appeared to be at ground level.

'You are an insult to educated people,' Mrs Elaine Townend now told Albert in front of the gathering crowd. The constable Sid had come up to listen but drifted away again in deference to Albert's feelings. She went on: 'You may be a great success with shop girls, factory girls, receptionists and barmaids and lonely little slap-and-tickle housewives –'

'And three High School girls and a woman solicitor,' Albert said, shamefacedly.

'What?' she said. Then as though it didn't matter, she went on. 'Don't bother to apply to us for a job, Mr Argyle. Our customers are not in that category. We deal with people of status, with persons of some importance – we conduct business which is right out of your class.'

'Exactly,' Albert said. 'This is more or less word for word what I was telling Cally.'

'You may be big game in this neck of the woods,' Elaine Townend went on, 'but in the selling game let me tell you, smart alick, you've never been out of the bargain basement.'

Albert stared at her while she seemed to be thinking whether or not she had said it all; then she added:

'Did that sound convincing?'

'Perfectly,' Albert said. 'I'm a slob.'

'Yes,' she said. 'Will you *please* move your car.'

'Yes,' Albert said.

Albert got into the Ford and backed it away. He watched the woman drive off in the Jaguar, then drove away himself.

Five minutes later Albert joined Mrs Elaine Townend in the American Bar of the White Hart Hotel. She was already at the bar with a drink lined up.

'Scotch on ice. Is that all right, Albert?'

'That's lovely, Yvonne. It is Yvonne, isn't it? I'm good at putting names to attractive women.'

'Elaine,' she said. She smiled at him as they drank. 'I'm glad you got the message.'

'In the last few seconds,' Albert said. 'What was it all about?'

'My husband was looking out of the window,' she said. 'I just saw him in time.'

Albert gave his face a dry-wash as he understood. 'Of course. That's why I parked there.'

'Don't worry. It was a nice trick.' Her eyes wrinkled as she smiled and he liked it. 'Have you used it before?'

'Several times,' Albert confessed. 'It was used on me to start with.' He gave a coy wriggle. 'Nice feller.'

Elaine laughed. 'If you can reach somebody in a moving car then you can reach anybody.'

'So what about a job?' Albert said.

She looked at him sadly, but with a certain warmth. 'Darling, it's going to be difficult. My old man's pathologically jealous.'

'Is he violent with it?' Albert asked, nervously.

'Well. He knows how to use his knees in a fight,' she said.

'Oh, manly.'

'The only manly thing in our family is carried by the dog,' Elaine said. 'I shouldn't have said that,' she added, without conviction.

Albert pressed her hand. 'We must do something about that.'

'It's going to be difficult. He keeps tabs on me.'

Albert said seriously: 'We can't help it if we're thrown together by our work.'

'Mmmm!' she said. 'That sounds violent!'

Albert smiled at her. 'Just make me your new area manager, darling.' He looked into her eyes, then drifted his gaze down her body and looked at her knees, crossed as she sat on the high stool. 'I can think of a few areas I'd like to manage,' he said.

She just stared at him with a mingling of warmth and weakness.

'Have this again?' Albert said.

She emptied her glass and he ordered again. He liked the picture in the bar mirror. A sophisticated pair.

'Give me one of those Havanas,' he told the barmaid. 'I'll save it for lunch,' he told Elaine. 'I like a cigar with coffee and liqueurs.'

'You don't have to sell me, darling. Mr Callendar did it very successfully. You don't think I'm usually like this with strangers, do you? The worse he made you the better it sounded. You'd have had the flags out if Clive hadn't been there. Anyway, I have to lunch with him. He'll be here at half-past one – he's busy trying to popularize himself with the reps. at the moment. Buying drinks and telling foul stories. He can't bear for people not to love him and everybody hates him. Sad really. Even the dog only does as it's told.'

'I thought you were the boss,' Albert said.

'I am. But every time I rub it in – like engaging somebody without his say so – he gets nasty. You see, I was secretary to Mr Jago – he founded TTT after the war. One of the first gift stamp companies in this country – of course it's all over America. Anyway – you're not drinking – when Jago drank himself to death he left me the majority of shares. Embarrassing, really. It was in the paper. For services rendered.'

' I see.'

She sniffed, ruefully. 'So did Clive. He'd been running a chi-chi dog parlour in Chelsea – oh, he tried lots of things. Gastric enteritis wiped out all his capital and he went bankrupt and moved in on me. But for him TTT would have been the biggest stamp company in the country – instead it's the smallest. You know how we operate? Move in before the big companies have got here, do some ground work, then sell out our franchise to the big boys when they arrive. We've never operated in one town long enough to give away a pair of nylons.'

'I would have thought you were doing all right,' Albert said. 'Plenty of shops giving your stamps.'

'Not enough,' she said. 'You've got to have one shop in four to make it worthwhile. Worthwhile for everybody – us, the shops and the customers. I mean in the first instance we just get the stamp money – you might sell twenty pounds' worth to a small shop if you're lucky.'

'There's no profit in that!'

'That's only the beginning. After that we work on a percentage of increased profits. You allow him a minimum increase on his average profits without taking anything from him. That's to encourage him and let him get his stamp money back. Then over an agreed level we take fifteen per cent – that can be quite a lot. Some shops increase their turnover by two hundred per cent.'

'Do you have to take their word for what they're making?'

'We get audited accounts if possible,' Elaine said. 'But you can't expect elaborate accounts from back-street grocers.'

'That's dicey,' Albert said. 'I wouldn't trust 'em.' Elaine smiled. 'They're not all Alberts.'

'So why can't you get more clients? It only wants a bit of lavish publicity – you can get the shops to pay for that.'

'No you can't. You'd be surprised how reluctant they are to pay for advertising. You can never prove the value of advertising to them. And after all, if they're doing all right why should they bother? It's no sinecure being in business these days. Not for the small man.'

'How I hate small men,' Albert said.

'Well, that's the point about the stamp business,' Elaine told him, with a flicker of enthusiasm she could not suppress. 'You get a grocer, you get a baker, you get a hairdresser and a chemist and a garage and a draper all giving stamps – well it means they have all the resources and advantages of one big departmental store. Do you see what I mean? *And* without the overheads *and* keeping their individuality – which is what lots of people like as distinct from the multiples and supermarkets.'

'It's a damned good line,' Albert said with frank admiration.

'It's not a line! It's the truth!' She blazed at him for a moment.

'I mean a selling line. A spiel. You know how to put it over, love. You ought to be doing well.'

'Well you put your finger on it. Advertising. Publicity. Stunts. The big stamp companies offer them massive local tie-ups and so on – I mean it's an investment if you can do it. We haven't got the cash.'

Albert said: 'Have you ever thought of letting a Public Relations firm handle it for you?'

Elaine laughed at him. 'No, but you have. You've got a nerve, Albert. "May I speak to Mr Argyle – your area manager," he said.'

Albert shrugged. 'A bit previous, that's all. I suppose you told him?'

She smiled at Albert in a hazed way. 'I didn't as a matter

of fact. I don't know why. I honestly don't know why. I had a feeling about you. After all, it takes a bit of initiative to do what you did.'

'I'm ambitious,' Albert said. 'What did you tell him – the PRO?'

Elaine Townend looked down at her glass, a little ashamed. 'I said you'd just taken a plane up to Manchester to initiate a crash programme for TTT. I shouldn't have said that.'

Albert laughed at her and she met his eyes again. He said: 'What I like most about you are the things you shouldn't have said. We've got a lot in common, Elaine.'

'Yes.'

Albert moved his knee to rest lightly against hers. 'We both know how to fly kites.'

She nodded and blinked in a shy way. Obscurely, this tiny defenceless act moved Albert with a familiar, sharp pleasure-pain of emotion. He got something of this from every woman but a lot of it from only very few. Grace had it and so did Treasure when she wasn't throwing things at him and whenever it happened they all flooded into his heart together and made a fool of him.

'What's the matter?' she said.

She knew what was the matter and that was a part of it too. It was a communication neither sex nor love. It came from the drop of an eyelash or the quiver of a mouth and always in silence. It could happen in moonlight or on top of a bus or in an American bar. Whatever people thought Albert was looking for, this was really what he was looking for.

'How about dins?' he said.

'I can't do any meals,' she said. 'It would have to be something sneaky.'

'I'll be sneaky,' Albert offered.

They looked at each other in the anticipatory way people look at new possessions before using them.

'Forget about the job, Albert. It would be better if you didn't meet Clive. He dirties everything up.'

'I need the job,' Albert said.

'You've got some money to be going on with.' She stopped. 'I shouldn't have said that either.'

This jolted Albert. 'Did Cally tell you about that?'

Elaine laughed. 'He was livid. Although really he was tickled pink. It's a funny thing. He goes round slandering you but subconsciously do you know what? I think he's secretly proud of you. It's as if he's talking about his own glorious youth. I'm sure he doesn't realize.'

'Nor do I? Do you mind?'

She shrugged. 'I think some people are like some people. But I can't be natural with him. I have to keep up the sales act – classy dame stuff. Do you know he keeps calling me "madam". He's a bit of a social climber really. Of course, he'll never get anywhere.' And after a moment as if in the light of her previous remarks she had now made a *faux pas*, she added: 'You will, Albert.'

Albert had already picked up her line of thought. 'Well, I'm not a Liverpool Irish Jew, am I?' To leaven it he said: 'Mind you, he hasn't had an easy time. One of the under-privileged. He often told me about running with the kids on the Cast Iron Shore – you know, Merseyside as it was. They called it the Cassy. "There were rats as big as cats," he used to say.' Albert glanced around the American Bar. 'In this town, I told him, there are rats as big as people.'

Elaine laughed. 'Why don't you leave it?'

'I would if I got the right opportunity – or a bit of cash.'

'Where would you go?'

Albert was looking at the bright cocktails, the glittering glass, the cherries; he saw a land that was one big American bar with deep-pile carpets, soft lights and beautiful girls.

'Stateside, I guess,' he said, with an unconscious American accent.

'I'd come with you,' Elaine Townend said, wistfully; then she laughed at his expression. 'Sorry – that frightened you. You don't like being tied down, do you, Albert?'

'I wouldn't be tied to the Crown Jewels,' he said.

'I'll remember that,' Elaine said. 'Tell me your address –'
He started looking for a pencil but she stopped him. 'I'd
rather memorize it.'

'Five Railway Street – top floor.'

Elaine was looking into the mirror, speaking swiftly and
clearly. 'I'll make a hair appointment for four o'clock – that
will give us through to seven.'

'I'll be waiting –'

'Give me your drink, turn away and order another one –
my husband is just coming in,' she said in the same flat tone.
'Play it cool, Albert.'

Albert turned his back on her and made a sign to the barmaid, then looked in the mirror. Clive Townend came across
from the door with the dynamic, up-and-down walk of the
handicapped; a big Alsatian at his heels. There was an
electric smile on a red, bearded face, a glow of six baths a
day, Savile Row suits and silk shirts, artificially waved hair
and an urgent, violent and desperate demand for celebrity
status in every crooked step; he reached the bar with the
triumph of swimming the channel.

Elaine was waiting for him with Albert's whisky ex-
tended: it was like a grown-up encouraging a baby to walk
by holding out some favourite toy. 'I got you a Scotch darling.'

'Wait!' the man said. Then to the dog: 'Sit!' Elaine
waited, the dog sat down.

'He can't come in here, sir,' the barmaid said. She was
giving Albert his drink.

'I beg your pardon?' Clive Townend said. 'You must be
new. Biff has got more right in here than you have.' An unpleasant hate-smile was fixed on his face like a mask. He
looked down at the dog. 'Outside!'

The Alsatian loped across to the glass door. Somebody
sitting near got up to open it. Clive Townend rasped: 'Leave
him!'

The man near the door sat down. Everybody was watch-

233

ing. The big dog went up on his hind legs and put his weight against the door, which yielded. He went through, then stood staring back at his master. Clive snapped his fingers. The dog sat down outside the door. Clive Townend now turned to take the drink from Elaine. The smile was varnished on, his hand with the glass was trembling. Everybody relaxed as he drank the whisky; it was as if a spotlight was still playing on him but the high-wire walk had been accomplished, the exhibition over.

'Have you ordered a wine for lunch?' Clive Townend asked his wife.

He spoke loud and clear like a ringmaster announcing the next act. Elaine shook her head. She had glimpsed Albert watching and listening and was now avoiding his eyes, embarrassed and diminished.

There was a menu on the bar and Clive Townend scanned it, at once nonchalant and lordly, reeling off a programme of menu French. Then he turned to the barmaid.

'Have you got a good Mâcon?'

She gave him the wine list.

'I asked you a question,' Clive said. 'Have you or haven't you?' It was all spoken with the fixed smile and the glint of venomous friendship.

'We've got everything on the list including Mâcon,' the girl said.

'How amazing!' Clive said. 'Let's take it in with us. Finish your drink, Elaine.'

They both finished their drinks and he was turning away with the menu when the barmaid said:

'That menu belongs to the bar, sir.'

Clive had to turn right round on one foot to speak to her. The handicap made every simple movement a muscular exercise and oddly deliberate. 'Then you can come and fetch it when I've finished with it, can't you?'

He bulged his eyes at the rest of the occupants, inviting them to laugh, and strutted out with Elaine following.

'Stay! Stay!' his command came through the glass door.

The barmaid was still staring after them. Albert grinned at her.

'It's all done by kindness,' he said.

The girl pulled a distasteful face.

Albert sat for a moment getting his hate up. All that energy, all that hate, all that desperate effort to make a dog sit down and a girl look silly. A big inflated tycoon, empty as a shell; one dose of gastric enteritis and he's bankrupt. Albert hated Clive Townend for Elaine but most of all and inexplicable to himself he hated him for the red tooth marks on Cally's wrist.

Albert drove from the White Hart Hotel straight round to the hire garage in Butterhall Street, knowing that Jackson would be at lunch. He went into the driveway and parked close up to a brick wall to conceal the damage.

'You're two hours overdue, sir,' the garage mechanic said. 'Should have been in midday – you've been uninsured since twelve o'clock.'

'Good job nothing happened, then,' Albert said. 'Where's Mr Jackson? He knows me.'

'He's at lunch, sir. How much deposit did you put down? Ten?'

'Ten,' Albert agreed. He didn't mention that the cheque had been torn up. 'That's Saturday, Sunday, Monday, three days at two pounds a day –'

'One pound insurance,' the mechanic added.

'Three pounds change, then,' Albert said.

He went to the office and collected it, gave the car a grateful farewell pat as he came out.

Albert browsed around the men's clothing shops for an hour with money to spend. He rather fancied the picture of the dilettante author that Alice Finbow had put into his head; or he had put into hers. He bought a pair of light rayon slacks, two cream shirts and a bright red smoking jacket with a tasselled sash. He invested in a few bottles, a set

235

of new glasses, a jar of olives and a box of potato crisps. Then he got a taxi from the rank outside the Town Hall and went home.

When the taxi had driven off Albert stood outside number five, Railway Street, holding his parcels and taking stock of the houses. 'What a crummy dump to ask anybody into,' he said. He could just see a Jag. Mark 10 parked in this street. He looked at his watch; he had one hour and a half to do something about it.

Albert started by cleaning his room out, putting all the portable furniture outside on the landing to give him elbow room. He filled a bucket with hot water from the Sadia over the bath, sprinkled into it talcum powder, lavender water and a few bath crystals; this mixture, well stirred, he splashed all over the top floor of the house before starting to sweep. He had pawned his vacuum cleaner long since.

In ten minutes he had cleaned and perfumed every parallel surface right to the top of the stairs. Tables, dressing table, sideboard, chairs, radiogram, the wardrobe-cum-cocktail cabinet. Everything got the treatment and came up shining and fragrant.

To get clean linen for his bed he went downstairs and ransacked the drawers of the girl who lived below. There were two bachelor girls in the house, for Albert couldn't bear to sleep very far away from women. With one of them he had already had an affair and was now on friendly, neutral terms; the other was a new girl preparing for marriage and it was to her bottom drawer that Albert's sure instinct led him. It furnished not only bed linen, best quality Irish still wrapped in cellophane, but also such pretty extravagances as table centres, pillow cases, a bright blue candlewick bedspread. He carried all those upstairs and beautified his bedsitter.

His mother's old ornaments were dusted and polished and replaced; two china horses rampant of neo dart-stall vintage which stood as book-ends to the alarm clock, two mermaid vases in gilt glass, a carved wooden baboon with its young on its back which his father had brought from Gibraltar, a desk lighter, still unused, which Treasure had given him. Only the bent brass knobs of his bedstead resisted his attentions; he concentrated on these for several minutes, using various ineffective cleaners scrounged from other rooms, but the knobs remained obstinately brown and yellow with hints of cankerous green in the cracks. Then Albert, with a bright idea, stopped rubbing. He went into the bathroom and came back with the lethal after-shave lotion. He poured some of this onto his cloth and applied it to the bed knobs. The result was alarming and miraculous; the very metal itself seemed to dissolve without any hard rubbing. Each tiny splash of the stuff instantly turned brightest gold tending towards platinum silver.

Albert stood at the door of his room and stared, dazzled, at the four shining gold knobs as they caught the afternoon light; and he felt his own, tenderly and with compassion.

'You see those brass knobs?'
'Yes.'
'They were as black as your hat and I cleaned them with after-shave lotion.'
'I must remember that.'
'Last Saturday night I spilt half a bottle of it on my courting tackle.'
'Oh, Albert! You poor thing. That must have been terribly painful.' She did not find it amusing. She reacted as his mother might have done to such an accident.
'I'm out of action for a week. I had to tell you before you got properly in,' Albert said.
'I understand.'
'You looked so sexy standing on that doorstep.'
'Don't let it worry you,' she said. 'I made a special effort.'
'You got a special result,' Albert said.
She was wearing a three-quarter-length fluffy oatmeal coat open over a tight scarlet dress, black figured stockings –

which turned out to be tights – and five-inch heels. Her fair hair was brushed back from her face and her skin was naked of make-up except where she had deeply painted her lips. She was standing quite still, just inside the door, looking around. Albert had been circling with his hands in his pockets, his head down, getting it off his chest.

'I *like* your little room,' she said, putting him at his ease. 'I thought I might be revolted, but I'm not.'

'Good.'

'I thought I might feel like one of a procession. But I don't.'

Albert stopped circling and looked at her. She smiled, kindly.

'You must have made a lot of love up here, Albert.'

'Yes.'

'It's left a nice taste in the air.'

'That's bath salts.'

Elaine Townend laughed. 'No it isn't. It's a happy room.'

'I'll get you a drink,' Albert offered.

'No. I don't want anything yet. And then I'll have a cup of tea.'

In bed together they played a gentle, satisfying love game and as soon as it quickened or became ungentle they stopped it and talked.

'Nobody will come in?' she asked.

'Nobody comes up here without me.'

'I mean one of your chums or somebody? I noticed your door doesn't lock.'

'I haven't got any chums.'

'But who do you talk to? You have to talk to somebody.'

'I'm talking to you. I talk to myself.'

'Do you talk to your girls?'

'Sometimes. I don't think they listen. They run as soon as it's over as if they've done something wicked and want to forget it. Or else they stay as if they've done nothing.'

'That's not much good to you.'

238

'I get most of what I want. Some of them are too young.'

'What about me?'

'You're the oldest woman that's ever been in this bed with me.'

'I know. It makes me feel important.'

'And you're lovely.'

'Do you mean well-preserved?'

'No.'

'Good.'

'How old are you? Twenty-nine?'

She said: 'Thirty-one.'

'That means thirty-six, say it quick.'

She said: 'Thirty-seven.'

'What about him?'

'He needs me, Albert. He needs me more than anybody needs anybody in the world. He's useless and he needs me. If I deserted him, if he thought I'd been with anybody like this, naked in your arms, he would kill himself.'

'I know that one.'

'No. It's true. I know it is because he's never said it. It's about the only thing he's never said.'

'Cigarette?'

'Yes, please.'

They smoked.

'Nobody knows we're here,' she said. 'I never felt so peaceful.'

Then she said, 'Albert.'

'Yes?'

'Thank you, Albert. You've made me feel normal. Thank you,' she said.

When the knocking came at the downstairs door they did not at first hear it. Their conversation had moved out of the cluttered backyard of their immediate lives and into the quieter fields beyond. She had asked him how he came to be called Albert, such a prosaic and ordinary name, and he had told her that he was named after his father who in turn had been named after a township in Belgium where Albert's paternal grandfather had been fighting at the time. They had moved on to Albert's mother whose faded photograph was sandwiched incongruously between the pin-ups over his bed. Albert was making Elaine laugh with his memories of her just as he laughed himself.

'She used to say, "You can always get another sweetheart but you'll only have one mother." Bless her heart, she said it every time she sewed another button on for me. She's out-numbered now,' he added, laughing up at the parade of tits and navels. 'Still, she was a good worker.'

Elaine laughed. 'You sound like a farmer talking about a favourite cart-horse. Didn't you ever do anything for her?'

'I let her keep me until I was eighteen. No, honestly, that was doing her a favour. It gave her a kick. She liked me being dependent on her. She said I wouldn't grow up too quickly.'

'But didn't you ever take her anywhere? Buy her any-thing?'

'I got her a television set. She didn't like it. She used to say: Sex sex sex sex sex, nothing but sex, yet they keep on sending up all those rockets!'

Elaine Townend shouted with laughter. And it was in the silence that followed that they heard the knocking at the downstairs door.

'Oh Christ!' Albert said.

The knocking came again.

'This is what I hate about married women,' Albert said.

'Don't be silly. It can't be him. Nobody knows I'm here. I left the car at the office. I didn't say which hairdresser I was going to. I came halfway in a taxi and walked the rest.'

These elaborate precautions did nothing to reassure him.

'It's the dog that scares me,' Albert confessed. 'I've always been frightened of them ever since this.' He showed her a scar on the palm of his left hand. 'I was eight or nine and mum was in hospital having a varicose vein operation. I got bitten by a dog and the blooming neighbour took me to some back-street quack chemist. D'you know he made such a mess of my hand – it came up like a balloon. Well, he was mad – he used to buy cats a shilling each and kill them and then bring them to life with some cayenne pepper embalming formula.'

'Listen,' Elaine said.

'He lanced it nine times before I was carted off to hospital. My mum was raving when she knew about it –'

'Listen!'

'He used to send in eight *News of the World* crossword coupons every week –'

'Stop babbling, Albert!'

Now there were footsteps ascending the top flight of stairs outside the door. Elaine looked at Albert who was sitting bolt upright in the bed, his face whiter than the clean pillow-case. The footsteps came across the landing.

'It's not him,' she said, expertly.

'I'm not f-frightened,' he told her, with a deliberate stutter to cover his funk.

There was a tap at the door and Albert shot out of bed. He had kept his underpants on to hide the embarrassing bandages and now he started getting into his trousers. The tap came again. Elaine also got out of bed and pulled on her coat.

'Who can it be?' she whispered.

Albert whispered back: 'Dunno. Bailiff, creditor – somebody like that.'

'I'll answer it then,' Elaine said. 'I'll tell them you've moved.'

Albert watched her go to the door. He was too worried to appreciate for the moment the delightful things a short fluffy oatmeal coat and high heels did to a naked woman with bedrough hair. Elaine opened the door a fraction and put her head round. Albert was already pushing his shirt into his trousers. It was a situation that rang many alarming bells with Albert and he never ceased to panic. When a woman was married everybody was in the right except you.

He heard a girl's voice and Elaine looked round at him, closed the door. She was amused.

'A Miss Finbow. For you.'

'Oh God! Income Tax!'

'Really?'

'No. I mean it. She's from the Inland Revenue office.'

Then: 'Coming,' he called. He put on his shoes and went out, wiping his mouth hard.

Elaine was smiling. She looked round the room, saw the kettle and picked it up, checked for water and stooped to the gas ring. She could hardly contain her laughter. The situation was funny and normal and good.

Out on the landing Alice Finbow was looking nervously at Albert; she had come straight from the office and was wearing a white mac over a rather lumpy green costume. There was a smudge of ink near the mole on her cheek.

'I'm sorry,' she said.

'Ah, that's all right love – it's only my ex.'

'Your wife? Kathleen?' Alice was frightened.

'Who? Oh, yes. She's just called in to put her things together.'

'Oh, dear!' Alice said, speaking in a hushed, terrified voice. 'She hasn't found *my* things, has she? My umbrella and gloves – I left them here.' She gave her nervous cough.

'It doesn't matter if she has. It's all over. She's married to someone else. Anyway, they're not here, dear. I cleaned the place out this afternoon. Is that what you came for?'

'I must have left them in the car,' Alice said. 'I wouldn't worry about them only – dad – my father gave me the brolly for a birthday present. It was just before . . .' She coughed again.

Albert put his hand on her shoulder but she drew away, conscious of the visitor. 'I'll get 'em back for you.' He knew that she had lost them for good. He didn't want to take Jacko on again. Another garage he couldn't go to. The town had been quite big once but now for Albert it had narrowed to one or two coffee bars, a couple of pubs and half-a-dozen shops; the rest of the town he had lost with broken promises, con tricks, lies and downright fraud.

'There is another thing,' Alice Finbow said. 'That's really why I came. In case they get in touch with you.'

'Who?'

'Mr Bellamy – the chief tax collector –'

'Oh, don't worry about that – I've got that in hand. My accountant's taking care of it.'

'No. It's serious, Albert –'

'Let's take it in the bathroom.' Albert scented trouble and was conscious of the thin door.

They crossed the landing and entered the bathroom. Albert closed the door and sat down on the lavatory, holding her hand. 'What is it, love?'

'There's a file missing,' Alice Finbow said.

It was just behind her head, the box file itself, the cover removed and the box containing a tidy array of toilet bottles and jars. It made a nice little bathroom cabinet.

'Go on!' Albert said. 'What file?'

Alice rushed on, spilling the worries of a ghastly day. 'I know it's nothing to do with you and they said I had the only keys and somebody – you see they think somebody came in – broke in – to the tax office I mean, over the week-end – the police have been in this afternoon. They've been asking me questions – do you remember I had the keys?'

'What keys?' Albert asked.

She was relieved. 'I knew you wouldn't remember – I didn't even bother to tell them I'd told you. You see they asked me and I said no –'

'Just a minute, dear,' Albert said. 'Sit down and take a breath. If I can help you I will, you know that.'

'Yes,' she said.

She sat on the edge of the bath. Her incoherence came from trying to avoid the point; not wishing to offend Albert. 'I told them – well I had to tell them – that I was with you. I hope you don't mind, Albert? They kept asking me, you see.

It would have seemed funny if I hadn't told them. As if I had something to hide. Well, we haven't got anything to hide.'

'As it happens,' Albert said.

'I hate asking you, Albert – you don't mind, do you? I mean it's only for myself. You see I didn't tell them. I knew you hadn't got anything to do with it. You even told my mother before we went – you know, about having to go somewhere. That business appointment.'

'Oh, that?' Albert said. He thought deeply. 'Was that Saturday?'

'You remember–you left me at the reception. Well I didn't tell them that – not Mr Bellamy. Well, nor the detective. But if they ask you – well, remember you were with me all the time, Albert.' She was close to tears. 'I'm sorry I lied about it. I didn't want them to come asking you questions – well, it's spoilt the evening. It was a lovely evening, Albert. Giving me that buttonhole and everything. It's still alive. I was afraid you wouldn't see me again.'

And the biggest worry of all was off her mind; the question she had set out to ask, still unasked. What was his business appointment? Where had he gone for those two hours?

'And now my income tax file is missing, you mean?' Albert said, as if trying hard to understand.

'Oh, not yours! That's just the point. In fact that's what the detective said –'

'Was it George Beeson. Plump feller – Detective Sergeant?'

'Well I'm not sure. Yes I'm sure it was a Detective Sergeant – I think it was. I didn't catch his – I wasn't listening – oh, it was awful, called into the office in front of everybody – I'd been telling all the girls about Saturday. Well, the reception and so on. About that carnation.'

'Old George wouldn't go asking questions about me,' Albert said, incredulously. 'He was in my class!'

'I bet it was him,' Alice said. 'He didn't half give Bellamy a straight talk – well Bellamy did I tell you, he knows you?

Well that is your returns – the expenses and the children and – anyway it doesn't matter and this detective said it's not even Albert's file – I'm sure he called you Albert.'

'That was George,' Albert said. 'Good chap, George.'

'So – where was I? Oh yes.'

'Comfortable, are you?'

She smiled at him adoringly and he stroked her wrist.

'Yes, I'm sorry, Albert. I expect I sound silly. I can't talk straight when I'm excited.'

'I like you when you're excited,' Albert said.

She knew what he meant; she had lived through those moments a million times; she got breathless remembering them again. 'I ran all the way from the office. In case, you know. In case they – somebody – well, they might.'

'Whose file was it then?'

'Somebody named Carpenter. Galahad. Colindale.'

'Ah. Don't know them.'

'They got me out of church on Sunday. Or was it Carpenter? Well it doesn't matter. Did I tell you? They got me and my mother out of church on Sunday morning. Only about the keys. I'd forgotten all about it. About them. I didn't think a word more about them! The caretakers couldn't get in and there was this flap and then today – anyway.'

Albert pressed her hand. 'Don't worry about it, love.'

'I'm thinking about you.' It was all she was thinking about. 'I don't want to get you into trouble.'

'How about you?' Albert said.

'Oh, it doesn't matter. It's only a job.'

Albert stared at her: 'Do you mean they've fired you?'

'It doesn't matter –'

'Of course it matters! What about the civil service exams and everything – your father's good record, your mother –'

'It doesn't matter, Albert – I can get a job. I can get a job. It's not that – it's getting you into – well if they come asking you must tell them. I mean don't forget you were with me all the evening and oh yes – that I didn't mention the keys to you – I don't want to make you lie –'

Albert calmed her down. 'Now don't you worry about that. I don't like lying, naturally, but I'd lie my head off if it means protecting you. You know that, don't you?'

She nodded, dumbly grateful. 'Yes.'

'Upsadaisy, then.' Albert got off the lavatory and lifted her off the bath. He brushed his mouth against hers then kissed her forehead. She was trembling in his arms.

'Oh, *Albert* . . .'

He led her out of the bathroom on to the landing. She was trying to say something more.

'Sorry I – you know,' she said, looking at his door. There came the friendly rattle of teacups.

'That's all right, dear. She'll be gone in a minute.'

Alice drew away towards the top of the stairs : 'I'd better go, then –' then in a rush again: 'Mother wondered if you'd come round to see me – I mean to supper, dinner, one night. Anytime. When you're not busy. Tonight if you like?'

'Well, that's nice of her. I like your mum. Not tonight, though – I'm a bit pressed.'

'Yes, of course. But you will come?'

'Soon as I get me head up. I've got this new job. Area manager for TTT stamps –'

'Oh Albert!' her eyes shone with admiration and happiness for him. 'That's wonderful!'

Albert had a thought. 'I may be able to fit you up with a job.'

'If only you could!'

'I'll pop round and see you in a few days,' Albert promised.

'If I'm out job-hunting you'll always find mother at home.'

'Good.'

He was really foul. He knew this and there was nothing he could do about it.

'Ta ta, Janice love,' he said.

She was turning away but now she turned back again.

'*Alice*, I mean,' he said. 'D'you know what? I'm *sure* you mentioned the name Janice?'

'Of course I did!' She was laughing. 'It's your daughter's name. Your own child! You are funny!'

There was nothing funny about it. He had told her so many lies she would have to go the way of all the others. So many people, so many girls, so many old friends who'd be glad to see him if only he could remember what he'd told them.

'How *is* the writing going, anyway?' she asked, this excusing everything.

He wished he had the scarlet smoking jacket on but he had instinctively kept it out of Elaine's sight.

'Fine,' he said. And he shaped his mouth into a farewell kiss.

Alice blew him a kiss and then, overcome at her own boldness, she scuttled down the stairs, falling the last three. The sound of Alice falling downstairs stirred something deep in Albert's mind about Treasure, and he stood there, sentimentally, until the street door slammed below. Then he got a vivid retrospective picture of his ring on the third finger of Alice's ungloved right hand as she had blown him the kiss.

Albert shivered.

4

Albert got the job.

Not directly through any of his lunatic plans. Not entirely
because Elaine wanted him within easy reach. Albert's plans
had never come to very much; his women were never the
kind to move mountains; his achievements were always
short-lived and he preferred them that way; it depressed him
to see further ahead than one week and bandwagons are
notorious for their short journeys. But nor was it entirely
accidental that he got the job. Rather was it the result of
random repercussions of the things he had started, lucky
ricochets hitting the target; a bit of the Callendar tax
swindle, a touch of the engineered car crash and just a
sprinkling of after-shave lotion.

A girl brought the letter in to his room on Wednesday
morning while he was still in bed. She was holding a cup
of tea in the other hand. She wore a dolly face painted on to
a pugilistic bone structure. The static, painted face was
pretty, but it was the boxer who smiled.

'Wake up, Romeo!'

'Hello, Wendy. You might've knocked.'

'Don't be daft. I always know when you've got company.
It's like trains going by all night. This old place is going to
fall down one of these times.'

'Ditto, darling.' He opened the letter and she stood by,
watching him, still holding the tea. 'Is this all there was?' he
asked.

'Tore the others up. They're still on about that typewriter.'

Their familiarity came from a brief passion and a long
and pleasant neighbourliness. She was in the room directly

underneath his. She was looking at him, curiously, as he pondered on the letter; the unruffled bed, the spare pillow.

'What's the matter with you these days, Albert? Given it up?'

'Only for Easter.' He was staring at the letter. Now he handed it to her to read and got on with drinking his tea.

'This job any good?' she said, looking up from the letter.

'I dunno, do I?' He gave her back the cup. 'Thanks, mate.'

'Ta, ta,' she said. 'Oh, and good luck.'

He watched her, broodingly, as she tottered out; a good generous female rump, her big knees shackled by a tight hemline. There had been no involvement. She happened to be living downstairs, they were both sleeping around and it would have been silly – even unfriendly – not to do it. He was thinking in fact that Wendy might be the one to start up with again when he was ready. He could take his time and he wouldn't feel self-conscious with her.

The letter was short and formal, typed on TTT headed notepaper. It referred to his recent application for employment with the company and suggested an appointment for five-thirty that afternoon. It was signed by Elaine Townend, Managing Director, and it was impossible to find any secret message in it for him, personally.

Dorothy showed Albert into the conference room at five twenty-five and left him. Elaine looked up from a desk full of papers.

'Oh, it's you. Take a seat, please. I'll tell my husband you're here.'

Albert again failed to find any secret message in it for him, personally. Sitting there alone in the big room he got a very prickly feeling around the nape of the neck. He remembered Monday's trust and the elaborate safety precautions she had taken to get to his room. There was a funny sort of undercurrent about it; as though clandestine romance had somehow got mixed up with the French Resistance.

'Ah!'

The single explosive word and the loud handclap that
went with it had Albert leaping off his chair.

'Mr Argyle?' Clive Townend was extending a hand and, it
seemed, trying to hypnotize him with a piercing, searching
stare.

Clive Townend was not a man to wait for answers any
more than a ringmaster expects a reply from the audience;
he was already stomping noisily around the desk fiercely
concentrating on the next trick. Albert could see the top hat
and the whip and was grateful the Alsatian dog was not in
this particular act. With a series of sharp commands, ejacu-
lations and a few waves of his hand he got Albert to sit, take
a cigarette and listen.

'I want to put you in the picture as quickly as I can because I'm expecting a telephone call and might have to
run . . .'

He seemed to be telling Albert that he could also put
people in pictures, take telephone calls and run.

'Let me put it this way.' Clive Townend banged the desk
with his fist. 'This is not my desk. This is not my office.
Interviewing you is not my job. My wife is the managing
director of Treasure Trove. She is absolute boss. And she
hates your guts.'

'That's nice,' Albert said. 'I've got a big future here.'

'But wait,' Clive Townend said. There was a dramatic
pause, then he said: 'We have somebody to thank for this.
Somebody we both know . . .'

Your friend and mine! Albert was filling in, none other
than! Wait for it!

'Yes,' Clive Townend was saying, 'Mr Theodore Callendar!'

'I see,' Albert said. He could hear the shouting and clapping and stamping. Bring on Cally the lying old sod.

Clive Townend was laughing. There was no real sound; he
seemed to do it with his lungs. 'What an escape!'

'What was?' Albert asked, feeling that he had missed
something important.

'Mr Argyle, I don't know whether or not you gathered this

from the brief interview you had with my wife in the street on Monday? Anyway, to put it mildly, Mr Argyle. To understate it, that is. Your friend Mr Callendar – your old boss, I believe? – Mr Callendar, while waiting for us to sign a contract with him, has been systematically destroying your character. What do you say to that?'

'Naughty!' Albert said.

'He has said things about you,' Clive Townend said, 'that I wouldn't say about my dog.' Before Albert could comment on this he went on: 'Now I think I know why. He knew that we badly needed a local man as area manager and he was afraid of competition. Well naturally. It's a very good job. It could be worth, say, eighty or a hundred pounds a week. Five thousand pounds a year plus expenses.'

Albert pulled his nose and tried to look only modestly impressed. 'Worth considering.'

'Briefly, he said that you were immoral, dishonest, a liar, a cheat and a thief –'

Albert waved it down. 'I can imagine!' He gave Townend a serious, earnest look then. 'How did you find out it was all a pack of lies?'

'Ah!' the ringmaster exclaimed, clapping his hands again. 'Mind you,' he added, 'Elaine – that's my wife – is still not convinced. Personally, after what's happened, I want to hear your side of it.'

'What's happened?' Albert asked.

Clive Townend frowned, suddenly puzzled. 'I don't know why she isn't convinced. She's a shrewd woman. Of course, Callendar worked on her more than on me – probably his technique.'

'He's wily,' Albert agreed.

'Do you know . . .' Clive Townend had difficulty in talking about it. 'Do you know what happened? You probably know Wilkinson's?'

'Biggest family grocers in town,' Albert said.

'Yes. The essential shop to start a stamp chain – well, you've worked in stamps, you know . . .'

Albert had never worked in stamps; there were things about the background to this interview still veiled in mystery. He had to go on playing it by ear.

'Well, not to draw it out,' Townend said, 'we had Mr Wilkinson himself up here on Tuesday – yesterday – together with the principals in the firm. Do you know what happened right in the middle of the conference? Just when we were beginning to impress the Wilkinsons with our facts and figures? Just when we were beginning to convince them of our record of sales promotion successes? Of our integrity and reliability when it comes to advertising support and the mustering of customer goodwill? Do you know what happened?'

Albert shook his head. He could hear a roll of drums.

'The police arrived! Yes, the police marched in and arrested our new area manager! Mr Callendar was whisked out of this very room from under their very noses and carted off to the jug!'

'Oh no!'

'Oh yes!'

'Oh my gawd!' Albert said.

'Some *tax* fiddle!' Clive Townend said, disdainfully.

'Stupid!' Albert said, his face a mixture of pain, compassion and sheer disgust.

Clive Townend smiled at Albert. 'And that's why I wrote to you . . .'

Albert was only half listening for the next little while. He knew, of course, that Cally had not been arrested; that was said merely to make it a better story and he would have done the same himself. But slotting in with what Alice Finbow had told him he realized that Cally had been questioned, was in trouble, would have to pay the two thousand odd tax after all and had parted up with fifty pounds to Albert plus, probably, his job. Quite unintentionally Albert had done Cally a bad turn when in fact he had set out to do him a good turn by working for him. Albert felt quite badly about this for the next five minutes.

'There is one little thing else,' Clive Townend was saying. He presented Albert with a foolscap sheet of paper. 'This application form. You filled it in but you forgot to sign it.'

'Ah yes,' Albert said. He was staring at the form and trying not to show that he was reading it for the first time. Somebody had filled it in on his behalf. Apparently he *had* worked for two trading stamp companies, had attended a minor public school and could furnish references from two banks and several previous employers if required.

Albert quickly signed his name to it.

'You must be careful about that little detail,' Townend told him. 'Forget to get the signature on a customer agreement and it could cost a lot of money.'

'That's right,' Albert said. He felt it was time to be knowledgeable. His bona fides as detailed on the form had given him a new confidence. 'By the way I was wondering about your methods. Your working methods. I imagine you're after a franchise of one shop in four, aren't you?'

'Yes. What's your opinion about that?'

Albert said: 'One in four in the town centre, one in six in the suburbs. You get this inverse differentiation where the population reduces with the square of the distance.'

'Eh?' Clive Townend blinked for a moment then took control again. 'You're quite right. You may like to discuss that with my wife and the reps in the morning. Say nine o'clock?'

Yes, he had definitely run a poodle shop in Chelsea, Albert was glad to discover; it meant he had only Elaine to contend with and from the way she had filled out his form anything he did was going to be all right with her.

'But suppose she doesn't want me?'

Clive Townend gave Albert a worldly, man-to-man smile. 'You'll have to win her over. I'm sure that's not beyond you. She wouldn't let personal animosities stand in the way of a good business proposition.'

For the past few minutes Clive Townend had been glancing at his watch and then at the telephone. When he did it this time Albert got up.

253

'See you in the morning, then?'

'Just a moment – sit down.' Clive Townend opened a ledger. 'I'd like you to glance at our existing sales pattern.' He pushed the book round so that Albert could look at it. The pages were headed in shopping areas throughout the town. Each area had a list of tradespeople in various groupings: grocers, butchers, dairies, drapers, radio and electrical, sweet and tobacconists, shoes, leather goods, hairdressers, fashions and clothing, bakers, garages, every kind of merchandise considered essential to a community.

'You probably know what the stars mean?' Townend asked.

'Sure. The ones with the biggest profit potential.'

'That's right. We start by working on the best and then have to make do with what we can get. You know there's a lot of anti-stamp feeling in the town.'

Albert nodded. 'That's the local Chamber of Trade boys. It's only sour grapes. Because they can't all have a cut of the cake they don't want anybody to get a piece.'

'That puts it in a nutshell.' Townend smiled his appreciation of Albert's understanding but at the same time seemed to be short of anything else to say; as though Albert had short-circuited a subject that he might have enlarged on.

'You won't find any opposition from the public,' Albert said. 'Not in this town. They'll pay through the nose for any rubbish if you give them a windmill or a toy balloon. I mean, if they haven't got through their housekeeping money by Wednesday they get neurotic –'

'Yes.' Townend was staring at Albert, uncertainly.

'And when they've got everything they want they'll spend their last sixpence just to get a free gift stamp.'

Albert was away on a homily which was diametrically opposed to the business he was trying to woo. But in an apathetic world Albert's hot partisan disgust with the buying public – and therefore with himself, for he could never resist a sales trap – was such as to confuse his audience into the belief that he himself had a god-like detachment and was speaking objectively. He could sell a carpetless woman a carpet-sweeper, call her a moron and then leave her laughing; or leave her any way he wanted to leave her. Had he known it, Albert's doorstep sermons were not far removed from those of his grandfather on the village green; method, motive and achievement were identical; both possessed and were possessed by the genial and endearing art of deploring the apple right down to the last bite.

'The secret of a slave population today,' Albert said, 'is to put everything, anything that is, in a coloured packet – keep the germs out and the profit in – charge a high price for it then slash twopence off. Or give them one of your gift stamps.'

'That's perfectly true. You must tell my wife.'

'You take Easter,' Albert went on. 'This is an Easter town – did you know that? Hats,' he added, at Townend's groping expression. 'That used to be our chief export but now it's tractors. Easter is always boom time in this place. Money money money. You watch the factories go on full time before Good Friday. It's not just hot cross buns and Easter Eggs now, you know. Chocolate chickens, chocolate houses, chocolate chocolates – toys, flowers, cards, clothes and hats.'

'That's perfectly true.'

'Easter is bigger than Christmas already,' Albert said. 'It means that to humanity at large the crucifixion is more popular than the birth.'

The telephone rang at last.

'I'll come right away!' Clive Townend said thankfully; he had even forgotten to ask who it was. 'No, don't go,' he told Albert. 'Sit somewhere comfortable and browse through some of our literature.' He was plumping brown corduroy cushions on a big old-fashioned leather sofa which obviously went with the furnished offices. 'I'll get Dorothy to bring you the full brochure.' He gave Albert the kind of smirk reserved for male society. 'Familiarize yourself with our routine – not with Dorothy. Though mind you,' he added, 'you can't go wrong there, either.'

'Where?' Albert asked.

'With Dorothy. Don't be put off by her face. After all we don't look at the mantelpiece when we poke the fire.' And he laughed the lung-laugh again, went out.

'Ugh!' Albert said. Telling Albert in advance that a girl was a cert. was as unwelcome as telling Christopher Columbus that America was three thousand miles across the Atlantic and that having climbed a tree he might be able to see an ocean which looked like the Pacific. Even if he had not been incapacitated Albert would not have summoned very much enthusiasm for Dorothy when a moment later she came in and sat down beside him.

Clive Townend looked in; now he was wearing a cheese-cutter cap and had the big dog at his heels. 'Sorry to have to leave you – see you both tomorrow. 'Night night!'

Albert and Dorothy were left alone.

'Eeeee!' said Dorothy.

'Oh, I dunno,' Albert said.

What he meant was that Clive Townend had not interrupted. Albert out of work was Albert without an audience. He was making up for it now and grateful to anybody no matter who within listening distance. He had not yet quite forgiven Elaine for telling him to stop babbling.

'You're joking, of course,' Dorothy said.

She went to the window. Albert joined her and together they watched Clive Townend drive the Alsatian away in a Mini-minor van; a car that might have been built for the two of them. They were not at the window two minutes later when Clive walked back and quietly entered the building.

Put simply, Clive Lloyd George Townend was trying to keep up. He was a First World War baby made homeless by the boarding schools of the twenties. The links in his life included the blow of a hard ball on a cricket pitch at Horsham with nobody to rub it better; the wallpaper in his vacation room at the Rutland Hotel in Newmarket with a gramophone playing *Hallelujah* somewhere near; standing in wet grass on the July Course wearing a sailor suit and holding the hand of somebody not his mother; the pictures on the dormitory wall of Fairway, Gloria Swanson, Hyperion and Al Capone; a Chinese girl sudent in Grantchester Meadows; the movement in the branches of an alder tree in a French fen just before a bullet smashed his kneecap with nobody to rub it better.

Ever since then in a world that moved faster and faster Clive had been trying to keep up with the rest and if possible give the impression that he was just that much ahead. It was all an illusion now and had been ever since the moment of the bullet and the shock that followed and the final interruption of whatever complicated nervous process ended participation and turned a player into a spectator.

He sat now, smoking a pipe, one hand on the head of his dog, watching Albert and Dorothy through a one-way mirror. It was an unlikely thing to do, but no more unlikely than the manufacture of one-way mirrors for fitting in secret places. There was a steady demand and supply of practically anything if you knew where to go. Behind this locked office door and with the bookcase pushed aside Clive had spent a lot of time keeping up. He had kept up with his wife and discovered that she did not have sexual intercourse with her reps. in the conference room, but that female employees often did. Dorothy, for instance, he had seen spreadeagled on the sofa, the floor and even the conference table, with one or other of the men and particularly with Geoffrey Evans, TTT's senior salesman. Clive had watched them, curiously and enviously, much as he had watched the coupling of animals in his Chelsea kennels.

'I've got the feeling we're not alone,' Albert said.

'That's not the feeling I've got,' Dorothy told him.

'Another time, love,' Albert said.

She sat close, she touched him, sometimes she yawned back amongst the cushions, spreading her body, but Albert stayed grimly with the sales literature.

'Give me a big grocer's somewhere near Butterhall Secondary Modern,' he asked her.

'I don't work after six o'clock,' she said.

'Taylor's,' Albert said. 'That's the one ...'

Dorothy walked across to the mirror and adjusted her bra right in Clive's face without knowing it. 'What a liar that Callendar turned out to be,' she grumbled.

Clive Townend was equally disappointed in Albert. It was reassuring to know that he would be no threat to Elaine, but his entertainment value was likely to be low. Funny chap. All that talk. Looking at the two on the sofa, the girl wriggling and the man immersed in coloured bumf, he thought how different he had been; he and his friends in the thirties. These youngsters were aggressive to an almost frightening degree; they were both after what they wanted; they wouldn't be *put* was the closest he could get to it. No parents would ever inhibit them – quite the reverse. They didn't accept things. They didn't just accept things. Neither government nor church nor law, decree nor morals. They questioned every bloody thing. What they didn't like they banned. They weren't communists or fascists, they weren't concerned with queen or country or the world. They were concerned with themselves. It was healthy and Clive Townend, unhealthy, looking through the looking-glass into the new world, could only envy them.

'Christ!' Dorothy said.

Albert wet his finger and turned to another page of shops.

Early the next morning Elaine Townend entered Albert's house, taking bottles off the doorstep and papers and letters off the mat.

The house was a chatter of get-up-and-go. A pallid youth was watering his hair from a vase of lilacs in the hall, shouting to someone upstairs about seeing her again. A radio blared the BBC's morning count-down of music, news, weather, headlines, trailers, fish prices all punctuated by the minutes to eight o'clock.

'Are you with Albert?' Wendy was waiting outside the bathroom, her large feet bare, a towelled dressing gown over a shortie nightie, her face greased, more than ever the boxer. 'Thank God he's back to normal.' She wiped her nose on the back of her hand and peered at the things Elaine was carrying. 'Don't take him those bills. He's ordered his yoghourt and papers, has he? Must have got that job.'

'Bye, Wen!' came the shout from below.

'Ta ta!' Wendy yelled. Then to Elaine: 'Dead loss! You go to bed with a prince and wake up with a machine-minder.' She banged the bathroom door: 'Hurry up!' There came a muffled groan of despair from inside and Wendy looked to heaven. 'What we all come to. Constipation, morning sickness. Still, she's getting married soon. Beat the tax bride with a communal honeymoon at Butlins. My God!'

Laughing, Elaine went into Albert's room.

Albert was doing a slow dance to *The Thought for Today*. He was eating a hot boiled egg held in a handkerchief, was dressed and shaved and ready to go. He was surprised to see her.

'What are *you* doing here?'

'Come to give you a bit of priming. About the job.'

'Oh. I gotta win you over – did Clive tell you?' He talked with his mouth open on a hot piece of egg.

'I'm won,' Elaine said.

'How did you fix it?' Albert asked. 'That form and everything? Getting rid of Cally? It wasn't the police, was it?'

'No. They did call, but only on a friendly basis – nobody likes the tax collector. Still, it was a good excuse to get rid of him. And I told Clive he'd been making passes at me. That's really what did it.'

'Poor old Cally,' Albert said.

'I thought we might give him a job later on,' Elaine said.

'I'll think about it,' Albert said.

They smiled at each other and Elaine kissed him lightly, afterwards wiping the egg from her mouth.

'How are you, Albert?'

'Nearly better,' he said. Then he said: 'What's today?'

'Thursday.'

'Two days more then,' Albert said. 'It's pretty grim, you know. That bed rattling downstairs all night.'

Elaine said: 'I bet you've got a backlog of crumpet to catch up with.'

Albert said: 'I don't like women to use words like that.'

'Sorry,' she said.

But Albert was moving again, tidying, putting out the gas, putting the bed straight. 'I got one or two ideas,' he said.

'Good. We need 'em.'

'Got to go now.'

'There'll be nobody at the office till nine.'

'This is groundwork,' Albert said. He took a piece of paper from his pocket and showed it to her. 'A list of shops who are going to take Treasure Trove Trading Stamps in the near future.'

Elaine scanned the list, then looked at him. 'I hope you're right. We've tried most of these.'

'You probably went straight in the front door,' Albert said. 'That's not the way to do it. You've got to make them want you. You've got to make 'em send for you. You've got to get 'em down on their knees.'

He took the top off the yoghourt and starting eating it with two fingers. With the other hand he was turning the pages of the papers.

'Do you read all those?'

'When I'm in business.' He sucked his fingers. 'This is what I call gracious living again.'

'But why so many newspapers?'

'You have to keep abreast.'

She was amused to see that he went straight to the strips, glancing at neither news nor articles. He noticed her amusement and shrugged. 'This is the real stuff. *Peanuts* in the *Sketch* for instance. That Schroeder kills me. Here we have

Four D. Jones against the establishment – never miss the *Express* if I can help it.'

'And *Garth* in the *Mirror*, I suppose.'

'No – Cassandra. More contemporary.' He scanned the column, muttering a little, then turned to other papers. '*Daily Herald* for the stars – let's see what Diana's got to say to me.' He read it first, then repeated aloud: 'You don't lose your independence when you push partner's or best friend's plans – with success!' He grinned at Elaine. 'That's us, partner.'

'Auspicious,' she said. Then: 'What about the *Telegraph*?'

'Situations vacant and Business opportunities.'

'And the *Mail*?'

'*Flook*. And that's the one I carry.'

'I'll give you a lift,' she said.

They went out together.

Albert came out of the house, stopped and stared: 'Blimey!'

He was confronted by a bright pink Consul with a mock-rock cave on the roof. In the mouth of the cave a washing machine and a bicycle in cardboard mock-up and bright colours. Rainbowed over the set piece was the cut-out:

SAVE TREASURE TROVE STAMPS TODAY

'Where's the Jag.?' he asked.

'The Jag. is mine. This is yours.'

Albert brightened. 'Really?'

'That's why I called. Wanted to give you a surprise.'

'It does that all right. Talk about a circus!'

'We are a bit of a circus, Albert,' she said. 'Hadn't you noticed?'

'Albert!' The voice came from above and they both looked up to see Wendy leaning out of a window. She was holding something out. 'This was in with your mail.' She dropped a postcard which came fluttering down. 'Ta ta!' She withdrew.

Albert picked up a view of Brighton showing the Aquarium and Palace Pier in Raphael Tuck's forever summer.

He glanced at the back, then slipped it into his pocket. He started walking round the car to the driver's door.

'Don't I get my door opened?' Elaine asked.

'Sorry,' he said. He came back. Then again, as if rejoining her. 'Sorry, darling.'

She got into the car and he closed the door on her, went round to the other side, got in behind the wheel, slammed his door, started the engine, jerked away at high speed.

Elaine looked at him. 'What makes that one so important?'

'She's on honeymoon,' Albert said.

'Don't they ever get you out of their minds?'

Albert smiled without humour. Then a moment later, driving fast, he asked her: 'How much can I make?'

She looked at him again, connecting the card with the urgency of his thoughts. 'You think money can solve everything, don't you, Albert?'

'You can't buy it,' he said.

'They think everyone you know. They think everybody *you* know. *Everybody* you know must be – *must* be – a tart or a whoremonger. They forget you once used to know *them!*'

The speaker was a blonde, Colonial-looking man. big-boned, paunched, haggard-faced. He turned to find that Elaine Townend and Albert had just come into the conference room.

'I think we've got mutual friends,' Albert said.

'I was talking about wives,' the man said. His breath was loaded with morning brandy. 'About marriage.'

'This is Geoffrey Evans,' Elaine introduced, 'our senior salesman.'

'Are you Jewish?' Geoffrey Evans asked Albert. 'You look Jewish. Doesn't he look Jewish?' He referred the question to Elaine and the four other men in the room. 'You stand over here near the light.' He took Albert towards the window, looked at him critically, then turned him half-way from the light. 'No, that's not right. Switch that light on somebody. That's better. Now look at his face from this angle. You could be Jewish.'

'This is Albert Argyle,' Elaine said.

'Argyle?' Geoffrey Evans said. 'That sounds like a good old Clan cover-up of a name?'

'It's my professional name,' Albert said.

'Professional what?' Evans asked. 'Professional Jew?'

'Not professional anything,' Albert said. 'I'm just a professional person as distinct from an amateur person.'

'What's your real name, then? Not Goldberg or Welensky or something like that?'

'What's it matter?' Albert asked. 'You won't be using it.'

'Go on then,' Evans persisted. 'Albert what? What's hiding under those kilts? Cohen? Bickstein? Something without a foreskin? Look at the light on his nose. I know what it is – Green! It's always Green! How green is my lolly!'

'Harris,' Albert said. 'Albert Harris.' •

Geoffrey Evans roared with laughter. 'What did I say? Harris is another. What do they call you at the synagogue, Albie boy? Anyway, it's the nineteen sixties now – let's shake hands, Albie boy.'

Albert shook his hand. 'What's the matter? Don't you like Jews?'

'Of course I like 'em. I'm kidding. It was different in the old days. I had friends then. These days the party is strictly non-racial. I really mean that. It's no good hating people, Mr Harris. It doesn't pay. Especially in this business. The bastards are everywhere. What are you, anyway? A bloody landlord or a filthy tenant?'

Elaine had been smiling at Albert's bewildered expression and she now rescued him. 'Mr Argyle is a-political, Mr Evans. He is the high priest of his own personal religion – making money and getting girls.' And then apologetically to Albert: 'You have to treat them in their own coin.'

'Are you a girl-getter?' Geoffrey Evans roared. He shook Albert's hand all over again. 'Join the hearty-hetero club.

263

I take back everything I said, Mr – Argyle. I'm going to call you Albert, you can call me Geoff.'

Elaine said: 'Now introduce him to Dick, Tony, Steve and Matty. Incidentally it was Matty he was getting at, Albert, not you.'

Matty's smooth Jewish face was smiling steadily as he shook Albert's hand. Elaine left the conference.

'Professional person, eh? I like that, don't you?' Geoffrey was saying. 'What's your profession? Oh, I'm a person. A *qualified* person.'

'You're a big twat, Geoff,' Matty said.

'That's better than a little one . . .'

Behind the mirror Clive Townend was envying them their hates and aggressions and antipathies and sheer male roughage. He envied them their ability to laugh the secrecy out of what was inside them; the communal umbilical cord of laughter that joined them to the world. He envied the people on the other side of the one-way mirror; he gazed at them with all the frustration of the ringmaster who wants to perform and can't.

Elaine Townend accompanied Albert that afternoon on his first assignment for TTT.

'It's not that I don't trust you,' she had told him over lunch with Clive in the White Hart. 'I just want to be there if you dry up on your statistics.'

Clive had said: 'Most of our new men have a week's training before going into the field.'

'Well, I don't need it, do I? Still, I want you to be there. Just to show you how it's done.'

'I like confidence,' Clive said.

Behaving naturally in the presence of a husband was a separate art. Albert was inclined to like husbands and get them to like him. It was an insurance and sometimes gave him the benefit of the doubt in the event of a leakage.

Elaine had said: 'I never know how to distinguish it from conceit.'

264

'You'd better be good,' Clive warned Albert while Elaine was out of the way.

In the light of his relationship with Clive's wife Albert secretly agreed.

Sitting in Albert's pink car outside Taylor's the family grocers, Elaine started assembling the literature, stamps and books.

'Leave those for now,' Albert said. 'Go in with a handful of bumf and they think you want them to buy something.'

'What about this percentage reckoner?' Elaine was holding a coloured slide rule device which showed graphically and clearly instant estimations of profit increases for any given turnover in a given time.

'Figures tie you down,' Albert said. 'I'd rather be vague.'

'But we don't have to be vague. These figures are proven.'

'But you can only *tell* them that,' Albert told her. 'Don't worry. I'll give them the picture.'

Elaine stopped trying. She went with Albert into the shop.

'Albert!'

About to speak to one of the counter assistants, Albert now stopped with a 'shot in the back' look; Elaine glanced at him, questioningly. A middle-aged woman came hurrying from the cash office, pushing wisps of hair back into a bun, her homely face wreathed in a smile of welcome.

'Hello, Hetty love,' Albert said, without enthusiasm.

'Albert!' She held both his arms for a moment, studying him. 'It's lovely to see you! You do look well!'

'Thanks, dear. Didn't know you worked here.'

'Oh yes. Ever since Callendar's. Just looking after cash and accounts. Well, you've got to do something. Haven't we had a slump? Still, things are looking up now – I knew you'd be in, I told Mr Taylor.' She laughed loud and long. 'You are a one! We've had at least a dozen of your old girl-friends in today all asking for TTT stamps!' She laughed again and looked at Elaine with her eyes streaming with mirth. 'He is a card! Hello, I thought meself – Albert must be on the stamp racket and sure enough here you are, large as life.'

Again she looked at Elaine, then at Albert with pride. 'It's typical of his tricks! Create the demand, he always used to say – didn't you, Albert?'

'Did I?'

Albert exchanged a foolish smile with Elaine.

'Is this your new wife?' Hetty said then. 'You are rude. Why don't you introduce us? I heard you'd got married – last Saturday, wasn't it?'

'That was Treasure,' Albert said. Then to Elaine: 'My girl.'

'I see,' Elaine said. It explained the card.

Albert tried to scrape up the remnants of what impetus might be left to scrape; he patted Hetty's shoulder and looked round. 'Tell Mr Taylor I'd like to see him, there's a dear. You know – business.'

Hetty looked her regret. 'You'll be wasting your time, Albert. I suppose I shouldn't have told him about the girls coming in. Well, he didn't take it very well. Not much humour. Oh, I do miss those laughs we used to have, Albert! Have you seen old Cally lately? Somebody told me he was in prison! Never surprise me.'

'I think we might as well go,' Elaine said.

'Yes, *he'll* never give stamps,' Hetty said. 'He wouldn't give the pickings from his nose, Mr Taylor wouldn't. Though I don't want to be disloyal. He's chairman of the Chamber of Trade, you know. All very snooty. They don't like this gift stamp business. They keep having meetings. Still, eh?' And she beamed at Albert again.

'Well thank you very much,' Albert said bitterly.

Hetty followed them to the door, reluctant to lose a bit of the happy past. 'He'll never change, you know,' she told Elaine Townend behind Albert's back. 'He's always been the same. Tell her what you used to do with the penny your mum put on your belly button because of your navel rupture, Albert. He used to take it off and spend it, bless him! Only three he was.'

'Goodbye, Hetty love,' Albert said. 'See you.'

'Don't leave it so long!' she cried as they walked back to the car.

She stood sighing at the door long after the car had driven away.

'Down on their knees, eh?' Elaine said as Albert drove. 'Sorry about that.'

'Let's just say you overdid the groundwork,' Elaine told him.

He looked at her; she turned her head to hide her laughter. Albert ran his finger around the back of her neck.

'You don't care, do you?' he said.

She looked at him with affection, shaking her head. 'You're the most fortuitous thing that ever happened to me.'

'What's fortuitous?'

'Something that crops up just when you need it most.'

The value of an area manager was his knowledge of the area; Albert's drawback was the area's knowledge of him.

'I've been in this dump too long,' was one of his favourite complaints. 'I'm what we call in show business "over exposed".'

It was the same at Joe Keppings' greengrocery shop in Market Street. Joe, a plump, pleasant, florid young man, was making his shop window look beautiful. He was an artist rather than a business man; he won the town's window-dressing prize every Whitsun, yet he couldn't make a profit. A hard worker, he would get up and off in the lorry to the Covent Garden Market in London and back by mid-morning with a load of beautiful fruit, vegetables and flowers. The trouble was, Joe bought more for beauty than for what would sell. At the bidding he would be looking at the crates with an artist's eye, seeing his window like a landscape garden, all pyramids of scarlet Worcesters, Cox's in their suede green and orange, canary yellows and Spanish blues. In a working-class district living, especially since the slump, on potatoes and little else, Joe would buy peppers and uglis and exoctic expensive mysteries just to make his window glow.

This afternoon Joe was too busy creating in the window to notice Albert and Elaine Townend come in. Mrs Keppings, his mother, small, neat, attractive and desperate, was scooping soggy de-frosted fish and meat and vegetables from a deep-freeze cabinet. The bailiff was sitting on a sack of potatoes, looking on, gloomily.

'Hello, Mr Weatherhead,' Albert exclaimed to the bailiff. 'After your onions again?'

The bailiff, an elderly man, enjoyed Mrs Keppings' company and often dropped in just for the pleasure of it; he gave Albert an unfriendly stare.

'What are you up to, Albert? I should've thought you'd have left town, once the money ran out. Making a living, are you?'

Mrs Keppings, upside down in the deep freeze, now came out holding a pound of wet sausages. She stood in a pool of water, looking at Albert and his companion, apprehensively.

'He hasn't ordered anything else, has he?' And turning to the window: 'You haven't bought that automatic scale, have you, Joe?'

Joe, his tongue in his cheek, put the last orange on top of a pyramid before turning round. His face lit up at the sight of Albert.

'Hello, Albert boy! Nice to see you!' He wiped his hands on his green smock then shook hands with Albert, smiling at Elaine.

'This is Mrs Townend,' Albert said. 'Joe Keppings, Mrs Keppings and Mr Weatherhead.' Then with introductions complete he turned again to Joe. 'We've come to do you a good turn, Joe.'

'Oh no!' Mrs Keppings exclaimed. 'Not today, Albert. We can't afford it. Look at all this.' She pointed to the pile of messy wet food lying in the pool of water by the empty deep-freeze. 'The electricity's been cut off,' she explained. 'We've been living on wet food for the past two days. Mr

Weatherhead is waiting for some customers to come in so we can pay off a writ. The Building Society are foreclosing on the mortgage on the shop.'

'Everything normal, then?' Albert grinned. He looked at Elaine. 'This is a shop that really needs us.'

'I don't know how you've got the nerve to come in,' Mrs Keppings said. 'What about that round you started up for us on the new estates? Put us on our feet, you said.' She looked at Elaine: 'He left here one Monday morning six months ago with a big Commer van packed full of green-grocery – we haven't seen him since until today!'

Elaine looked at Albert, reproachfully.

'There was no demand!' Albert said.

'He's right, mum,' Joe said. 'I knew he wouldn't sell it. Not up there. Those council house rents are higher than luxury flats. They can only buy fruit at Christmas.'

'What did you do with it all?' Mrs Keppings asked Albert. 'Forty pounds' worth of fruit and vegetables! What did you do with it all?'

'Well, you know,' Albert said. 'Perishable goods. I carted 'em round for four or five days. Well, naturally, they perished.'

'They would,' Joe said. Then he said: 'What do you think of my window, Albert?'

Albert and Elaine admired the window display.

'Very nice,' Albert said. 'Only one thing missing though.' This time they had brought a display case in with them and Albert took out a coloured poster and held it up.

TREASURE TROVE TRADING STAMPS GIVEN HERE it said.

Joe beamed at it, then at Albert. 'Is that what you're in now? How are you getting on, then?'

'We're not having them!' Joe's mother exclaimed.

'My oath!' said the bailiff. 'What? Hah!'

Albert gave the bailiff a cool look. 'What d'you mean "My oath what hah?" How long have you been running the business? He hasn't proposed yet, has he Mrs K.?'

'Don't be cheeky, Albert!' Mrs Keppings said, blushing deeply. 'Mr Weatherhead's quite right. We can't afford to give anything away.'

'You're not giving anything,' Albert told her. 'We do the giving. You just make an extra profit. Fill this shop, these stamps would. You'd get queues a mile long.'

'Of course we wouldn't,' Mrs Keppings said. 'There's not the money about. That's the answer.'

'There's not the money about,' Joe said.

'That's just the point,' Albert told them. 'What money there is will come to you. How many greengrocers in this area? Six? Seven within half a mile – Johnson's, Wheatley's, Pilsworth's, Edwards', Curr's, Sears' and the Supermarket. You'd take all their customers. They'll be bankrupt within the year –'

'And go on the black list of the Chamber of Trade,' Mrs Keppings said. 'Then try getting credit from the wholesalers!'

'You won't need credit,' Albert said. 'You'd be paying cash – *and* getting all the price advantages that goes with it. What? You'd be opening branches before the year's out. Joe Keppings and Co. Ltd. Can't you see it?'

'Yes,' Joe said, always the visionary. 'He's right, mum.'

'He's not right! Are you out of your mind? Tell him, Mr Weatherhead –'

Albert said: 'You can't take Mr Weatherhead's opinion, Joe. He always sees the black side. The black side's his job. Besides that, if you got out of debt he wouldn't be able to come and see your mum –'

'Yes I would!' the bailiff said.

'There you are then,' Albert said, 'now we're all in agreement. How many books of stamps would you say?' he asked Elaine. He was already offloading the books of stamps and the customers' collecting books, the gift catalogues and display posters.

'Two books should be enough to start with,' Elaine said.

'How much a book?' Mrs Keppings asked.

'Twenty pounds each,' Elaine said. Unaware of the silence that had intervened in the transaction, she went on: 'That'll cover thousands of pounds worth of business.'

'Well we haven't got twenty pounds,' Mrs Keppings said. 'We haven't got two pounds. Otherwise Mr Weatherhead wouldn't be sitting here, would he?'

'Oh, I see,' Elaine said. 'I'm sorry.'

'Don't be daft,' Albert told Elaine. 'We can come to an arrangement. Who's asking for cash?'

Elaine said: 'But that is the initial investment in the scheme. They get it back with the first twenty pounds of increased profits.'

'Well, we'll wait for that,' Albert said. Then, winningly to Elaine: 'Special favour. Friends of mine.'

'But the town's full of friends of yours.'

'Don't you believe it, madam,' Mr Weatherhead said. 'I have personal knowledge of people who have had dealings with Albert and are at this moment in the debtors' prison.'

'Well, we shan't go to them, naturally,' Albert said. Then again to Elaine: 'How about it?'

'All right. One book of stamps.'

'Two.'

'All right. Two.'

'The deal's closed,' Albert said. He shook hands all round. 'Get the old posters up, Joe, stand back and wait for the rush!'

'Thanks, Albert,' Joe said.

'That's all right, Joe. You've got the TTT franchise for the area. Congratulations. Let's get you signed up.' Albert clicked his fingers at the managing director of the company. Elaine sighed, spread out the forms, avoiding the puddles of water from the lifeless deep freeze.

'What happened to the van, then?' Mr Weatherhead asked as Joe was signing up with Elaine.

'Yes,' Mrs Keppings said. 'What *did* happen to our van, Albert?'

'I left it,' Albert said. 'I had to. You can imagine the smell. Anyway it was an old one. Not worth its tax.'

It created a mental image of a big old van full of rotting vegetables and fruit standing derelict and putrid and unnoticed in some side street in the town for the past six months; it was an image that remained unmentioned between the three of them long after Albert and Elaine had completed the transaction and left.

'We could have palm trees in tubs along the back of this window,' Joe Keppings said, caught up in Albert's dream. 'A sort of tropical grotto.'

His mother and the bailiff exchanged a look of deep despair.

'Bit slow,' Albert said.

Elaine nodded. 'That's how it's been.'

They sat in the High Street Lyons drinking a cup of tea. Besides the Keppings' greengrocery shop they had recruited one hairdresser's and a small general store; to do this they had covered many miles of the town and called at twenty shops. They were both tired.

'Albert . . .'

He looked at her over the table; he was sitting across two chairs with his feet up, smoking and enjoying the tea.

'Let's go back to your place?' she said.

'Ah no, love. Not today.'

'Didn't you like it?'

'Of course I did. But it's a bit of a strain. I mean it's not fair. At least it's not fair on me.'

'Perhaps you're all right now?'

'Not quite,' Albert said. 'Don't worry. I'll know when I'm all right.' He smiled at her over his cup. 'What-o next week!'

'You can never depend on next week,' Elaine said.

'I tell you what. You take a taxi back to the office and I'll go on.'

She looked at him, suspiciously. 'More of your ideas?'

'Could be.'

'Let's go back to your place.'

'Oh, blimey!'

She gave it up. 'I suppose you're right.'

'We'll make up for it, darling.'

Teasingly that wasn't teasing, she said: 'You're not fooling me, are you?'

'Of course I'm not. Remember Monday? Would I have all that will power?'

'Who's Miss Finbow?'

'You know. The tax girl. You saw her.'

'What did you do in that bathroom all that time?'

'Do you mind! Cor!' He winced as though with a broken back.

'Then why does she phone you several times a day?'

'Who, Janice? Alice I mean? She hasn't phoned me.'

'Oh yes she has. You just haven't got the calls, that's all. She's in love with you, isn't she?'

'I dunno. Well yes, I suppose so. Do you blame her?'

'Be gentle with her, Albert,' Elaine Townend said.

'I haven't been anything with her yet.'

'That's all the more reason,' she said. 'Whatever you are to her, let it be something she'll always thank you for.'

Albert looked at Elaine seriously.

'I mean don't spoil it for her,' Elaine said. She looked down at her teacup.

'Did somebody spoil it for you?'

She looked up and then blinked her lashes quickly looking down again in that way that affected him. It was as if he might catch a betraying glimpse of some kind of unwelcome truth about her. He stood up when she went, which was something Albert rarely did for women. He watched her walk right out of the shop without looking back. It was the best walk he had ever seen. As he sat down he found that a black waitress collecting trays had been staring at him.

'As for you!' he said.

It was five o'clock when Albert parked his pink car in the

273

Butterhall Secondary Modern School drive, crossed the play-ground and entered the building. It was odd to walk the corridors where he had once jostled and ragged, marched or waited in disgrace. It was pleasant to ignore the notices: 'Keep your coat on your peg.' 'Quiet, please!' 'Do not run.' 'Wash your hands before classes.' Albert put two fingers up at the notices and came to the door marked 'Headmaster'. He knocked.

'Come in, please.'

Albert entered and Cedric Mason looked up from his desk with delighted recognition.

'Hello, Albert!'

'Hello, sir – Cedric.'

Cedric Mason stood up and shook hands with Albert, then indicated a chair. 'Sit down, Albert, sit down. Sorry I can't offer you cigarettes or anything –' And as Albert took out a packet '– no, you go ahead.' He sat back at his desk and pushed his work aside; studied Albert with earnest pleasure and enjoyment. 'This is nice, Albert. I was beginning to think there was something missing in this town – everybody hard up and depressed. Now I know what it was. It was you, Albert. Where have you been? What've you been up to? Marjorie's always asking after you.'

'Oh, really? That's nice of her. Tell her I miss her, too. One of my best customers. How is she?'

Cedric's tired, middle-aged face was illumined for a moment and he tried quite unsuccessfully to be blasé. 'She's fine. She's marvellous. You'd never guess, Albert – we're going to have a baby!' He laughed at Albert's momentarily crestfallen expression. 'Unbelievable, isn't it? After all this time!'

'I wouldn't say that, sir. Cedric.' Albert was mentally counting the months to his last visit. 'When's it due, then?'

'August, she says. It should come just before the summer camp.'

'That's wonderful, Cedric. Congratulations.'

'Yes.' Cedric blinked his rich pleasure across the desk at his favourite old boy. 'And that's not all. Do you know what she wants to call it? If it's a boy?'

Albert knew.

'She's going to call it Albert,' Cedric said. 'After you.'

'That's a compliment,' Albert said. 'Tell her ta.'

'Well, I've often said to Marjorie – she'll tell you – if I had a son I'd like one like our Albert. Of course, I'd try to get him into a decent career. What *are* you doing now, Albert? Not that cheapjack selling any more?'

'No, I gave that up,' Albert told him. 'I'm working on sales promotion now. Area manager for Treasure Trove Trading Stamps. That's really why I'm here . . .'

Albert gave Cedric a brief summary of his job and his enormous prospects. Cedric listened in a kindly but at the same time deploring way.

'But isn't it a parasitic occupation? I mean you're still not producing anything, are you, Albert?'

'Oh, I wouldn't say that,' Albert said. He said it in a dead-pan way that people like Cedric accepted as earnestness but his more worldly friends would detect as humour.

'Well, it's no use preaching to you,' Cedric said.

'Gift stamps are good for business,' Cedric said. 'This town needs a shot in the arm.'

'You can always justify yourself. You always could, Albert. All right, what can I do for you?'

'It's what I can do for you, Cedric.' Albert leaned across the desk. 'I bet you still haven't got a decent piano here?'

'Not yet,' Cedric said. 'The new schools are getting all the equipment. I expect it's only right. Our turn will come.'

'And what about a trampoline for the gymnasium?' Albert asked. 'You always wanted one of those.'

'What are you getting at, Albert?'

Albert said: 'Get your kids to collect our stamps and we'll give you a new piano. And a trampoline. Any other equipment you want.'

'They'd never do it, Albert.'

'Of course they would. They love collecting things. See who can get the most.'

Cedric laughed. 'Well, that's true. I used to collect cigarette cards, birds' eggs, car numbers.'

'Ah, but they weren't worth anything.'

'They were to me, Albert. They were to us. You couldn't have put a price on "Cries of London" or "Famous Jockeys". I remember once –'

'Listen, Cedric. I'm not doing this just for me. It's for you. It's for the old school. I'll give you some stamp collecting books, you put a notice on the board. All they've got to do is to get their parents to shop at the TTT shops – they're everywhere now. Soon mount up with five hundred boys collecting. You could have a new piano inside three months.'

'It's worth thinking about –'

'I knew you'd do it,' Albert said.

'But it's not as easy as that, Albert. I have to be careful. I can't afford to put a foot wrong. With the Education Committee I mean. There was a lot of opposition to my getting the headship here – because of my CND work.'

'What's that?' Albert asked.

The headmaster looked at his old pupil, appalled. 'You amaze me sometimes, Albert. You seem so worldly and yet you don't seem to know what's going on.'

'I only read the strips,' Albert said. 'What is it – political?'

'It's the Campaign for Nuclear Disarmament, Albert.'

Albert smiled. 'Oh that! You're not mixed up with that crummy old lot, are you?'

Cedric sighed at him. 'You've got the image, anyway.'

'Sorry,' Albert said. 'But I thought they were all communists? Or pacifists or something?'

Cedric said: 'There'd be no such word as "peace" if there was no such word as "war". Still, I don't want to bring it into the classroom. That's one of the things I had to promise. Odd, really, the most important issue since Christ and we mustn't tell the children.'

'You can tell me,' Albert said. 'I've got an open mind.'

'You think you have but you haven't. You probably think that giving up the bomb means Britain becoming a weak nation. Well it doesn't, Albert. Giving up bows and arrows in 1066 might have meant that, but not the atomic bomb today. We have lost the world's leadership – for what it was worth – in power politics, but by being the first country to abandon atomic weapons we would be leading the world again on the only path left.'

'Why doesn't somebody else do it, then?'

'Well exactly. That's where the courage comes in. That's leadership,' Cedric Mason told his old pupil.

'You're dead right, Cedric,' Albert said.

'Oh, everybody knows we're dead right,' Cedric told him. 'But at the moment being dead right is dead wrong. It doesn't fit in. It's not popular. And there's no money in being unpopular, Albert. You can't stay in power, you can't sell newspapers, you can't even keep your job. That's what I mean about these stamps of yours. They can't sack me for being a CND supporter, but give them any other excuse . . .'

'Nobody's going to object to this,' Albert told him. 'It's a way of fitting up the school without spending rates.'

'I'm thinking of Major Simpkins to be quite honest,' Cedric Mason said. 'You see he's on the Education Committee and in charge of Civil Defence. Civil Defence is an acceptance of the idea of a nuclear war. Don't make any mistake about that, Albert. Fall-out shelters are for our children.'

'You're right.' Albert had an odd feeling of mutual paternity as he said it.

'Disarmament to the Major means dishonour,' Cedric said. 'He's still muttering about Suez.'

'You toe the line for the Major and you might as well be in the army yourself, Cedric. Bomb or no bomb, this is your big opportunity to prove that you're not.'

Cedric Mason thought about this for a moment. Then he said: 'Do you know I think you're right.'

Albert gave the headmaster an admiring handshake. Although not a man himself for large unprofitable issues,

Albert had discovered that practically anything could be cut down and quickly adapted to serve a more useful purpose.

'Do you mind if I use your phone?' Albert was already dialling and looking at the PRO's visiting card given to him in the pub. 'It's worth a bit of a splash,' Albert said. Then to the telephone receiver: 'Hello – Peter? Albert Argyle – TTT. What are you doing for the next half hour – don't bother, I'll tell you. You know the American Bar of the White Hart?' Aside to the headmaster he said: 'You're coming out for a little celebration. You tell Marjorie you were with me ...'

Watching his prize old boy's slick telephone performance, Cedric Mason's weary face was a battleground of daring and doubt.

5

'Jonquil!'

Police Constable Sidney Cook's wife came to the breakfast table where her husband was reading Friday's local news.

'Look at this!'

She looked.

'I knew he was up to something,' Sid said, delightedly. 'I knew there was trouble brewing.'

It was a photograph of Albert Argyle, area manager for Treasure Trove Trading Stamps, drinking champagne out of a teacher's upturned mortar-board at the American Bar of the White Hart Hotel. Half obscured in the background was headmaster Cedric Mason's worried face.

'BENEVOLENT OFFER TO LOCAL SCHOOLS,' ran the headline.

'Init marvellous,' Sid said. 'It takes old Albert to get this town out of the dumps. I told you I saw him with that bird in the car? Didn't I tell you? Then that bump up in the High Street with that blooming woman driver? Then the Tax people making those unpleasant insinuations about him. Well, look at that picture! Soon as he starts, everything starts. Look, all on one page: two break-ins, four road deaths, Colonel accuses Scoutmaster. And now look at the situations vacant! What?' He started turning the leaves. 'Four pages of jobs! No kidding, look! See for yourself!'

'There's a sale on at Hobday's,' his wife exclaimed.

'Of course there is. Of course there's a sale on. What do you expect?'

'That's wonderful, Albert,' Elaine Townend said.

'Oh, I dunno,' Albert said. 'Any brilliant mind could've conceived it.'

'Do you like the coverage?' Peter Fisher asked. 'Three column photograph, you know. I had to fight for that.'

'Splendid, Peter,' Albert said, in one of his voices.

'What's the main idea, then?' Dick Haynes asked; and since Albert was talking to Elaine he turned to Matty: 'What's the main idea? I mean, what's behind it? I can see its immediate advantages, of course, but I don't quite see . . .'

The conference had been convened by Elaine on the strength of Albert's enterprise. The five TTT reps., two steps higher than tally boys, neat and inclined to be natty; five in their over-thirties who Albert could never tell apart unless from their ties. Geoffrey Evans, Dick Haynes, Tony Harper, Steve Laidlow and Matty Matthews, sitting around the conference table; Elaine was with Albert who had taken the chair at the head of the table. The guest, Peter Fisher, the PRO, was standing beside Albert's chair.

Clive Lloyd George Townend sat behind his mirror, watching and smoking, his dog at his feet. From being a furtive pleasure it had now become a kind of compulsive occupation. Sometimes he watched the cleaner shooting the dirt under the carpet and sometimes he sat there and watched an empty room, like a television addict who watches the blank screen long after the Epilogue has faded away.

Elaine was saying: 'Well, it gives TTT a bit of dignity which we badly needed. It creates a demand for our stamps. It conquers the snob thing. People don't mind pretending that they're collecting gift stamps for a charity. Isn't that right, Albert?'

'Well, that's only part of it,' Albert said. 'That's just a beginning. I mean, they're not going to let those kids collect our stamps. I can tell you that. I know this town.'

This got immediate attention from them all.

Geoffrey Evans, now sober, said: 'Then I must confess I'm baffled.'

'So am I,' the PRO said. 'Enlarge, old boy.'

'It's dead simple,' Albert said.

There was nothing unusual about Albert's plan as Albert's plans went. Had he been talking to a group of his old tally boy chums they would have found it dead simple. Just a few smart moves. Had the conference comprised Jacko and Arnold and more particularly Cally – well, Cally would have been ahead of him. Albert was still assuming that TTT was a crooked racket in spite of Elaine's discouraging assurances that they were legitimate. Albert was beginning to see the gift stamp business as a subtle variation on the traditional and well-established protection racket. You take our stamps or we'll close you down. Or better still, the chap next door will.

'This is really local politics,' Albert said. 'I don't know whether you lot know much about it ...'

Albert spoke to the assembly with a dignity and sense of occasion that came from this oft-dreamed situation of holding the chair at a business conference. He wished some of his friends in the town could see this; a few of the higher class girls; Grace, perhaps, and Treasure; and his mother. The bank manager who had had faith in Albert to the point of imbecility but had finally lost his nerve and frozen his overdraft six months ago. Who would have thought that six days ago Albert had been sitting in a barber shop ready to die?

As he talked Albert took out the cigar he had bought to impress Elaine on their first meeting. She took it from him, cut off the end, gave it to him back, watched him with some pride and affection as he lit it. Behind the mirror her husband noted this and wondered about it; she had certainly changed her mind about that chap! Elaine turned and looked at him, appearing to meet his eyes, defiantly; he sometimes suspected that she knew he was there and it didn't seem to matter.

Albert simplified local politics for his audience in a few thoughtless words. 'A lot of little men run this town. Little men with little grasping minds and little ambitions. People who have stopped growing. People with hats on. I mean it's the same in any town. The only way they can make their mark is to get their name on a hospital bed or a park bench. You know the type. You'll find them on the council, on the bench, on this committee and that. Chamber of Trade, Civil Defence, Education Committee. Shopkeepers, most of them, a few gibbering old soldiers, local landed gentry, hereditary lunatics and so on – you know, backbone of the nation.' He dismissed the social structure according to his generation. 'Well, as soon as they read this little lot there's going to be a hell of a stink. I mean they live in each other's grubby little pockets. The Chamber of Trade is going to complain to the Education Committee and this stamp scheme is going to get sat on.'

'I think you're right,' Elaine said.

Albert said: 'Well, that's where Peter comes in with a few well-chosen letters to the press. Protests and that. Stir it up a bit.' He mimicked: 'Why shouldn't our children collect stamps? Why shouldn't the school get a new piano? Why can't we shop where we like? You know? Signed "Mother of Five", "Disgusted", "Unemployed" and so on?'

The audience began to buck up.

'Very good,' the PRO said. 'We might get a big thing going.'

'Well that's not all,' Albert said. 'With any luck old Cedric will get the sack through this. I mean, that's why I had the picture taken in the bar, drinking out of his hat. Clever stuff.'

'It would be really marvellous if he got the sack,' the Press Relations Officer said. 'I could do a lot with that.'

'You don't know the half of it,' Albert said. 'If Cedric Mason gets the sack we can start a big rumpus with the CDN. The ban-the-bomb crowd.'

'You mean the CND,' Elaine said.

'Yes. Cedric's one of their biggest banners. He's already had trouble. See what I mean? I don't have to spell it, do I? Victimization?'

'That's brilliant, old boy,' the PRO exclaimed. 'We could hit the nationals with that! Front page all over the country.'

'And quite right, too!' Steve Laidlow said. 'I think it's disgusting the way a man gets pilloried for his political leanings in this country.'

'Sold to the gentleman on the right,' Albert said.

Elaine was laughing at him. 'If your plan is only half successful, Albert, we shall have the big boys bidding for our franchise. It could mean a lot of money for all of us.'

'It'll work, love,' Albert told her. 'My plans always work. Usually for other people.'

Dorothy came in, looking puzzled. 'Mrs Townend. I've had three calls from shops who want to take our stamps!'

Albert stood up, clapped his hands, stared round at the circle of radiant faces. 'There you are, you see – down on their knees! Well, I've done my bit. Now it's up to you.' To Elaine he said: 'Let's go and have a coffee, love?'

'Telegram for you, Mr Argyle,' Dorothy said as Albert and Elaine came past.

Albert looked at the message: 'VERY MANY CONGRATULATIONS LOVE A.F.'

How stupid, he thought. How square. How well-meaning. How sick.

There was a jubilant gathering of the reps. in the bar of the George that evening. It had been a good day for TTT with a dozen more shops enrolled into the gift stamp scheme.

'I'm in the chair,' Albert said.

'No, I am,' said Geoffrey Evans.

'Fight you for it?' Peter Fisher offered.

They had all been paid and the money in their pockets still had that everlasting quality that comes with anything over fifty pounds in notes.

'Let me go on,' Clive Townend said.

'Clive, must you?' Elaine said.

Clive had had enough to drink to disregard inhibiting influences. He was telling the one about the woman who had bought a boxer puppy from him, believing it to be a bitch. All of his stories had the betraying element of being one hundred per cent masculine; a certain desperate straining to talk about the sort of things men talked about.

Geoffrey Evans had been watching the back view of the barmaid each time she stooped to the lower shelves, and he could see the tops of her stockings. 'I feel like a party,' he told Albert. 'Non-political. Can't you rustle something up?'

'I like the sound of that, Geoff!' Clive said. 'Rustle something up! The sound of a rising skirt!'

'Clive,' Elaine said, tiredly.

'Sorry, dear.' He bulged his eyes at the rest. ' 'Fraid you're in the wrong bar, dear.'

'Or else you are,' Elaine said.

Albert said to Geoffrey: 'I might.'

Matty said: 'You can count me in. How many girls have you got?'

'Only two,' Albert said.

Peter Fisher said: 'I'll bring mine. Hah hah what? She does this marvellous limbo dance. Gets everybody started.'

'Is that the redhead?' Albert asked.

The PRO gave him a sharp look. 'Do you know her?'

'I just caught a glimpse of her,' Albert said. Then: 'Anyway, plenty of time, let's think about it ...'

Albert had been thinking about nothing else for the past few hours. The point was – Albert was better.

He took Elaine aside a moment later. 'You don't want an orgy, do you?'

'No. You obviously do.' She smiled at him. 'Congratulations! How long is it? A whole week? Who's it going to be, then? The little tax girl?'

'What! With this lot?'

'I'm glad to hear you say that. You're more moral than you think you are.'

'I know I am,' Albert said righteously. Then he said, furtively: 'Keep Peter here for half an hour or so, huh?'

At seven-thirty Albert was in a telephone box consulting his little book. He dialled 60452 and heard a girl's voice. 'Lois?'

'Yes. Who's that?'

'Albert.'

'Albert who?'

'We met last Sunday at The George – you were with Peter Fisher and I was going out.'

'I remember. But he didn't tell me he knew you.'

'I got to know him since then so that I could meet you.'

'What am I supposed to say to that?'

'That you'll come to my party tonight.'

'Sorry, I'm seeing Peter.'

'You're not, darling. He's been called away on business.'

'How do you know?'

'I did the calling.'

'Oh.'

'What time shall I pick you up?' Albert asked.

'Oh look! Look Wendy! That's what *I've* got. A blue candlewick bedspread exactly like Albert's.'

The girl was looking with passionate admiration at the contents of her own bottom drawer. Albert put a drink into her hand.

'Don't splash it, eh?' he said. 'It's new.'

He had quite forgotten to put back the things he had borrowed on the day of Elaine's visit.

'This is Elsie, Geoff.'

Geoffrey Evans had been staring hideously at the girl: 'Is that mine? It's a bit skinny.' And he made a foul suggestion to the girl.

Albert had to hold on to her to stop her running out.

'That's it then!' Wendy said. 'We're going!'

Albert said: 'Don't go! He'll apologize. Geoff, just mind your bloody tongue. I have to live with these girls!'

'What, both of them?' Geoff said. He laughed. 'Two at a time, I bet.'

'He's drunk,' Matty explained to Wendy.

'I don't want to stay,' Lois told Albert.

Geoff snarled at her: 'You bloody hypocrites. What are we here for then? Get on that bloody bed.'

Albert put his hand over Geoff's mouth. Geoff brought his knee up and Albert collapsed on the bed. Wendy flew to him, tending him, blazing round at Geoffrey Evans.

'You've hurt him! Get out! Go on, get out!' And to Albert: 'Where did you pick *him* up?'

'He's drunk,' Matty explained. 'That's all. Don't let it worry you. I know old Geoff. He doesn't mean any harm.'

'You Jewish bastard!' Geoff said.

'He'll drink his way through it,' Matty said. 'Come on, Geoff, drink up . . .'

The party started.

By eleven o'clock the mood had started catching up with Geoffrey Evans who had started slowing down. The light was out. In the glow from the electric fire Lois had been dancing a self-concentrated limbo for the past half-hour. Albert lay on his back on the carpet watching over his head. Somewhere in the darkness Matty had Wendy on a chair, Geoffrey Evans had Elsie on the bed. Only gradually did Albert become aware, through the bleating of the record, of Elsie's rhythmic breathing; a sibilant sucking of breath that became louder as if keeping time. Albert grew cold and sober and somehow revolted.

'Elsie,' he said. 'Elsie!' More loudly. Then he said: 'That's your own bloody bedspread. Your bridal trousseau!'

There was a sudden commotion, a squeal, a swift and violent fight and the light went on. Elsie stood by the door clutching her blue candlewick bedspread. Her thin face was flushed, her hair tousled.

'You rotter!' she shouted at Albert. 'You rotten devil!'

She ran out of the room, sobbing. Geoffrey Evans went to the door and shouted after her.

'Come back!' Then he shouted, unfairly: 'P.T.!'

Wendy had got off the chair. 'Let her go!' Then flamed round at Albert. 'You ought to know better. You know what condition she's in! What else have you got?'

Albert gave Wendy the table-centres and the linen.

'Give her these,' Geoffrey said, handing Wendy her friend's

panties. Then he turned to Albert: 'Nit! What you want to do that for? I'd just got her going.'

Wendy said: 'I never want to see you crummy lot again!'

Matty got off the chair, straightening himself. 'Let's go down to your place, Wendy?'

Geoffrey gripped his arm. 'Bugger them. You come with me. Come on, Albert – over to my place. We'll have a real party.'

The music stopped. Lois stopped dancing, looked at them with a glazed eye. 'Where's everybody?'

'You'd better have a rest,' Albert said. He lifted her on to the bed.

'Come on, Albert,' Geoffrey Evans said. 'You can have that when you get back.'

'I don't want to go anywhere,' Albert said.

'Ah, come on!' Geoffrey Evans said.

'You'd better come,' Matty said.

'You shut your snotty Jewish mouth,' Geoffrey Evans said.

Behind a bolted door Wendy and Elsie heard the men clump down the stairs and out of the house.

'Dirty rotten trick!' Elsie said.

'You'll meet him again,' Wendy said, comfortingly. Then she smiled: 'Old Albert's getting back into his stride, thank goodness. Make you some coffee, dear?'

'Hot milk,' Elsie requested.

'Here,' Wendy called from the kitchen. 'Have you heard? Agricultural Tractors are back on full time next week.'

'Thank Christ for that,' Elsie said. 'Honest to God I'll never get everything in time.'

'I'm thinking about Easter,' Wendy said.

They walked to The Dolphin, an inexpensive commercial hotel in Butterhall Street. With each step of the way Albert wanted to return to Lois. He needed her with every deprived, underprivileged, over-excited fibre of his body. He was visualizing the consummation with such intensity that he felt ill. He wanted her – or somebody – quickly. After such a week and after such an evening's titillation Albert needed a woman.

'Who have you got up here?' Albert asked as they walked up the stairs of the hotel.

'You'll see,' Geoffrey Evans said.

He let them into his hotel bedroom and Albert's first depressed impulse was to get out. It was just a hotel bedroom, a carpet, a bed, a wardrobe, a bedside table, three overstuffed chairs, a gas fire with a gas meter and a wooden thing for cleaning shoes on.

'Where are the women?' Albert said.

'Wait till I make a call,' Geoffrey Evans said. He picked up a telephone and dialled the operator. To Matty he said: 'Get the fruit out, the drinks – the record.'

'You can't play music in a hotel,' Albert said. He could see Lois, lying in his bed, her red hair against the striped caseless pillow; tanked up, half-asleep and ready for him.

'Get me Pinner, miss,' Geoff was saying to the phone.

Albert looked at Matty who was now, for some odd reason, putting dishes of fruit all around the room; bananas, oranges, apples, plums of different sorts.

'Have an apple,' Matty said.

'I don't want a bloody apple.'

'Ssssh!' Geoffrey said; then, sweetly to the phone: 'Mabel? Are you still up?'

'That's his wife,' Matty said, proudly.

'Just ringing before by-byes,' Geoffrey was saying to the telephone. Then: 'I'm sorry tell her. You know what to do. Hot mineral bath with Reudel Salts, rub her chest with camphorated oil and get her to bed nice and cosy with a hot water bottle, hot milk and aspirin. She'll be as right as ninepins in the morning ...'

'That's his daughter,' Matty told Albert, with equal pride.

Grumpy, Albert sat on the arm of a chair chewing an apple and drinking a glass of neat whisky. Was Lois still there and if she was would she stay there if she woke up?

288

'I'm going,' Albert said.

'Just a minute,' Matty said. 'He's nearly finished.'

'Come and have a word with my wife, Mr Tomlinson,' Geoffrey said to Matty, who took the receiver.

'Hello, Mrs Evans?' Matty told the telephone in a jolly, elderly and false voice. 'I hope the weather's brighter in Pinner than it is here. Your husband's been home all the evening watching the television – we couldn't even go out for a drink ...'

Geoffrey Evans whispered to Albert: 'She thinks I'm lodging with a family – Matty is the landlord. Suspicious bitch she is. Never happy unless I'm in the rain.'

'Ah, he's always in bed by twelve, never worry,' Matty was saying.

'Lying Jewish bastard,' Geoffrey Evans said. Then he went close up behind Matty and tickled him.

'Shut up!' Matty hissed. Then to Geoffrey's wife: 'I've got the cat jumping all over me. Didn't he tell you about the cat?' He gave Geoffrey a warning glance.

Geoffrey looked fed up. 'Now I have to remember a cat.'

'How old's your daughter?' Albert asked.

Geoffrey thought about it. 'Oh, I don't know. How old was that bird I tried to jump tonight? Seventeen? Eighteen? Ida's about the same age.' He shook his head and sighed. 'Great responsibility, daughters, Albert,' said Ida Evans's father.

'When are we getting the girls in, then?' Albert asked.

Geoffrey Evans had said goodnight to his wife and they had been sitting in the room nearly half an hour drinking whisky and eating apples.

'This is better than copulation,' Geoffrey said, munching his apple. Then he said: 'Do you like these apples?'

'Not very much,' Albert said.

'Still,' Geoffrey said, 'you're eating them, that's the main thing. Tell him what they are, Matty. And the rest of the fruit.' He pointed around the room. 'Bananas, oranges, apples, plums – three sorts of plums –'

'It's all South African,' Matty explained. 'You know – the Union.'

'Oh?' Albert said.

Geoffrey Evans said: 'Ate it right through the boycott you know. Undercover supply through Ireland. Remember the first night of the boycott, Matty?' He grinned at Albert. 'We sat up all night eating South African peaches. All the drink is South African too.'

'Are you South African, then?' Albert asked, confused.

'Of course I'm not South African. Dutch bastards. Sound, though, mind you. All sound men. Matty's sound, aren't you, you sod? Matty's got a big black minah bird that says, "I hate Kruschev!" – true as I sit here. Put the record on, Matty . . .'

Albert was out of his depth and not interested. It was not a kind of passion he understood.

'I hate Kruschev! Plain as you like! He does too. I swear he'd peck his bloody Russian eyes out if he saw him.'

The record started with crowd cheering noises. A German voice started shouting a speech. Martial music started playing in the background.

Geoffrey Evans and Matty Matthews had stopped eating and drinking and were concentrating on the shouting voices.

'Hitler!' Matty told Albert, proudly.

'For Christ's sake he knows that!' Geoffrey said. Then he said: 'Beer Cellar . . .' The voice died away and then started on a new note with new background noises. 'Burning of the Reichstag,' Geoffrey said, flat and cryptic, like Gracie Fields giving the next chorus. The voice went on and on and both Geoffrey and Matty were staring into space with bright eyes.

'I'd better be going,' Albert said.

'*Anschluss*!' Geoffrey Evans barked.

The music swelled again into a march with a full-throated German choir. Geoffrey and Matty were both singing in German and stamping their feet.

290

> *'Die Fahne hoch, die Reihen dicht geschlossen*
> *S.A. marsehiert mit ruhig festem Schritt*
> *Kam'raden, die Rotfront und Reaktion erschossen*
> *Marschieren im Geist in unsern Reihen mit . . .'*

Albert chewed on his apple, staring at them resentfully. Whatever stirring visions they were seeing he was seeing Lois alone on his bed, waiting. Geoffrey got up and started marching up and down the room, swinging his arms, goosestepping his legs. Matty fell in behind him.

'You can join in,' Matty offered.

'Where's the bog?' Albert asked.

But the two TTT reps were singing with the massed German choirs again and Matty could only point towards the door as he marched.

Albert could still hear them marching and singing, a steady, solid, thumping rhythm as he left the hotel.

'Raving!' Albert muttered.

Across the street Police Constable Sid was staring up at the lighted window and listening, puzzled. Albert came hurrying by and stopped at the sight of his old school chum. Sid laughed.

'Well I'm blowed! I knew you were up there! If there's anything going on, I thought! What is it, musical chairs?'

From above came the recorded mass-singing in some German square from voices long silent, people long dead or preferring to be, and superimposed the nostalgic duet of the Treasure Trove reps. as they marched back and forth past the window.

> *'Bald flattern Hitlerfahnen über allen Strassen . . .'*

A hymn of the Third Reich dedicated to the martyr Horst Wessel, son of an army chaplain killed by the communists; ode to the first drop of blood in the opening of the flood gates and a restatement of final victory, all pouring down Butterhall Street over the roof of the Town Hall and into the High Street.

'Very musical,' said P.C. Sid, beating time.

'*Die Knechtschaft dauert nur noch kurze Zeit* ...' came the uplifted, inspired voices.

'Long as they don't create a disturbance,' said Sid.

'It's only folk singing,' Albert told him.

'Well, it makes a change from all this old rock,' said Sid.

'So long, mate, then,' Albert said.

Sid watched Albert hurry away, looking after him with a benevolent smile; then the constable marched on his beat, unconsciously adopting the infectious rhythm of the Third Reich and pom-pom-pomming the tune.

Albert crept up the stairs and into the bathroom. Keeping the after-shave lotion safely out of the way he had a quick wash and brushed his teeth, gargled and used a little fragrant talcum. 'Forty days and forty nights!' he muttered. That's what it seemed like since last Saturday. Now it was Saturday again and one o'clock in the morning. He left the bathroom and tiptoed across to his door, listened. He opened it just a crack and listened again. Inside was the red glow of the fire and the sound of hard breathing. He opened the door wider still. The hard breathing stopped and a familiar voice spoke softly and complainingly:

'Don't put the light on, old boy!'

Albert stood there for a moment; then he closed the door and walked away. Hah hah. What? He thought, furiously.

Two minutes later he was driving out of town. Driving fast out of town. Speed was for emergencies. He was sick of the whole sordid lot of them. He wanted someone clean and fresh and loyal. He wanted love.

'Very many congratulations!' he muttered.

Stupid, perhaps, but welcome. Sweet of her, really.

The point was, sex alone was not enough. He needed sweetness, kindness and love. The physical thing didn't matter any more. He was beyond it. Purity was what he wanted now. Her eyes would shine. She would give her nervous cough. He could see the yellow hair, the rough eyebrows, the childlike

292

eyes, the curving mouth, the spot of brown fur near her ear. She had grown on him, crept up on him; the girl who was not his type was suddenly the only person in the world he wanted.

He parked the pink car in a side road and walked quietly to the semi-detached. The whole road was in total darkness. He stepped over the low gate so's not to risk a creak, walked across the lawn and looked up at the dark front window. That would be the best bedroom. The widow's bedroom, Mrs Finbow's bedroom. The other end of the nice Spring Double. Half an hour ago he would have been throwing pebbles at that window. Straight sex with no involvement.

Albert walked quietly round to the back of the house and looked up at the back bedroom window. He could picture Janice asleep in her little bed. Alice, he meant. Probably wearing a white cotton nightie with a frillie neckline. Sweet untouched, earnest, dreaming of Albert. That was love. That was romance, pure feeling, sincerity, generosity, hearts and flowers. That was the thing that lasts. That was all involvement and no sex.

He thought about this for a gloomy moment then walked back round the house and threw pebbles at the front bedroom window.

Almost immediately, as though she had been half-expecting him, Mrs Finbow looked out of the window.

'Who's that?'

'Albert,' he called softly.

'I'll come down,' she said.

He stood in the small dark porch by the front door, dry-washing his face. I'll come down and let you in, cried the fair young maiden's mother. He was foul. He meant really foul. If you needed proof, this was it.

The hall light went on and the door opened. Mrs Finbow smiled at him. She had Alice's face plus twenty years of modest experience in it; her eyes larger and softer, her figure a little fuller, her attitude less afraid. No nervous cough. She was wearing a quilted robe over her nightdress and she carried a faint perfume which seemed to indicate to Albert a swift dash into the bathroom on her way downstairs.

'What do you want, Albert?' she asked.

'I didn't get you out of bed, did I? Sorry, Mrs Finbow. I thought perhaps Jan – Alice might be up. Felt a bit lonely. You know. A little chat. Don't have much time in the day. Bit pressed.'

'Come in, Albert. I'll just see if she's awake.'

He entered the hall, she closed the door very softly, then turned and smiled at him. She whispered: 'I don't think she's awake. I'll just see.'

He watched her tiptoe up the stairs and tiptoe down. 'No, she's not awake,' she whispered conspiratorially.

'Ah,' Albert whispered. 'Better go then. Another time, perhaps.'

'I'll make some coffee,' Mrs Finbow whispered. 'You never know, she might wake up.'

She led Albert into the front room, drew the curtains together before putting on a soft light.

'Make yourself comfortable,' she said. 'There's some cigarettes in that box. Think I'll have one.'

She stood close to him while he lit her cigarette, then gazed at him with her big soft eyes. 'It's rather naughty, isn't it?' She pressed his arm. 'But I'm glad you came. I was feeling lonely too. Nice to have somebody to talk to.'

'Yes.'

'Sleeping alone in that big bed after twenty years,' she said.

Albert expressed his sympathy.

'I'm glad you got my message, Albert,' she said then. 'I got yours.' She laughed at his lack of response. 'The way you looked at me that night!'

'Sorry,' Albert said.

She gave him a mock punch in the stomach: 'You're a naughty boy at heart . . .'

They drank instant coffee and smoked an instant cigarette and made instant conversation for five minutes.

'I don't know whether you might like to just see her before you go?' Mrs Finbow said, then.

'Yes.'

It got them both upstairs.

'I'll just see if she's awake now,' Mrs Finbow whispered.

Silent and cautious as a safe-cracker she opened the back bedroom door and peeped in. Albert stood behind her, touching her, his hand around her waist, looking over her shoulder. The frustrations of the week built up like an unexploded bomb inside him.

The oblong of yellow light fell on Alice Finbow's yellow hair. She was lying high on the pillow, halfway to meet her dreams in a white cotton nightie with a frilly neckline. At her head, near her upturned face, was pinned Albert's photograph as though recently kissed. It was the photograph cut from the newspaper and stuck on the headboard as Albert's pin-ups were stuck to his wall.

'She's fast asleep, bless her,' Mrs Finbow whispered. 'It's all right.'

She quietly closed the door and turned in his arms. Albert kissed her.

'Daughters are such a responsibility,' said Alice Finbow's mother.

He kissed her again.

'We'll have to whisper,' she said.

'There's nothing to whisper,' Albert now told the mother.

Albert picked up Mrs Finbow by knees and waist and carried her into the best bedroom, put her into the lonely double bed, undressed as though about to rescue a drowning child and then dived in with her.

During an ensuing period of calm in the stormwracked bed she said: 'I expect you think I'm promiscuous?'

'No, darling,' Albert told her fervently. 'Just fortuitous.'

There was something about the dawn walk away from a woman that filled Albert with self-loathing and self-disgust. This Saturday morning's journey back to town was a hell of remorse from which he would never recover. That sweet child lying in the next room dreaming of her untarnished knight, or whatever it was. What had he done to her? Well, what had he done to her? Looked at categorically it was monstrous. There was her father, Mr Finbow, dear old Finbow, not a bad chap looking back on him; you could grow fond of the people who chivvied you for money; it was a kind of relationship. And people like Albert and Callendar contributed to nothing except the death of tax collectors and national insurance officers. That was her father murdered, you might say, at five in the morning driving away from Mrs Finbow's bed and early tea. Then there was the girl herself brought to within a shade of seduction, ruined but for the intervention of a most unlikely providence. Then he had stolen her keys, robbed her office and got her the sack; ended her career which she had planned and worked for. Comptometer and Office Routine at Further Education, most likely. And now he had been to bed with her mother.

'Oh my Gawd!' Albert said as he drove along the deserted streets. 'I'll have to do something for that girl,' he said. 'Something really nice . . .'

Unknown to Albert – more unknown than most things – he was just driving past the church where he would eventually marry the girl he was talking about.

Also unknown to Albert was Dean Swift's evocative description of what met Albert in his little top room when he went in; the stench of an adulterous bed. Peter and Lois had gone at some furtive night hour but their absence was hardly noticeable, such was the state of Albert's bed. 'Ugh!' Albert said. It was like being faced with the washing-up after a good meal. He flung open the window wide, turned off the electric fire and went out.

Wendy came to the door in reply to his knock and stood there, fogged with sleep, her face greasy, looking more than ever the boxer returned to his corner just in time to avoid a knockout. Her hair stood in cylinders around her head and she was wearing a plastic sweat-and-slim round her waist, holding her hand over her breast and keeping the door over the rest.

'I don't know why they want to go to Mars,' Albert said. 'They should come up here. You look like a bloody rotary engine.'

'What are you doing dressed?' she said. 'It's half-past five in the morning. Haven't you been to bed?'

'How can I go to bed with them up there?'

She looked up the stairs affronted: 'Cheek! What, that red-head and that feller? Are they still at it? We've had the ceiling in twice –' She stopped him going in. 'You can't come in here – Elsie's sleeping here. She daren't go to her room alone in case that nut comes back –' she looked past him. 'He's not with you?'

'Course not. I've been pacing the streets all night.'

'Go and sleep in Elsie's room. She won't mind.'

'I'm lonely,' Albert said.

'You don't half look pale. Did he hurt you? When he kicked you in the privates?'

'I'm crippled for life,' Albert said.

Wendy giggled. 'You can come in then.'

Albert went into her room. Elsie was asleep and snoring on the far side of the bed against the wall.

'It's going to be a bit of a squash,' Wendy said.

This was another Saturday, different again. Albert lay in bed till noon, the sunlight streaming across the morning papers while he read the strips. The two girls had waited on him hand and foot, continuing the competitions of the night. Albert was catching up.

'Got to go and get my train now,' Elsie said at last. 'I can't miss it. My boy friend's meeting me off the other end. We're going to look at houses.'

Albert blew her a kiss, watched her go out with her week-end case, heard her call goodbye to Wendy who was upstairs cleaning Albert's room and changing the bed.

297

He turned back to yesterday's local paper and after studying his photograph for yet a few more minutes he went on to
the other pages. That meant 'What's on at the pictures', 'Cars
for Sale', 'Situations Vacant' in case there was an opportunity
and 'Situations Wanted' for a different kind of opportunity.
Albert was in the habit of bringing girls up to his room on
the false pretext of granting an interview; it was yet another
source of supply. Not much, but a steady trickle; typists,
secretaries, domestic workers, linguists, part-time teachers of
pianoforte. This was how the High School girls and the
woman solicitor had been harvested; the latter from the
'Missing Pets' column.

Then suddenly, like a cloud going over the sun, Treasure
was there. Last week's 'Marriages'.

> *Bluett: Hunter – On Saturdady 9 April at St*
> *Stephen's Church. Charles Joslin to Terese, by*
> *Rev. E. Thoday.*

'Saturdady!' he said bitterly. It was the only legitimate
criticism.

And he put his face in the pillow.

He watched her get out of the train with the stranger who
was probably a bloody Aussie with a name like Bluett. He
watched her follow him across to the news-stall and buy the
local paper and look on the back page for their name in print.
Typical of bloody Aussies to get married to get their name in
print. He watched the moment when she caught sight of his
own face on the front page and the moment when she was
going to tell her husband and then decided to keep it to herself.

He met her eyes when she looked straight into the tearoom
window knowing where he would be.

She had always known where he was.

Between the love and the hate, the fights and the make-
ups, the walk-outs and the come-backs which had been their
life together, they never lost sight of each other for long.
They both knew exactly where to be seen, with the people

they used – like props in a play – to hurt each other. Now that she knew she took her husband's arm and rested her head against his shoulder, using him for a little while as they followed the trolley of luggage down the platform.

Albert brightened. It meant that she still loved him. That she was still lost without him.

He watched her as far as he could see her and then he went to the door and watched her again. She turned with that split-second timing that only lovers know to make sure that he had done this.

'Bless her,' Albert said.

He strolled after them, arriving outside the station as their taxi turned out of the station yard. She looked back from the rear window. Albert waved, giving her the victory and feeling generous about it.

'Mrs Bluett,' he said. And there would be five kids in five years or less.

Fundamentally that is where they had differed; he content with what they had, she always getting pregnant. She was careless about it. He had to keep her dates in his pocket book so that he could remind her in time to do something. And afterwards when she was all right he had to give her a special treat to make up for it and it never quite did. A bit of jewellery, a dress, a pair of shoes; a week-end here, a day there. It had not always been easy. And her moods of frustrated motherhood would last for weeks. It was as if he had taken the future away and given her a doll. He could never quite reach her at those times. Even in the pleasures of their love-making, which was better with each other than with anyone else, she was reaching for something galactic, cosmic, bigger than both of them.

'Don't you ever feel anything besides my body?' she used to say. 'Don't you feel any kind of continuation?'

Strange girl in many ways. His type to the point of being his prototype. She could exchange joke for joke, crack for crack; she could keep him company five hundred feet above ground level for hours at a time; she could remain in glorious

299

technicolour all night long; they were tuned in to each other so closely that in sex, love, pain and misery it was snap snap snap every time.

'And yet you don't see any meaning in it,' she would tell him. She meant that he did not want her to have a child; marriage was something else. It could be put off forever.

I'm not old enough. I'm not ready for it. These were the kind of jokes he had made. He had not even decided what he was going to be when he grew up. It was the way Albert's mind worked; he really meant it. He looked at men and he saw the finished article. Albert was not yet, thank God, a finished article.

She had tried to get him tuned into this one last little bit of herself. She had taken him under the sky. They had made love in woodland and field and lying under a towel in sand dunes at Littlehampton. With her he didn't mind. He liked it anywhere with her.

'That's not quite the point,' she used to say.

Over Box Hill they once saw a rag of golden cloud suddenly turn black and she said: 'It's like life going out.'

At Hemingford Grey they saw two swans flying into a sunset and she said: 'All that sky and nowhere to lay their eggs.'

On Burwell Fen they saw two lonely horses touching noses in a rainswept field and she said: 'The last creatures in the world.'

Bored in a crowded room they would play horses, stand with their noses touching until they were laughing again and nobody knowing what they meant.

And now she was Mrs Bluett.

6

In the mock-log-cabin golf-clubhouse on Sunday morning
Major Simpkins was holding an unofficial court-martial of an
absent public enemy already doomed. Present and correct
were Wilkinson of Wilkinson's stores, councillor and JP; Taylor of Taylor's stores, chairman of the local Chamber of Trade;
Solly Cowell, owner of the biggest departmental store in town;
and Colonel Wainwright, retired chairman and shareholder
in Agricultural Tractors besides having that rare double-
distinction: hero and survivor of the Battle of the Somme.

The club was assembled in their usual haunt by the fire.
The old Colonel, bundled up in a tweed suit of plus-fours,
was directing the steward with a tray of drinks.

'Over here. Little to the right. There we are. Move in now.
I've cleared this whole area for you. Splendid.'

He stood, precariously, on ancient bent legs, his rheumy
eyes assessing the drinks. 'Here we are, lads. Scotch for the
Major, gin for you, sir . . .' He was a well-known figure in the
town, tottering around the streets, inclined to direct the
traffic if given the tiniest encouragement, always looking for
a command.

'Dammit,' Major Simpkins was saying, 'it wouldn't be so
bad if Mason had the grace to admit his own crass stupidity.
He will take a stand! I mean, what does it boil down to in the
public eye – it's the public we've got to think about. It's our
job to watch out for them. What Mason's done is tantamount
to putting the Council's seal of approval on this gang of
charlatans!'

'Hear hear,' said Mr Wilkinson. 'Besides encouraging unfair trading.'

Mr Taylor said: 'That's what concerns me. Goodness knows it's been hard enough to make a living out of a small shop this past six months. Break an egg and you're bankrupt!'

'Heh heh!' Colonel Wainwright laughed. 'I like that, Taylor of Taylor's stores, chairman of the local Chamber of Trade; Always good conversation in this place on a Sunday morning. Don't know what it is. Got your supplies sir?' He gave Solly Cowell his drink. He had known Solly for years but had never quite accepted him nor remembered his name.

'TTT is right,' said Mr Taylor, thus encouraged. 'Stands for Tinpot Trading –' He groped for another 'T' without success. 'I mean they gull the public into buying cut-price goods with a lot of rubbishy gifts. Trash, most of it. Make it themselves, you know.'

'Oh, not this firm,' Wilkinson said. 'They're not big enough. Bankrupt stock more like it.'

'Stolen goods,' said Major Simpkins. 'That's what it is. Where do all these hijacked lorries go? You don't have to make any signals. Little more than a gang of crooks. Did you see that female Callendar brought up here? Gangster's moll! Been all the same if I'd had my good lady with me! And that's another thing.'

Mr Callendar had drifted up to greet them; he now listened resentfully.

'We should force him to resign,' Solly Cowell said. 'He only uses this place for contacts. Have you ever seen him play golf? What? You'd think he was threshing corn.'

The old Colonel laughed again. 'Damned funny, sir! Heh heh! Keep it up. I had a joke myself somewhere . . .'

Mr Callendar now went on to the bar.

'There he goes,' said Solly Cowell. 'What a twister!'

'No salutes, Colonel!' Major Simpkins said.

'Oughtn't we to say something?' Mr Taylor asked.

'I've already spoken to the secretary. Keep it regular.'

Mr Callendar had blown the TTT trumpet so loud and long that any crime now committed in their name would be laid at his door. So far as the golf club was concerned he was TTT stamps and always would be.

'Remember that dreadful stamp business,' they would be saying about him ten years later, standing in the same place by the fire. Except the Colonel.

Mr Taylor now spoke to Wilkinson: 'I had heard that you were contemplating taking up their wretched stamps, Wilkinson? Of course I didn't believe it. Reputable shop like yours?'

'Of course not,' Mr Wilkinson said. 'Certainly I explored. Just to judge their tactics.'

'Very sound,' said the Colonel. 'You can't beat a good recce.'

'Corrupting little children,' Major Simpkins said. 'Those are their tactics. Correct me if I'm over-stating the case.'

'You're perfectly right, Major,' Taylor said. 'Once you start children collecting those stamps there's no knowing where it will lead them.'

'We're beginning to feel the pinch already,' Wilkinson exclaimed, thoughtlessly. Adding: 'Not that profits are important. It's a principle that's at stake. It's a moral issue.'

'One big con trick,' Solly Cowell said, looking across at Callendar's back.

'And the clever thing is,' Major Simpkins said, 'they start their conning where they know it's easiest – among the ranks of the CND. That explains Cedric Mason. I don't have to say more than that. Thank God there's a committee for dealing with things like this.'

'Civil Defence?' Taylor asked.

'No no!' said the Major. 'The Education Committee! This is purely an educational matter.'

'Of course,' said Mr Wilkinson.

'A headmaster's job is to teach the three "R"s' said Mr Taylor, having worked it out again. 'Not the three "T"s!'

'Heh heh!' laughed the old Colonel. 'Keep it up.'

The Major said: 'Do you mind if I make a note of that?'

At the bar Mr Callendar called for another large Scotch. The Steward came up for a quiet, anxious word.

'I wonder if you'd settle your account, sir?'

Callendar stared at him resentfully. 'It's not the end of the month.'

'Just getting the books straight sir.' Then remembering that he was talking to an expert collector of money: 'Stock-taking?'

'Listening through keyholes?' Callendar hazarded. 'I'll pay you next week. Failing that, when I feel like it.'

'Do you still want that drink?' the Steward asked.

'No. I think I've just about had enough!'

The Steward watched Callendar stalk out. So did the fire-place club.

'And sending all those little popsies into my place,' Taylor said, 'asking for his stamps.'

'A man of his age,' said Mr Wilkinson, adding pensively, 'I don't know where he finds them.'

'La Paloma,' Major Simpkins said. 'A coffee bar cum dance hall in "The Ribbon" – the basement under that betting shop that got burnt down.'

'I know it,' Taylor said. 'Tatty little street. All dustbins.'

'That's the place,' said Major Simpkins. 'Nowhere to park at night.'

They drank for a moment in reflective silence, then Mr Wilkinson said: 'What's happened to Willy? On the door?'

'Fired,' said the Major. 'Left yesterday. Getting past it, y'know. Then there was that mix-up with the cars last Sunday. Members are not going to stand that kind of thing for long.'

'Still,' Taylor said, 'I liked Willy.'

'Well, yes we all did,' said Major Simpkins. 'But he took a stand. I mean there was quite a bust-up. The secretary got his wing dented. Willy would have it wasn't his fault. I admire a bit of spirit, mind you, but you can't have them taking a stand. Not employees. Not in a place like this. Had to go, I'm afraid.'

'Understandable,' said Mr Wilkinson.

'Pretty old to get another job though,' Taylor said.

'Oh come now,' said Major Simpkins. 'Isn't that a fallacy? These days I mean? There's a nasty tendency to molly-coddle the old folk. They've got their pension. They're not helpless. Look at my old lady. Bless her goitre, there's an example for us all! Seventy-eight! Seventy-eight and still up and down, up and down from the Mill House to the Guild and right out to the Manor on Wednesdays for the eggs. Still driving her own Rolls Royce!'

'Drives herself too much!' quavered the old Colonel.

'Dammit the chauffeur's always there if she wants him!' said Major Simpkins.

'Heh heh!' laughed Colonel Wainwright. 'Always a laugh on Sundays. Don't know what it is.' Then, looking at his glass: 'Who's ready for another volley?'

'Cunts!' said Mr Callendar, as he drove away from the golf course in a hired car.

It was especially galling to see Solly Cowell rubbing shoulders with the hierarchy; standing on the bit of carpet Cally coveted for himself. Cally had worked for Solly just after the war. In those days Solly had run a tally house, Cally had scraped enough of Solly's customers and stock together to start a place of his own. Ever since when Solly had been gunning for him. You would think a man who had so much would be able to forgive the occasional trespass. But not Solly. Solly had gunned Cally out of his dreams, one by one; he had out-manoeuvred Cally in everything. Solly had made a great success, overcoming the shape of his nose with a substantial bank balance and a mass of collateral. The feud between them had reached such a pitch and was so widely known throughout the town that whichever of them died first the other would surely be hanged as a matter of course.

'Threshing corn!' Cally muttered. He was proud of his game, such as it was.

In the darkest cellar of his mind, waiting like a bit of mushroom spore for germination, was the idea that one day, when circumstances were right, he and Albert Argyle together would get the better of Solly Cowell. He sometimes felt that he had nurtured and bred Albert for this one purpose. It was not something he cared to think about too much. He had to be down to his last idea and somebody else's last penny to even give the thought an instant's acknowledgement. He could do nothing with Albert riding high; but Albert riding low was a different matter. On the road they travelled the cycle of prosperity and desperation was inevitable, the see-saw of their affairs as constant as the seasons.

But the time was not yet. From Friday's paper he could see that Albert, using Cally as a stepping stone, leaving him stuck in the mud with the Inland Revenue breathing down his neck, was now soaring on the high end of the board. It couldn't last. He couldn't stay there. He could only come down. There would come a time when once again Callendar would be in the satisfactory position of twisting Albert's arm.

Pity he's not married with a starving family, Callendar thought. Or coming out of prison without a friend in the world. Something that would make Albert manageable and easily harnessed. The thought was almost paternal.

Driving through the town he concentrated on ways to get started again. The sun was shining, the church bells ringing from the loudspeaker on the ice-cream carts; the Sunday traffic was faster and noisier, the pubs busier, girls prettier and more laughing going on. The town was quickening towards spending another Easter, prosperity inflating like a pie and Mr Callendar wracked his brains for a way of getting his finger in.

On Monady the local *Daily News* placard read:

GIFT STAMPS IN SCHOOLS: HEADMASTER
SUSPENDED

'The headmaster is there to teach the three "R"s – not the three "T"s – H'rumph! What!' Albert was reading a quotation from Major Simpkins in the paper.

'That's excellent,' Elaine said. She smiled at Albert and Peter. 'Congratulations to both of you.'

Albert said: 'But I don't think much of your letters, Peter.' He held up the front page which had been devoted to public reaction. 'That's four letters knocking us – three in favour.'

Peter said: 'I didn't write those. They're genuine, I'm afraid. They didn't print mine.'

Elaine said: 'Well it doesn't matter. TTT is now a talking point. That's the great thing.'

Cedric Mason had been relieved of his duties pending a special meeting of the Education Committee on Tuesday. Cedric's worried face stared out from the top of the page.

'Mr Mason refuses to comment until after the Committee's decision is made known,' Albert read. Then he said: 'Just like old Cedric. Too cautious.'

Elaine looked at Albert without smiling: 'I hadn't noticed that.'

If it was a criticism he ignored it. He was elated and happy. The plan was clicking like a fast game of snooker; one thing cannoning off another; in off the red and the white and yellow. The reps. had been out all day signing up shops and garages. The anti-stamp feeling in the town was becoming pro-stamp.

'We can afford to reduce the franchise area now,' Elaine told Albert. 'Some of our present shops couldn't accommodate the kind of boom they'll be getting. They're not big enough, they haven't got the staff.'

'You're not cutting across Joe Keppings' area, are you?'

'I think we'll have to, Albert. Oh, they'll get more customers than they want. But Geoff's working Shaw's Super markets now – that's eight big shops.'

Albert said: 'That's worth a hundred and twenty quid to Geoff in one go – you could have given that to me.'

Elaine smiled at him: 'You're getting an overall bonus, sweetie.'

'I bet he is!' Peter Fisher said; then at their mutual distaste, he added weakly: 'Hah hah. Sorry.'

Elaine turned to the mirror and shouted: 'Clive! Why don't you sit in on this!' She looked down at her papers. 'He never *does* anything . . .'

'Now let's get down to this victimization gag,' Albert said to Peter. 'We want it to go off before the Committee Meeting tomorrow.'

'It's no good us putting up the idea,' Peter Fisher said. 'It would smell a bit, wouldn't it?'

'Anonymous letter to the paper?' Albert said.

'No,' Elaine said.

Clive Townend came in. 'Elaine's right,' he said, as if he had been sitting in on the conference, which he had.

Albert and Peter looked at each other in brief bewilderment.

Clive Townend said: 'It's a big issue. No local rag is going to take the responsibility for making an accusation of that kind. It'll have to come from a CND source or from Cedric Mason himself.'

'Or from his wife,' Albert said, suddenly inspired.

Elaine was smiling at him again.

At five o'clock Albert stopped outside Cedric Mason's house in the outer suburbs. He sat there for a moment in nostalgic reflection. Marjorie Mason had been one of his special regulars in his tally boy days. How much he rated with her now he wasn't sure. Their attraction had been on many levels. Physical, certainly, for she was much younger that Cedric and with a strong appetite. She also saw herself as a mother figure to one of her husband's old boys. But beyond that she was addicted to the things Albert had to sell; her house was a museum of electric gadgets, wrought plastic and fibre glass, a monument to her endurance and capacity for quick half-hours.

He walked across a neat front lawn on which stood the ambassadors of every garden ornament factory in the country; a gnome, a dwarf, a wishing well, toadstools with plastic toads, a water sprinkler which she switched on from indoors if she saw anybody coming. It started into action now, sprinkling the April-wet lawn. She gave him time to start the carillon of chimes and then the door opened.

'Albert! This is lovely!'

'Nice to see you, Marjorie. Missed me, have you?'

Marjorie Mason pouted. A modern, slim-line number nicely painted and dressed like a French maid in English farce. 'A lot you care!' Then she prodded him with her finger. 'You've been putting on weight!'

'All solid fat, not an ounce of muscle,' Albert said, striking an Atlas pose. He tapped her stomach: 'Talk about me. What's this, then?'

'Not in front of the neighbours, petal.'

She took him inside.

They kissed in the tiny hall and she ran her fingers around the back of his neck.

'I've missed this,' she said.

'Thought you'd had enough.'

'I don't mind, Albert. I want him now.' She looked around at the bric-à-brac of her home as they went through to the living-room; the little wall shelves, the hanging vases, the pictures, the bits of brass. 'He'll fit nicely into that back bedroom,' she said. It wanted something, was the thought.

And sitting on Albert's lap, playing with his eyebrows, she said: 'I hope you'll come and see him sometimes.'

Albert said: 'You'd better enter him now if you want me to put him on my round.'

Marjorie Mason laughed. He kissed her.

'Cedric's not here, then?'

'Any minute, petal – sorry.' Albert took his hand off her leg. 'He's over at the County Education Offices.'

'You're not going to let them get away with this, are you?' Albert said, coming to the point.

'Make him attack me, then,' Geoffrey Evans was saying when Albert came into the conference room at six o'clock. 'Go on, Clive, tell him to fetch me.'

Geoffrey and Matty were looking at Biff, the Alsatian. Clive Townend was holding the dog's collar as he sat by the window. Elaine was working at papers and ledgers, catching up with the day's enrolments and impatient of the messing about going on.

'Come on, boy! Fetch me!' Geoff said.

The dog stirred under Clive's hand. 'Don't do that,' Clive Townend said. He knew he was being got at. The reps. didn't often go as far as this; it seemed to indicate that Elaine had been disloyal to him; that they were losing what little respect they had for his position as the managing director's husband. Perhaps it meant that they knew she was having an affair with one of them.

'If he went for you he'd kill you,' Clive said, thinking perhaps it might be Geoff.

Geoffrey Evans said: 'Why train a dog to do that, then? What are you afraid of? Burglars?'

'I like training dogs,' Clive said.

Geoffrey Evans said: 'You like to be the only one he'll obey, Clive, is that it? What is it? An inferiority complex?' He laughed at Clive's pink face above the beard, glowing like an angry sunset over a privet hedge. 'That's made you mad – go on, set him on me! Why keep picking on little fellows?'

Elaine looked up at Albert. 'Callendar's been in. The dog got him again.'

'Bloody brute!' Albert said. 'If I'd been here I'd have kicked it in the gut.'

'You can't do that,' Clive said, expertly. 'He'd come straight at your throat.'

'Go on then,' Geoffrey Evans persisted. 'Prove it.'

'For God's sake shut up!' Elaine said. 'Take that bloody animal in the other room, Clive. This is a business meeting.'

310

Clive Townend finished his drink, got up, led the dog out; Geoffrey Evans watched him go, distastefully. 'Grrr!' he said.

Matty laughed at his friend.

'What did Cally want then?' Albert asked Elaine.

'What do you think? A job. Feel sorry for him, really.'

'What did you tell him?'

'I told him to see you.'

'Oh, that was nice and easy,' Albert said.

'Why don't you go round and see him?'

'Good idea. Yeah, I will. Good idea.'

Elaine glanced up at him again, knowing what happened to his good intentions. 'What about Marjorie Mason?' she asked.

'No comments,' Albert said.

Geoffrey Evans punched him. 'You old ram! Here, have a drink, build yourself up.'

While Albert got his drink he told Elaine that the Masons refused to make any accusations against the Major.

'Chicken lot,' Geoffrey Evans said.

'I wouldn't say that,' Albert said. 'He wants to get his job back – or else a transfer. No good bucking the Education Committee. I don't want to get my friends into trouble.'

Geoffrey Evans said: 'But he's being victimized. Somebody's got to say it. I mean if you're going to get your two-pennorth. What about the CND crowd?'

Albert sat on the desk, thoughtfully drinking. He didn't know anybody in the movement. And any approach would warn them they were being used.

'What it really wants,' Albert said, 'is a nice big demonstration outside the Town Hall tomorrow night. While the Education Committee's meeting about Cedric.'

Geoffrey Evans clicked his fingers.

'No!' Matty Matthews said, staring at him.

'You don't know what I'm going to say yet!' Geoff said.

'Yes I do,' Matty told him.

Geoffrey Evans looked at Albert. 'I've got just the boys for

311

this job. Why didn't I think of it before? You want a bit of rabble-rousing? You come to Uncle Geoff.'

Albert said: 'What d'you mean, Geoff? CDN supporters?'

'CND,' Elaine said.

Geoffrey raised the palms of his hands: 'CND, CDN, disarmament shamarmament – whassa difference so long as ve got banners?'

He picked up the telephone and asked Dorothy for a London number. Albert was looking at Elaine who was staring at Matty who was gazing on his friend with fear.

That evening Albert took Peter Fisher along to a jobbing printer whose business premises were in a disused church hall in the heart of the town's condemned area.

'This is the part of the town I don't like,' Peter Fisher said. They had parked Albert's car and were crossing the dreary street. On the old church notice board could be seen the weathered memories of some biblical quotation '– Christ forever –'. Superimposed on that was a barely discernible 'BINGO TONIGHT' sign. This in turn had been covered up by: 'J. K. Moore – The Garden Press.'

'Got your cards, Albert,' Jack Moore told him. He was a skinny north-country tradesman of forty; he wore a carpenter's apron over an ink-stained suit.

'Let's have a look.'

Albert studied the card with pride and pleasure, showed it to the PRO.

'Very nice,' Peter said. Then he said: 'You're late getting these, aren't you? How long have you been with the firm?'

'How's your cabaret work getting on?' the printer asked. 'Did you do that broadcast?'

'We haven't got time for a lot of questions,' Albert told them. 'Let's get these posters mapped out.'

'I've been busy since you telephoned,' the printer said. 'Just come over to the silk screen. This is not the finished job, you understand . . .'

Albert left Peter working with the printer. 'I might call in again about eleven to see if you've got anything finished,' he told them.

'I shall be here, old man,' Peter Fisher said.

That was what Albert really wanted to know.

'This is nice,' Albert told Lois half an hour later.

'You have got a nerve,' Lois said.

They were in her flatlet overlooking the Beakley Park on the London Road. She had made him coffee, turned on the television and turned off the lights. They lay together watching the screen. The sound was off.

'Known Peter long?' Albert asked.

'About two weeks. I did some photographic modelling for one of the stores. He was doing the publicity.'

'He's a good worker,' Albert said.

'What about you?'

'I'm a good organizer,' Albert said.

All Tuesday morning the six TTT cars toured the town bearing Peter Fisher's posters. In place of 'SAVE TTT STAMPS' was 'SAVE CEDRIC MASON'. And: 'TONIGHT AT SEVEN: EDUCATION COMMITTEE MEETING IN TOWN HALL – PROTEST MEETING OUTSIDE'. And: 'HEADMASTER VICTIMIZED'. And: 'DON'T BE TOLD WHERE TO SHOP'.

Besides bearing some of these posters, Albert's own car had a public address system fitted and he drove around the town making speeches, some of which had some bearing on the victimization of Cedric Mason, but some were curiously mixed up with his private convictions.

'Are you being brain-washed?' he asked a startled crowd of shoppers in Butterhall Street as he kerb-crawled along, steering with one hand and holding a hand-mike in the other.

'Let him alone,' Police Constable Sid told his sergeant. 'Old Albert's in his element.'

'What do you want for your children?' Albert's voice boomed along the busy street. 'Major Simpkin's fall-out shelters – or Cedric Mason's TTT piano?'

'We're going to have to stop it,' the sergeant said, regretfully.

'Pity,' P.C. Sid said. 'I swear if there was a General Election now old Albert would get in.'

Having by-passed the small formality of getting council permission for the street announcements, Elaine was visited – belatedly – by the local Chief Inspector and the cars were withdrawn by midday. By this time they had covered the town and distributed ten thousand 'Save Cedric Mason' leaflets. The leaflet struck a nice balance by having the TTT trademark at the top and the CND sign at the bottom while neither issue was actually mentioned in the text.

In the bar of The George, after a hard morning, Albert was drinking a quiet one with Geoffrey Evans.

'We'd better stay out of it tonight,' Albert said. 'Don't want to get the firm mixed up with a lot of rioting.'

'That's all right with me,' Geoffrey said. 'I fancy screwing that skinny one at your place. What's she like? Does she go?'

'I dunno, do I?'

'I don't like taking them up to the hotel,' Geoffrey said. 'They know what they're there for. Not subtle enough for some of them.'

'I know,' Albert said.

The infinite variety of sex talk could go on for hours without once repeating itself. Albert didn't mind it. There was a difference that not everybody would understand between smutty talk with basically sexless men and straight sex talk of the enthusiastic connoisseur kind between two actual practitioners. Then it became an exchange of notes which could be educational and valuable. This was the hearty-hetero type and Albert was a full member. The two kinds of men could be distinguished by their habits. The non-participative, often much-married kind congregated in groups and told dirty stories with dirty laughs; the hearty-heteros met quietly in pairs and never raised their voices.

'Of course,' Albert said, 'after the way you acted the other night I can't guarantee anything with Elsie.'

314

Geoffrey stared at him, apprehensively: 'What did I say? What did I do? Nothing ungentlemanly I hope?'

'You're joking of course.'

'Oh Christ,' Geoffrey Evans said. 'That's the trouble. After ten Scotches I have these black-outs. Sometimes nine Scotches. I never know the next day even. What did I do?'

'Ah!' Albert said.

'Of course, it can work wonders. I mean bashing straight in.'

'Oh yes,' Albert said. 'What is it – same again?'

'One more, that's all. I've got to organize this press gang.' Geoffrey Evans looked at his watch.

'Wendy might take you,' Albert said.

'Didn't fancy her. Is that the big bruiser? I didn't fancy her.'

'Anyway, clear up after yourself,' Albert said. 'Bloody mess the other night with old hah hah yes.'

'Don't you worry, sport,' Geoffrey Evans told him. 'I pride myself on that. You won't know the place has been used. Take Matty's place in Campden Hill. Lovely shagging ground but only one bedroom. He used to hang this board on the door to keep people away on Saturday afternoons. Well, I can't afford a flat. Family man, you know. Still, I've bought lots of bits and pieces of furniture for Matty's place. He's a quiet one old Matty but he gets there, you know. The only anti-semitic Jewboy I know. No fuss, not much talking. Bastards, they are,' he said fondly.

The barmaid came round to collect their glasses. The men reacted according to their group; the D.O.M.s, the wholly-males, the dirty story club nudging, watching with sly suggestive eyes. The hearty-heteros openly admiring, unsecretive and crude.

'Look at that lovely arse,' said Albert, his voice hushed with reverence and respect for woman.

During the afternoon a strange assortment of people began to arrive by car and rail. Mostly men. Some had the Chelsea

315

beatnik look, others were elderly and intellectual, some oddly European and without a word of English. They arrived at the TTT offices singly or in pairs and groups.

Cedric Mason was entering the door next to the gift shop when a big open Lancia of the early thirties vintage stopped with a squeal of brakes and disgorged a gang of thugs; Cedric squeezed himself to one side to allow them to go in. He half expected to see them pulling on nylon masks and knuckle-dusters.

'I did a stretch about the same time,' one of them was saying.

'I didn't even know he'd been topped,' said another.

'Well, Liverpool! What a place to get topped in! You don't hear about it, do you?'

Cedric followed them up the stairs, careful not to offend. 'Save Cedric Mason' posters and banners were propped around the reception desk.

'Mr Argyle?' Cedric asked Dorothy.

'He's terribly busy,' she said. 'What name shall I say?'

'Cedric Mason.'

'Who?' she said. 'Well, just a minute, I'll see . . .'

Cedric sat on the edge of a chair, waiting. The noise coming from behind the door of the conference room was like the sound of a boxing match at the Albert Hall.

Albert came out to him after a moment, bringing two glasses. 'Hello, Cedric, nice of you to drop in – have a drink?'

Cedric stood up in his old mac, his shoulders stooped. 'Albert you've got me worried! What are you doing?'

'Just fighting your cause, Cedric. You know, honour of the old school and that.'

'You're getting me into terrible trouble! Major Simpkins thinks I'm behind it! He's threatening to sue me!'

'Good,' Albert said. 'That means we've got him worried. You wait. This time tomorrow you'll have your job back – read the papers in the morning. Not the local – the London papers. You're going to be a hero, you are, Cedric.'

'You've got to stop it!' Cedric Mason said.

The door burst open and two men fell out, fighting furiously.

'I can't stop it,' Albert said.

'Oh my God!' Dorothy exclaimed. She was standing on a chair.

'Geoffrey's action committee,' Albert explained half-heartedly.

Some men came out and dragged the fighting pair to their feet, held them apart.

'Now apologize!' somebody demanded.

'All right all right – you was in Budapest!'

'Certainly I was in Budapest!'

They were dragged back into the room and the door slammed shut.

'So long, Cedric, then,' Albert said. 'Got to go. Bit pressed. See you at the school. Get the old stamps buzzing in, that's the main thing.'

Albert went back into the room. Cedric gazed at the door for a moment. It seemed that the fight had started again.

The procession left the TTT offices at six o'clock. Amongst the banners held aloft by the wild assortment of people were ten demanding Cedric Mason's reinstatement, three demanding unilateral disarmament and two telling the public to start saving Treasure Trove Trading Stamps Today. At the front jogged a life-sized photograph of Cedric Mason, mounted on a kind of crucifix.

Between High Street and the Town Hall the nucleus of fifty had grown to several hundred; more CND banners had appeared and traffic, always quiet at that time of the evening, came to a dead stop. P.C. Sid and half a dozen other uniformed officers stood in line abreast in front of the Town Hall approach, holding up their hands. The procession, with a hard core of the action committee in the forefront, walked straight through them.

'Friends!' shouted a man from the Town Hall steps, holding up his arm in a manner vaguely familiar to the watching crowd and speaking with a heavy accent. 'Friends and fellow citizens!'

Inside the Committee Chamber in the Town Hall Major Simpkins and the Education Committee stopped talking to listen.

'Down with these council dictators! Are we going to let Major Simpkins crucify Cedric Mason? Is this the way to run a town? Are we going to let him bully us? Are we going to let the Civil Defence militarists destroy a man of peace? Are we going to be told where to shop?'

'Live for Free with TTT!' came the answering chant.

'Friends!' cried the voice anew.

'This is quite ridiculous!' said Major Simpkins.

Somewhere near came the crashing of breaking glass.

'Oughtn't we to adjourn?' somebody suggested.

'I think we're safer where we are,' Major Simpkins told the meeting.

'This is a good idea,' Alice Finbow said. 'Whatever made you think of it?'

Albert and Alice were parked in a country lane, eating fish and chips from a newspaper. They sat in the dim glow of the dashboard light with darkness all around. Far below, like an upside down sky, were the lights of the town.

'Me and Treasure used to do this,' Albert said.

'Oh.'

Albert looked at her as he popped another chip into his mouth. 'I shouldn't have said that, should I?' He tried to diminish its importance. 'She was only a girl.'

'That's all I am.'

'You're different.'

'Was she different?'

'In a way. It lasted nearly two years.' He shook out of the memory. 'What are we talking about her for?'

He turned her head towards him and kissed her, both with their mouths full. He had decided to get out of town for the evening. In case anything went wrong. In case there was trouble. He wanted a witness that he was somewhere else. Alice had been telephoning him without success steadily for the past few days and now she had got her reward.

'No, I won't call for you,' he had told her. 'See you outside the Ritz, seven o'clock.'

They had driven round the villages, called at several pubs, bought the fish and chips and retired into the darkness.

He wiped his mouth, then cleaned his hands on his hand-kerchief. He wiped her mouth and hands, screwed up the newspaper and put it out of the window, then kissed her again with more concentration.

'There's more room in the back,' he said.

'Is that what you used to do with Treasure?'

Albert stopped kissing her.

'Sorry Albert,' she said. 'But I don't think the back of a car – I don't think it's very nice.'

Not the first time, anyway, Albert thought, cynically.

She knew that she was losing him and she grew desperate. 'I mean. It would make me feel cheap. I didn't mean Treasure – well, it's just me!'

He took out cigarettes. 'That's all right, love.'

'Albert. Albert!'

He looked at her.

'I'll come back to your place if you like?'

'We'd better not.'

'Albert. If you want me. Well – I will if you want me.'

He shrivelled up inside, feeling like a monster. He put his arms around her and kissed her again. 'I think you're wonderful.'

'Do you mean it? Really mean it? Do you think about me when I'm not with you?'

'All the time.'

'No, I mean really. I know you don't. I know you don't think about me, Albert. You even forget me when I am with you. Oh, I don't mind. It's just your way. You've got these little ways.'

'Tell me about them,' Albert said, always finding himself engrossing.

'I expect Treasure knew them all?'

'Yes.'

She was talking quickly and keeping her head averted, as though intent on what she wanted to say. He could hardly see her face at all in the shadows. 'I don't think I shall ever quite understand you, Albert. Do you think you have to understand people? I mean – for it to come to anything?'

'I dunno, do I?' She *was* different. He would run a mile to get away from a talker. Yet he was enjoying it and was touched. She loved him. She was shouting it. It didn't often happen. You couldn't dismiss it.

'I'm not very good at explaining,' she said. 'Sometimes – for instance, that is – sometimes when you say something serious you're really making fun.'

'I wouldn't make fun of you, dear.'

'No, I know. Not of me. Not of anybody. Not of any*body*. I didn't mean that. I meant sometimes when I'm in bed – that is, anytime when I'm thinking about you. About what you've said. Well I only just get it. Your mood. What you're thinking. Hours afterwards. Then it's too late and I wonder what you think about me. You must find me dull,' she finished, hopelessly.

She was out of breath.

'No I don't, darling. I like being with you.'

'No you don't! Well yes, perhaps you do. But not enough so you want to be with me again. I'll catch up when I get more used to you.'

There was an air of having long-term plans; inevitable plans; plans they couldn't escape; as if they had found themselves marooned on a desert island together with no hope of rescue. A bit alarming, Albert found it. Then it was partly explained, as if she had been listening to his thoughts. And that was alarming too.

'You see the thing is. Well, I haven't been out with many

boys. Well, not any, really,' she said, wretchedly. 'Oh dear,' she said, almost crying.

Albert stroked her hair very gently. 'Stop worrying. I love you.'

She fairly flung her arms around him like a long-lost child. 'Oh Albert! I love you. I love you. I love you. I love you ...'

She went on saying it into his throat till it had become a desperate, despairing moan; as if by repeating it as constantly as breathing it would become indestructible.

The emotion of it held Albert silent and contented and elevated for a very long time. He went on stroking and kissing and soothing her and he didn't need a cigarette or to look out of the window nor even any kind of thought in his head. Her skin, her hair, her lips, the love she was radiating possessed them both for more than half an hour by the dashboard clock and there was nothing sexual more than the tips of her fingers against his chin, her hair brushing his eyes, the ribs of her back through the summer dress. When it was over they were both exhausted.

Albert sank back behind the wheel and smoked a whole cigarette in silence and wonder. It was a new experience for him. What did they call it? It was something you couldn't talk about in a bar.

From the darkness at the other end of the bench seat, she said: 'You never call me Alice. Don't you like it? My name?'

Funny you should say that, he thought. Given two names, Alice and Janice, he would never get them right. Just as he was about to use one of them he had the doubt and then it was too late. You could go right through a lifetime with a person and never use their name. Later, when she was trying to gas herself and the child, the baby curled up in a cat basket with a shawl over it, Albert had pounded on the door and with some curious amnesic lapse had shouted the wrong name.

'Alice,' he said now.

'That's better.'

'Alice Finbow.'

'Yes.'

'A.F.'

She laughed.

'Very many congratulations!' Albert said.

Alice squealed with dismay and embarrassment. 'Now you've made me feel awful! Did you think it was silly? Truthfully, Albert! Truthfully!'

It seemed to demand the truth.

'Yes. I did at first.'

The truth horrified her. 'I *knew* you would! Soon as I'd sent it I knew! I wished I hadn't sent it! Oh dear! You see? What I said? I'm hopeless. It was seeing you in the paper. When I saw that picture and – well, I felt so proud. I mean I wanted to share it – well I can't explain.' She stopped talking and summoned every reserve. 'Yes I can. I wanted you to think I cared about your work and I don't really and I knew you would know that. Because you don't care about it yourself.' Then she looked at him. 'There! That's exactly what I meant to say and I said it.'

'Congratulations,' Albert said.

They laughed joyously together, kissed on a brighter, less contractual note.

'Let's go back to your place,' she said, in a chummy way this time. 'I'll make you some tea and look after you.'

'No, not tonight, eh? Another night. This has been a good night.'

'Oh yes!'

'Yes, it has,' Albert said.

She laughed. 'You sound so surprised.'

'Oh no. No.'

She looked at him as though daring herself, encouraged because she had found his wavelength, then said: 'There's a reason you don't want to take me back to your place to-night and you don't want to tell me what it is. You see? I'm beginning to catch up with you. Did it take Treasure very long?'

322

'You're a funny girl, mate. If you know there's a reason don't you want to know what?'

'Yes. But you'd only tell me some funny lie.'

'I don't tell lies!' Albert's voice cracked.

'Not really, I know.'

It meant that she knew that he did and didn't mind. It implied an infinite licence: it lubricated the future; it made her accessible again. He could rub out the marriage, divorce, children, Kathleen, Bahamas, everything. For an innocent girl her instincts were fantastic, he thought. He must be terribly important to her. He could even tell her the truth now.

'I've lent my room to a pal and his girl.'

'Oh.'

His hand went out to the ignition switch but she held it. She said: 'Let's get in the back of the car.'

Albert looked at her, steadily, and she did not flinch. 'You'll get yourself into trouble.'

'I don't care. Not with you.'

'Look ... look —'

'Alice,' she supplied, helpfully.

'Look, Alice —' He broke off, finding her humour ahead of his; he tickled her and made her squeal. 'Now who's taking the micky?'

She came back to watch him again, with his own mockearnestness: 'I love to watch you talk. Go on.'

'Look, all they told you to do was deliver that bloody writ! Now look at you!'

Seeing the whole thing like that, starting so cold and now being so perfect filled them both with an excitement that nothing matches. The excitement of two humans who suddenly knew each other.

'It's the most wonderful thing that ever happened!' she said.

She was in his arms again and they were merging into that unity of emotion again.

Albert murmured: 'You'll have me falling in love with you.'

'Yes, please. Please, Albert. Please try.'

'I don't have to try,' he whispered.

'Yes you do!' She pushed him away and stared at him with a bright and alert expression, her insight and wisdom and knowledge squeezed up to a tripos level; as though to capture and clarify something left obscure; pinning an important fragile moment as you would the last vital butterfly in a collection. 'We must be realistic. You do have to *try* to love me. I'm not your type, I'm not what you *think* is your type. You don't know for sure. I might be a good lover. I think I shall. I feel it. It's all instinct, isn't it? There's no ABC. I love you so much I feel that I shall be a good lover for you. I want to be, Albert. I *want* to be. I shan't rest until I know.'

Albert held her hand tightly. Now it could be left. They smiled a secure smile and relaxed.

There was a red glow down by the canal, outlining the gasometers.

'Have you seen Geoffrey?' Matty asked. He was talking to Peter Fisher who was at the American Bar of the White Hart with Lois and a stranger. They were deep in conversation and Matty had to repeat it. He was staring round the crowded bar, looking through the glass doors at people passing by. 'Have you seen Geoffrey Evans?'

'Hello there,' Peter Fisher said. He was apprehensive of the distraught look in Matty's eye. Warningly he said: 'This is Roger Acock – Fleet Street man.'

'Have you seen Geoffrey?' Matty asked. 'He's not in his room, he's not at The George – Elaine's in a tizz. They're breaking the town up!'

Roger Acock nodded. 'I just came in. Never saw anything like it.'

'He must be with them!' Matty said.

Peter Fisher said: 'He should leave it to the police.' Then, giving Matty the message: 'We don't want TTT people to get mixed up in this.'

'They're breaking windows!' Matty said. 'Somebody's going to get hurt!'

'The point being,' Peter cut in to interpret, 'that anti-CND factions are getting out of hand.'

'It didn't seem like a CND thing at all,' Roger Acock said. 'I mean, nobody was sitting down.'

'Well of course there's a lot who'll go anywhere for a good old riot,' Peter said, in a jolly way.

'Where does TTT come into it, then?' the Fleet Street man asked.

'Well, they don't!' Peter Fisher said. 'That's the beauty of it! That is, they're just being used as an excuse to get rid of Mason.'

'I must find him – excuse me.' Matty ran out.

'Let me get it straight,' Roger Acock said. Then he turned and stared after Matty. 'Who was that?'

'One of the TTT reps,' Peter Fisher said.

'What's their worry, then?'

'Let me try to give it to you in clear,' said the Press Relations Officer. 'At the bottom of it you have a CND headmaster – Cedric Mason –'

'I must try to get hold of him.'

'He's away,' Peter said. 'As I say, you have the Civil Defence boys trying to get him out – I mean, whatever you believe and I'm easy – well, you have to be in this job – that's the fact of the matter. Now it so happens that Major Simpkins wears two hats.'

'I beg your pardon?'

'Simpkins – councillor and so on. Local big shot. He knows it would be unpopular to sack Mason on the CND grounds, so he puts on his other hat and backs up the Chamber of Trade boys against this gift stamp thing – do you remember?'

'Ah, yes. Yes, I think so. Go on.'

'So in order to get at the ban the bomb crowd,' Peter Fisher said, 'the Civil Defence fellows are using the Chamber of Trade boys' hatred of Treasure Trove Trading Stamps.'

'What does it all add up to?' the reporter asked.

There came the crump of a distant explosion; drinking and conversation ceased for a moment.

'Just this,' Peter Fisher said, crisply: 'If the public wants TTT gift stamps, then they should be allowed to have them.'

'I'll make a note of that,' said the Fleet Street man.

As he did so, Peter Fisher turned back to Lois. 'It's all very well,' he said, 'but where the hell's Albert?'

Lois gave him his drink, sympathetically.

'Bit unfair, after all,' Peter said. 'Him and his stunts.'

Outside the hotel six policemen were trying to lift an overturned patrol car.

'Albert!'

Wendy had opened her door as Albert went upstairs.

'Hello. Nobody up there now, I hope?'

'They're all looking for you,' Wendy said. 'That woman came and fetched Geoffrey. There's bin an accident. They want you down at the office.'

'Twelve o'clock at night? What sort of accident?'

'To that little one, that Jewboy Matty.'

Albert came down to her. 'What's happened to Matty?'

'He got thrown through a plate glass window,' Wendy said. 'Init awful?'

'Not dead, is he?'

'I think so. She was in a terrible state. So was Geoff. They went off together.'

'What time was this?'

'Hour ago – 'bout eleven. You might have told me he was coming! I had all me hair up.'

'He was a TTT rep,' Albert said.

'He was a Jew,' Elaine said.

'That's got nothing to do with it,' Albert said.

'He's right, Elaine,' Peter told her. 'We'd better stick to that. I've already done the handout. He was a TTT rep thrown through a TTT window – then you get the persecution thing.' '

'Burning of the Reichstag,' Geoffrey Evans muttered.

They were in the conference room at one o'clock in the morning holding a quiet inquest.

'It would really look better if the gift shop window was smashed, you know,' the PRO said, thoughtfully.

Albert exchanged an understanding glance with Peter Fisher; there was a team spirit between them.

They waited for the morning news, much as a theatrical company would wait for the first crits. There was the same feeling of bonanza in the air; the same scene of desolation on stage. The town looked as though a pillaging army had passed through several times. By appointment Elaine met Albert, Geoffrey and Peter for a transport café breakfast by the bus depot; the only one open at seven-thirty in the morning.

'These are all the morning papers,' Peter Fisher said. 'Whatever else has been printed I'll get through the cuttings agency.'

Elaine said: 'I think this will do.'

ASTONISHING SCENES IN GIFT STAMP BATTLE

CASUALTIES IN HIGH STREET CUT-PRICE WAR

This was the general trend.

'I like this one,' Peter said. He showed them:

TOWN FIGHTS FOR FREE GIFT SCHEME

'Marvellous,' Albert said.

Elaine said: 'They don't mention Cedric Mason or the CND at all?'

'Ah yes they do,' Peter said. 'Look on the back page here.'

A small item gave: 'EDUCATION COMMITTEE RE-INSTATES HEADMASTER'

'They've separated the issues as news items,' Peter explained. 'Well they are separate really.'

'They probably smelt something,' Albert said.

'This is rather good,' Elaine said.

It was a quiet, rational editorial headed: AN ENGLISH-

She read: 'We live in a country that prides itself on freedom of thought, speech and action. The Englishman's home is his castle, they say. And rightly so. If he chooses to fill it with free gifts or cut-price food then he should be allowed to do so. If he chooses to believe in uni-lateral disarmament, then let him. Unlike many other coun-tries this is no police state. We treat our minorities with tolerance and respect. Co-existence, like charity, should begin at home.'

Outside, the big double-decker buses were filling up with workers for the tractor factory.

'What now, then?' Albert asked Elaine.

She smiled at him. 'You've done enough. Now it's my turn.' To Geoffrey Evans she said: 'I want the sales pattern brought right up to date by midday. I'm taking it in to Red Sword – that means the twelve-thirty train.'

'Take me to your leader!' Albert said.

They watched Elaine Townend walk out.

'Grrrr!' Geoffrey said.

Albert looked at him.

'Okay, okay,' Geoffrey said. 'Not for me. That's trouble, sport.'

Albert said: 'What's Red Sword?'

'Only one of the biggest stamp companies in the country,' Geoffrey told him. 'They usually take our franchise. This'll be the biggest yet.'

'Then what do you do?' Albert said.

'Move on,' said Geoffrey Evans.

Peter Fisher said: 'What about Matty?'

'He'll be out in a few weeks,' Geoffrey said. 'Taking him some fruit this afternoon. Did I tell you they're giving him a new nose?'

Albert said: 'It's an ill wind . . .'

'I'm sorry to keep you waiting, sir, but we only have three lines – just a moment, please.' Dorothy looked round as Albert went past. 'Taylor's and Wilkinson's now.'

'Don't make any appointments,' Albert said. 'We're sorting it out.'

Whatever the truth behind last night's rioting, and it was never likely to emerge for only locals had been arrested and nobody had seen the going of the London task force, it had had the effect of bringing the public and after them the traders on to the side of gift stamp trading. Shops already lucky enough to be giving stamps were getting overcrowded with customers; shops not giving stamps were being neglected; traders were down on their knees and begging to be let in.

'Stick to the shops with the stars,' Clive Townend told the reps. 'Cut the franchise down to one in three.'

Albert said: 'What about our arrangements – it's been one in six, one in four at the most.'

'Never mind that, boy,' Geoffrey Evans said. 'Offload all the stamps we can and leave the trouble until after the take-over – we shan't be here.'

'That's right,' Clive Townend said. 'We ought to shift two thousand pounds' worth before the end of the week.'

Albert turned and looked out of the window, deep in thought. He had enjoyed working for TTT. He had enjoyed using his wits and getting the business off the ground. He was satisfied with the rate of pay – he would have cleared over a hundred pounds in commission already. But there was something missing and Clive's last command had given the clue to what it was.

Albert had driven down Market Street half an hour ago and seen Joe Keppings' greengrocery shop stiff with customers and more queueing up outside. He had told Joe that this would happen, but Albert had not for a moment believed it. He had taken it for granted that it was a spiel. Well, it wasn't just a spiel; Elaine was right. Treasure Trove Trading Stamps *did* help the ordinary man to fight the cost of living. In fact the gift stamp business, depressing though he found it, was legitimate. Albert had looked into Joe's teeming shop and he had been depressed. Albert had not been clever at all; his skill and his wit and all the work he had put into yesterday's publicity stunt had all been wasted. TTT had all the appearance of a fiddle but it was not a fiddle. And no doubt, looking back on it, this was the thing that had been depressing Callendar.

'Well let's get cracking.' Albert turned from the window. He had just got another idea.

When he drove away from the office following the other pink cars on their rounds, Albert had the ten books of stamps on the back seat which Dorothy had issued to him and another twenty books locked in the boot.

Elaine Townend came off the London train at four o'clock. She was tired and sweaty but triumphant. She hurried to the station car park, impatient of every slight delay in telling somebody about it. The traffic was heavy and she sat a fretful five minutes in the usual afternoon High Street jam. She pulled the roof back, found the sun too hot and closed it again. Outside the office there was nowhere to park, the service road full, bumper to bumper. She cruised round the block twice, then finally double-parked and hurried into the building.

There was an air of suspended excitement in the conference room; the thick smoky atmosphere of a party going on and all work put aside. The occupants of the room wore the statued, guilty expressions of a dirty story interrupted. Dorothy sat on the sofa, Albert on one arm, Geoffrey on the other, the rest grouped around. Clive and his dog were in pride of place and both seemed frustrated at being interrupted.

'Well?' Clive said.

Elaine faced them for a moment, just to keep them guessing.

'Go on with your story, don't mind me,' she said.

They all laughed.

'It was that time I was in the hotel bedroom in Madrid with that American woman and the lift boy brought the *Guardia* in. I'd forgotten to tip him.'

'Perhaps it was as well,' Elaine said.

Albert was staring at her. 'Did you clinch it?'

'Of course.'

'How much?' Albert asked.

Clive Townend said: 'I don't think it's something to discuss in front of the staff.'

'I always do!' Elaine said.

'And he always says that,' Geoffrey told Albert.

'Is it right we get a bonus?' Dorothy asked.

'Travelling staff only,' Geoffrey said. 'You locals are only temporary after all. You haven't got a real stake in the firm.'

Elaine smiled at Dorothy. 'Take no notice of him, Dorothy. There'll be a bonus and a staff transfer arrangement for you.'

'What about Argyle?' Clive asked.

Geoffrey punched Albert: 'This boy's travelling, aren't you, Albert?'

'I'll think about it,' Albert said.

Elaine said: 'Isn't anybody interested in the deal?'

'You haven't made it?' Clive said.

Elaine laughed. 'I have.'

'Twenty thousand?' Clive said.

'What?' Geoffrey Evans exclaimed, 'for a ninety per cent franchise? Are you kidding? Fifty thousand! Am I right?'

'No,' Elaine said.

Albert said: 'Seventy-five thousand pounds.'

'And ten per cent of their profits for the next five years!' Elaine said, her voice trembling.

There was an astonished silence.

Albert said: 'You'd have done better to sit tight. They know what it's worth. A town this size.'

'No,' Elaine told him, 'they've got the organization, we haven't. We've got more business than we could ever start to administrate. We'd want new premises, a big staff – I don't want that sort of life.'

'The excitement's in the killing,' Clive Townend said.

Geoffrey Evans said: 'Elaine likes wildcatting!'

Clive Townend looked at him.

Geoffrey added: 'In the nicest possible way.'

There was an atmosphere that came of what everybody in the room knew or suspected about the Townend marriage. Somebody always tries to leaven an atmosphere and usually makes it worse.

'You knew what you were doing when you married her,' Geoffrey said.

Clive smiled but the atmosphere was thicker; did she know what she was doing when she married you, was the mutual unspoken thought. Steve, Tony and Dick formed a chatting group by themselves, centring on the drinks table.

'I've got to park my car,' Elaine said. 'Fix me a drink.'

'I'll park it for you, love.' Albert got up.

Again Clive Townend looked at a possible lover.

'No, you won't,' Elaine said.

She looked her thanks at Albert and she went out.

'Seventy-five thousand pounds!' Dorothy said, to break the silence.

'And ten per cent!' somebody else said.

Steve Laidlow had a better idea and turned to Clive Townend. 'So what happened when the *Guardia* came in with the lift boy? I expect you all had her?'

The laughter was louder than warranted. Clive started the fight to prove himself a man again.

'Don't be silly. I'd had her five times before they came in.'

The men laughed the hard laugh of disbelief in sexual bragging. Dorothy looked at Albert.

'As good as my honeymoon night!' Clive Townend said. He wanted to tell them, now, while they were all together and with the subject, usually smouldering and resented, now brought into the open; he wanted them to know once and for all. They watched him hoppity click across to the open window and look down. 'Bless her,' he said, to put her clearly into their minds.

Albert was tensing with the anticipation of something

332

worse to come. He was not informed in the ethics of chivalry but had an acute instinct that sex is private. Is a shared two-way secret.

'Seven days and nights in a hotel room at Brighton,' Clive Townend said. He was staring down into the street. The people behind him in the room were uncomfortably silent. Albert had grown cold and his head was buzzing as if to shut out any more. He still had the view of Brighton front in his pocket. He had had the honeymoon in his head ever since the wedding. He had successfully calmed himself with the fog of optimism that obscured any actual mental picture of Tres and that stranger in bed together. A car door slammed and the engine revved and Clive Townend looked down at his wife. 'Oh boy! I left it looking like a plasterer's bucket!' he said.

Albert did not afterwards remember hitting Clive Townend or swearing at him. Townend swivelled on his good leg and almost fell over. Nobody moved or spoke. Then the Alsatian dog, who had been standing at his master's side, sprang at Albert, knocking him flat on his back. The dog's teeth were at Albert's throat and he was trying to keep his hands there for protection.

'Call him off!' Geoffrey Evans yelled at Townend.

For a moment Clive Townend watched his dog trying to kill Albert and did nothing about it; it was the final proving act in years of training and a difficult one to resist. Then he shouted:

'Hold! Hold boy!'

The Alsatian withdrew its jaws from Albert's bloodied hands, but kept its weight on its forepaws across his chest, its teeth bared. Albert's face was strained away, his cheek on the tatty brown carpet, afraid to move a muscle.

Geoffrey said: 'Well get him off, for God's sake!'

Clive Townend paused on each manoeuvre to prove his mastery.

'Stand back! Come here! Heel! Sit! Stay! ...'

The dog obeyed reluctantly and with a dog's imprecision.

333

Albert sat up and looked at his hands.

They all stared for a moment, embarrassed by the sudden violence. Then Dorothy knelt down beside Albert.

'Are you all right?'

'I think so.'

Clive Townend said: 'What the hell made you do that?'

Albert allowed Dorothy to help him to his feet and escort him out of the room. Clive Townend was looking at the others.

'What did I say?'

'You were talking about your honeymoon,' Geoffrey Evans said; he spoke as if by honeymoon he meant horseshoes and silver bells.

Clive Townend dwelt on this. So did the others. They again looked at each other, but in a different way. It looked as though Albert acted through jealousy; as though perhaps there was 'something there'.

Elaine crossed the reception room on her way back and heard running water and voices.

'That's your job gone, Albert!'

The reception room was a creaky landing with a table on it and the bathroom was a bathroom; it served as washroom and lavatory for both sexes. The door was open and Dorothy was bathing Albert's hands in the basin.

'He'll never forgive you for that.'

'For what?'

Elaine was on the threshold looking at what seemed like a basin full of blood.

'You called him a filthy, rot-mouthed bleeder,' Dorothy said. 'Or was it bastard? I think you said both.'

'I hope I said both,' Albert said.

They saw Elaine, said nothing, but watched her as she looked at Albert's hands, then at the bloodied water. She looked up at Albert.

'Just grazes and scratches,' he said. But he looked very worried about it. 'Have you got any antiseptic? Anti-tetanus?' He started working his mouth, checking for the first signs of lockjaw. The women were already conferring in eye language.

'Albert went for Mr Clive,' Dorothy said. 'Biff went for Albert.' Then, vaguely: 'He said something about your honeymoon.'

'Who, Albert?'

'No – Mr Clive.'

'What honeymoon?' Elaine said, faintly incredulous. Then: 'All right, don't tell me.' She turned to Albert. 'Thank you.'

Albert shrugged, implying an acknowledgment of his championship and chivalry which was not strictly accurate. He did not know what *was* strictly accurate.

'Go to my office and make yourself comfortable with a brandy,' Elaine told him. Then to Dorothy: 'You can get off home if you like – you all can. Will you tell the others?'

'My jaw's a bit stiff,' Albert said, anxiously. 'I think I'll pop down to the hospital for a check.'

'Wait for me,' Elaine said. 'I'll drive you.'

Elaine went on to the conference room.

Dorothy finished drying Albert's hands. 'I think I'll give her a minute before going in there.' Then impulsively she kissed him and, unusually for her, smiled like a pretty girl. 'You're very brave, Albert. I would never have guessed.'

Albert already had lockjaw and was unappreciative. He was trying to inspect his glands in the dusty mirror.

Elaine ignored the embarrassment in the conference room. 'Get this place tidied up,' she said, 'put the bottles and glasses away then you can go home. You all can. See you in the morning.'

Clive was staring at her. 'I expect you've heard his side of it?'

This stopped the migration towards the door. They had all been trying to escape a scene as a cinema audience tries to escape the National Anthem. Steve Laidlow, on the threshold, managed to duck out.

Elaine said: 'I wasn't going to mention it in front of everybody, but since you've brought it up, Clive, I will. If you have to invent sexual anecdotes please keep *me* out of them.'

'That's a nice thing to say to your husband. What sort of relationship have you got with that fellow?'

Elaine said: 'What do you know about relationships? You've never had one. Except with that stupid dog.' She turned to the rest, but was looking at Geoffrey. 'Sorry – but I'm sure that's not news to any of you. Goodnight.'

Clive Townend had gone very white. He snapped his fingers at the dog then limped out as if to do something important. The sound of his lop-sided walk remained in the room, dwindling; came the crash of his door.

Geoffrey gave Elaine a pained and sympathetic look: 'We have this in every bloody town.'

'Not quite this, Geoff,' Elaine said.

Elaine drove Albert to the hospital and waited outside.

'Not you again!' the sister said.

'I'm accident prone,' Albert told her.

She dressed his hands and gave him an injection.

'Is it better?' she asked. 'I mean the other?'

'Yes.'

'How do you know?' she asked.

Albert grinned at her and she looked to heaven in the theatrical manner which, with the popularity of medicine with the viewing public, many medical people were beginning to adopt. Addicted to television, people were now dying on the operating table happy and secure in the sure knowledge that, eternity apart, in the Nick of Time everything would be All Right.

The sister said: 'I think you just like us.'

'I do, sister. Most of my family die here.'

Albert's mother had died there, not twenty yards from where he was flirting with the sister. It was his regret that he had not been with her at the end because she had always enjoyed his company even though she did not always understand it. He had spent an hour with her that last afternoon

336

of her life, holding her hand and making the other patients laugh.

'Don't go!' he had called, as he went out. It was the last funny thing he had ever said to her. Two hours later she was gone.

'Come back to my place?' Albert asked Elaine when he rejoined her in the hospital car park.

'Do you want me, Albert?'

'Yes.'

'Then we'll do it my way,' Elaine said.

She drove him back to the office.

There were only two cars left outside; Albert's pink company car and Clive Townend's Mini-minor.

'I don't want to see him again,' Albert said.

'He's not there, darling. You know Clive. He'll be catching up on his popularity with the boys. Slandering the two of us and buying all their drinks. He usually leaves his car here to save re-parking. I'll check if you like.'

'You check,' Albert said.

He waited for Elaine to go in, then looked up to find her at the conference room window, beckoning him. When he got up there she already had the drinks poured out and two cigarettes alight. They embraced. Then Albert withdrew from her, unhappily.

'Not here. I get goose-pimples in this room. Do you think somebody once died here?'

Elaine sat down on the sofa. 'We'll exorcize that. Come on.'

Albert took the cigarette out of her mouth. Elaine lay with her face turned towards the big mirror on the wall. Neither of them commented on the sound of the gunshot in the next room; Albert because he didn't know what it was and Elaine because she did.

After it was over for the first time Albert salvaged the cigarettes and wouldn't meet her eyes.

'You want to say something,' Elaine said.

Now Albert looked at her. 'I must be wrong.'

337

She smiled. 'No you're not. Say it.'

Albert said: 'You were a virgin until now.'

'Yes.'

'But you've been married how long?'

'Ten years.'

'What's the trouble?' Albert said.

Elaine ran her hand over him. 'Well, it's not me. Thank God.'

'You're wonderful,' Albert said.

'Then let's leave it at that,' she said.

Soon he took her cigarette away again.

She was not watching the mirror this time.

When they were smoking again she said: 'Albert – can I say something to you?' Albert waited. 'For your own good I want to say this. Because in the future I'm going to worry about you.'

'That's nice.'

Unlike Alice's implication of a long future together, this implied a long future apart.

She was choosing her words, holding his hand, looking at him sometimes; they sat sedately as guilty lovers do, side by side, demonstrably proper.

'I waited all this time because I never before found anybody quite as criminally unwary as you.'

'Unwary?'

'Unwary of women,' she said. 'This "big deal" Don Juan approach of yours covers the most appalling innocence.'

'Innocent? Me?'

'You've a baby innocence, Albert. Sexually you're not fit to cross the road.' She smiled at his shadowed face. 'You're a marvellous lover – I should say, anyway, I've known no other. It's not how you do it. It's how you lay yourself open. No ordinary man would be idiot enough to take me on – you ask Geoff. Some people are never innocent from the day of birth. Some people never lose their innocence – you're one of those. I'm one of the others. It's not what happens to your

338

body. It's your relationship with the world, with life. It's where you stand in the universe. In the street of life, Albert, you can't see over the kerb.'

She was happily mixing her images as she had after their first collision.

'You're wrong! I'm five hundred feet above sea level.'

'Stop babbling,' she said. 'One day, if you don't watch out – and I think you're probably generically incapable of watching out and it makes me shudder – *one* day you'll meet somebody like me and your life will be ruined. But somebody more ruthless than me. No, I've been ruthless. Not that. Somebody who happens to want something else.'

'I'm not quite as simple as that.'

Elaine sighed her despair and looked at the mirror. 'You see, when it happens you won't even know. You'll think it was something you planned.'

'Tell me about it tomorrow.'

'No, Albert. I've done my best. There isn't any tomorrow for us.'

Albert frowned at her. She laughed in a friendly way. 'Don't look so despondent. You didn't want to come with us. You won't want to leave this town. You only think you do. You wouldn't be tied to the Crown Jewels, remember?'

Albert said: 'It's not that. I'm just not sure about the job. I mean this stamp business really works. That's not my kind of job. It's on the level. It doesn't need me. It doesn't give me enough scope. That's all.'

'I want you to cut clean, Albert. Now. Tonight. Believe me, it's best for you.'

Elaine Townend opened her handbag and took out a cheque book. She wrote on it neatly and clearly, folded it in half, gave it to him. 'That's my rough calculation of what I owe you. In salary and commission and bonus, I mean. I can't repay you for other wonderful things.'

Albert put the cheque into his inside pocket.

'Aren't you going to look at it?'

'Money!' he said, disdainfully.

She was amused by his sulkiness. She watched him stand up, hoist his trousers, start circling the room with his hands dug deep into his pockets.

She said: 'You're not accustomed to the other party doing the brushing off, are you? Don't let it lower your ego. This is for your own good. Go and find that nice girl from the tax office. Janice.'

'Alice,' Albert said.

Elaine stood up. 'I want you to go now, Albert. Quickly.'

Albert came to her and kissed her, then walked straight out of the room. She listened to him descending the stairs and when the front door had opened and closed she went to Clive's office and opened the door. The gun smoke still remained in the room. The one-way mirror had been covered again by the book case. Clive Townend sat in his viewing chair, looking down at the big Alsatian which lay dead at his feet.

It was not exactly what she had expected; but then it was. It was a kind of suicide. A relinquishing of command.

'Can't have him savaging people, old girl.'

Elaine went to Clive and took the gun out of his hand, laid it on the table.

'I had to do it, Clive,' she said. 'I had to prove myself to myself. I'm sorry I had to prove it to you. It was the first time. It won't be the last. I'm sorry.'

She held his face against her. It would be another memory link in his life, crying his acceptance of what was left, feeling against his mouth the breast of a woman not his mother.

7

Albert woke up at what time he didn't know when. He was in a dream sweat brought on by nothing more than Elaine's unkind remarks. It took less than what she had said to undermine his self-confidence. Lying there in the darkness he tried to get the dream back but it remained a membrane's thickness out of reach, like voices in the next room, like activity in the next brain cell. But he knew what it would be, by the panic and the sweat. There would be the bright lighted window with the laughing crowd inside and he unable to find a door to enter. Or it was the one where he was going to a party with friends who suddenly disappeared on the garden path and he found an overgrown door and knocked for a long time but nobody came and then he found that it was a disused summer house. Walking away he was called back by an old crone with whom he shook hands and whom he took great pains to impress, but she got on with cleaning a huge dirty cast-iron oven stove under a crumbling brick archway. Then he disappeared on the same garden path and was suddenly with his friends and rows of people eating and drinking. They lounged at long feasting tables and wore eating and drinking clothes like Romans as though banqueting and laughing and talking cynically was their career. Albert told the sneering chief-looking man that he had already met his wife and the man laughed to make a fool of Albert and said that he was not married, did Albert mean his bird. Albert apologized to a fat woman wearing a laurel wreath who turned out to be a Mrs Diefenhozer whose husband then got terribly angry. His friends were now pretending not to know him and everybody went on eating and drinking and laughing and talking as though he were not there. Then the old crone who was a different colour came through and Albert tried to engage her in conversation but instead found that they were surrounded by a wall of washing up. He had then told all this to a man who interpreted dreams who had told Albert that the dream meant that Albert really wanted to do something else. But that was in the dream too and added to the infinity of confusion and fears. He had worked out, also in the dream, that the dream meant that he would never be important and that only nonentities would look up to him and love him and applaud him, people like Hetty and Police Constable Sid.

'Dorothy!' Albert said.

She had her back to him and took a great deal of waking up.

'Hello, Mum? Is that you? Oh, I'm sorry, Mum, it couldn't be helped.' Dorothy sat at the telephone board trying to keep her eyes open. 'We worked till all hours last night again – well you know what time I got home the night before and you worried to death, so anyway the scooter was out of petrol and not a single garage open and you know that girl? Wendy, who I have sandwiches in the Wimpey sometimes with – I thought I told you her name? Well it's Wendy, she's got this friend Elsa – no, Elsie. Oh, I thought I'd mentioned them. Well they were nice enough to put me up in a little spare room where they live near the station – well, I couldn't let you know very well. Anyway I was all right and I knew it would stop you worrying only I couldn't let you know – just a minute, Mum.'

Geoffrey came hurrying up the stairs.

'Mrs Townend wants you, Mr Evans.'

'I want her!' Geoffrey said.

Dorothy was putting her fingers across the phone in case he was obscene; she waited until he had gone through, then resumed the composite of truth that made lies acceptable to parents.

'Anyway – Mum? I was saying, they've got this little room and it's got everything I want so you'll know where I am if it does happen to happen again and then you won't worry about me on the roads. . . .'

'This is Scudamore over again!' Geoffrey said.

They both remembered the red-headed rep. in **Keighley** who had over-sold their stamps at cut prices for cash, killed the take-over and forced them to fly to Ireland till it all died down.

'Damn him!' Elaine said. 'I won't be conned!'

'You conned him,' Geoffrey said.

The news amongst the reps that morning was that the dog had been put to sleep and Clive Townend had gone back to London and was starting another business of his own. Where yesterday the big mirror had hung, there was now a large reproduction of three horses galloping across the moorland.

'Six butchers in the High Street all giving our stamps,' Geoffrey said. 'They're flaming, I can tell you.'

'Three grocers in Butterhall Street,' Elaine said. '*Every* garage in town! It makes us look ridiculous!'

'It makes us look crooked,' Geoffrey said. 'He must have cleared four or five hundred quid for himself.'

'Well it's all he'll get,' Elaine said. She picked up the telephone and asked for her bank.

'You're not going to shop him, are you?'

'Hit him where it hurts,' Elaine said. Then to the telephone: 'The manager, please. . . .'

She stopped payment of Albert's cheque for one thousand pounds.

'No comment,' Geoffrey Evans said.

'How are we going to get those franchises back, Geoffrey?'

'You won't, sport. They're all doing good business at the moment.'

Elaine said: 'They'll have to be conned. Somebody's got to drop the hint that our books won't be honoured – then buy back the stamps. Give them twice the value if necessary.'

I'm not going to lose this take-over now I've got Clive off my back.'

'Don't ask me to do it,' Geoffrey said. 'It would take another Albert.'

Elaine thought about this for a moment, then picked up the receiver again.

If there was one thing Albert could do comfortably, no bother, it was spend money. Given twenty pounds a week he could just get by. Given forty pounds a week, he could just get by. Given a hundred pounds a week, he could just get by. Given a thousand pounds in the bank and four hundred in his pocket he had to restrain himself. He had to go easy or he could be in trouble.

His first call that morning was at the bank where he paid the thousand pound cheque into his current account. The clerk took the cheque into the office where he and the manager, Mr Wisbech, held it up to the light.

'Mr Argyle!' said Mr Wisbech, coming forward like everybody's friend. 'How nice to see you again. I was afraid we had been deserted!'

He went on to make it plain to Albert in the nicest possible way that he could not draw any cash immediately, it would take a couple of days to clear the cheque. Albert did not want any cash immediately.

'I'll cross off that little overdraft straight away, however,' he told Albert.

'Well that's taken care of,' Albert said.

'How much do you owe?' the manager asked. 'I mean – altogether?'

'I dunno, do I?' Albert said. He didn't know. He had so many tired debts that had trailed backwards and forwards through the county court that nearly everybody had been glad to forget them. In the end they cost more to collect than they were worth.

'I might let you in on a little proposition,' Albert told him. 'Get a bit of excitement out of life.'

344

'Yes, well we have missed you,' the bank manager told him. 'Our Miss Peters was always asking after you.'

'Oh?' Albert looked worried.

'She had to – well, that is, she got a transfer to Worthing in the end.'

'Ah,' Albert said.

'Now go easy with this cheque book until we've got this cheque of yours cleared, that's all I ask.'

'You know me,' Albert said.

When he had gone out Mr Wisbech went into a hurried conference with the chief cashier. 'Let's get this cheque cleared by tomorrow,' he said. 'I shall feel happier. . . .'

But twenty-four hours was more than enough time for Albert to write twenty-four cheques. The first was to the car-hire firm in Butterhall Street.

'I had to pay that out of my own pocket, old chappie!' Jackson told him. 'And the damage – and that change you got out of Smith!' he watched Albert fill in the firm's name on the shiny new cheque. 'Call it twenty pounds altogether.'

Albert looked up. 'Just a moment – we might do a deal. What have you got in the way of used cars?'

'Are you shopping?' Jackson asked. 'Here, come with me. . . .'

Mr Callendar was getting ready to go when he saw a Jaguar Mark 9 arrive outside the block of flats. It was in royal blue and shining chromium, and had every external gadget it was possible to crowd on; fixed spotlights, movable spotlights, flashes, badges and hub spinners.

'Albert!' he said. And he rubbed his hands.

'I've been worrying about you, Cally,' Albert said as Callendar let him in. Then he looked his old boss up and down. 'I don't know why. You look as though you've dropped sixpence and picked up five hundred quid.'

'Well you never know! You never know, Albert!'

Albert felt Callendar's suit, touched the suede waistcoat

and silk tie, tipped the homburg back on his head. 'That's nice!'

'Thanks, Albert. You look smart yourself.'

'I vish you vell to vear it!' Albert said.

Callendar's smile took on a slight glitter. 'What do you want, then? You're not here for nothing, Albert?'

Albert looked at the rolled umbrella on the table and the pigskin briefcase lying next to it; he wondered how much more of the stock Cally salvaged before the bums got in. 'I'm not keeping you, am I?' he asked.

'Depends,' Cally said.

'Job hunting?' Albert asked.

'Little business,' Cally said, obscurely.

'Does that mean you're still broke?'

'Well, you know.'

Albert had come to give him the fifty pounds back, then he had changed his mind, but now once again he could not resist the gesture.

'How much was that you gave me?' Albert asked. 'On that deal that went wrong. Forty was it?'

'Sixty,' Callendar said.

'That's right – fifty. I remember now. I'll give it to you back while I think about it.' He took out his cheque book.

'Ah ah,' Callendar said.

Albert grinned at Cally and flapped the book in his face. 'There's three thousand quid behind this,' he said.

Divide it by two and stop the cheque for a thousand leaves how much. Callendar worked it out in the duration of his answering smile, taking into account a deposit on the new car and all the trimmings.

'Still, I'd rather have cash, Albert – my account's a bit difficult at the moment.' He added: 'If it's convenient.'

Albert put away the cheque book and took out a bundle of fivers, peeled off ten and handed them over. 'Thanks for the accommodation, Cally,' he said.

'Any time for you, Albert. Tell me,' he said then, feeling Albert's lapel: 'Where do you buy your suits? You could do better than that. You know County Tailors in Station Road? Savile Row suits all fittings off the peg – thirty-five quid you mention my name. And ask to see their suede – you like this waistcoat? Another thing would suit you is the suede coat with the sheepskin collar – like a film director, you know?'

'I like those,' Albert said. Then, suspiciously: 'Have you got shares?'

'You do me a good turn, I do you a good turn. Got a radio in that car? Get the new transistor radio and tape-deck combined for car fitting. Show your Callendar card and it's thirty off. Go on, Albert, have a good spending spree. It's been a long time. Don't stint yourself. You got a good day for it, eh? Would you like to drop me off?'

'Sure,' Albert said.

They drove through the centre of town in the Jag., looking, unknown to both of them, like two peas in a pod.

'What are your plans, Albert?'

'I'm going in for property,' Albert said. 'That's the big thing now. You can't lose. It only goes up.'

'The trouble is it's already up,' Callendar said.

'Not the way I work,' Albert said. 'You buy an investment. The town's full of crummy little houses and old people living in them. Thousand pounds a pair. Get a partial mortgage to reduce capital outlay, get rid of the tenants, spend a minimum on conversion and you come out with five hundred per cent profit. Argyle Properties Ltd – I'm getting some cards printed.'

'How do you get rid of the tenants?'

Albert gave him a sinister grin. 'All ideas welcomed. After all, why should they be shut away in those crummy little rat-traps when there's that lovely cemetery on top of the hill?'

'Well, that's the snag,' Callendar said.

Albert rubbed thumb and finger together: 'Not if they've got hard-up relations. And who hasn't?'

'Interesting,' Callendar said. Then he said: 'Sound your hooter, Albert – quick.'

Albert blew the twin hooters, looking round. He saw two

pairs of legs and whistled. But Callendar had seen Solly Cowell and Major Simpkins entering the White Hart. It was the difference of twenty years.

Callendar sat back, happily. 'Things are popping again, Albert, I'll give you that. Just here will do.'

They were outside the TTT offices.

'Coming in?' Callendar asked, blandly.

Albert had a sudden revelation and snapped his fingers. 'You've got my job!'

'Just considering it,' Callendar told him.

Albert smiled at him, admiringly. 'You're quick off the mark, you old sod!' Then he felt into his pocket. 'Here, now I'll do you a favour.' He gave Callendar a small plastic container. 'Any more trouble with that bloody mongrel and just squirt this straight between his eyes. After-shave lotion. I can recommend it. But for God's sake keep the top on. Not that it would change your way of life.'

Mr Callendar stood outside the gift shop long enough to watch Albert drive the sleek blue monster up the High Street. He felt proud and elated. Albert's cheques would be bouncing all over town in a couple of days. He would get two years for false pretences – no. Knowing Albert twelve months with remission. Even so.

'Now I would like to see that boy get married,' he said, mistily.

If there was a wife and kids waiting for him when he came out then he might be ready to do business.

It was the dream that took him to the undertakers in 'The Ribbon'. He didn't know why. Was the old crone supposed to be his mother? You would never know. It was worse than the Sunday night play. Lot of bloody scribble. Albert had more this day than he had ever had in his life, perhaps more in cash and kind than he would ever have again. Yet all the while he was shopping, spending, parading in the shiny car, the dream stayed like a dead weight on his mind. If he had had a conscience he might have thought it was that.

By twelve-thirty he had bought the essentials and grown tired of shopping, tired of writing cheques; there came a moment when you found the wad of cheques remaining thin and the wad of stubs thick and it was time to leave it for a day or two. He had shirts, underclothes, two Savile Row suits, the suede waistcoat, the film director's coat which he was now wearing and sweating in; he had shoes, socks, ties, a hat which he would never wear, a stuffed tiger for the back window of the car and the radio-cum-tape-deck with a Monte Carlo Rally flag flying on the antennae. Why did the dream keep coming back, why was something pricking him?

'I want to pay ten pounds owing on my mother's funeral,' he told the woman in the undertaker's parlour.

'Oh yes, sir? What name, please?'

She was dressed in black but wore a piece of white lace on the shoulder to suggest that one shouldn't take it too seriously. Behind her on the wall next to a kind of serving hatch was a big painting of a landscape which could be taken for heaven and also, therefore, not too bad.

'Argyle,' Albert said. Then: 'No – Harris.'

'First name?'

'Albert.'

'Your mother's first name?'

'Oh.' That stumped him for a moment. If there was one thing he had a head full of it was women's names. 'Don't tell me,' he said, snapping his fingers, 'oh yes – Margo.'

'Margo?' The woman opened a book. 'Margo Harris . . .'

'No, wait a minute,' Albert said, 'that's what I used to call her. It was Harriet.' He gave her an apologetic smile. 'Bit old-fashioned. You know?'

'Date of interment?'

'Eh?' he said.

'When did she pass away?' the woman said, embarrassed.

'Oh Christ, you've got me there,' Albert said. 'Do you have to know that?'

'It will help me to find it more quickly.' She gave him a forced, encouraging smile. 'Roughly will do.'

'It'll have to do. I'm no good on dates. Where are we now?'

'Was it this year?'

'No, of course not.' It seemed a silly remark to Albert, who never paid any bill until a decent time had elapsed. 'No no. It'd be about five or six years ago.'

She covered her shock by saying: 'Then I might have the wrong book –'

'Tell you what – tell you when it was. It was the year that whatsit horse – whatsit – won the Grand National. Give me a few winners,' Albert said. 'I'd know the name if I heard it – started with an "M" I think. They nearly all fell that year.'

'It's a very cruel race course,' the woman said.

'Good prices, though,' Albert said.

'I'll just skim through,' the woman said, desperately.

As she turned the pages of the dead Albert was trying to remember. Nothing was simple, he thought. Everything was complicated. It was one of the reasons he didn't bother about paying old bills; it was like opening old wounds. Nobody thanked you –

'Margo!' he said suddenly, that was it. 'The winner of the National?'

'No, that was what you used to call your mother –'

' That's it!' Albert said. 'I mean, that's why – she was always racing around like a bloody racehorse. Never stopped working. Well, not until that year.'

'I'm afraid I still don't know when that was – hold on just a minute.' She turned and put her head through the serving hatch. Albert admired her backside which wasn't bad for her age. 'Fred!' she called. 'Look up the details on Harris for me – Harriet Harris. About six years ago.' She turned back to Albert. 'It won't take long.'

'Well I know it's ten quid – I paid twenty-two from her insurance and this was left over. Big fraud, those tin-pot insurances.' He took out the cheque book. 'What name is it?'

'Harris,' the woman said. Then: 'Oh!'

Albert laughed at her. 'I've got you at it now!'

A voice came from the darkness beyond the serving hatch as Albert was writing the cheque.

'Ten pounds eight shillings outstanding. Harriet Harris – six-one-one-double-three.'

'Eh?' Albert looked up.

'Her grave number,' the woman said.

'Blimey. For a minute I thought you had her telephone number – nearly had me Believing!'

Giving her the cheque Albert felt depressed. Somehow while the money was still owing on his mother's grave she was never quite at rest; never quite out of things.

After leaving the undertaker's Albert felt better. But it wasn't enough. Looking at all the purchases, all the loot in the big boot of the Jag., Albert felt that he had to counterbalance it. Who else could he do something nice for? It didn't take a lot of thought.

At one o'clock he arrived outside Alice Finbow's house with enough out-of-season red roses in the back seat to seduce a nunnery.

'Albert!' Mrs Finbow exclaimed when she opened the door. 'I thought you were never coming.'

'I'm out on business really.'

'Well you must come in, dear.' She said it as if it was now a condition of their relationship.

Albert went in.

When she had closed the door and put the catch on Mrs Finbow flung her arms round him and kissed him. He broke as soon as he decently could.

'What about Alice?'

'Who?'

'Janice,' he said. 'No, I mean Alice. It *is* Alice. Isn't she here?'

'No, it's all right,' she said. She laughed at him. 'I love to see you so nervous – such a boy!' She punched him playfully in the stomach again.

Albert knew what that meant. He looked at his watch: 'Sorry – got to push.'

'You'll come back, won't you?'

'Oh, sure.'

'I haven't forgiven you for the other night yet – you didn't come in.'

'Well, I couldn't, could I? Been no good.'

'Well next time,' she said, having worked it out already in exact detail, 'after you've dropped Alice off wait just up the road in your car. When I switch the light on and off in the front bedroom you'll know she's asleep.'

'Okay,' Albert said. So will the neighbours, he thought.

'She soon drops off,' Mrs Finbow said. 'I think she likes to dream. They do at that age.'

'Good,' Albert said. He looked again at his watch. 'Have to go now. Bit pressed.'

'If you must,' she said. She embraced him again, holding him against the bannisters. 'Give me a long, long, long kiss . . .'

'Phew!' Albert got behind the wheel of the car, exhausted, disgusted, revolted and sorry for Alice. 'That's it, then,' he said. He meant it was all finished. It had to be. Whatever Alice meant to him in his sentimental moments it wasn't going to be worth all this. The girl with the yellow hair would have to go.

He looked round at the roses, thought for a moment, then started the engine and put the automatic to 'D' for drive and said 'F' which was not for fast.

Surprisingly, Alice was in the graveyard. Wearing a white dress, floating between the shrubs like a butterfly. Albert saw her from the lych gate just in time. He swung right round and went back to his car, threw the roses back on to the rear seat, went round to the driving seat.

'Albert!'

352

He looked round, crimson with guilt. He sometimes hated his own name. The vicar was coming up, smiling.

'Hello, vicar? How goes it?'

'I have a tiny bone to pick with you, Albert,' the vicar said. Then he looked at the car: 'My goodness, what a lovely machine. Is it yours?'

'Well, you know – it will be. I'm in a bit of a hurry.'

'This won't take a moment, Albert. Just look down there in the gutter – do you know what that is?'

'Confetti,' Albert said. 'Had a wedding, have you?'

'You threw that, Albert,' the vicar said, gravely, 'two weeks ago. Isn't that true?'

'Oh yes! Sorry! Time they swept it up.'

'They won't. They sweep round it. You see, it's illegal. Try to remember in future?'

'There's not any future, is there?' Albert said. 'I thought you'd done away with all that?'

'You may be right, Albert. I may be wrong. But in the gamble for a kind of immortality, this is my throw.'

'Nicely put,' Albert said.

'Hello, Albert!' Alice had come to the lych gate from the graveyard.

The vicar bestowed a kindly smile on them both. 'It'll be your turn next,' he said. 'I hope you'll remember.'

'Sure,' Albert said. 'No confetti!'

Alice and Albert looked at each other without speaking until the vicar had entered the church.

'Hello, mate,' Albert said. 'You look lovely.'

He reached into the car and threw the new suede coat to cover the red roses in the back. There must be no encouragement now.

'Wherever did you get this,' Alice said, staring at the car.

'Bought it,' Albert said.

'Oh, Albert! It's lovely!' She smiled at him, admiringly. 'It suits you. It just suits you. It's the car you ought to have.'

It was this kind of thing that made her irresistible.

'Just been round to your place.'

'Did mother tell you I was here?'

'Yes. No, I mean. It was just luck.'

'You're such a wonderful liar, Albert,' she said happily.

And this kind of thing made her irresistible.

'Come and see,' she said then.

She took Albert by the hand and led him into the grave-yard. She pointed across the gravestones.

'I hope you don't mind. I found the number in the church register. I've been putting flowers on your mother's grave – and my father's.'

And this kind of thing made her irresistible. Two big bunches of white chrysanthemums stood out amongst the untended graves like Easter bonnets on a rubbish tip.

'His and hers,' Albert said.

She laughed at him, fast catching up. He kissed her lightly.

'Thanks, duck.'

She said: 'Why did you want to see me?'

'Take you for a spin.'

'Oh yes! I'd love to. What about your work?'

'I've resigned,' Albert said. 'Got something better in line. Come on.'

'What have you done to your hands?'

'Bitten by a dog.'

'You don't want me to ask questions, do you?'

He grinned at her, held her hand, pulled her after him. And this and this and this ...

Things were not what they seemed. As Albert's affairs seemed to be going up, his spirits with them, his end of the see-saw was actually crashing down faster than ever before to desolation and destruction and ruin.

They spun out to the country and watched gliders circling and ate ice cream. They spun along to a nearby Stately Home and parked on a steep hill, watching the deer grazing and the swans on the lake.

'What's the time?' Albert said. 'Four o'clock. How about a nice cottage tea somewhere?'

'Come home to tea, Albert?' Alice said. 'Please. Mother would love it. You've made a great hit with her. She never stops talking about you. When are you coming? Why haven't you called? Have I said something wrong? Well, you know what mothers are.'

'Sure,' Albert said.

'All right,' she said. 'A nice cottage tea shop.'

He looked at her. She was with him completely. He didn't have to say no or yes or perhaps.

'Or should we go to your place? I mean, is that all right today? We could take some things in and I could get your tea?'

'We'd better not,' Albert told her, solemnly. 'You know what you are.'

'No! No, I didn't mean that! I'll be good.' Then she saw the humour of it and blinked a fresh Sunday-school smile at him. 'We'll be good.'

This is where it became too much for him. About now. What he had been looking for was there in such abundance that it choked him.

'Give us your hand. Not that one, the other one.'

He took the ring from her right hand and slipped it on the third finger of her left hand. She tried to stop him. 'Albert, no! You know what I said!'

'This isn't a trick, love,' Albert told her. 'I love you. I want to marry you.' Blast it! he could have added. He had had no control over what he had done. He had not done it to impress anybody.

She was staring at him, half-frightened. 'Are you sure?'

It made him laugh but she was not laughing.

'Albert, don't do it. You'll regret it. Think about it. No, I mean it. You're not yourself today. I've noticed. You've quarrelled with somebody or something.' She said it as though to say 'think, try to think of something'. She was looking at his bandaged hands. 'Let's talk about it to-morrow,' she said. 'You know how you change.'

She was going to take it off but he stopped her; held the

355

hand with the ring on it, then held her face cupped in his two hands and kissed her gently.

'I love you, Alice Finbow, and I want to marry you,' he repeated, taking pains to get her name right. Not that getting her name wrong meant anything, he knew who she was.

'Oh Albert!'

They were together again once more on high ground but in daylight. Again she said many times that she loved him.

Albert said: 'That means we're engaged. You're my girl. We're going to get married. Soon as we can.'

'Can I tell people?' she said. 'Oh Albert! Can I show the ring – well, I have shown it, but – Albert, can I tell mother? She'll be so excited. She'll be more excited than me! I think it's what she really wanted! I daren't tell you that before, dare I? But I know it is. She even asked me if you would come and lodge with us –'

She broke off at the look on Albert's face.

'Did I say something wrong? Oh, you mustn't now – I wouldn't want that, would you? Of course you could if you wanted to. Anything you say, Albert. She's bound to offer us the best room until we get a house –'

'No!' Albert said.

'No!' she exclaimed. 'I was going to say no. Have I said something wrong?'

She was trying to pick her crime out of his mind, set it right; she knew that something had happened to spoil it, she was desperate again.

Albert stroked the hair from her eyes. He said: 'It's not the best way to start, that's all.'

'Oh,' she said, relieved.

They clung together for a long time but the unity was not there.

'Have you got an appointment or something?' she asked, suddenly.

'Yes,' Albert said. Then: 'How did you know?'

'I could feel it,' she said, simply, and with pride.

'Yes, I know,' Albert said.

He kissed her again very tenderly and she said: 'I'm not going to tell anybody, Albert. Not yet. I'm going to wait and see how you feel.'

'You can tell everybody, darling,' Albert said.

'Well, I'll keep your ring on,' she said.

But they were going to get married and they both knew it.

He was starting the car when she said: 'There's just one thing I ought to tell you. I think I should.'

'You're already married?' Albert hazarded.

'It's about my father – my dad. You don't read the papers or you'd know. He committed suicide.'

'I'm sorry, love,' Albert said.

'I just thought you ought to know. All the worry of his job and so on.' And she added a casual throw-away: 'It doesn't run in the family or anything.' A casualness that said that she had looked it up. Albert's mood on that first day had been no joke to her; the talk of the railway line, the scream from the bathroom. Suicide had damaged her and she would always be ready for it.

'Forget about it,' Albert said.

'I will now.'

The appointment was at twenty-three Marshals Drive. He had made it suddenly when he realized what marriage to Alice Finbow involved. How much of this she guessed he didn't know. Certainly she did not mention tea again. He had dropped Alice at her gate and gone straight off. They had made a date for the pictures that evening.

There were footsteps in the hall, the rattle of a pail, the front door opened and Treasure threw a bucket of cold water over him, drenching him and the bouquet of red roses.

She stood placidly and watched him gasp and brush the water from his face and hair.

'I've been waiting all the week to do that,' she said.

'Very funny. I hope it was worth it?'

357

'You never give complete satisfaction,' Treasure said. She noticed a woman staring from a window across the road. 'Come inside and dry off.'

'Now I see,' Albert said. 'It was your way of getting me undressed. Always did do things the hard way.'

'Leave those roses in the bucket,' she said as they went inside. 'You can take them with you.'

'Yes, Mrs Bluett, certainly Mrs Bluett, okay Mrs Bluett, I will, Mrs Bluett.'

Albert looked around him as she led him through to the living room. The hall was nice. No wallpaper, all white walls and ceiling. Carpet twenty-seven-inch plastic-backed thirty shillings a yard. Couple of tasteful Chinese prints on the wall. Gold bannister on the stairs. Cheap, simple, nice; a girl of taste, he always had said so.

He looked around the living room and said: 'Oh my Gawd!'

He shielded his eyes from the wallpaper, looked at the dining-room suite and lounge suite, all formica and lacquered brass and green glass, coloured veneer which had never seen a tree, spindle legs, shocking pink nylon-fur hearthrug and against the mock-rock, mock-brick, mock-wood-panelled jigsaw of the wallpaper several of the hideous wallpaper murals – Canadian Rockies, Botanical Gardens with Fountain.

Treasure tried to look severe but failed and put her knuckles into her mouth to stop laughing. 'He let me choose the hall,' she said defensively.

'What do you do in here? Wear sunglasses?'

'I'm in the kitchen most of the time.'

'That's nice.'

She had all ready for him a towel and some clothes. 'That shirt's never been worn, these flannels are back from the cleaners – drop them in again in my name. Here are some socks, take your pick.' She talked as Albert had talked, like somebody whose friends no longer dropped in.

Albert stood there towelling his head. 'It was well-planned, chest?'

She watched him undress without embarrassment. They knew each other better than they knew anybody.

Standing in the clean shirt, he said: 'Shouldn't we take this upstairs?' He meant this situation.

'We're not going upstairs. I'm waiting to throw you out. I just wanted you to know where we stand. I knew it was no use telling you.'

Albert did not make a come back. This registered with her and she looked at his face when he was turned away, tucking the shirt into the trousers.

'What's the matter, Albert?' she asked.

It was the catalyst needed to release the self-pity. Albert ducked his head so that she would not look at him and pulled her to him, holding her painfully tight, burying his face in her hair.

'What's the matter?'

She knew that he was not trying to make love to her. For Albert to break down it took a crisis. He had held her like this when his mother had died. And when he had seen Treasure crash to the bottom of the stairs. He had held her like this.

'What is it!' she said.

'I've got engaged.'

'Oh Albert! I thought that was just a gag!'

He sniffed, noisily, rubbing his eyes on her hair. 'It was. It backfired.'

'Can't you get out of it?'

He shook his head.

'How many weeks is she?' Treasure asked, wondering if she could help.

'It's nothing like that!'

'It must be!'

'It isn't, Tres, I swear it. I'd tell you, wouldn't I? I haven't even touched her. You won't believe it but she's a virgin.'

'Oh my God!' Treasure said. 'Oh, Albert, I am sorry, you

359

know I am. I've wished you dead, but not this. However did it happen?'

'I dunno, do I?' Albert said.

They separated a little and she looked at him with genuine compassion. 'Sorry I threw that water.'

'Ah,' Albert said. He shook her shoulder. 'You don't change, anyway, mate.'

'Who is she? Alice, wasn't it? She looked quite nice.'

'She's a nice kid,' Albert said. 'Have a fag?'

'I'd better not start again,' Treasure said. 'You go ahead. Are those trousers all right?'

'Trouble is her old woman's after me,' Albert said as he lit his cigarette.

'What's she like?'

'All right.'

'Well, that's not quite so bad,' Treasure said.

'It's gonna be dead dodgy, Tres,' Albert said. 'Flashing lights, corridor creeping, notes under the clock – blimey, I'm getting too old for that sort of thing.'

'You look old,' Treasure said. 'You look terribly old.'

'Thanks. That's what Grace used to say.'

'It's what every woman says when a man is too busy else-where. Have you told Grace?'

'I never go there now,' Albert said. 'I think about her. I expect she's all right. I got too fond of Fred. You know? And the kids. It's always a mistake. Mind you, she always reck-oned I should settle down.'

'She meant with me!' Treasure said.

'Yeah. Well . . .'

Unknown to Albert in his life there were the women he had used; the women who had used him; there were the two women he had loved, Grace and Treasure – who had been Grace again and, now married, had gone the way of Grace. Unknown to Albert he had missed the two perfect marriages and was about to dig a pit with Alice.

'I'll make you a quick cup of tea and then you'll have to go. Got the dinner to see to.'

'What, for Charles Joslin Bluett?'

She smiled at him and he followed her into the kitchen. The whole house suffered from having been furnished and equipped in one go with one lump of money; nothing in it looked like something somebody had fallen in love with; everything had been bought to 'go with' something else.

Albert couldn't help comparing it with the precious personal rubbish she had had in her bed-sitter when he first went to live with her. Only now did he begin to understand why she had fought every h.p. addition he had tried to make and why she had not minded when the unpaid for part of their home was periodically reclaimed.

He watched her getting the tea things out. She had not changed. With every slight step she had a way of swinging her skirt that drove him mad. And yet she must be going on twenty-four, now, he thought. She was not quite as pretty as Alice but much more composed and sure of herself. Her ash-blonde hair never looked as if she had to decide how to wear it; just a short, grammar-school bob, quickly combed. She had a way of composing her features, her mouth and eyes and jaw to say something which would require words from other girls. She could turn a look on you and say something without speaking; question or answer. She did it now, over the teapot. It meant this was a funny situation to find themselves in but it was mostly Albert's fault.

'I know,' Albert said.

'Never mind,' she said.

They took their tea on to a mosaic-topped table with brass screw-in legs. He could remember her kicking the identical model when he brought it home, eight shillings a week, to her room. 'It's all impersonations with you,' she had told him.

They had as much as most people could ever hope to have in common, but she was deeper; there were more layers to her. And she wanted more than he did although at face it would appear to be the other way round. When she appeared to go along with his immoralities, when she showed her understanding of his present predicament, his engagement to a girl who was not even pregnant, she was really understanding at his level, not her own. Like Grace, she knew Albert right through and therefore to help him with his problems she had to think with him. They had both loved Albert for the way he was and were both finally defeated by the way they were. The complicated relationships had not included the simple trick which every simple girl knows of bringing him up to scratch, getting him to the altar. They had indulged him too much, treated him too well, understood him too deeply; they had gone too far with Albert in the course of years to do what Alice Finbow had done in two weeks. They would go on looking for Albert in everyone they met; he would go on looking for them.

'What have you done to your hands?'

Albert held up the bandaged hands. 'Dog bite. I was attacked by these three big Alsatians.'

'One poodle,' she said. 'Is it all right? You know what happened with that dog bite before.'

'I'm a bit worried,' he said.

Treasure smiled at him, fondly. 'Such a liar.'

'Well. I need all the sympathy I can get now.'

'You and me both,' she said. 'No, I didn't mean that.'

'Yes you did. He doesn't actually ill-treat you, does he?'

She gave him a look that asked him what he was likely to do about it anyway.

'Fancy marrying a bloody Aussie.'

'He's not an Aussie!'

'I thought he was?'

'I wouldn't marry an Aussie!'

They were both young enough to have decided about Australians; about the Labour Party; about the world.

'I thought you had to get married, anyway?' he said.

'I thought I did,' she said. 'Then it was all right. Then I thought what the hell.'

'Did you get rid of it, then?'

'No.' She did something with the teacups that told him there was something to hide. 'It got rid of me,' she said.

362

Albert laughed. 'There you are, you see. You try and you can't do it, you don't try and you do it.'

Treasure was not laughing. 'Have some more tea.'

'What's the matter, Tres?' he asked.

'Nothing!'

'Oh, sure. I know that bite. What is it?'

'And then you'll have to go,' she said, pouring it out. It meant that the subject was closed.

'Nice house,' Albert said. 'Like living here?'

'Stinking neighbours.'

'Of course,' Albert said.

And about neighbours they had decided.

'What's he like? Charles Joslin?'

'Wonderful, kind, generous, reliable, secure, loving, punctual,' Treasure said. 'And I can't bear him to touch me.'

'But that's the main thing!' He did not mean love-making. She knew what he meant.

'I know,' she said. 'I feel guilty. He must guess.'

'Oh, Tres.' He touched her hand and she curled her fingers to hold his. It was part of touching.

Albert gave her a cheery smile. 'Be all right when you get some kids.'

'I can't have any children.' She said it casually but being Treasure it was like saying she was going to have her leg off on Friday.

'Don't be ridiculous!' Albert exclaimed, his voice cracking. 'If there's one thing you can do it's have kids. Try to stop you. You conceive if I sneeze at you. What is it – him? Well have one of mine, then – have two or three. I can recommend them.'

'It's not him, it's me,' she said. 'They told me when I had that last miss.'

'They're wrong, Tres!'

'They're not wrong!' She shouted at him, then said: 'They're right.'

'I don't get it. Why? What happened? You didn't do anything daft, did you? I mean I was always telling you.'

'I didn't do anything,' she said. And she looked at the clock.

This told him the truth. She had been trying not to let him know. Protecting him.

'It was that last fall!' he said. 'When you went into hospital. Wasn't it?'

She shrugged. 'I don't know.'

'You know!' Albert said. 'All those bloody abortions – a dozen in two years!'

'Yes,' she said.

'Oh Christ! It was me! I've done this for you!'

She squeezed his hand comfortingly. 'It wasn't you, Albert. It was me. It was us.'

'Oh Gawd!' Albert said. Then, as if to excuse it: 'We were having a good time, Tres.'

'I know,' she said.

She got up and went across to the window to knuckle her mouth again but not to stop laughter. The feeling of continuation was stronger than ever and it was too late.

Albert remained sitting for a moment by the tea cups. And was that a part of you? Were all those aborted lives forever a part of you no matter down what drain in the universe? He closed his eyes and gritted his teeth. Then he opened his eyes and relaxed his muscles and breathed deeply. He got up and walked across to her.

'Don't cry, eh?' he said.

She turned on him the look that said no.

'It's time to play horses,' Albert said, 'that's all.'

She gave him the glance that said yes.

They stood in the barren home in the newly-wed room amongst the newly-wed furniture and they rested their noses and foreheads together, their hands hanging limply down, like the two lonely horses in the big wet field.

THE URBAN
DISTRICT LOVER

For Janice with affection

Chapter One

On the Thursday, one week to the day before the inquest on Albert Argyle and while he was still alive, he called to pick up Mrs Bluett and take her into town to collect the materials for her husband's basket-making at charity prices.

'I don't care what anybody says, they should never have told him that it was hopeless and there's nothing left to live for,' she told Albert while he was kissing her in the hall.

It was a kiss of compassion rather than passion these days, for the open fire had been changed for a slow-burning stove.

'Yah brah Sahnah ah nah Kahsahtah, Ahbah,' Charles Bluett told Albert when he saw the two packets of twenty cigarettes Albert had brought him.

'He says thank you but you shouldn't have done it,' Charles's wife explained to Albert.

'No he didn't,' Albert told her. 'He said he wanted Kensitas and I've brought him Senior Service – ' he laughed at Charles ' – I understand you better than she does. You're talking better now, Charles.'

'He is talking better.' Then she said to her husband: 'Will you be all right?'

'Wah yah tah mah tah thah lah?'

Albert caught the fleeting, stricken look in the young woman's eyes. 'I'll wait outside in the car.' And to Charles: 'Cheero, mate – see you later.'

Albert went out of the house, leaving Treasure to take her husband to the lavatory.

'Funny really. You always wanted a baby,' Albert said, later.

'And now I've got one. It's a punishment.'

'Don't start talking balls. Mate,' he added. And putting

her into his car he nipped her knee and told her that she looked marvellous, which she did. She had always known the art of looking beautiful on pennies and now, with the kind of life she had got, it had paid off.

'He's getting worse,' Treasure said.

Albert nodded.

One evening five years ago Charles had come home from work and been relieved to find Albert sitting in his chair, reading his paper, smoking his cigarette, eating one of his kippers, chatting with his wife.

'Watch me walk across the room,' Charles had requested.

Albert watched Charles walk backwards and forwards across the living room. Treasure had come from the kitchen with his hot plate in her hand and also watched.

'Very nice,' Albert had said.

Charles had laughed at him then. 'I know it sounds daft, but I keep walking as though I'm a bit drunk. Charlie Wright said so. I tripped over the guillotine.'

'You know your trouble,' Albert had said. 'You're a bit drunk.'

One evening several months later Charles Bluett said something to Albert which he didn't quite catch.

'What?' Albert said.

Charles, a normally placid, gentle toolmaker, a man of systematic mind and habits had astonished Albert by blowing up in a troubled, angry way at Albert's not catching what he had said. Treasure, to whom it had already happened, swiftly turned off the television sound.

'It's time you went, Albert,' she said.

'I was just going.'

And in the hall he asked Treasure if her husband was fed up with him calling. Albert had been calling ever since his marriage as somewhere to get away from his mother-in-law. At first he had called to try to crumble Treasure's resistance and get back the relationship they had had before her marriage. But Treasure had remained faithful to Charles and Albert had become a friend of the family just to be near her.

'No, it's not that,' Treasure had told Albert. 'He's not angry with you. He's frightened.'

'Albert!' Charles had called from the doorway. And then the two words formed separately and with difficulty: 'Come – back ...'

That was the beginning, as Albert remembered it, of Charles Bluett's *multiple sclerosis*. During the past five years Albert had watched Charles gripped by the creeping paralysis and Treasure gripped by the Welfare State.

'I hope you are not putting the cane through the holes for him, Mrs Bluett?' Mrs Cornwallis told Treasure, accusingly that morning in the Welfare office. 'He must use his fingers as long as he can. It's most important. And is he doing up his own buttons? The doctor says he's still quite capable of personal things. Tell your brother to have a strong word with him. ...'

Swiftly adaptable, Albert had become Treasure's brother to the busy, efficient people in the local welfare machine, many of them predatory clerics who could find the God-hungry only amongst the dying.

'And make him use that wheelchair,' Mrs Cornwallis told Treasure. 'He's very lucky to have it. There's a long waiting list. ...'

She said it as though having *multiple sclerosis* was becoming increasingly popular.

'Wah dah yah thah?'

When Albert and Treasure went in Charles held up a finished canework tray in pallid, trembling fingers which had once skimmed the last ten-thousandth of an inch from whirling steel.

'I'll take that,' Albert said. However many trays Charles completed, however many woollen rugs, Albert always had a pound ready and a customer waiting.

'No you won't,' Treasure said, 'it's already sold.' However many pounds Albert had she was always ready with a reason for not taking them.

'You do enough,' she often told Albert when Charles was out of the room.

369

'Only because I want to take you to bed,' Albert would tell her, before Charles came back.

'I have enough charity, thank you,' Treasure would say.

They still loved each other but they had put their needs in abeyance.

Later in the morning Albert was knocking at the door of a tumbledown terraced cottage in Bute Place. At the absence of any answer his spirits lightened a little. He noticed a bottle of milk still on the doorstep and a newspaper stuffed through the letter box. This he pushed through and then put his nose to the slot, sniffing for gas. While he was doing this an old lady came up behind him and watched him for a moment before speaking.

'Now what are you doing?' she asked him.

Albert was depressed at the sight of her. 'Thought you might have gassed yourself.' And as she unlocked the door, he added: 'It's easily done at your age – especially living alone.' And following her in, he went on compiling a further list of hopeful possibilities. 'Or slipped over and broken your leg with nobody knowing. Or tripped over the oil stove. For instance what would happen if you locked yourself in the loo? There's no window.'

'We went all through this yesterday, Mr Argyle,' Mrs Judd told him, patiently. 'Now will you excuse me while I feed Jimmy?'

Dolefully Albert watched her take a packet of sunflower seeds from her shopping basket and sprinkle some on a saucer.

'Don't tell me you're starting a family?'

'Jimmy's a sweet little rat.'

She went around the room with the saucer making tweeting noises. A large brown rat appeared on the hearthrug and sat up to beg.

'I found him under the harmonium after you'd gone yesterday. He came out in the middle of *All Things Bright and Beautiful.*'

'Well there you are then! You can't live in a house that's

370

got rats. They'll come out in the night and tear your throat out.'

'Not while Jimmy's here.'

Albert watched the rat taking the seeds from the old lady's fingers and nibbling them between its fore-feet, delightedly.

'You can stroke him if you like. He's very tame.'

Albert knew he was tame. He had dropped the rat behind the harmonium on his visit yesterday.

'Its nice to have a bit of company now the knocking's stopped,' she said.

Albert had spent several nights in the empty cottage next door, tapping the walls with a hammer.

'You're holding up my plans, Mrs Judd,' Albert told his only tenant, bitterly.

The headquarters of Albert's business empire was based over the pet shop in the High Street.

'Come to Mummy!' A confused, middle-aged woman, her smile as homely as a rock bun and dressed in a badly stained green overall, was lifting some small creature out of a box as Albert came in.

'What the hell's that?' Albert asked, staring at the animal and holding his nose against the awful smell of the shop.

'I'm not sure,' Hetty said, equally puzzled. 'They keep getting into each other's boxes.'

A small boy was waiting to receive it into his arms. 'It's a sort of hamster,' he explained, expertly, adding, vaguely: 'Except for the tail and the tusks.'

Albert said: 'You'd better take a packet of birdseed to be on the safe side.'

'Seven and sixpence,' Hetty requested. And as the boy went out she laughed at Albert: 'Doesn't matter what it is there's a customer for it.'

'How do you know what to charge?' Albert asked. 'I mean if you don't know what they are you can't have a price list.'

Hetty became businesslike. 'Oh, I don't do it that way. No,

I've got fixed prices – seven and sixpence children, fifteen shillings grown-ups.'

Albert thought about this. 'But those chinchillas cost ten quid each!'

'But the mice only cost sixpence,' Hetty explained, 'so it evens itself up. Anyway,' she burbled, happily, 'we've got quite a lot in the kitty and three times more stock than we started with – I mean, you can't lose!' She got busy scraping out a rabbit hutch with a table-spoon. 'Mind you it's all go. It takes all the morning to get 'em up for the day and all the afternoon to put 'em to bed. . . .'

Getting used to the smell now, Albert looked around the over-stocked shop with a proprietorial eye. He had started the business not with any love for animals – he had always been more sentimental about meat – but because the derelict old building happened to contain an empty shop and because Hetty, an old friend and colleague, happened to be out of a job.

'It won't cost anything,' he had told her, 'so we can't lose anything. It's up to you to make your wages.'

It had turned out to be the one business that made the most of Hetty's only qualifications – a kind heart and a muddled mind. Given a gold mine with an established yield she could have made Albert bankrupt, but starting the pet shop with a litter of kittens saved from drowning and a few mongrel pups she was now making fifty pounds a week clear.

There came the sudden terrifying scream of a woman being murdered in the back room.

'Christ!' Albert exclaimed.

'It's them peacocks,' Hetty told him, worriedly. 'There's more everytime I look and they're the one thing there's no demand for.'

Albert was not surprised. What did surprise him was that everything else found a market. Besides the mainstay of puppies, kittens, rabbits, rats and mice, hamsters and guinea-pigs, there were tortoises, lizards, snakes, monkeys, bushbabies, chinchillas, birds of all kinds, tropical fish, all

waiting motionless as though paralysed by their own combined stink and the warm, humid, faintly exotic and slightly
sinister steam of atmosphere.

The peacock gave its unearthly scream again and Albert
found an excuse to come to the point.

'I need a bit of petty cash, Hetty love. Make it ten quid.'

'What again? I wish you could wait till Saturdays so I
know what we've took.'

'Be all right on Saturday. The old woman gets paid.'

'Shut your eyes and turn the other way, then.'

Albert turned away and closed his eyes. Hetty quietly
lifted the lid of a biscuit tin labelled 'Poisonous Snakes'
and took out some banknotes. It was a system that kept the
profits safe from burglars, Albert, the inland revenue and
her own haphazard book-keeping.

'It's not very businesslike,' Hetty told Albert, giving him
the money. 'You ought to give me a recipe.'

He left her galumping about the shop, dolloping out food
and water indiscriminately, scolding the lively animals,
jollying up those more inclined to hibernation, oblivious of
smell, atmosphere, and a hundred red, resentful eyes that
watched her, singing *Beulah Land Sweet Beulah Land* at the
top of her voice and answering the screaming peacocks with
an occasional 'Oh shut up you soppy things!'

Albert went out of the shop and entered the door at the
side, pocketing the money. What had been started as a side-
issue, a catch-prop merely, had turned into a life-saver.

He had gone into business on his own account after a long
and chequered apprenticeship in selling for other people,
with a sizeable investment and a lot of hope. It had started
with the top brass plate on the doorpost, now turning green:
ARGYLE PROPERTY MANAGEMENT. As money went out
and nothing came back and time went by he added the
second plate: ALBERT ARGYLE (INSURANCE). The indus-
trial insurance book, obtained on a swap for a second-hand
Vauxhall Cresta, turned out to be full of rapidly lapsing poli-
cies and Albert had added: ARGYLE MUSICAL PROMOTIONS,
ARGYLE DOMESTIC EMPLOYMENT BUREAU and a desper-

ate all-embracing ALBERT ARGYLE ENTERPRISES; a lot of
brass plates all screwed up the side of the doorpost, once
shiny with optimism and faith in the future but now looking
like a lot of badly-aimed life-belts around a drowning man.

It was typical of Albert that he had spent more time and
money on the brass plates than he had on researching the
business.

'If you know the town and you know the people you can
make anything pay,' he used to tell his mother.

His mother, who had kept the home going for ten years
after her husband's death in action with a multitude of
menial jobs and without a single brass plate, had made no
comment.

'A bit of capital and you're away,' Albert used to tell her.
And: 'Money makes money.' And: 'Only fools work for
other people.'

His mother, tortured with varicose ulcers, housemaids'
knee and bunions, was usually too tired to argue after a hard
day scrubbing other people's houses. It was her greatest
regret that Albert didn't learn a trade like his father who
was a master plumber just coming up for top rates when
Hitler started the war in Europe.

'You should've flown to Munich instead of Chamberlain,'
Albert once told her. 'You had a stronger case....'

Reginald Corby sat on the edge of Albert's desk keeping
his feet off the floor as he watched a crowd of coloured
mice playing along a hot-water pipe.

'Take no notice, Mr Corby,' Albert said as he came in,
quickly sizing up the situation, 'they're only pets. Sit down,
have a cigar, tell me how much you want to borrow.'

Albert sat down in his swivel chair, put his feet up on his
desk, opened the cigar box and showed surprise that it was
empty.

'Ah well, I'll have one of yours – thanks, old man.'

Through the social preliminaries and the first few minutes
of Reginald Corby's conversation Albert sat back puffing
the cigar and savouring the situation and not the slightest

bit interested in a word that was being said. Here was Reginald Corby, distinguished local citizen – also a rat who had driven his wife to suicide, but never mind that – a town councillor, leading estate agent and a member of Toc-H and all the best rotaries; here he was coming to Albert, sitting at Albert's desk, frightened of Albert's mice; there was his Bentley parked outside with his chauffeur behind the wheel and his second wife sitting in the back seat waiting for Albert to finish with him. It was something to savour. It was a kind of social recognition.

'Why learn a trade,' he would tell his mother at other times, 'when you've got an executive mind?'

'I leave it up to you, Mr Argyle,' Corby was saying.

'Can we have it again?' Albert requested.

Corby stared at him blankly.

'I didn't quite get the gist,' Albert apologized. 'You know how it is. Head full of business.'

'It's that property of yours in Bute Place,' Corby told him. 'I believe I may be able to negotiate a sale for you.'

'Which property's that?' Albert said, vaguely, as though he had a hundred. He began sifting through a box file filled with – in fact – bills, demands and threats.

'You've only got one,' Corby said, tiredly; then with a glance of revulsion towards the mice: 'Besides this.'

'Oh, that row of houses in Bute Place?' Albert said.

'Those two condemned cottages,' Corby said, heavily. Balding, running to fat, Reginald Corby had an air at once fastidious and suffering; occasionally he dampened his finger and moistened a tentative moustache as if some extra activity was demanded which would partly divorce him from this kind of room and people like Albert. As though he wanted you to know that he was not giving this business all his time and that he was partly elsewhere. You were lucky to have him there at all.

Albert the executive could no longer tell people like Reginald Corby to go and stuff themselves.

'Very nice of you to call, Mr Corby,' he said politely, it being part of the price you had to pay for success, 'but I'm

375

not interested. To tell you the truth I'm playing around with a few ideas myself.' And he added after a moment's playful conjecture: 'I may build a supermarket.'

The estate agent's only reply was to look at the sole of Albert's shoe, still lodged up on the desk; a hole in the leather showed a dry, dusty circle of nylon sock.

Resentfully Albert took his feet off the desk and lost his executive manners. 'All right, Corby, who's after it?'

'Nobody's "after it",' Corby told him, distastefully. 'The brewery has shown a slight interest, that's all. They've got planning permission for an extension of the George in the High Street.'

'Oh I see!' Albert exclaimed. He sat up and rubbed his hands. 'That's nice, old man! I thought you wouldn't be running after me for nothing. Well, well, tell me more.'

Albert had come to life. His dream of a swift, rich pay-off to his one and only property speculation had always been something like this. Selling what he had bought for nine hundred pounds freehold with a sitting tenant to some grasping chain store or millionaire speculator. No, not immediately selling it to them, but holding out until the price skyrocketed Albert out of all his troubles – his marriage, his mother-in-law, his accumulation of moribund businesses and debts, his own personal torpor. Only money could help him now and only money was what he looked like getting. What was richer than a brewery? What was another hundred thousand pounds to them?

'They'll give you what you gave for it,' Reginald Corby told him.

Albert stared at him incredulously for a moment of silence. 'You're joking of course!'

'Plus probably your conveyance expenses.'

'You must be mad,' Albert told him, his voice cracking on a high note of scorn. He stabbed his finger towards the window and the noises of the town. 'Do you know how much – are you mad? That tatty little butcher's shop across the street? Do you know – one hundred and fifty thousand pounds! One hundred and fifty thousand pounds they paid for that – a multiple draper – you're mad, you must be, Mr Corby! What I *gave* for it? One hundred and fifty thousand pounds for the lease of that crummy little shop – how big was it? Thirty-foot frontage? What I gave for it? Nine hundred quid? Ha ha ha!'

Reginald Corby had sat through all this with a good deal of moustache dampening. Now he said: 'But they are not buying a High Street frontage. Bute Place has no shopping potential. The brewery want your land for a car park enlargement and rear entrance – that's all. It doesn't affect their building plans. It's not even essential.'

'Well that's good,' Albert said, 'because they're not getting it.'

Corby did not get up. He adopted a reasonable, friendly tone. 'You could do worse, Mr Argyle.'

Albert leaned across the desk, cupping his chin in his hands and asked with genuine interest: 'How?'

'You can't do anything with it while you've got a sitting tenant.'

Albert couldn't do anything with it while Mrs Judd refused to budge. He had already spent sixty pounds bribing her grasping children to take the old lady into their homes. All he'd got were promises that came to nothing. Either they'd changed their minds or she wouldn't go. He'd taken time and trouble trying every trick he could think of short of fire flood and famine to get her out but without success. And for the past twelve months since the rates re-assessment he'd been paying twenty-five shillings a week on top of the seven-and-sixpence rent he got from the old lady – not counting running repairs and painting the exterior. The only ideas Albert had been playing with in relation to his speculation were ideas for killing Mrs Judd without getting found out.

'You sell to the brewery and they'll have her out in no time,' Corby told him, as though reading Albert's mind.

'How disgusting!' Albert said. 'What? That poor helpless old lady of eighty-nine – well, seventy-nine – out on the

377

pavement with all her sticks of furniture round her and rain getting in her harmonium?'

'No, no,' Reginald Corby said. 'There'll be alternative accommodation available naturally. The cottage is already condemned. Once the demolition order is signed she'll automatically qualify for an old persons' council flat.'

'Well let's do that then,' Albert said, 'and forget about the brewery. How long would it take?'

'It's not quite as easy as that.'

'No, I didn't think it was,' Albert said. 'What you mean is that you can't get a demolition order until a redevelopment plan has been approved by the council and the only plan that's going to be approved for my property is the brewery's.'

'I wouldn't say that –'

'Well I would,' Albert told him. 'You've got it all sewn up, haven't you? Another little perk for Councillor Corby – how much are they paying you?'

Reginald Corby flushed. 'That's a libellous suggestion. I came to you in the interests of the town – the public. That property of yours is dirty and unsightly – the whole of Bute Place will eventually come down. Money doesn't come into it, Mr Argyle. It's up to all of us, every citizen, to try and enhance the amenities of the town.'

Albert said: 'You don't run that Bentley on duty.'

'I came here to do you a favour – there's no reason why you should lose over this.'

'I'm bloody certain *you* won't,' Albert told him.

'I won't get a penny,' Corby said. 'It would be more than my position is worth.'

'No, I don't suppose you will,' Albert said. 'But how about a quiet transfer of a few brewery shares through your stockbroker to a nominee?'

The estate agent turned deepest scarlet.

'For instance?' Albert added, having struck home. Then he said: 'No, don't go –'

Corby was on his feet and heading for the door; Albert got between him and it.

'Let's see if I can outbid them. No, I mean it – look, I'll make you an offer. I mean I'll do business with anybody. You get fifty thousand pounds for that property and take a half-share – say twenty-five thousand each? As one property tycoon to another? Call it split commission?'

'Good day, Mr Argyle,' Corby said, trying to get by. 'You know where to find me if you change your mind.'

'I've changed my mind,' Albert said. He went back to sit behind his desk and finish smoking Corby's cigar.

About to go out, his visitor now looked round at him.

Albert said: 'I'll take five thousand straight cash – no cheques, no records, how about that?'

Corby went out. Somewhere below the peacock screamed again. Albert sat dreaming into the cigar smoke. Five thousand pounds. ... It would take him to Tobago. A bungalow on the beach, turtle soup every day, lovely girls in his bed every night. On second thoughts he could do without them. No point in starting all over again.

Albert only now noticed the big over-stuffed suitcase standing on the floor by the filing cabinet. He called after the estate agent but was answered by the slam of the outer door below. He picked up the case, which was quite heavy, and carried it out and down the stairs. Either there was a time bomb in it or Corby wanted an excuse to come back to see if Albert had changed his mind about the deal – to come back without losing face, that was.

'Mr Corby – you've forgotten something!'

Corby frowned round at Albert; his wife was watching out of the car window. She did not look pleased.

'It's not mine,' Corby said.

'Well, it's not mine,' Albert said.

'Come on, Reggie!' Mrs Corby exclaimed. 'However much longer – what have you been doing?'

'Hello Albert!' called a passing policeman. This was Sid, an old school chum of Albert's. Then, seeing the company Albert was in and catching Albert's evasive expression, he changed the greeting to: 'Mr Argyle.' And then: 'Sir.' Now Albert condescended a nod of acknowledgement.

'He's changed,' Sid was thinking, sadly. 'Getting stuck up. Not like the old Albert. Pity.'

'Mr Argyle!'

Albert looked round and up. So did Reginald Corby and his wife. So did the policeman. In fact, to Albert's consequent embarrassment half the street seemed to be looking up at his window where, inexplicably, a girl who appeared to be quite naked was standing.

'Where are you taking my things?' she called. 'I want to get dressed!'

'Get in!' Mrs Corby hissed at her husband. And as the door slammed shut almost on Reginald's fingers she said: 'I *thought* you were a long time. . . .'

'Aye aye!' P.C. Sid said to Albert, relieved again, his belief restored.

Albert went back to his door and entered it. Once inside away from curious eyes he gave the case a closer examination. There was a label on the handle which he now read.

> 'Miss Patricia Gort,
> Lansdowne Girls' School
> Oxted, Surrey!'

'Oh my gawd!' Albert muttered and he glanced back out of the door to make certain that the law had passed on. Then, going up the stairs he had the saving thought that perhaps she was a teacher.

'I'm most frightfully sorry. They couldn't see me, could they? I forgot I was starkers!'

Patricia Gort's pink face was visible round the edge of the partly-opened bathroom door. It was not used as a bathroom and there was no floor covering; it was the place where the aquatic pets were kept until there was room in the shop below. The room now seemed to be filled with steam and Albert could glimpse bits of washing draped around.

'My name's Gort – Patricia Gort,' the girl's face told him. Then: 'If you could just push that case in to me I'll get dressed behind the door.' And then apologetically: 'It's going to take a bit of explaining. Just give me a minute. Terribly sorry.'

Albert pushed the case through the doorway and she pulled it the rest of the way, then disappeared behind the door.

'I put all the fish and frogs and lizards and things in the hand-basin – I hope that's all right. . . .'

Albert sat down at his desk to wait.

'It's been so jolly hot today, hasn't it?' the girl called.

She tried one or two more attempts to leaven the situation as if anxious to break him down a little before facing him.

'You haven't got a looking glass, have you?' she called soon. And when he didn't answer she muttered: 'I'll just have to guess.'

Two cigarettes later Hetty came up the stairs and into the office, all out of breath:

'Oh, Albert – I meant to tell you. There was this girl after furnished accommodation – I told her to wait for you.' She laughed. 'Well I knew you'd fix her up if anybody could! Did you see her?'

Albert nodded.

'Ta ta, then,' Hetty said. 'I've locked up the shop. Feed the lot in the bath, will you – just tip a packet of something in, that's all I do. Night night.'

Hetty went, her big Baptist Chapel shoes pounding down the stairs.

'So there you *are*,' the girl said, stepping into the office, dressed now, glad that Hetty had broken the ice for her. 'I've been dragging around all day and there was all that lovely hot water and nobody here.' She studied Albert's dead face for a moment, then switched on a bright, confident smile: 'You don't mind, do you? You look as though you need cheering up.' Then, more seriously: 'If it's that offer from the brewery, I wouldn't sell! That was a try-on if ever I heard one. You couldn't give me a cigarette, could you?'

Albert was giving the girl a cigarette when he heard his car horn being blown loud and long outside in the street.

She followed him to the window. A woman was sticking 'L' plates on Albert's car. She looked up, smiling:

'Are you ready, petal?'

Albert waved, dispiritedly.

Patricia Gort had kept discreetly out of sight.

'Your wife?' she asked now.

Albert shook his head. 'Got to go,' he told her. 'There's a gas ring over there, tea things in the cupboard, some blankets in the filing cabinet if you want to use that couch.'

'Oh I couldn't possibly impose on you!' the girl told him. Then she followed his glance towards the open bathroom door and the line of washing and suddenly laughed. 'You're terribly understanding,' she said.

Albert managed a smile for her. He was just dead tired and fed up. The motor horn blew again as he went out.

She watched from the window as Albert went away down the High Street, sitting next to his pupil and apparently falling asleep.

'Dear Mummy,' Patricia Gort said to herself, dragging back the case and starting to unpack some more things. 'Arrived safely. ...'

She took out two packets of sandwiches, a bottle of Guinness, some plastic crockery and a police whistle.

'Turn left,' Albert said.

'Too late, petal – I don't know how to do it when you say it quickly like that.'

'Christ,' Albert said.

They were now committed to a mile of one-way streets through the centre of town.

'Look at the road not at me!' Albert snapped.

'Well really,' Marjorie Mason told him, deeply hurt; 'you used to be so sweet.'

'You used to be in a bedroom.'

'We've matured.'

'So that's what happened to us.'

'You know you're always welcome.'

'I don't get time, do I.'

382

'Cedric's always asking after you.'

Albert yawned, dry-washed his face. 'That's exciting.' Then he blinked away: 'Not that way!'

'Too late,' she said.

'Now you've got the level crossing. Good luck!'

'Oh my God!'

'Just what I could do with,' Albert said. 'A nice diesel train in the middle of my back.'

He looked at his watch as though estimating the chances but in fact he was thinking tiredly of the next commitment. Marjorie flashed him a smile but it did nothing. Even her legs only led down to the clutch and accelerator these days. He couldn't think about sex any more. All those years collecting women and now look.

'Married, harried and bloody nearly buried,' Albert thought as they came up to the level crossing.

He was too miserable to think about making love.

It would be like trying to break into song.

At six o'clock on the dot Albert was parked outside the electric blanket factory. A girl left the outcoming crowd and hurried to join him in the car. Albert watched her throw a hold-all into the back seat.

'Where're you going?' he asked.

She looked at him with large, tragic eyes. He started the car. There was the anger between them which came of mutual worry and being separated and the certainty that the other was not sufficiently worried. Was somewhere laughing.

She refused to tell him what he wanted to know.

'So what's new?' Albert asked.

'We got a bonus,' she said. 'Production's gone up.'

'Naturally,' Albert said. 'The electric blanket has taken the place of love.'

'Love!' the girl said.

Albert looked at her with compassion. The compassion was for himself. 'No luck?'

'What d'*you* think.'

Albert sighed deeply. Everything he touched turned to worry, is what he thought.

'Where're you going?' she suddenly asked.

'Taking you home – my early night.'

The girl said, flatly, staring straight ahead: 'I can't go home.'

Albert stared at her.

'Me mum knows,' she said.

She bit her lip. So did Albert.

This was Dorothy.

There was a time when Albert did outrageous things with panache and audacity. He was now inclined to do the same things through sheer habit. When he drove straight into the garage beside the semi-detached house and waved to the French onion man coming out, Dorothy was lying on the floor of the car behind the front seats.

'I'll get you some tea,' he told her after he'd closed the garage doors.

'I won't be gassed by the exhaust fumes, will I?'

Albert gave this a moment's consideration. 'Not with the engine off,' he said, regretfully.

He made her comfortable on the back seat and put on the car radio, softly.

'You'll get the news headlines at half-past six,' he told her, comfortingly.

'I can't wait!' she said.

The problems of the world as listed by the announcer mingled with the gloomy mathematical gropings of her mind; murder, famine, earthquake and disaster overlaid her calculations like a bit of dismal wallpaper holding dismal scribbles and unwanted telephone numbers. Supposing she was a day early the last time – that would make it the sixteenth – add seven for the end and then thirty take away seven more – or was it eight? That's sixteen and seven makes twenty-three, add thirty –

'Oh shut up for Christ's sake!' she told the BBC.

She was certain you weren't supposed to add thirty. It was

something divided by two and then a day either side. She held her face in her hands and the tears came through her fingers. To make it worse she could hear Albert whistling in the house.

'Is that you, darling?'

The lady of the house had just been to bed with the onion man and she came down the stairs waving a smoking incense stick to take away the smell.

'Oh blimey!' Albert told her when she came into the kitchen and smiled at him. 'Madamoiselle from Armentieres.'

She wrinkled her nose at him. 'Parles vous?'

'Them night classes'll be the ruin of you,' Albert told her.

She laughed with pleasure and delight and teased his nose with the smoking incense stick; a pretty, vivacious woman of forty-two, her cheeks and lips and eyes shining bright and mischievous as a puddle, her black hair with the grey dyed out done in a rumpled poodle-cut.

'Like it?' she asked, about the yellow chiffon drift of house-coat she was wearing.

Albert, washing up cups at the sink, gave her a 'once-over' leer. 'I love it. Aren't you supposed to wear something underneath?'

She came closer to him. 'Why don't you find out?'

'My hands are wet,' Albert told her.

She looked at the cups. 'They've all been washed once.'

The scene was little more than a tired re-statement. She ever-ready for sex, Albert washing up. He let her see the little brown stains she left by hanging up the cups wet with detergent water.

'Anyway it doesn't taste. Not in coffee anyway.' And 'Tea tea tea!' she said, following him around as he made it, still waving her little smoking sticks. 'You're so bloody English,' she said.

'Alice ought to hear you talk like that,' he told her. 'You'll be swearing in front of the kid.'

'Well who started me? You started me. Who started me? Perhaps Alice ought to know that! I was a different woman.' She plunged the incense stick into the washing-up water as a gesture towards her old respectable self, that pre-Albert widowhood, that smouldering limbo of grief and freedom. 'You showed me a new world,' she used to say, before Albert had grown tired: 'you opened a door. . . .' She never mentioned how many had come in.

'Where are you taking that?'

Albert with the tea on a tray had paused to pile a few dough-nuts on a plate. 'The garage,' he said. 'Got a bit of engine trouble.'

'I'm not surprised the way you run around.'

'Yeah.'

'You never seem to do anything except run around.'

Albert agreed so much he could cry.

'One thousand two hundred and fifty-three miles since last Friday tea-time because I checked your speedometer,' she told him, taking off one of the doughnuts.

'Jesus!' Albert said, his voice choked with self-pity.

'One thousand two hundred and fifty-three miles in a town no more than five miles wide!' she said, bitterly. 'Don't tell me it's all business – one tumbledown cottage and half-a-dozen rents to collect. Women, that's where your mileage comes from . . . .'

It was another tired re-statement of the facts. She was beginning to think there wasn't a woman in this town he hadn't been with. It was an embarrassment to go shopping with him. He couldn't go five steps without 'Hello Albert love – Albert sweetheart – Albert darling – Albert petal' whether he was pushing the pram or not. It was never Mr Argyle or Sir.

'Look at that girl in the Church Choir last Sunday making those vulgar sucking noises at you!' she told him.

'I told you I didn't want to go to church. I'm an atheist. You're supposed to respect other people's beliefs.'

'Even Alice has noticed it,' she said, refusing to be side-tracked with a religious discussion. 'Stupid and besotted

386

with you though she is. It's no way to treat your wife. She's a simple, trusting girl, just like her father.'

'She's never here!' Albert exclaimed.

'And all you do is complain, Albert – I don't know where we'd be without her wages. Look,' she added, on a softer note, as though realizing that she was repeating herself; 'why don't you bring that tea up to bed? Alice won't be home for ages – I've sent her off to the literary society straight from work. Well, she needs a break – all those nice, educated young men.'

'I'm busy,' Albert told her.

'All right. I'm sorry,' she said, in the placating tone of one who can afford to wait. 'I'll make up the fire, draw the curtains and put the light out,' she said, 'then we'll see.' She giggled. 'I know you don't like making plans.' And following him to the door: 'I hope you know how lucky you are, Albert – a pretty wife and a beautiful mother-in-law.'

When he had gone out with the tea tray to the garage she picked up a string of French onions from the table and hung them up on the wall beside half-a-dozen others, softly singing to herself in gay nightschool French the song *Alouetta*.

This was Albert's mother-in-law, Mrs Finbow.

'Sit here with me, Albert,' Alice said.

'No, you sit with me, Albert. You can't talk and eat,' she told her daughter.

'I'm not very hungry,' Alice said.

'That's not a compliment, Alice. Now just look at your food and stop moon-gazing at Albert. Alice, you're putting that soup in your lap!'

Yet another tired reiteration of the family circle.

Alice got on with her soup. She looked like the girl in the advertisement who is never asked to parties. A pretty girl with yellow hair and a good figure, but terribly tired; a tired skin, tired hair, tired eyes. In their five years of marriage in her mother's house the only week she had been able to relax was the time in hospital having the baby.

'That skirt is revolting,' Mrs Finbow said. 'I can see the tops of your stockings.'

'Marvellous,' Albert said.

Crimson faced Alice pressed her knees together and moved them away from her husband.

'You shouldn't dress her like that,' her mother told Albert. 'She's not the tight-skirt type.'

It was another old battle. The first thing Albert had done after he'd married Alice was to take her out of her tweeds and shirt-waisters and dress her according to his own taste in blondes. Unknown to Albert this had caused Alice, a shy girl, more suffering than anything else.

'Chaps keep whistling me!' she told him, tearfully, in those first months.

He dressed her in tight skirts, figure-hugging dresses, lace blouses and undies and nighties that she had to wash, dry and iron behind locked doors. It had complicated her life more than she had ever admitted to Albert. At the library where she worked she had had a special request to wear a high-necked overall and glasses. Men had started changing their books two or three times a day.

'I'm not going to the literary society any more,' Alice said now.

Albert looked at her. 'I'm glad to hear that.'

'Well, *I'm* not!' Mrs Finbow said. 'You can't give it up, Alice. A home is not enough for a woman. You shouldn't lose contact with intellectual pursuits just because you're married.'

'It's not as intellectual as it used to be,' Alice said. 'They get all sorts of odd people there.' Then, embarrassed under their gaze, she added: 'Well, men I mean. They only come to talk about – well, you know the sort of books. In front of us girls. I don't know where to put myself, sometimes. When they read bits.'

Her mother said: 'You mustn't be narrow-minded, Alice.'

'Oh, it's not the books. It's them. Well, they keep trying – they sit next to you – well there's only those little school desks and. . . . Anyway.'

388

Albert grinned at his wife. 'A bit of kneesy going on, eh?'

Alice flared at him angrily: 'I wouldn't 've thought you'd have wanted it – I am your wife.'

'No harm in it,' Albert said. 'I mean, it's better than Oscar Wilde all the time – he's dead.'

To his dismay Alice was crying over her food. Albert put his arm around her. 'Come on now, lovey – it's not as bad as that?'

Alice sniffed into his shoulder for a moment but conscious of her mother's disapproval she drew away and composed herself. 'One fellow follows me home.'

'Nonsense,' her mother said. 'It's your imagination.'

'I don't see why,' Albert said. 'I'd follow her home if I wasn't here already.'

'You could come and meet me,' Alice told him.

Mrs Finbow laughed scornfully. 'What in broad daylight?' She added: 'Or even in the dark! You're twenty-six Alice – a married woman of twenty-six.' Then to Albert: 'You're not to baby her – that's what I was always telling her father. What sort of man – is he nice?'

'He walks about six paces behind me,' Alice said, as if giving a sufficient description.

'You should slow down and walk with him,' Mrs Finbow said, rationally; not to suggest that she would be glad if her daughter would find a lover and give her a little more time with Albert, but as if she was shining a healthy light on bogies for her child.

Albert said: 'I don't want my wife walking home with other chaps, thank you very much.'

Alice smiled at him gratefully. It was the closest she had ever heard to an admission of jealousy; and it wasn't very close. Albert put his arm around her again; not so much in affection for Alice as an open defiance of her mother.

'You're so unworldly!' Mrs Finbow told them, furiously. She picked up a copy of the *Paris Match* and stared at it, uncomprehending but with an appearance of sophisticated interest.

Albert said: 'We're going to get out of here before we get corrupted.'

Angrily his mother-in-law got up. 'I can see you want a minute to paw each other!'

She stalked out of the room.

'You shouldn't hurt her feelings, Albert,' Alice told him.

'Hah,' Albert said.

'We are in her house.'

'Yeah.'

'She's very understanding really.'

'Oh yes,' Albert said. Then he leaned close and ran his hand between her knees: 'Come on, we've got forty seconds.'

'Don't Albert! No! Shut up!'

Mrs Finbow came back with a loud cough. 'I've started your bath running, Alice. Albert, you left the television on in the front room and the garage door is open. I don't feel terribly well. I think I'll go up. Don't let the water run cold, Alice. Albert, you did promise to help me with my phrases tonight.'

'I thought you were going to bed?' Albert said. Then he said: 'Oh, I see – silly question.'

Alice said: 'You could sit with mother while I'm having my bath.'

'That's what I mean,' Albert said.

He gave his mother-in-law a disgusted glance which she pretended to find mystifying.

'You haven't finished your wine, Alice,' Mrs Finbow now said, looking round for last things to remember.

'It's my third glass,' Alice told her.

'Well drink it up. You know what the doctor specially told me to tell you. It will do you good. Make you sleep. . . .'

'Chee!' Albert said to himself as he got up.

HURRY UP. Mrs Finbow formed the words with her mouth above her daughter's bent head as Albert went out of the door.

'He doesn't seem to have any *go* in him these days,' she told Alice when the door had closed.

390

'Could you see all right?' Albert asked Dorothy.

The television left on in the sitting room and the garage door left open was no oversight on Albert's part but yet another of the small chores he had to think of. By arranging the angle of the garage door Dorothy had been able to watch a reflection of the television programme in the garage door window.

'What were they talking about when that chap came in and that tall woman slapped his face? Was that Jeanette Sterke! I bet it was Jeanette Sterke. I like her. What was it about?'

'I dunno, do I? We were in the dining room.'

'Lucky to have a bloody dining room.' The tea tray and the remains of a doughnut were on the back seat.

'I hope you don't think I've been relaxing,' Albert said.

'Well aren't you going to get in?'

Albert, haunted and hunted, looked and listened towards the house before getting behind the wheel. Dorothy sat heavily at the other end of the seat as if rooted with cold.

'Was that your wife came home? Gave me a heart attack. Footsteps sound as if they're coming right in. Who was that with her?'

'Nobody.'

'Don't be daft. It was some chap. They were talking.'

'One of her literary society friends,' Albert said; it was faintly derogative of the girl stuck in his car when he wanted to go to bed.

'Why did he stand outside for half an hour, then?'

'How do I know?'

Dorothy said: 'Albert, how do you know she's faithful?'

Albert laughed a mirthless laugh.

'What was that for?' she asked.

Albert could not tell her. They were all bloody faithful. You would think he was the only man in the world.

'I've been faithful ever since we – well, started.' Dorothy spoke with a new-found loyalty; a sense of belonging and togetherness and dedication. 'I wouldn't look at anybody else. Or have chaps hanging round. Waiting outside the house till you go out.'

'Oh my gawd,' Albert said.

'Well you don't know what goes on when you're not here.'

'I couldn't care less,' Albert said, fervently.

This defeated her. It gave her nothing to work on. The desperation engulfed and paralysed her. She was in no position for breaking up marriages.

'Not that I'd marry you even if you were free,' she said.

Well that's something, Albert thought.

As though detecting this she straightened in the seat and looked at her watch by the dashboard light. 'Where are you taking me, then?'

'Nowhere,' Albert said, thoughtlessly. Then as she convulsed as if electrocuted, he added: 'Not yet.'

'Nowhere you said! And that's what you mean!' she exclaimed. 'I knew that's what was in your mind. If you think you can dump me in your bloody garage all night while you go to bed with her and me in my condition –'

'Shut up!' Albert said. This shocked her into silence and he urged: 'They'll hear us – no, listen,' he added, placatingly, 'I've just got to pop back. Soon as they're asleep I'll get out.'

'Then what?' She spoke bleakly, sure that Albert had no plans for her.

'I'll find somewhere.' He touched her to renew contact. 'Honest.'

With simple, trusting faith, Dorothy said: 'I thought you'd take me away.'

'You're joking!' Albert said. 'You must be.'

'It's not unheard of,' she said, with pride and dignity, 'when you love somebody and they're going to have your baby.'

'I would if I could,' Albert said. 'You know I would. Like a shot. But I can't just walk out. Not straight away.' It seemed a marvellous idea for a moment; a longing for the freedom of the old days. It did not include Dorothy. 'I'm a married man – with a family,' he reminded her. 'And what about my business? We can't live on air.'

'We could both go out to work. Get a flat or a house somewhere. Rent it furnished.' She faltered at Albert's expression. 'Sleep together every night?' she threw in.

'You wait here, love,' Albert said, 'then we'll see.'

Dorothy sank back heavily into the seat. 'Bring a blanket. I'll use your office.' Albert was getting out of the car when her mind reached the next staging post. 'Why didn't you take me straight there? That's where you usually take me. I suppose you don't want me any more. Now I'm like this. It serves me right, doesn't it? Creeping up and down those stairs. Now I've got to stay there.'

'Shan't be long,' Albert told her.

'Will you bring the cat, again?' she asked, urgently.

Albert stood by the car, sandwiched against the concrete wall, listening to sounds from the house; somewhere a door closed; running water stopped.

'She's just getting into her bath,' he whispered to Dorothy. 'Soon be asleep.'

'Don't go in there!' Dorothy told him. 'You don't go into the bathroom when she's in it, do you?'

'Nothing like that,' Albert said, tiredly.

'Does she get into bed before you go into the room?' Dorothy asked. 'You don't see her undressed, do you?'

'For goodness sake,' Albert said, 'she's only my wife.'

'Well,' Dorothy said. 'Me sitting here. I haven't even had a wash or done my hair.'

'You're beautiful,' Albert said, stifling a yawn.

'Don't forget the cat, then.'

Albert started closing the car door.

'Albert!'

He looked back.

'What about the tray?'

'Oh, yeah.' He opened the door again and lifted the tray from the back seat. 'Don't want anybody coming out for it.'

393

'Albert,' Dorothy said again. And when he looked at her: 'Kiss me.'

Albert leaned over the seat to kiss her – the crockery fell onto the car floor with a china crash. They both froze. Then Dorothy, staring at him, lost her fright and replaced it with disdain.

'You're terrified!'

'I don't want any more trouble,' Albert said, defensively.

'You're henpecked! You're a jelly-fish!' she said. 'I'm going to get rid of this and be independent of you. You've changed, you have, Albert. You even look shorter. You'll never leave her. You're stuck for life, you are.'

'Don't say things like that,' Albert told her.

Dorothy was sitting higher in the seat with a new determination born of Albert's uselessness. 'What's eight from thirty?' she asked.

'Twenty-two,' Albert said.

Dorothy started counting on her fingers, then said: 'Have you got a pencil and paper?'

Albert found her a pencil and paper and watched for a moment as she started scribbling her desperate calculations. He left the crockery where it was and tiptoed away.

'Oh God! It *can't* be,' he heard her whispering.

But it was. Albert knew this better than she did. He had been through this depressing situation many more times with many other girls. It was always going to be the last time and it never was. He knew when she had conceived, he knew when she would find out about it and when she would give up trying. He knew with a dead, leaden certainty the worries of the next few weeks. Renewing contact with people he never wanted to see again, the furtive chain of furtive people, the arrangements, the visits, the passing of money – God, the money! A hundred and fifty pounds – no, guineas – was the latest price. His and Treasure's first abortion had cost only twenty – in fact had cost him nothing for he had slipped somebody a record player from the shop where he worked.

Albert let himself into the house, tired, exhausted, beaten.

There was a time when he could take this kind of thing in his stride. Very quietly he by-passed the sitting room and crept up the stairs to the bathroom door, listened for a moment to the splashing of water inside.

'Pssst!' he whispered at the bathroom door. What a way to conduct a marriage, he thought.

The bathroom door opened and Mrs Finbow smiled out at him, leaning from the bath. 'You're just in time to rub my back,' she whispered.

Albert, his resistance gone, went into the bathroom and washed her all over with as much passion as he would wash his car. She was too clever for both of them and he might as well give up. He always saw her move one move too late. Of course Alice was too tired for her bath. Looking for Alice was like looking for the pea under the conjurer's nut-shell. Alice only got her husband when her mother had finished with him or didn't want him and by that time one or other of them was asleep.

'Dormez-vous?' Mrs Finbow said, a little later, sitting up in bed in a pink negligee. 'Albert!'

'Eh?' Albert blinked awake. He was sitting on the edge of her bed, the French reader drooping in his hands.

'Were you asleep?' she asked, complainingly. 'It's not much of a compliment. Still, I expect you find French a little boring. Well, you don't have any practical use for it. Put the book away. Let's just see if Alice has gone off and then you can get undressed.'

She pulled back the eiderdown and the covers, taking her time about covering her legs as she got out of bed and walked past him, running her fingers through his hair, eneveloped in clouds of *Je Reviens* and burnt incense with the middle-aged approach to sex. Albert dutifully followed her out, crossed the landing, waited while she very carefully turned the handle and peeped into their room ... another old ritual that had started on Albert's first visit and never faltered.

'Bless her,' Mrs Finbow whispered, 'right off....'

Alice lay with her eyes closed, her tired face on one tired

arm. Not according to ritual was the sudden loud blast of Albert's car horn from downstairs.

'Heaven's!' Mrs Finbow exclaimed. On a frightened reflex she slammed the door – then swiftly opened it again.

Alice looked at them.

'Are you awake?' Mrs Finbow said, crossly. Then: 'I should think so. Enough to wake the dead. It sounded right inside the house –'

Albert was anxiously trying to avert another: 'I'll go down and see if –'

'No, it's all right, they've gone past.' Mrs Finbow had crossed to the landing window and was peering out.

'I'll get to bed, then.'

Mrs Finbow turned swiftly but too late. Albert was already inside the bedroom and undoing his shirt.

'Good night, Mrs Finbow,' he told her. It was his way of insulting her.

'Good night, Mother,' Alice called.

Albert closed the door.

'*Merde*,' Mrs Finbow muttered angrily, then: 'Shit!' in case she had got the wrong word.

'You look lovely, mate,' Albert told his wife.

He came to the bed and stooped over her, put his hands on her breasts, kissed her on the mouth. She was the first girl he had wanted in days.

'Albert. ... Oh, Albert,' she said.

They whispered as though sinning and Albert pulled the headboard of the bed a little away from the wall. Alice became apprehensive at this.

'You won't make a lot of noise?' she asked.

Albert stopped getting undressed. 'That kills me, that does.'

'I'm sorry,' she said, wretchedly. 'I'm sorry.'

Albert lit a cigarette.

'Come to bed, Albert,' she said. 'I said I'm sorry.' He turned his back on her. 'I want you, Albert. I don't care how much noise you make.'

'The story of our bloody married life,' Albert said. 'I'll never understand how we got that kid. No wonder it can't talk.'

There was a silence. He turned and looked at her. Alice was crying, silently. He went to her, stroked her hair.

'Ah, he's all right. Not old enough yet.' He put on one of his old voices to make her smile: 'I was being beastly. Come on, move over.'

He lay down beside her and the bed creaked. They heard Mrs Finbow cough in the next room. The warm beginnings of an embrace went cold and he sat up again.

'Sorry, Albert,' she said.

'It's not your fault, love.'

'I don't think she wanted you to come to bed yet.'

'Marvellous,' Albert said.

'She can't go to sleep unless you're in the room.'

'Is that what she told you?'

'I know it's not very fair on you,' Alice said.

'It's not very fair on you,' Albert said.

'I'll come home early tomorrow night. She'll be at Bingo,' Alice said.

'And so the weeks passed,' Albert said, in his narrator's voice, 'the summer slowly changing to Autumn and then Winter and later on the Spring.'

Alice laughed at him. 'That was like you used to be.'

'Okay,' Albert said, 'let's get divorced. Happy days.'

Alice just looked at him, sadly, from the pillow. 'I think you're right, Albert. No, I mean it. I worry about you. You're not the same Albert. Marriage doesn't suit you – or else I don't. You don't get inspired like you used to. Rush around with crazy ideas – big ideas, Albert, you used to have.'

Albert had caught her sadness for the death of his vintage years. 'They didn't come to anything, did they?'

'That didn't matter! That was the whole point – that didn't matter. You were terribly ambitious. And you used to get angry more – about silly things I mean. About the public and social conditions and hire purchase. You were always bouncing, Albert.'

'I must be getting old,' Albert said.

'I don't think it's age. I think it's marriage. I think it's me.'

Albert looked down at her, soberly, and she met his eyes.

'I'm not your type,' she said. 'I never was. Tax office girl. Librarian. I fell in love with you and you were sorry for me. It's true. I couldn't keep up with you so you slowed down for me. You're not yourself any more, Albert. You should have married Treasure.'

'Ah!' Albert said, scornfully.

'You dress me like her,' Alice said, 'but it's no good. I don't give you any sparks.'

Albert quietly slid his hand under the bed-clothes. She wriggled but refused to change mood.

'I don't even know how to make love,' she said. 'I'm inhibited.'

'Have a bloody job to be anything else in this room,' Albert told her. 'What with the bed squeaking and your mother with her ear to the wall – that's what's ruined your love life. We'll get the hell out of here. She can keep her semi-detached and her Spanish onions – where did that one come from?'

Albert looked at an onion which lay on the dressing table.

Alice shrugged, bewildered. 'It was in the bed.'

'A virility charm or Black Mass – I wouldn't put anything past her.'

Alice reached for his hand. 'Put the light out, darling.'

The sound of Albert switching off the light brought a new spate of coughing and the rustling of pages from the next room.

'You'd better just pop in and see her,' Alice suggested. 'Then she'll go to sleep.'

'Well just make sure you don't,' Albert said.

He slipped out of the bedroom. He also slipped past his mother-in-law's room and straight down the stairs, collecting the cat on the way.

Amongst all the disadvantages of having two women in the house was the single advantage that if he was not in one bedroom they took it for granted he was in the other.

Three policemen were grouped like blots of ink in the darkness by the garage door when Albert went out with the cat. Police Constable Sid smiled his relief at Albert's appearance.

'Hello, Albert.' And to his colleagues: 'I told you it was Albert's house.' Then to Albert: 'Did you know there's a bird asleep in your car?'

'Yes,' Albert said.

'There you are,' P.C. Sid said to his comrades, 'I told you he'd know.' And to Albert: 'Didn't want to wake up the family, eh boy?'

'Thanks,' Albert said. Then he said: 'Don't go, you lot. . . .'

He got the three policemen to pull the car silently out of the garage and down the road without starting the engine or waking Dorothy who was now slumped as though dead, her head against the cold door window.

'Do the same for you,' Albert told them.

Two of the policemen went off laughing, Sid hovered around, hopefully.

'You got something on, Albert?'

'No, mate.'

'I thought you'd got something on,' Sid said, disappointed. 'Been a long while. Is she all right? Not dead, is she?'

'I don't think so,' Albert said, regretfully.

'No individualism any more,' the constable said. 'She was blowing that horn earlier on. It's illegal after sunset. Still, it's all we've had tonight. Dull old world.'

Albert nodded. 'We're all in the same boat, Sid.'

Sid said: 'Yes, but you never used to row the same way, Albert.'

'Got married, didn't I?'

'That was a mistake!' the constable said, fervently. 'I said so at the time. Tie you down and everybody's tied down. You heard about Cally?'

'Who?' Albert said.

'Cally Callendar. Old Cally!' There was a note of shocked

reproof in the policeman's voice that Albert had forgotten him.

The name came to Albert like a breath of life from a previous existence. 'He's not dead, is he?'

'Worse than that,' Sid said, 'he's working at the tractor factory.'

'Oh my God!' Albert exclaimed.

'Yes,' Sid said, mournfully.

They dwelt in sad and silent communion on what might have been patent evidence that the world had indeed come to an end.

'Poor old Cally,' Albert said.

'There's always somebody worse than you are,' Sid said. 'I should get her home if I were you.'

He sighed and shook his head as he watched Albert drive away with the sleeping girl and the cat. He couldn't think of many places you could take them in this town after midnight.

'It sometimes takes a stranger to get things into perspective,' Patricia Gort said.

'What do you think then?' Albert asked.

'I think you're in an absolutely ghastly mess,' she said, lightly. 'I don't honestly think you stand a chance. Well, you are your own worst enemy, aren't you? You've spent all your life collecting women – now you've got them. Logical, isn't it? I don't know whether you know anything about logic.' She looked at him, critically. 'No, I shouldn't think you do. Motivation? Sublimation? Consequences? That sort of thing? It's all a question of applied thought – that's why we have brains and animals don't. Not in the accepted sense. Why did you bring that cat up here?'

'*I* never stop thinking,' Albert said.

'But you probably think in circles,' Patricia Gort said, knowledgeably. 'Lots of people do. Mummy does. She's a beautician so it doesn't matter – I mean it's all right thinking in circles if you're not going anywhere. Daddy's a doctor so he can't afford to. Do you see what I mean?'

'I suppose so,' Albert said.

'I don't think you do, I don't think you're capable of thinking. You're absolutely bogged down. I shouldn't say that, it's a meaningless cliché. The absolute fact is – I use the word in its proper sense – where you once used to propel yourself you are now being propelled. And by the same force – if you can call them that.'

'Don't you ever stop talking?' Albert asked her.

'I'm only trying to help you. You come in here looking like death and absolutely – not strictly absolutely – at your wits' end. Well, I am a woman, you know.' She laughed and then said, abruptly: 'That doesn't help you, does it?' Now she clicked her fingers: 'Yes, I think that's given it to me.'

Albert just looked at her and she went on:

'The logic of your situation. You see the logical consequence of being a womanizer – a *successful* womanizer – is that in the end you will be completely and utterly hagridden! Well that's you, isn't it?'

'Approximately,' Albert said.

He was lying full length on the office couch watching the amateur psychiatrist pour out two more glasses of Guinness. She shot him a serious glance as if she had just operated on him and wanted to see if he was dead. She gave him then an encouraging smile when she saw him watching her. It seemed to say, 'Don't worry, you are going to get better.'

It was not at all a cosy situation; the rickety make-do furniture, the shade-less fly spotted bulb, the smells from the pet shop; the girl dressed from head to toe in a faded and crumpled pink woolly siren suit which had everything except ears and clashed hideously with the red in her hair and the freckled pink of her skin and was only the worse for matching her over-applied and half-removed-for-bed lipstick. He had found her asleep in it and he had no doubt he would find her shopping in the High Street in it; it was a sort of general purpose wearable sleeping bag handed down from Mummy's wartime fire-watching wardrobe. Albert, who had undressed a bit in three bedrooms so far that night was wearing trousers with a pyjama jacket instead of a shirt, carpet-slippers with no socks and a fur-collared short over-coat, a relic of a long-past affluence. Come upon suddenly the scene might have been 'Survivors from total war' or, except for the cat washing itself in front of the workable bar of the rusty electric fire, 'Another attempt on the North Face of the Eiger'.

'Ding dong!' Patricia Gort said, cheerfully, giving him his glass of Guinness and raising her own.

Cally working in a factory! Albert was thinking. It was like lions in a circus. Elephants in a zoo. It was a long time since Albert had gone trumpeting through the jungle of this urban district but until now he had always had the saving, comforting feeling – which every noble marauding animal must have even in captivity – that the jungle was always there to go back to if ever the chance came for escape. Now he was not so certain. Cally Callendar working in the Agri-cultural Tractor Factory! It was like finding the king of the beasts whom you had left in charge keeping the path trod-den and the undergrowth back now sitting in the next cage and eating a bun.

'Well don't cry!' Patricia Gort told him.

'I'm not crying,' Albert said.

It was not merely personal concern for Callendar for they had always been at each other's throats, always ready to double-cross, blackmail, lie, cheat or steal in their efforts to rook the public whether in tally selling or trading stamps; it was not that Albert felt any particular loyalty for the man who, more than anybody else, had encouraged and helped Albert's latent talent for making money. No, Albert's deepest distress came from the certainty that if Cally had given up, had started working for a living, had become a wage slave, then it meant that what Albert suspected was true: there was no more opportunity in this town. The game wardens had finally taken over. The Corbys were in charge. The Solly Cowells owned the town. The chain stores and the monopolies had moved in and put their uniform stamp on every shop in the High Street and anything left over went to the big tally boys blooming in the Mayfair penthouses who could afford full-page advertising in the national press.

'Git the goods in the 'ouse!' had been Cally's war-cry when Albert worked for him, but now you couldn't get the goods. Private enterprise at Albert's and Cally's level was blocked by borrowing restrictions, trading associations and council committees, all with their finger in the pie. If Cally was getting up in the morning and clocking in it meant that there was not a sixpence left under any pebble. The town was sewn up.

The girl in the siren suit raised her fist like a pantomime rabbit: 'You must get out there and fight!'

'Eh?' Albert looked at her, woozy and uncertain as a Chelsea pensioner now too deaf to catch the order to charge.

It was the news about Callendar that finally pricked the bubble of his misery and set him offloading all his troubles on to this stranger. He had only popped in to drop the cat to frighten away the mice before bringing Dorothy in – it had become a routine – and somehow he had stayed with the feeling that he couldn't go on. What was waiting for him down in the car and back at the house was all at once too immense; it was paralysing.

'And that brewery might be the place to start, matey!' Patricia Gort exclaimed, militantly.

Blah gah mah rah blah gah, Albert thought, listlessly.

Oh *dear*! Patricia Gort was thinking, touched with pity at the sight of Albert leaning weakly on one elbow as he drank like a casualty in a road accident. Hot sweet tea would be more the thing, she thought.

'Dear Mummy,' she composed, 'I think I've found myself a job....'

Chapter Two

The time of day when Albert stopped loving everybody was first thing in the morning when he badly needed another six months deep sleep. He had been in bed four hours when the motor horn woke him at seven. He left Alice sleeping and crept down to bring Dorothy into the house.

'I'm freezing cold,' she complained. 'Thought you were going to take me to the office? I knew you wouldn't get up once you got into bed with her.'

'Have to get you some more blankets, duck,' Albert told her, thoughtlessly.

'You don't think I'm going to spend another night in that car, do you!'

'Ssssh!' Albert said. They were climbing the stairs. And at the bathroom he said, softly: 'I'll have to come inside with you in case somebody wakes up.'

'No fear!' Dorothy said.

'I'll give you five minutes then,' Albert said.

He waited outside the bathroom door, hugging himself and freezing and hoping nobody would appear.

'Don't listen!' came Dorothy's voice from inside. And she set the taps running; in the quiet house it sounded like Niagara.

Albert did not know what he was going to do with her but whatever happened they would have to come to some other toilet arrangement.

At five minutes to eight Albert stopped his car outside the factory. Dorothy was eating a bacon sandwich and drinking from a jug.

'I shouldn't be working really,' she told him, aggrievedly.

'Don't be mad,' Albert told her. 'You've got an overdue period, not a baby.'

'Not according to my calculations,' Dorothy said. 'And I feel ever so sick.'

'You're just talking yourself into it.'

She wiped her mouth, set the jug down on the floor, then looked at him, pitifully. 'What am I going to do, Albert?'

Albert opened her door: 'I'll try to think of something while you're at work.'

Dorothy put her legs out of the car slowly and reluctantly like an invalid, grumbling all the time. 'Freezing cold all night and electric blankets all day – I can't move my neck –' she broke off, staring round: 'Just a minute, here's my sister. Marge!' she called. 'Over here.'

A young girl with sleepy eyes came towards them from the factory gates, loaded down with cases and parcels and a record player and leading a dirty-white dog by a piece of string.

'Oh lor – she's brought all my stuff!'

Albert, dismayed, looked at the girl piled high with her elder sister's belongings.

'Mum won't have 'em in the house!' Margery told Dorothy on a note of suppressed excitement conjured from the unusual read-about drama in an undramatic family life. She gave Albert a quick throbbing glance, half afraid that to meet his eyes would make her pregnant too. 'Is this your chap? I think you're rotten.' Adding to her sister: 'But he can't take all the blame. You shouldn't go too far.' And having dispensed with the duty she rushed on: 'I've brought your new Dusty Diamonds record that John give you.'

'Put it in the back and shut up,' Dorothy told her sister.

'I always said he was the nicest one,' Margery retorted. And as an object lesson: 'He didn't even kiss you the first night.'

'I wish he was here,' Albert said.

On the back seat the dog was scratching violently with

such intense concentration and effort that its spare rear paw flailed the air as though muscularly synchronised.

Albert ran out of petrol at the bottle-neck and traffic lights where Butterhall Street intersected with High Street and in the middle of the morning panic rush of workers who calculated their journey to the last ten seconds before clocking-in time. An angry symphony of horns struck up and then, as he got out, fell momentarily silent; Albert was wearing pyjamas and bedroom slippers with his raincoat; he had not expected to get out of the car. He looked around at the watching faces, shrugged helplessly, walked away.

'Here, mate –you can't leave it there!'

'Push it!'

Albert turned long enough to put up two fingers: 'You push it.'

The dog stopped scratching to poke its nose out of the window and bark after Albert as if to remind him of his new responsibility.

He was relieved to find a girl on the petrol pumps and didn't mind her laughing at him.

'What you doing – sleep-walking?' she asked.

'Just escaped from a lunatic asylum,' Albert told her and then when her smile faded he added: 'Give us a gallon in a can, love.'

'It's ten bob deposit.'

Albert clapped his hands to his pockets. 'Call in and pay you.'

'You won't,' she said. 'That's the idea of the deposit – we was always losing these cans.'

Albert said: 'You tell Jacko it was me – Mr Argyle.'

'Jacko?' she said.

'Mr Jackson,' Albert told her. 'We're old buddies.'

'Old Jackass in the store?' the girl said disdainfully. 'You better talk to him yourself – wouldn't trust myself in there.'

Instead of gaining prestige by claiming friendship with the boss, safe in the knowledge that he wouldn't be in until nine o'clock, Albert found that he had degraded himself by admitting that he knew the storekeeper. Trust old Jacko to slide down the ladder. You couldn't rely on anybody.

'Jacko!' Albert called at the store hatch inside the garage.

A fat man came along a corridor of spare-part bins, holding an armful of rubber tubes. Albert's heart sank at the sight of him; a fat nondescript man with whisky eyes and nose and all hope gone. Callendar in a factory, Jacko wearing a brown oil-stained cow-gown.

'It's Albert, isn't it?' he said.

Albert just stared at him, dismally. Things were worse than he thought. Jacko, colleague and salesman with Albert in Callendar's Warehouse, used to be the poor man's Lord Roote complete with 'old man' and 'old chappie', fifty-guinea suits on H.P., carnation buttonholes and a university accent – he had the whole façade of success; everything that used to be considered necessary if you wanted to inherit the earth.

'Nice to see you, old chappie,' Jackson said, as though suddenly remembering who he used to be.

'You look well,' Albert told him.

'So do you, old man,' Jackson said.

They each meant that at least the other was not actually dead.

'Off the sales lark, then?' Albert said.

'Oh yes,' Jackson said, as if he had been promoted. 'Well, the wife died,' he added.

'I didn't know you were married!' Albert said; there was a note of congratulation in it that seemed out of place.

They had known each other intimately but not at that level. Not at any level as low as marriage or children or home. Selling glamour and glitter and gloss they had lived in the sodium and neon limelight. They had had to be what people wanted, not what they'd got. They had had to be where people wanted to get, not where they already were. It seemed ludicrous to think that after all the dreaming housewives Jacko had had or had said he had had, lifting them for a moment out of their drab lives into a bright and beautiful labour-saving world; after all that there had in fact been a woman behind Jackson and that when she had died Jackson was finished.

Perhaps Cally had been married? Albert thought with horror. Supposing Callendar had been married all that time. They had none of them known where the others had driven away to in their shiny cars after six o'clock – Max, Arnold, Albert, Jacko and Cally. Had they all gone to homes? Had they all turned grey once the lights were off? Was it all a trick of reflections? Had Albert been the only one actually living the dream?

'Then of course there's the money,' Jackson said. 'I get a steady wage here with extra for overtime You can't live on commission. ...'

'Live on commission,' Albert used to tell his mother, 'and you live on faith in yourself.' Or he would say: 'You *live* on commission—you *exist* on a wage.'

From his mother's point of view it was all abstract for she never saw either commission or wages from him.

'I hear you're doing well,' Jackson said. He said it in the tone he had used to tell Albert that he looked well. A sort of sympathetic politeness.

God knows what he had heard, Albert thought. Whatever it was it suddenly became difficult to ask Jackson to get the petrol on tick.

'Oh yes,' Albert said.' You can't go wrong with property, Jacko – it only goes up.' Well other people's property did. If it was your own it went down or did nothing; it was somewhere nobody wanted to build anything except, perhaps, roads. Then you lost it under a compulsory purchase order for what the Council laughingly called 'current values'.

'I wonder if you could do me a favour, Jacko,' Albert asked, suddenly.

'Could you lend me a pound, old chappie?' Jackson said, just as suddenly. Then: 'Sorry – what were you saying?' And he added in the split second available: 'Fact is I came out without my lunch money. It doesn't matter if it's difficult. Or have I just got it? Yes, I think I've just got it – stop looking.'

The whole performance had lost Albert his petrol and sent him diving deeply into his mac pockets; his hands now came out with sundry folded papers, cigarettes, matches.

'Have a fag, anyway,' Albert said.

'Not for me, old man!' Jackson said. Then, seriously: 'Five people I know personally have died of chest cancer in the past few years.' And suddenly recollecting: 'You remember Baxter?'

'Who?' Albert said.

'Here come and look at this,' Jackson said.

He put down the pile of rubber tubes on the remark: 'Can't shift these things. It's all tubeless now.'

Albert followed him from the store to the workshop, a big concrete and steel erection with one or two bits of work going on in odd corners.

'Make a nice skating rink this would,' Albert said.

Jackson led him to the mangled wreck of a two-seater sports car. What had looked like solid gleaming metal in the showroom was reduced to crumpled paper-thin tin and shattered glass.

'Took his head off – clean as a whistle!' Jackson said.

'Who?'

'You remember Arnold? Course you do! Old Arnold!'

Albert remembered with a shock. 'What that stupid one? Always picking his nose!'

'That's the one. Cut his head off. Only doing about sixty. The other chap must have been speeding.'

They both dwelt briefly in the past.

'Used to bring those birds up to your flat,' Jackson said, sentimentally.

'Poor old Arnold,' Albert said.

'He got it in the end, you know,' Jackson said.

'What?'

'Your flat – you know he was after it?'

'Was he?' Albert said.

'You remember you had to do a flit – somebody told the creditors you were there,' Jackson laughed. 'You were always in trouble.'

'And I was always getting out,' Albert said, nostalgically. He seemed to have lost the art of getting out of trouble. Then he smiled at his old self. 'Anonymous phone call!' he said. 'Somebody telephoned the bailiff.'

'That's right!' Jackson said. 'Now you've got it – that was Arnold. That's how he got you out.'

'Fucking bastard!' Albert said. He kicked the remains of the car. 'A lot of bloody good it did him.'

'Clean as a whistle, old chappie,' Jackson said. 'Straight through the windscreen.'

'I hope he left his balls on the radiator cap,' Albert said. 'Anonymous phone call!' Then he said: 'Is he dead?'

'It cut his head off!' Jackson said.

'Poor old Arnold,' Albert said, fondly.

Albert lit a cigarette. Jackson, staring moodily at the wreck, put out his hand and also took one. It didn't seem to matter in the long run.

'Mr Argyle?' The petrol girl came running into the workshop. 'The police want you!'

Jackson looked at Albert in sudden alarm. 'See you then old chappie,' he said, and left abruptly. Halfway back to the store he stopped and turned round, only now recollecting that Albert was wearing pyjamas.

'If I were you, Sid,' said the police sergeant, soberly, 'I wouldn't be quite so friendly with that chap.'

'That's what Jonquil's always saying,' the constable said, regretfully.

They stood by the petrol pumps watching Albert drive away. Sid had furnished the money for the petrol and had pushed the car all the way from the traffic lights. A traffic jam half a mile long stretched from the centre of town outwards in each direction.

'He don't carry it off the way he used to,' Sid said, still regretful. 'Still,' he said, and he laughed. 'There aren't many of 'em left.'

There was Old Charlie the tramp who thought he was a trappist monk and walked through the town wearing a brown blanket; he never spoke but sometimes sat for hours on the marble steps of the cinema, some people said he was the cinema manager's brother trying to get his own back. Then there was a little shrivelled half of a woman, just shoulders and arms and face, wheeling herself around the town in an invalid chair. Then there was Daft Dick, a strong-looking man who cycled around the town in khaki shorts wearing socks with scout garters and a flat cap. Then there was a little square man who seemed to have his clothes painted on him like a jointed doll and wore a scarlet bowler hat and called himself Mr Japhet. Then there was Albert who called himself Mr Argyle and whose real name was Harris.

'A joke's a joke,' the police sergeant said.

'You're right,' said Police Constable Sid.

And a lot of jokes weren't jokes any more, Sid thought.

'He may be harmless,' said the sergeant, 'but I wouldn't like to bet.'

'He nearly saved a woman's life once,' the constable said.

'I bet she died,' said the sergeant and then when Sid admitted that she did he said: 'I know the type.'

Police Constable Sid tried to think of some nice things to remember about Albert but he knew that they wouldn't sound nice in the telling. You had to be Albert.

'For instance, how do you know that girl wasn't dead last night?' the sergeant said. 'Or doped? Or drugged?'

'She kept blowing the motor horn,' Sid said.

'His dog's got fleas,' the police sergeant said.

Patricia Gort was waiting to go up to Cambridge and had decided to 'pig it', as she called it, in the provinces rather than spend the long vacation doing the holiday spots of Europe.

'Statistics are people,' she had told her parents.

It was no use studying economics or anything else unless you had first-hand experience of what they were about. A bed-sitter and a job and making ends meet was also economics, she told them. Of what use to live with the cream in a world flowing with Pepsi Cola, she told them. She told them that the ruling class today was hoi-polloi and she intended to rub noses with them until the beginning of term.

'As long as you don't let it go any farther,' her mother said.

It was her mother who had given her the police whistle while her father had given her a cheque for fifty pounds.

'That's really the difference between Mummy and Daddy,' she told Albert over the gas-ring breakfast later that morning. And then she said: 'Come on, matey, you must eat something.'

Sitting back on the couch and being waited on, Albert felt oddly helpless and grateful towards her. Of all the women who were making his life unbearable, Patricia Gort was the first to have perceived that he was an invalid and treat him like one. An invalid and mentally deficient. Or mentally sufficient. At any rate something that made him different from the norm. His child with Alice had only confirmed this.

People who knew, neighbours or friends of Alice or Mrs Finbow, never asked about Albert's family. They sometimes got as far as: 'How's your fam—' and changed the subject. Or: 'How's the family –' then quickly switch to asking how the car was running or if his wife was keeping well. People were frightened of mental sickness and this could include genius, brilliance, spastic, polio or any other kind of restriction of communication. Like multiple sclerosis. Treasure had been boycotted by her neighbours ever since Charles' illness. They crossed the road rather than meet her. No wall in the urban district was higher or thicker or more impregnable than the wall around the sick. The intelligent dumb and the intelligent deaf were left to themselves. The mentally alert sitting in the invalid chair with neck awry was left to gape at the sky. The raving maniac, the sex pervert, the raper and strangler of small children was accepted warmly so long as he could smile and had a ready flow of small talk about the weather.

'While you're out on business today,' Patricia Gort said, munching in a noisy, healthy way and looking around the room, critically, 'I'd like to get a pot of paint or two and brighten this place up.'

Albert laughed and it sent some strength through his veins. 'I think I will have something – give us one of them hot bangers.'

He laughed because he remembered when he used to be like that; going around cheering the place up; always on the buzz, bucking things up, pushing, seeing what happened.

She detected something of this and smiled at him with a mouthful of toast and marmalade that made her look suddenly about ten years old and impish and not wise at all. This brought a kind of masculine dominance, a paternity into his eyes and this in turn made her shy; one of those fleeting chain reactions that bring people together in spite of what they say and do; the fundamental that splinters through and makes a mockery of the struggle to communicate.

As if on the basis of this unspoken moment she said, warmly: 'Oh, you'll get better!'

With the food eaten and the tea drunk right down to the last cold cup and the tea-leaves spat out which they both did without reticence and with cigarettes alight, Patricia Gort took control and Albert reclined in his illness as though by appointment. He liked it. They both did.

'Tell me about your son,' she said.

'Which one?'

'The one in your marriage. Alice's baby. You keep skipping it? Is he mental?'

'He's backward, that's all.'

'Is he autistic?'

'Don't be bloody silly,' Albert said, 'he can't even talk.'

Patricia Gort patiently explained the word.

'Well I dunno do I? Nobody does. That's what he's there for.'

'I should think he's autistic,' Patricia Gort said.

413

'Do they get better?'

'Well it depends. It's a mental block. Sometimes because a child is unwanted – from conception, I mean. They get their own back by rejecting the world. They come into the world but they remain unborn. Somehow they have to be encouraged to get born again – you know, welcomed. It's a new field. Children are being saved now who ten years ago would have gone into a loony bin. I've got an idea about those peacocks,' she added, noticing that Albert had become emotionally moved.

'So have I,' he said, darkly.

They both laughed.

'Mummy's got a terrace,' she said. 'They seem to demand a terrace, don't you think?'

'It's not what I thought they were demanding,' Albert said. Then he said as she laughed again: 'Why don't you put something decent on?'

She was still wearing the sleeping sack.

'Not for painting,' she said. Then she said: 'Besides, we got off on the wrong foot – me naked. I just want you to think of me as a Girl Friday – a hot cup of tea, a paint brush, footprints in the sand.'

'I can't pay you,' Albert said.

'Not with a summer dress clinging around my thighs,' she continued, determined to remind him that she could be desirable if she chose or if he made progress. 'What have you got on today?' she said, to start him off again in the right direction.

'Nothing.'

'We'll think of something. How about that brewery business?'

'What about it?'

'Can't you raise a bit of competition for your property? Make them believe they're not the only ones after it? Get a syndicate interested – bump the price up.'

'There's nobody else interested,' Albert said.

'Haven't you got *any* friends?' Patricia Gort exclaimed, exasperatedly.

414

'They're worse off than I am,' he told her.

'It doesn't take money,' she said. 'A bit of initiative, that's all. A few signatures on a piece of paper – get somebody to make an offer for your property, send it through your estate agent friend, the one who came here. Surely somebody would do that for you? Somebody with some business-headed notepaper that's all.'

Albert thought about it and brightened. 'Old Cally'ld do it like a shot. Of course he'd want paying.'

'Give him a cut,' the girl said. 'Give him a percentage of the net – whatever you make on it above and beyond your outlay.'

'Five per cent?' Albert said.

'Twenty-five per cent!' Patricia Gort said. 'It doesn't matter what you give away if you haven't got anything – that's sound economics.'

Albert thought about it but grew depressed. 'They'd smell it a mile off. Besides, they wouldn't let anybody else develop that property. If the brewery's got Corby they've got the council.'

'And supposing somebody else wants to develop that site for the public good?' Patricia Gort said. 'Can't you do a bit of kite-flying in that direction? Do you know anybody on the local paper? There's always a councillor ready to catch votes on a controversial issue.'

Albert began to get excited. He sat up. 'Cally's the one,' he said, 'I mean for a sleeping partner. He'd never let on if there was money in it. Ideal man. Cunning old sod.'

'Well then,' said Patricia Gort. 'Go and see him.'

'Have to wait till he finishes work –' He stopped at her sigh of despair. 'No, you're right,' he said. He stood up. 'I'll get her stuff out of the car –'

'You'll leave it just where it is,' Patricia Gort told him. 'Make her comfortable here and you'll never get rid of her. Keep everything in the car including the dog. Let her see that you can't cope with her. She'll soon get fed up and go. Just don't worry about her any more.' She got up, wiped her mouth on the back of her hand, started examining the paintwork on the door. 'We've got to concentrate on work, Albert.'

'Don't forget she's pregnant,' Albert said.

'How disgusting,' Patricia Gort said. 'How bloody working class.'

Albert stared at her, incredulously. 'What, sex? Don't tell me you debs don't do it!'

'If we do then we know what we're doing,' Patricia Gort said. 'You've only got to look at the statistics for unmarried mothers. Ninety per cent are uneducated girls.'

Albert said: 'I don't know what education's got to do with it – you give 'em the right drink and a nice couch and a bit of technique.'

'Charming,' Patricia Gort said. 'Marvellous.'

'You know it's true,' Albert said.

'It's not true,' Patricia Gort told him. 'Sit down.'

Albert sat down: 'Is this part of the treatment?'

'It's a bit basic for you in your condition,' she told him. She took up a position behind the desk of breakfast things like a schoolmistress about to deliver a lecture, put one foot up on the chair. 'It's like applying artificial respiration to a corpse. Anyway – how many educated girls have you had sexual intercourse with, Albert?'

'About three. Well, I don't meet 'em, do I?'

'Well exactly,' Patricia Gort said. 'And they don't meet people like you – the great unlettered. Thank God. Oh, it's not just the three 'R's' you lack. It's background and character-building and self-awareness. It's the educated home.'

'Dorothy's parents are strict,' Albert said. 'They kicked her out.'

She allowed him to think about this for a little while.

'I suppose that's the wrong way round,' he admitted.

'I'm glad I don't have to tell you everything,' she said. 'You've got promise, that's why I persevere with you. Of course it's the wrong way round. If they've failed her, which they have, then they should succour her in her trouble. You see the working-class mum and dad think that being strict, as they call it, means pretending to their daughters that sex doesn't exist until they're married. Everything they see and hear says it does. Do you know what my father told us girls before we started menstruation?'

'Are you being filthy?' Albert said.

'That remark helps to explain what I'm talking about,' she said, and then: 'Daddy said – Mummy was there and I think he wanted her to hear because she'd got this thing on this wretched little Italian hairdresser at her beauty farm – he said: "I want you girls to know very clearly what will happen if you ever have sexual intercourse with a man while you are under my care. Sexual intercourse," he said, "in case you don't know and I'm sure you do, means letting a man put his thing inside you and wriggle it about. This causes you nine months later to have a baby. In the meantime your menstruation stops and your belly gets very big so that everybody knows about it. If this happens then you will leave this lovely home and go into an institution for unmarried mothers and scrub floors every day and live on bread and soup." '

'And that was an educated home?' Albert exclaimed.

'I shall always remember because my young sister Caroline said: "What sort of soup, Daddy?" and everybody laughed except Mummy who had almost fainted. Anyway she got rid of the Italian hairdresser and none of us has ever gone wrong in that silly, untidy way.'

'Blimey I should think not!' Albert said. 'Still, he's a doctor. You don't expect them to be very romantic about sex.'

'Well, that's the whole point,' Patricia Gort told him. 'You're so exactly in need of education that you keep making my points for me. You can't be romantic about sex. You can only be sexual about romance. Sex is an important part of love. Sexual intercourse without love is a betrayal of the human condition. A girl like your Dorothy won't find out until she falls in love and then it's too late. When love is new she will be second-hand.'

'Look, why don't you talk to her?' Albert protested.

Patricia Gort sighed and went back to examining the

paintwork. 'I've lost interest,' she said. 'If you don't get out of this bog and put your sex life straight you'll never do anything with your career.'

'You mean skip my responsibilities. Is that what Education teaches you?'

'You can't put one immorality right by indulging in another. That's not meeting your responsibilities.'

'I don't see that!' Albert told her, his voice cracking in protest. 'This has never happened to me before – I've never been landed with a baby. Not by a single girl. I've always had a strict rule – ask any of my friends.' He dug his hands deep into his pockets and walked up and down, glum with self-pity. 'Nothing wrong with my morals, darling. Married women only, that's what I've always stuck to.'

Patricia Gort turned to give him full attention but he did not notice her.

'After all,' he said, 'a baby should have a roof over its head.'

For the first time Patricia Gort could think of nothing to say. She started scratching inside the woolly siren suit, went into the other room and began to take the aquatic pets out of the bath and drop them into the hand-basin.

As Albert came out into the street he stopped as though shot. Across the road a man was aiming the barrel of a theodolyte at Albert's heart and Albert's premises.

'They been here for an hour.' Hetty had appeared from the pet shop doorway. 'Walking up and down, measuring up, carting chains about, looking. Well it's all coming down,' she said. 'Bound to.'

Albert nodded, grimly. Yes, it was all coming down. Soon as somebody wanted to put something up and there was a bit of dropsy available.

'Let's see,' Albert said, staring along the High Street, 'who haven't we got? There's Woolworths, Marks, British Home Store, Sainsbury's, Burtons, W. H. Smith, Fine Fare, Freeman Hardy and Willis – all present and correct. Oh yes, plenty more to come.'

'We could do with a Joe Lyons,' Hetty said, wistfully. 'Say what you like about their food you can't beat their cups of tea and coffee.'

On Albert's side of the street where most of the old property still stood several empty shops had dusty 'For Sale' signs in dirty windows; they could never be sold with the threat of demolition and development hanging over them. Not a direct threat. Nothing you could tie the council down to.

'It might be five years, it might be twenty years,' the health office would inform inquirers.

All they had to do was occasionally send out a team from the Borough Surveyor's office just to show the threat. No doubt Reginald Corby would be along to see him again, this time holding a theodolite to Albert's head.

'Stand and deliver!' Albert cried as he drove away; 'in the name of Town Planning Improvements, Developments and the Good of the Community!'

England's pleasant pastures green, Albert thought, bitterly. *What a carve up!*

The Agricultural Tractor Factory was Albert's private salt mine. Physically and spiritually it had loomed over him ever since leaving school. In the basin which contained his home town like a lot of dirty washing-up the tractor factory took up almost the whole of one steep side – making a contribution to the community which was both economic and gaseous; it provided work for half the town and contributed more than half of the yellow pall which formed the town's sky.

'Slavery or consumption,' Albert used to tell his mother, 'stay here long enough and it's bound to get you in the end.'

She never said so but had the tractor factory got Albert at school-leaving age her last years might have been financially bearable.

'Once they go through those gates and clock in you never see 'em again,' Albert would tell his mother.

There were times when this possibility only made his mother envious of other mothers.

Unknown to Albert many of his despised, stupid, unambitious, untalented chums he had seen dragged in and sucked under were now high-salaried executives enjoying a greatly plus-Albert life in exotic, tractor-tilled corners of the earth which Albert would never even see except on travel posters. Unknown to Albert there was a permanence about tractors which had no place in his way of life. His own private hire-purchase boom and trading-stamp campaign had finally fizzled out but the tractors kept on going. Unknown to Albert with all his knowhow, zing, personality, charm, ingenuity, initiative, shrewdness, talent and potential, there was a slot waiting for him somewhere in the grey, balding middle years, somewhere in the busy, heartless hinterland of a technocratic specialist and competitive society keeping up with the Ivanoffs when, had he lived, the question would have been asked and the answer duly noted:

'Experience?'

'None.'

'That's a laugh to start with!' Albert would have said.

Unknown to Albert nobody would have laughed. Luckily, dying when he did, he escaped this.

Now at the age of thirty-three, all the threes, Albert for the first time in his life was driving towards Those Gates. In all the years he had driven the streets of the town he had always made vast and complicated detours to avoid going within sight or sound or smell of the factory precincts. He had an inevitability phobia which came from he didn't know where except perhaps from one of his many dreams where he was sorting his visiting cards to impress a big West-end impresario who had, inconveniently, called him up to Claridges for dinner when, amongst such cards as: 'Albert Argyle –' 'Ventriloquist' 'Conjuror' 'Television Personality –' 'Celebrated wit –' 'Armchair philosopher –' 'Cabaret star –' and all the other achievements he had never achieved except wishfully or fictitiously in chit chat to this girl or that: well amongst all these glossy cards –

he was rather keen on things like gold Bodoni on pale green – amid all these printed lies as he shuffled and selected them in his dream he had come upon a grubby works clocking-in card bearing the name: 'A. Harris – 6113'. The dream had been shattered and the card had fallen into his coffee calypso. It had unnerved him for years and destroyed his belief in all dreams except the pleasant ones.

'Anyway, they got the name wrong,' he told himself, waggishly, for he had always been his own best audience. He meant that he had for many years lived under a pseudonym. All his success, all his vintage years, belonged to Albert Harris; and, of legal necessity, his marriage to Alice Finbow. Although he was Mr Harris only to the Finbow neighbours in his road, he sometimes wondered if the decline and fall of Albert Argyle had not started with the rise of Mr Harris. Hadn't Alice put her librarian's finger on it last night when she said that marriage had changed him? Funnily enough he felt like Mr Harris when he was at home now. A very ordinary, stick-in-the-mud, dead-end sort of person. All he needed was a hat and umbrella and he was finished. Suddenly having a girl living in his car was important – and the lousy dog and all the luggage; they belonged to Albert Argyle.

The main gates of the tractor factory could equally have been the portals of one of H.M. prisons. Big spiked iron gates ready to crash shut at the first hint of a break-out; a brick blockhouse with two uniformed guards and surely guns within easy reach.

'Who?' one of them asked at Albert's inquiry.

'Mr Callendar,' Albert told them. Then, to give Cally some increased stature which clearly he needed in a place like this, he elaborated: 'Mr Theodore Callendar.'

'Wait a minute, I've got it,' the other commissionaire said. He was flipping through a rack of clock cards and now withdrew one. 'T. Callendar: 40295 – Progress Department,' he read out. Then in an aside to his colleague: 'You know – that old Jew-boy....'

Albert bled. Thus were living characters of flesh and

blood reduced to numbers by the machine. Albert was sufficiently unconsciously anti-Jew never to have regarded Cally as a Jew. All Jews were strangers. If you got to know any they weren't Jews any more; this was as far as the Gentile world could educate its children in racial tolerance.

'Private or business?' the commissionaire asked Albert.

Albert stared at him. 'What?'

'If it's a private matter you have to be a close relative,' one of them said. 'To see them in working hours.'

'I'm no relation!' Albert said; it sounded like a protest after what they'd just said about Cally.

'Unless it's illness,' the other commissionaire said, 'then you'll need a medical certificate.'

Albert said: : 'His only son's just been killed in a car crash. Thrown straight through the windscreen – cut his head off.'

'I expect that'll be all right, then,' one of the uniformed men said. 'I'll get him on the blower.'

With the regulations satisfied the two commissionaires talked to Albert.

One said: 'I bet the ambulances have been busy today then. Used to be in the ambulance service. Before that I was in the fire brigade twenty-six years. My old dad drove the first horse-pulled fire engine they had in this town. They had to stop and let it eat the grass on the way to a call. It was all green fields then. Not like now.'

'It's all coming down,' Albert said.

'You're right, lad,' said the other commissionaire. 'Not a mouthful of fresh air left.' He coughed wheezily and then explained the cue: 'Got gassed in the first lot. We thought it was smoke bombs. It brought your lungs up. Still here, though. I'll be on again eight o'clock tonight to six in the morning – night watchman. Never sleep. Well, what is there to go home to? Nobody there.'

'It's all coming down,' Albert said.

He'll need watching, Albert was thinking. Let Cally in on a deal and he was liable to clean up and leave everybody else in the cold. There was part of Albert that wanted to rescue Cally, take him away from all this; there was also a part that felt apprehensive of the result. His apprehensions were banished or at least modified a moment later when he saw Cally emerge from the factory with a swift, frightened walk, like a small boy who's been given brief permission to leave the room.

'Oh my gawd!' Albert said. He went out to meet him beside the factory entrance. 'What have you done to yourself you poor old man?' Albert demanded, with real compassion.

It was an unhappy metamorphosis. To get the job Cally had had to take ten years off his age. The moustache had gone and with it the flourishes which had intrigued those lady customers with a nostalgia for the old-fashioned gallant; the mephistopheles eyebrows had been trimmed to a grey stubble, the wayward hair cropped short and dyed black; the nonchalant bits of suede and coloured waistcoats and tapered trousers and Italian shoes – essential to the middle-aged man in a teenage world – had vanished to be replaced by conformist off-the-peg Burton grey with a white shirt and black clerk shoes. Worse, far worse, the cheerful dishonesty of eye and expression, the rogue defences, the watching brain, instant for the main chance, were now all gone, all drowned in an unhappy mingling of slave weariness, boredom and fear.

The sight of Albert had turned Mr Callendar grey with shock. 'What are you doing 'ere, Albert? Here, Albert,' he corrected.

But Albert had not yet recovered. 'What have they done to you you poor old sod? You look like that chap they just dragged out of the gravel pits after he'd been missing two months. Have you been ill?'

'You got no right here!' Cally said. He was talking, Albert was unamazed to notice, in a convict whisper from the corner of his mouth. 'Want to get me the sack?'

'I want to help you escape,' Albert whispered in the same furtive manner. 'I've got a cake with a file inside it.'

Mr Callendar was already trying to edge away, disown Albert, get back into the factory. 'They shouldn't have allowed you in,' Cally told him, fiercely with a certain – Albert was dismayed to detect – proprietorial interest in the rules.

He tried to get between Cally and the factory door. 'No, wait a minute, Cally. Just a second. This is important – I've got a big business proposition right up your street –'

'I'm holding up production – you'll have to write to me – goodbye!'

Albert caught Mr Callendar's sleeve and held him back; this seemed to terrify him.

'There's no conversing on the forecourt – it's the executives' car park –'

'Bugger the executives,' Albert said, getting angry. 'Have you been brain-washed or something? I've got a big property deal on with the brewery. There's a few thousand in it for you, Cally.'

'Employees are not allowed to engage in outside business,' Mr Callendar recited. 'Goodbye, Albert.'

'See you up the road after six o'clock?'

'Is that your dog?' One of the commissionaires called to Albert. He was pointing to where Dorothy's dog was squeezing its hind quarters just inside the main gate. 'He can't do that there!'

Callendar took one horrified look at the offending dog then broke free from Albert's grasp and dashed into the factory. Albert came back to the gate and waited for the dog to finish.

'It's not that he can't read,' Albert told the two resentful keepers of the gate. 'He's just a rebel.'

Halfway back to the car Albert saw his chance to get rid of the dog and raced it the last five yards, got in and slammed the door, drove away at high speed. The dog sat down in the dust and scratched.

'He's got scabies,' one commissionaire said to the other. 'He ought to be in isolation!'

'*My* oath – remember that other old bitch then old 'un?

Finished up the whole town got it. Factories off work, rail-ways closing down. Bloody thing come from over Watford, that was the laugh.'

They each broke off to scratch; then hurried back into the blockhouse to watch the scratching dog through the window.

The feeling that Cally was not going to be of much use to him grew deeper when just after six o'clock Albert spotted his old boss approaching amidst a posse of office workers on bicycles.

'Bicycle!' Albert groaned.

To Albert nothing could have been more symbolic of Cally's ruin and degradation than the bicycle. In the human condition the bicycle and legs seemed as defunct as the appendix and tonsils. Albert had for years used a car instead of legs. One of the things that had always depressed him was the sight of groups of people on bicycles or walking or standing at bus stops or massing to and from railway stations. To be mobile and independent of time-tables to him seemed the first essential of being alive in the world. The bicycle was as out of date as the chamber pot. People who used either were dead fish. They were not even in the stream.

'What price the old Bentley now!' Albert called.

'Not here!' Cally hissed as he rode past.

Albert drove slowly along behind him getting overtaken by white-collar workers on their bikes and collarless workers in their cars. There was more skill in driving slow than driving fast. Albert could make his car sit up on its back wheels and sing songs; he and the car were one. Any car. He had done his shopping in a slow-moving traffic jam before now, jumping in and out.

'Hello, lovely!' Albert called to a couple of factory girls running for a bus. Uneducated girls with long uneducated legs.

A small dog following the girls stopped to look at Albert.

'Not you!' Albert shouted.

Dorothy's scratching mongrel switched his allegiance and raced alongside the car trying to get in.

Cally rode upright and steady. Not wobbly like a beginner but with concentrated caution in a straight line eighteen inches from the curb like a motorist who has hated bicycles for years and expected it to disintegrate at any second.

'Now where's he going?' Albert muttered.

Mr Callendar had turned a sharp corner from the main road into a side-street with an upright dexterity which gave an insane impression of a long Walt Disney car bending as it turned.

'What d'you want of me?' Cally said to Albert who pulled his car to trap the cyclist against the path.

'Come for a drink at the George,' Albert commanded.

'Not the George,' Callendar said.

'The Upper Red Lion,' Albert said.

He got out of the car and moved swiftly; not so much in case Callendar changed his mind as wanting to get back behind the wheel which had become home.

'Not the Upper Red Lion,' Callendar said as Albert bundled him into the car.

'The Lower Red Lion,' Albert hazarded.

He banged the door on Callendar's fears and went back to push the bicycle into the boot, its front wheel poking out. He knew the trick well from the girls on bicycles he had picked up in the past; the lid of the boot came down and held the machine safely by its own weight, the rim of the front wheel trapped against the back over-rider.

'The Flower Pot,' Mr Callendar said, when Albert was back behind the wheel. 'You don't get the workers or the bosses in there.'

In a very short time Mr Callendar had learned the habits of the factory and found his rightful place in the microcosm of feudal England that industry had become.

'You've had more experience than me,' Albert said, generously. 'In big business, I mean. It's not like selling a

426

cleaner to a stupid housewife. Right here,' he told Marjorie Mason. 'Watch your mirror.'

'Get your head out of the way then, petal,' she told him, taking the corner with her tongue out for better concentration and missing other traffic by several extraneous acts of self-preservation.

'Honest to God!' Dorothy said. And: 'Stop scratching!' to the dog.

'You know how to work on people like Corby,' Albert told his old boss, earnestly, as though willing him to remember some of the fast deals of the past. 'You say you're back in business he's going to believe it like a shot. I thought of one or two little projects that might impress him. For instance how about turning Bute Place into a covered shopping arcade? Pedestrians only. You'd get a lot of support for that. Worth a newspaper headline anyway. Bit of kite-flying, eh? Remember your emporium?'

'That bicycle's going to scratch all the paintwork,' Dorothy said, fretfully.

Unconsciously she had started getting house-proud about the car. She was taking out ash-trays and tipping them from the window, dusting the fascia, cleaning bits of chrome, rubbing the windows.

'You keep putting me off,' Marjorie Mason said.

'Get them worried,' Albert told Callendar. 'That's all you've got to do. Watch the price go up. I could clear twenty thousand. That's five thousand for you, Cally. I tell you what. Tell you what we could do. We'll form a company. Argyle and Callendar Developments. I'll get some paper printed.' He looked at his watch. 'I might get old Moore to do it tonight. We can see to the company registration afterwards. Get a few letters out first – one to Corby, one to the council planning office, one to the newspaper. Might be better if we tell the local rag first – let them read about it. I've got one or two good photos.' He laughed at Callendar. 'Be like old times!'

'I've got to get to night school by eight o'clock,' Mr Callendar said.

This strange remark from Mr Callendar only convinced Albert that he was still alone and talking to himself. He did not seem to be able to get started. The quiet drink at the Flower Pot had not materialised what with Dorothy who had to be picked up and Marjorie flagging them down with her 'L' plates and somewhere along the road the dog jumping in.

'All right,' Albert said, tiredly. 'What are you doing at night school?'

Mr Callendar became animated at last. 'The National Certificate course in mechanical engineering, Albert. You ought to come.'

'It sounds exciting,' Albert said.

'We're going all metric,' Callendar said. 'We got to conform to European standards – nuts, screws, sheet metal, drills, taps, all the different parts. No more inches,' he said, a little wildly, as someone who has had to accept something he doesn't understand. 'We've got a conversion factor of two-point-four five on all the old measurements.'

'What's twelve from thirty-seven plus seven?' Dorothy asked, turning to Mr Callendar as an authority on numbers. Then, to Marjorie: 'How many days were there in June?'

'I'll have to watch my signalling,' Marjorie said, as a fast-moving pick-up truck cut them up, its horn blaring.

'Oh God!' Dorothy exclaimed; she held her hands away from her body: 'I better not touch myself when I'm frightened.'

Marjorie said: 'You're not supposed to sit in the back when your pupil's in the front seat, petal.'

'I'm trying to talk business,' Albert said.

'Drop me at the two-two club, there's a flower,' Marjorie said.

'Nice for some,' Albert told her.

'Silly,' she said, smiling at him through the mirror; 'It's the Rover Scout rifle club – Cedric's there.'

'Point two-two of an inch,' Mr Callendar said. 'That's the calibre. What would that be in centimetres?' he asked Marjorie.

Outside the technical school Albert made one last try to engage Cally's interest. 'Remember I helped you when Solly Cowell was after your place, Cally –'

'Solly Cowell?' Mr Callendar said. He said it as if repeating a password; a strange look had come to his face; he had the appearance of a man who is groping to regain a long-lost memory and has just received the first spark.

'Solly Cowell,' Albert repeated on a note of hope.

'That bloody crook!' Mr Callendar said.

'That's better!' Albert said.

There was a flash of the old Cally; the dark gleam of anger, the quiver, the blood rising. 'What's 'e bin up to, Albert? It's time that old sod was dead.'

'I wish you would mind your language till you get outside,' Dorothy told them, primly, as though they were swearing in her house.

'He got me kicked out of the golf club. That bloody yid with his own tankard hanging on the wall.'

Albert had to keep the fire going now it was alight. 'Come and have a drink, Cally old man.'

'I can't skip classes – we're doing decimetric conversions tonight –'

'Blow all that,' Albert said. 'You can't start an apprenticeship at fifty-five –'

'Forty-five, Albert –'

'You'll have a nervous breakdown,' Albert pressed on. 'You want to leave all that hard grind to the yobs. They do the work, we get the money, remember?'

'You want to watch him, Albert,' Cally said, 'or you'll finish up where I am. Eight hours a day, night classes three nights a week, not a penny to call your own. That bicycle's on hire purchase.'

'Don't worry, I'm going to take you away from all this,' Albert said, fondly.

Dorothy gave him a quick, level glance.

Callendar had sunk back into dejection. 'You can't fight them. If I couldn't fight them you can't fight them, Albert.

You got to have money, capital, influence – no scruples, that's what you've got to have. I got scruples. That was always my trouble.'

'Yeah, I know,' Albert said. 'But now we've got something to fight them with – my property.'

'What property?' Cally asked.

'Let's go and have a drink. Just a quickie. You'll be back in time for the second house.'

'Got to go, Albert. The firm pay my fees. They'd know if I skipped. Plenty there ready to split on me. They don't like me.'

'We're tycoon class, Cally, and they know it. That's why. Get your blinkers off. Come in with me on this deal.'

'What deal?' Cally asked.

'Come and have a drink!' Albert implored.

'You're wasting petrol,' Dorothy said. Then, 'I think Aubrey wants to go somewhere.'

'Take him for a walk, dear,' Albert told her. 'A long walk. Look, Cally –'

Mr Callendar was following Dorothy out of the car. Albert also got out and hurried round to meet Cally at the boot.

'Leave your bike where it is –'

'I mustn't be late – they mark the register.'

Albert lifted the bicycle out of the boot and gave up, disgusted. The fire, such as it was, had gone out. He said: 'Old Solly would laugh if he heard you now.'

'What's he got to do with it?' Cally said, sharply.

'Do with what?'

'This deal,' Cally said.

Belatedly the inspiration came to Albert out of Cally's mouth, just as the original idea had come from Patricia Gort. He wasn't clicking any more.

'I told you,' Albert said. 'It's him that's after my property. I've got him over a barrel,'

'Let's go and have a drink,' Cally said.

Together they bundled the bicycle back into the car.

Mrs Finbow came up. 'What on earth!' she cried, merrily.

She was with a group of student-type young people who went around the town crying merrily. Mrs Finbow had on a pair of pink stretch pants with a white chunky and ballet shoes.

Albert turned to look at her with the bicycle in his hands, held horizontally. 'This is Mr Callendar – my old boss, you remember? This is Mrs Finbow, my mother-in-law –'

He was interrupted by squeals of delighted laughter from Mrs Finbow's young companions.

'Albert is so middle-aged these days,' she said, forgiving him with a smile, then saying to Mr Callendar: 'Topsy to you!'

Topsy, Albert thought. He said: 'And this is Mr Callendar's secretary's bicycle. That's her with the dog.'

'Pretty good!' Mrs Finbow congratulated him.

'But it's a man's bike!' a youth with her objected.

'The other way round then,' Albert said.

They went towards the technical school laughing. Mrs Finbow turned to call to Albert: 'Don't hurry up home, cherie! Alice has got company. You know, that man who's dotty on her. I invited him in. They're playing draughts. Tres cosee!'

She ran to catch up with the others going into night school, placed a hand on two shoulders and jumped between them.

'Further education,' Albert said.

'What's she trying to prove?' Dorothy asked when Albert and Callendar got into the car.

'Her old man was an income tax inspector – collector I mean. Used to drive her round on a motorcycle combination so he didn't have to talk to her. Or listen. That's why she shouts. Spent half her life in a side-car – now look at her.'

'Hurry up, Albert,' Mr Callendar said from behind him.

'I heard what she said,' Dorothy told Albert. 'About Alice and that chap. What did I tell you? Draughts! You're blind, you are.'

'Ah!' Albert said. 'Many hands make light work.' And

431

further to this thought. 'Why don't you sit in the back with Mr Callendar?'

'I happen to be doing my knitting,' Dorothy said.

She sat in the car as Albert drove away as though she were at her own fireside, plying her needles and half an ounce of wool by the dashboard light, the dog still on her lap and asleep with the day's exhaustion from running and scratching.

'What's Solly offering?' Mr Callendar asked.

Albert gave a scornful laugh. He quoted the brewery's figure; for brewery, read Solly Cowell to keep Cally biting.

'What's he want that dump for?' Callendar asked. 'He's got the biggest store in town – four storeys of multiple goods. That should've been mine, Albert. He gypped me.'

'We're going to gyp him,' Albert said, comfortingly. 'No holds barred!'

'Everything under one roof he's got,' Mr Callendar brooded. 'Copied my plans including the underground car-park.'

'We'll stick him for this,' Albert said.

'I put him where he is,' Mr Callendar said. 'When I joined that old bastard his turnover was nothing. I doubled his sales in six months – put him on the road, Albert.'

'I know you did –'

'Best salesman in the business he said I was – I remember his very words. He was talking to old Wisbech at one of Corby's parties –'

'Drink up and we'll get down to details,' Albert said.

'"He'd sell ice cream to Eskimos," he told him. That was just before Wisbech gave me that unofficial overdraft to back my business.'

'Good man, Wisbech,' Albert said. 'Best bank manager in the town. Lot of faith. Pity he's dead.'

'It should never have happened,' Mr Callendar said. 'Not like that.' He shuddered.

'Well, he was always a worrier,' Albert said. He topped up Cally's glass for the third time and paid for the third time.

'Now let's get down to details,' he said again. 'We've got to play it clever. You know what Corby's like – and Solly – and the rest of 'em come to that. You know their weaknesses. We've got to play one against the other.'

'Now he's got half a million pounds under one roof,' Callendar brooded.

'Something subtle,' Albert urged.

'One good fire and he'd lose the lot!' Mr Callendar said, fiercely.

This depressed Albert. Although still unaware of his own business limitations he now began to suspect why Solly Cowell had a half-million pounds emporium and Cally was cycling to work at the factory. The chaos that had been Callendar's Warehouse now began to make sense. Cally was not the man Albert thought he was. Never mind that Albert was not the man he thought he was.

'It's not a recognised business method, is it?' Albert said, with an attempt to laugh it off. 'Anyway, he'd be insured.'

'Of course, I'd want him to know I did it,' Callendar said.

'I don't think you'd have any trouble there,' Albert assured him. Then he said: 'No, come on, let's be serious, Cally.'

'I can see the flames!' Cally said.

All glass and satin walnut, Albert thought, remembering other dreams Cally had had; shop girls with his name on the collar. Callendar was just a dreamer, that's what it was. Albert had misjudged his man. He had dreamed his way to ruin and now he dreamed about revenge. Three whiskies and he was ready to bore you with his persecution mania.

'Drink up,' Albert said, despondently.

'Afterwards we could start a factory of some kind in Belgium,' Callendar said.

'Eh?' Albert had lost the drift.

'Light engineering, Albert,' Mr Callendar said, suddenly very wise and rational. 'Domestic appliances, for instance. You get very favourable financial concessions in Belgium at the moment.'

Albert sat back to smoke and drink and listen to Cally. He was now quite fogged.

'We could put the money in a Swiss bank,' Cally said. 'You forgot I know something about Swiss banks. I've got three empty accounts in Swiss banks. Well, they'll never be surprised to receive a substantial deposit. They don't know I'm out of business.'

'Good idea,' Albert said. He was still unwilling to believe that Cally was insane. 'You mean after burning down Solly's store?'

Cally smiled and Albert was greatly relieved to see it.

'That's quite by the way,' Cally said. 'That's my personal pleasure. You needn't know anything about that.'

Albert's relief vanished.

'You're probably wondering about capital,' Mr Callendar said. 'I wouldn't mind this drink again – thanks, Albert. I'm glad you come to me when you did. I was letting things slide.'

Pity you didn't, Albert was thinking. Poor old sod. Good job he couldn't afford much drink.

Dorothy came out of the Ladies with a scarf around her head. She stopped at their table: 'Will you be long, Albert?'

Albert was glad of the excuse. He finished his drink. 'Might as well come now – ready Cally?'

'Stay, Albert!' Mr Callendar said. He reached across and laid a hand on Albert's arm. Then he looked at Dorothy. 'Private business.'

Dorothy was not annoyed; she had a kind of happy glow and her smile towards Albert was warm. 'It's a lovely toilet,' she said.

'Good,' Albert said. 'Did you do everything?'

Dorothy laughed and indicated her handbag: 'All my smalls – clean stuff for tomorrow.' Then she became impishly secretive with a glance towards the bar. 'Can you tell I've shampooed my hair?'

'Blimey,' Albert said.

She said, 'Could I use your car heater if I switch on the engine?'

434

'You'll have to put your head down on the floor,' Albert said.

'That's all right,' she said. 'Lovely!' And then she said, 'Oh yes,' turning away and back again. 'Could you get a tin lid or something with some water – for Aubrey? They don't sell pork pies, do they?'

'I'll take care of it, love,' Albert told her.

'Ta ta,' she said, and walked out, happily.

He could tell that she was coming to terms with her living arrangements and would be happy for the night wherever he parked her.

Callendar was looking at Albert, sternly. 'You shouldn't let them get in the way of business, Albert. That was always your trouble. Here, look at this but don't let anybody see it.'

He passed Albert a folded sheet of paper from amongst a number he had taken from his inside pocket. Albert stared at it, mystified. It was a blown-up section of street map. Albert began to wonder if perhaps he had not misjudged Cally; missed something significant. There was a red line on the map and a heavy cross over Solly Cowell's corner site.

Albert said: 'What is it – development plans?'

'No, no!' Mr Callendar said, excitedly. 'You'd never guess. Nobody else has ever set eyes on that – except security of course. It's the route –' Cally broke off as someone passed their table, then continued in a whisper: 'It's the route the factory paycar will take next Thursday – from the bank to the factory.'

'Oh?' Albert said.

'No, wait a minute,' Mr Callendar said. He extracted another paper and took the other piece back. 'I've given you the wrong one – that's last Thursday. Different route every week, you see? And no wonder. Do you know how much they carry in banknotes, Albert – one hundred thousand pounds plus!'

Albert's fears and misgivings settled in an indigestible lump on his diaphragm.

Callendar was smiling at him, expectantly. 'Now do you

435

see what I mean? Given someone on the outside, I mean. With a reliable car and a few trustworthy friends – you might contact one or two of my old staff. People we know. Jackson, Arnold – Max, perhaps. Though I don't think he's very honest.'

Again, besides the route marked in red, there was a heavy angry cross over Solly Cowell's corner site; a cryptic diagram showing the means and the end, all in one.

Callendar, impressed by Albert's deliberating silence, went on: 'There are four men with it but no firearms. A wages clerk, two guards and the driver. Any questions?'

Albert shook his head.

Mr Callendar said, earnestly: 'Think about it, Albert. There's no hurry. Long as you agree in principle.'

'Oh, the principle's all right,' Albert said. 'I'm all for it.'

'Of course you are, my boy,' Mr Callendar said. 'Everybody is. Including the wages clerk.' He laughed, shortly. 'We get the man in the print room to turn out a few extra copies of these every week. One of these weeks it's going to come up for somebody – why not us?'

He made it sound like a football pool. Albert laughed. It made sense when he thought of all those zombies behind those gates.

'It ain't as difficult as all that,' Mr Callendar said. 'I got a big advantage – now I've almost mastered the metric system. We could go into production in Belgium straight away.'

'Well that's a start,' Albert said. 'And I can drive on the right-hand side of the road.'

'But no firearms,' Cally said, missing the point. 'We don't want no crime.' He went on: 'Look, I tell you what. You get things organized. I'll give you one of these maps every week – okay?'

'Okay,' Albert told him.

'Another thing,' Mr Callendar said, bright-eyed with enthusiasm: 'I thought of a way to get old Solly right at the top of the building at midnight. You know he's got a

shagging ground up there? Mind you I'm not serious,' he
added, unconvincingly. 'But don't come to the factory
again,' he said, getting jumbled in his anxiety to convey
everything at once. 'It's better if we ain't seen together too
much. Just in case anything goes wrong with your end of it.
By the way, you go out first and I'll follow. Leave my bike.'

'Sure you can ride it?' Albert asked him.

'I'm cold sober.'

It was the most horrifying thing he had said.

'Like it?' Dorothy said, when Albert slipped back behind
the wheel as if coming home.

'I used to,' he said, thoughtlessly; then, looking round,
'Now where are you?'

The girl was on her knees under the dashboard.

'You can come out of that straight away!' Albert exclaimed. 'The police love that position. They call it obscene behaviour in a public place – even if you're engaged.'

'I'm drying my hair!' Dorothy cried, outraged.

'That's just the sort of defence that'd get you laughed
out of court.' And he said: 'It's a cynical old world, darling,'
when she rejoined him on the bench seat.

The word brought her back into a good humour. Her
head was hanging down as she fluffed her fingers through
her drying hair; now she spared him a smile. 'Does it look
nice again?'

'Lovely,' Albert said.

He started the car and drove away from the pub.

'You know what I'm going to do?' She spoke as if promising herself a good time. 'I'm going to do my nails.'

There was a lilt in her voice and the dog was scratching
happily on the back seat. This together with the frustration
of finding that a man he had always subconsciously counted
on was useless and probably always had been made Albert
angry and bitter.

'Did you get anything?' she asked, as she massaged her
scalp. 'For me and the dog?'

'No.'

'All right. Don't snap at me. Plenty of time. I'm not a bit hungry yet,' she added, to make things easier for him.

'You can get something while I make a call,' Albert told her.

She looked up at him, disappointed. 'You're not going out again?'

'I *am* out!' Albert told her, angrily. 'This is not my home it's only my bloody car. You wouldn't think so,' he added.

Her cosmetics were balanced along the top of the dashboard. The driving mirror was slanted for her convenience. Two of her cases were open and odd bits of clothing spilled out ready for use; her radio was on, tuned to Luxembourg the station of the stars with a disc jockey spooning syrup for the millions who loved him; on the knob of the road fund licence hung a calendar and on the inside of the door window was stuck a picture of The Beatles.

'Bloody camel act,' Albert said. 'You're all the bloody same. Marriage mad right from the cradle. Any sort of marriage.'

'Albert's angry,' Dorothy told the dog, hanging on to her good humour.

It infuriated him to know that she was not yet miserable. 'Soon as you get tits you have to play mothers and fathers,' he said.

The girl stopped rubbing her hair and sat farther away from him. The silence satisfied him that he had destroyed her mood.

She said at last: 'I know I'm not wanted.'

Albert said: 'You wouldn't find an educated girl in this situation.'

Dorothy said, with dignity: 'If one hasn't got nowhere to go one can't very well go, can one?'

'Thah wah gah ma ah pahsah, Ahbah,' Charles Bluett told Albert.

Albert set down his cup of tea. 'Sorry, Charles, I didn't quite get that. Say it slowly.'

'Thah – wah – gah –' Charles began.

Treasure came in and interrupted. 'All right, dear, I'll tell him. We've had some bad news, Albert.'

'That's a laugh,' Albert said. 'How can *you* have bad news? I only come here to cheer myself up. Nobody's got what you've got, not even me and that's surprising.'

'They won't give him a pension,' Treasure said. 'It was diagnosed too long after the war ended.'

'That was careless of you, Charles,' Albert told him.

'He had the same kind of trouble – just the beginning of it,' she said, 'soon after he was discharged. But he had a wrong diagnosis and they delayed what was happening with drugs. His sister told me that.'

'Pity you didn't know before,' Albert said.

They met each other's eyes for a desperate moment. He meant it was a pity she hadn't known that Charles was doomed even when she rushed to marry him and get away from Albert's false promises. A pity for her and a pity for Albert. A pity for what they both knew happened between them when she did a simple thing like sitting down low on the settee opposite Albert and tucking her dress decorously under her thighs.

'You could have got all that back pension,' Albert said, explaining the pity of the moment to the watching Charles.

'He saw them wash his buddy out of the gun turret with a hose pipe,' Treasure said.

'Take less than that to paralyse me,' Albert said.

Treasure said: 'All those operational flights over Germany –'

'Bahgah, Frah, Pahlah –'

'Belgium, France –'

'All right,' Albert said, 'I'm not deaf.'

'Ah hah fahtah appahrahshahnah flah mah thah mah shah.'

'I know you did,' Albert told him. 'And came back.'

'Flahyah ahvah nah ahvah Hahbah, Cahlah, Bahlah – ah –'

'That's enough,' Albert told him. 'Sounds like a Cook's tour.'

'Have some more tea, Albert?'

'Mah tah, Ahbah?'

'Ta.'

Pouring it, Treasure said: 'And yet other people get a pension.'

'Well, if he had a leg off,' Albert said, 'something you could see. Old Charles may be a hero but we've only got his word for it – you can't understand that half the time.'

Charles Bluett laughed.

Chapter Three

Albert kissed Treasure good night in the hall and was alarmed to find her clinging to him and Charles only three feet away in the living room.

'Careful, mate,' he told her.

'God, Albert.' She shook her head, coming back to reality. 'You're the only one who talks to him. The only visitor. His people stay away. I need somebody, Albert.'

'What d'you mean?'

'Everything,' she said. Then, evading what was uppermost in their thoughts, she said: 'I soon shan't be able to cope. Getting him around the house. You know – sometimes he can't wait. It affects – well, anyway.'

'Can't you get somebody in? On the National Health?'

'No. I asked. They talk about a home – for M.S. When they reach a certain stage. I couldn't bear it.'

'Nor could Charles,' Albert said.

'No. No.' Then she smiled, apologetically. 'Sorry. Good night, Albert. I know you've got your plate full. Any news? I didn't ask.'

'There's a big deal coming up with the brewery. My property in Bute Place.'

'That's good.' She had known Albert for ten years. 'Good luck,' she said.

'Good luck, Tres.'

'Is that somebody in your car?' Treasure had opened the front door. And when Albert shrugged she withdrew from him. 'Lucky people,' she said. Then she called, softly: 'Albert!'

He came back to the front door. She touched his cheek

441

with her fingers. He held her hand for a moment, strongly. She closed the door and Albert turned away.

'Right then,' Albert said. He punched his hand with his other fist. His anger at what had happened to Treasure was now directed at the girl in his car. She would have to go. He would dump her and her dog and her belongings on her father's doorstep tonight. Positive thinking. Direction matey! No more thinking in circles.

He heard voices from the open window of the car before he quite reached it and stopped to listen and look.

'You are not listening!' Dorothy declaimed in a regal temper. 'I command your full attention!'

'A thousand, thousand apologies,' she said then, in a pinched, wheedling voice. 'If you please –'

Dorothy interrupted herself: 'If it pleases your gracious majesty!'

'If it pleases your gracious majesty,' she said, lisping her words, humbly.

Albert said: 'What the hell are you doing?'

Dorothy looked round at him, embarrassed. 'I'm talking to my subjects – that's Aubrey.'

The dog sat in Albert's seat under the steering wheel, scratching in a disinterested, part-time way now.

'I'm the queen of all the land and he's two of my knights – Justin who brings me jewels and perfumes and a fat one, Gustard, who brings me rich, exotic foods and that. They never know which mood I'm in so they're always trying to beat each other. He's also a serf who does the gardening and a wild gypsy called Saviour who lives in a private grotto and comes out at night. Sometime he's the king – my husband who beats me.'

'How d'you know when he's the king?' Albert asked.

'He calls me Mate,' she said. She giggled. 'My mum thinks I'm barmy. Me and Aubrey have always played this game together – queens and loyal subjects – ever since he was a puppy. He loves it.'

'Well ask him to take his fleas on the back seat,' Albert told her.

442

As he got into the car, Dorothy was saying: 'You heard the command of Prince Albert?'

'Ees,' said the serf, in her little voice.

Then, looking at Albert as he started away, she said: 'Are you still cross?'

He looked at her. 'I dunno,' he said.

'That's better,' she said. Then she said: 'I like being with you, Albert.' She settled herself more comfortably and went on painting her nails silver shimmer.

Albert put an arm around her suddenly and pulled her to him, spared attention from the road to kiss her neck.

'What was that for?' she said, surprised and delighted.

'I dunno, do I?' Albert said.

He really didn't.

The crash came as Albert was driving through the Bute Street factory area. It came from nowhere, a sudden shattering of the windscreen. One moment they were passing along the deserted street, the next all vision forward had gone and they were enclosed by the sheet of white glass pellets, still travelling at forty miles an hour.

'Albert!' Dorothy shrieked.

Albert's reactions were swift and based upon what he had heard rather than experienced; shattered windscreens were what happened to other people. He took both hands off the wheel, crooked his elbows and thrust them forward to smash a hole in the glass. He got a view of the lamplit street just before his car struck the kerb. He wrenched the wheel round and just avoided driving through a shop window into a display of typewriters and office equipment.

'Oh, my God!' Dorothy said.

'It's all right, we've stopped,' he said. He rested for a moment, half the car still up the kerb, recovering from the shock; a weakness and a trembling that grew momentarily worse instead of better.

'Oh Albert!' Dorothy said, in a strained, pained voice.

'It's all right,' Albert said. 'A stone or something. Flew up from the tyre. Ten quid's worth of new windscreen.'

'Oh God!' Dorothy said.

He looked at her now. She was holding her stomach and wearing a self-concentrated expression of intense pain.

'Didn't hurt yourself, did you?' he asked. 'What happened? Did you hurt yourself? Well for Christ's sake say something don't just sit there.'

'Oh my God,' Dorothy said.

She started rubbing her body, probing gently with her fingers. Her eyes turned in anguish upon Albert: 'I've got my pains!' she said. 'Oh my God!'

Albert's heart suddenly sprang with hope. 'You're joking!'

'Oh God,' she said. 'Awful twinges!'

Albert laughed. 'Well I don't know what you're grumbling about.' And as she fell silent he asked, anxiously: 'Are they still there? You haven't lost them have you? You'd better take something, quick. Can you have a hot bath?'

She blazed at him with unqueenly language. 'You don't bloody care, do you? If I lost my baby? All you think about is yourself.'

'You keep that pain going,' Albert told her, urgently.

He broke out some more of the windscreen, restarted the car, headed up the street fast. It would be worth ten quid's worth of windscreen.

'What on earth are you doing now?' Patricia Gort asked Albert.

He was squatting in the corner of his office heating gin in an aluminium saucepan over the gas ring.

And: 'What's it supposed to do?' she said, curiously, still discovering how the other half live.

'Bring her on,' Albert said. 'I think she's started.'

Patricia Gort said: 'Nothing you can do will do that – Daddy said so and he's a doctor. Don't worry, he made it very plain.'

'Doctors always say that,' Albert told her. 'Afraid of losing customers.'

'To the undertaker,' Patricia Gort said. 'She ought to be looking after herself, not abusing her body with hot baths and a load of poison and alcohol. Hyper-pyrexia is for killing blood viruses.'

'Hot gin is for getting rid of babies,' Albert said, stubornly. 'Everybody knows that. I've seen it work on Treasure. Not always, mind you, it depends how far it's gone. Sometimes salts will do it – Kruschens, Epsom. Or Cascara, Beechams pills, Witch Hazel, syrup of figs.'

'Then we criticize savages and their witch doctors,' she said. Then, hazily: 'What on earth do you do with Witch Hazel?'

'You get a twig and insert it,' Albert said.

Patricia Gort turned pale. 'How squalid.'

'Of course a fall is just as likely to do the trick – or running for a bus. Treasure broke her leg over the last one.'

'Poor things,' Patricia Gort said. And then, listening: 'Is she all right? Are you all right, Dorothy?' she called.

'There's something in this bath!' came Dorothy's anguished, tipsy voice. 'It's wriggling!'

'Oh lor,' Patricia Gort said.

She went into the other room followed by Albert with hot gin. Steam billowed out and the dog ran past them. Dorothy was trying to raise herself in the hot water and grope underneath her.

'Hold on,' Patricia Gort told her. She dived her hand deep down into the hot water.

'Here!' Dorothy exclaimed. '*Do* you mind!'

'I do beg your pardon!' Patricia Gort brought her hand out holding a wriggling lizard.

Dorothy squealed.

'I thought I'd got everything out,' Patricia Gort apologized.

'They get down the plug hole,' Albert said. 'Here, knock this back.'

'If it marks my baby I'll have you to blame,' Dorothy said, tearfully.

She drank the hot gin, pulling a face over it.

'Any more pains?' Albert asked, hopefully.

'My mother was frightened by a mouse when she was

carrying me,' Dorothy said, 'and look what happened because she touched herself.'

She showed them a mole on her stomach with whiskers on it. Patricia Gort sighed and went out.

'I don't think she wants to get better,' Albert grumbled.

'Only a man could call a miscarriage "getting better",' Patricia Gort said.

She was making some tea while Albert started pacing up and down like an expectant father. She was fed up with the whole thing and more than disgusted. It had gone midnight and downstairs in Hetty's jungle the peacocks had woken up.

'So this is your life,' she said.

'I don't choose it.'

'Don't tell me that. We choose what we get, matey,' she said. 'Frustrated peacocks in one room, you and your steamy sex in another. Talk about Tennessee Williams.'

'Do you like him?' Albert asked. 'I've got some of his records. I was going to bring him over for a big do at the Corn Exchange but he couldn't make it and it all fell through.'

'That's Tennessee Ernie, you're a liar and here's your tea. I just hope you know that I was in bed.'

'Nobody would know,' Albert said. She was still muffled up in her siren suit. 'What're you going to do when the weather changes?'

'And incidentally,' she said, 'and I use the word with accuracy, some business cropped up this afternoon – that man called Corby?'

'I knew he'd be back,' Albert said, with satisfaction, sipping his tea.

'You make everything sound like a master-plan.'

'Yeah – his,' Albert told her. He told her about the theodolyte aimed at his heart that morning. 'He'll offer to hold up the chopper on this place if I meet his terms about the other – you see.'

'I told him you'd had an offer,' Patricia Gort said.

Albert stared at her, resentfully. '*You* told him?'

'I said I was your secretary.'

'Hm. Yep, that's good,' Albert said, grudgingly.

'I said you were out negotiating with the prospective buyer – you were, weren't you?'

'Who? Oh, yeah. Old Cally. He's off his rocker. What did he say?'

'He wants you to ring him tomorrow. I told him you were busy tomorrow could it be the next day and he said yes. He wasn't very pleased.'

Albert laughed. 'Good.'

She gave him a worried look. 'He's very sharp.'

'So am I,' Albert said.

She said: 'But what do you know about property, Albert? Have you had any training?'

'Oh, Christ!' Albert exclaimed, scornfully. 'Not another!'

'You must have qualifications,' Patricia Gort said.

'Don't give me that bumf – you remind me of my mother.'

She said: 'It takes more than a brass plate to make you a professional man.'

'There's nothing you can't pick up, darling,' Albert said, confidently.

'Albert!' came Dorothy's cry from the next room.

To Patricia Gort it sounded like an explanatory footnote.

By twelve-thirty Dorothy was unconscious on the couch covered in blankets with the dog sitting at her feet, scratching.

'Now what am I going to do?' Patricia Gort asked.

Albert said: 'You can have the car if you like. The windscreen's out but you'll be warm enough in the garage.'

'I don't think so. It's very kind of you. What else do you do with your girls?'

'Very funny.'

A peacock screamed from below again and she said: 'I've an idea. If you're not too tired. Let's drive down to Mummy's place and take those birds.'

'What?' Albert said, tiredly.

'She'll be so pleased she'll give us breakfast.'

'What about my home?' Albert said. 'I'd get shot.'

'Your wife?'

'No – my mother-in-law,' he said. Then he said: 'Ah, what the hell – it'd be a happy release.'

'Come on, then, matey.'

'It's no good. I'm too tired. Anyway there's no windscreen in the car. I told you. We'd get blown to blazes.'

'Wake us up,' Patricia Gort said. 'Get some of those fleas out of the car.'

They were both scratching.

Albert spent ten minutes in the back room of the pet shop fighting four large peacocks and eventually came out, beaten.

'You wait here,' Patricia Gort said.

She left him in the shop and went upstairs. Albert was unused to being in his own shop without Hetty and he looked around to see where she kept the money. The tin with 'Poisonous Snakes' written on it struck him immediately as a possibility and he took it down, took off the lid.

'Chee!' he said.

The biscuit tin was half-filled with a higgledy-piggledy pile of bank notes of all sizes. It was something worth knowing. He felt happier at once, less trapped. There must be five hundred pounds there. He could always pack up and clear off.

'Good old Hetty,' he said.

Watched by a hundred gleaming eyes he extracted ten pounds, then another ten, thought for a moment and then put the tin back on the shelf swiftly before he was lost.

'You hold them,' Patricia Gort said when she came back. 'I'll use this.'

They went into the back room together and made a combined assault on the peacocks, Albert holding the wings while the girl, calmly and firmly as a nurse, stuck up their legs and beaks with Sellotape.

They drove out of town at one o'clock in the morning with a gale blowing in their faces and the birds, paralysed by the howling blizzard, sitting on Dorothy's luggage in the back seat.

'How far?' Albert asked as they cleared the town, coming up out of the built-up basin and heading into open country.

'I'll direct you,' she said.

'How far?'

'Just keep on the A5 for now.'

'How far?'

'Banbury,' she said. And when he looked at her in shock and dismay, she added, encouragingly: 'Just this side.'

He wore the blanket he had given Dorothy over his head and shoulders, peering out through a crack into the blizzard, his eyes watering. She was holding the all-purpose siren suit tightly beneath her chin.

'Do you know any Madrigals?' she asked him.

They were having to shout at each other.

'Only dirty ones,' he called back.

Patricia Gort started singing.

'Do you like it?' asked Patricia Gort.

'Very nice,' said Albert.

He had stopped the car just inside a wrought-iron gate and facing into a long drive which led to a mansion whose upper part could be seen above trees and foliage. It had taken two hours driving, the last thirty minutes through winding country lanes. They had also had an hour's sleep in the car. There was a red sky to the east of them and the dawn chorus had been started by the noise of the motor.

'What's it worth?' Patricia Gort said.

'Eh?' Albert said.

'You're a man of property,' she said, challengingly. 'What's this place worth? Today's market?'

'Oh well,' Albert said, cautiously, 'you'd have a job to find a market for a big old place like this today. What with the rates and upkeep. Take a lot of getting warm.'

'Just describe it. Go on, Albert Argyle, estate management, property development etcetera ad infinitum.'

Albert pushed the blanket off his head to get a better view. His face was red from the long cold wind, his eyes bloodshot, his chin and cheeks stubbled. He looked at the girl who was watching him, expectantly, her eyes bright with humour, her cheeks rosy.

'Go on then,' she said.

'Let's get a wash and brush-up, eh? What time's breakfast?' he said.

He went to start the car again but she stopped him.

'Come on,' she said. 'I want to see if you're as ignorant as I think you are. It doesn't seem possible.'

'Well, what d'you want to know?'

'The period, for instance?'

'Don't talk to me about periods, darling,' Albert said. Then he took another glance at the mansion. 'Well it's old. Pre-war stuff.'

'Pre-war!' Patricia Gort exclaimed. 'It's sixteenth century!'

'Well that's pre-war,' Albert said. 'Now then, what else?' He deliberated. 'It's big – four or five recep, ten bed, two bath, cloakrooms, usual offices. Hope there's some hot water.'

'It's incredible,' Patricia Gort said, 'that a man can be so wrapped up in himself that he can't learn anything about anything else. That's what's happened to you.'

'What you don't know you can pick up,' Albert said.

'You can't pick up education,' she told him. 'No wait a minute. Don't go yet. For your information this is a wonderful old Tudor mansion, enlarged in Georgian times and modernised in the twenties.'

'We've got some hot water then?'

'Those tall things flanking the long drive,' Patricia Gort continued, 'are trees.'

'I know that.'

'Poplars to be precise. The gardens are still as they were laid out by Capability Brown.'

'Mississippi Riverboat family,' Albert said.

'That was Caliope Jane,' Patricia Gort told him. She went on: 'The house has a galleried hall with open marble fireplace and sixteenth-century carved mantel, forty-foot drawing room – Mummy's gymnasium – six reception rooms variously converted into beauty parlours, sauna and Turkish baths, twenty-two principle bedrooms, fifteen bathrooms, a sun room and loggia.'

'I'd like a place like this,' Albert said. 'It gives me something to aim at. How old's your mother?'

'The grounds include twenty acres of arable and pasture, an acre of walled garden, terraces, swimming pool, stabling, garaging and gazebo.'

'What's a gazebo?' Albert asked.

'A sort of arbour commanding a view of the whole.'

'There you are you see,' Albert said. 'See what I've picked up?'

'Drive on,' Patricia Gort said. 'Mr Corby and his friends will make rings around you.'

Albert started the car up the long drive. He couldn't think why he hadn't done something about this girl. He sometimes felt that she needed it.

'You are not the man, that's why,' she said.

Then she pulled a goonish face, dropping her top lip down over her bottom lip as if mocking his crossness with her. Albert was seriously worried, however. This was the first girl since Treasure who had been able to answer his unspoken thoughts. And give the wrong answer at that.

The peacocks were numbed with cold and Albert was able to remove the sticky tape single-handed.

'I'm glad they haven't been clipped,' Patricia Gort said. 'They'll be able to roost in the trees. If not you have to put up some kind of box for them. When their toes get frostbitten they drop off.'

'How ghastly,' Albert said, in one of his voices.

'I'm glad Daddy's not here.' The girl was examining all the cars in the car port, a big converted barn. 'I'd have a job to explain you to him at this time of the morning. If I misbehave myself he's going to stop me going up.'

'Flying?'

'To university, clot.'

'I want a bed,' Albert said.

'Mummy will find you one, I expect. If you don't mind mucking in with the girls. There's about twenty here usually, all trying to lose weight.'

'I see what you mean,' Albert said.

'I hate cheap cracks. Do you know the wise-crack is old-fashioned, Albert? It dates you. The witty come-back went out when naturalism came in. You sometimes sound like an old movie. Shoo! Shoo!' she added to the peacocks.

But they remained quite stationary and glassy-eyed, exactly where Albert had put them by the car.

'Come on,' she said, 'let's go and have a swim.'

'You're joking! You must be! Do you mind?'

'Three outdated expressions,' she said.

Quite suddenly she unzipped her siren suit and stepped out of it, naked, laughed at his bewilderment, then went running out across the grass towards the swimming pool, leaping in the red light of the rising sun.

'Blimey!' Albert said.

Then, watching her, he wondered if that exclamation was dated; if he was dated; if it was dated not to strip off naked and run in front of half-a-hundred staring windows.

Albert stripped off. He ran across the grass and jumped straight into the deep end, sinking right to the bottom. As he came up Patricia Gort grabbed him and pulled him to the steps. Half-drowned, he could only gasp and splutter at her.

'Cramp?' She was patting and rubbing him, trying to get him higher from the water.

'No! Can't swim!'

'Then why jump in the deep end?'

'Only way to find out,' Albert said. 'Jesus, it's cold!'

'You're so conceited,' she said. 'You think you can do anything.'

452

'Give me five minutes,' Albert said.

He broke away from her and dog-paddled into deep water. She looked after him with some admiration for a moment, then the cold water offering relief from the colder air she followed him.

'Now like this!'

She showed him a crawl and Albert copied it. Standing in the shallow end together with the sun turning yellow on them, she laughed at him.

'It's hard to make a success of a man who doesn't know he's a failure,' she said.

'Wise-cracks date you.'

'No, I mean that, Albert, I really do. You remind me of that joke about the child who was asked if he could play the piano and he said "I don't know, I haven't tried". You think you can do anything. You're typical of those young people of today who think that fruit has only to be picked – not grown.'

Albert said: 'How can you talk such rubbish with your teeth chattering and your breasts all goose-pimples.'

'And don't forget I can see you,' she said.

She swam away from him and he followed, rapidly learning how to swim. Before they reached the far end there was the sound of a bell ringing. When they stood on the steps of the deep end again a dozen women were racing naked across the lawn towards them from the big house. They all plunged in except one who spotted the couple and waved.

'Patty! I thought I heard a car!'

'Hello, Mummy – I've brought a friend!'

'Be with you!'

Mrs Gort dived in and struck out swiftly towards them, diving under-water the last few yards and coming up perilously close to what Albert was embarrassedly holding tight.

'How d'you do,' he chattered, extending his other hand.

'These are the peacocks,' Patricia Gort said.

The four birds sat grey and colourless and immobile just as Albert had left them, as though made of stone.

453

'They don't look like peacocks,' Mrs Gort said. 'No, don't get dressed,' she told Albert. 'Come and have a good whipping.'

Albert dropped his clothes, guiltily, trotted after mother and daughter and the rest of the early-morning lunatics. He felt ill with the strain of keeping his eyes up and his mind clean.

'Is your friend amusing, Patricia? Are you amusing?' Mrs Gort asked Albert a few minutes later.

'I don't know,' Albert said, 'I'm not standing where you are.'

Albert was now being whipped with handfuls of branches and leaves in a room hot with steam and naked people. Next to him Patricia Gort and her mother were rubbing each other down with rough towels.

'My children collect amusing people and bring them to me like mother birds with titbits,' she said. 'How's the book coming, Patricia?'

'Afterwards we'll have breakfast,' Patricia Gort said, not wishing to put her raw material on guard.

'I've been reading C. P. Snow,' Mrs Gort said. 'They say he's a woman. He writes about this George Eliot. Do my back, darling. That's splendid,' she said, casting an eye on Albert: 'You're bringing him up in great weals. If you're allergic to sauna you get greater benefit,' she told Albert; 'Although I must say,' she continued to Patricia Gort who was now rubbing her mother's back, 'he doesn't look like a woman on television.'

Patricia Gort told her mother about C. P. Snow without offending her.

'For years I thought Charlotte Brontë wrote Jane Austen,' Mrs Gort confessed, delightedly.

'My wife knows Arnold Bennet,' Albert said.

They were eating hard-boiled eggs in the breakfast room with the sun pouring in when the peacocks walked past the french windows on the terrace with their tails spread out.

'Ooh!'

'Aaaah!'

'How perfectly beautiful!'

The beauty class left their breakfast and drifted out on to the terrace.

'They'll be much happier here,' Patricia Gort told Albert.

Albert nodded but he dare not look; everybody was still naked and he kept his eyes riveted on his egg.

'We go in for lots of eggs,' Mrs Gort told him. 'Any sort of cooking aroma will drive them mad – especially the three-weekers. I guarantee two stone off in three weeks or their money back.'

From outside came the sound of a peacock's scream – it was strangulated halfway through.

'You'll have to put up with a lot of that,' Patricia Gort told her mother.

Later in the garden they came across a few peacock feathers and later still Mrs Gort sniffed the breeze on the front terrace.

'Can you smell cooking?' she said. She started following the smell. 'I have to be very watchful. They smuggle things in and cook them on their electric fires. One good meal can destroy everything I've done for them. One good anything. I go in for complete irrigation – mind and matter. Are you a scientist?' she asked Albert. 'Is he a scientist?' she said to her daughter.

Patricia Gort laughed. 'Albert is what Godfrey called his last boss – the perfect example of negative-knowhow with hundred per cent supply-side lag.'

Mrs Gort's naked breast shook with her laughter and Albert, who was about to get angry, froze again.

'I never completely understood that,' Mrs Gort confessed when she had finished laughing, 'but some things Godfrey says you don't have to, do you, Patty. What was he telling you while he was whipping you, Albert?'

'Who?'

'Godfrey.' Then, appealing again to her daughter: 'What was he telling him?'

'I thought that was a girl,' Albert said.

'Really!' Mrs Gort exclaimed. Then to her daughter: 'Is he being amusing?'

'That was my brother Godfrey,' Patricia Gort told Albert. And to her mother: 'He's been petrified with embarrassment ever since he undressed.' Then to Albert, mockingly: 'Tut – and you a man of the world.'

Mrs Gort looked at Albert more objectively now. 'Yes, you are, aren't you? He is, isn't he? He could do with a spell here, couldn't he? Take a few inches off and free his mind. What sort of life does he lead? Has he got any money?'

'He's a property expert,' Patricia Gort said. 'Tell Mummy about her property.'

Albert said: 'You want to watch that damp course.' It was the only technicality he had mastered and remembered.

They drove the first fifty miles back in silence, the wind through the shattered windscreen blowing away any inclination to talk.

'All right, I'm sorry,' Patricia Gort told Albert in a transport café.

'Educated home?' Albert said, disgustedly, munching a piece of cold bread pudding. 'You take 'em peacocks and they have a bloody fry-up.'

The girl laughed. 'It wasn't completely a waste of time, Albert. It's shown us how badly-adjusted you really are, I mean. The great lover.' She laughed again and Albert chewed angrily on the bread pudding. She said: 'How many naked girls have you seen? I should say how many girls have you seen naked?'

'How many this, how many that!' Albert said.

'This is important.'

'None. We don't do that sort of thing. I'm not kinky,' Albert said.

'You see?' she said, hopelessly. 'You are kinky. That's just what you are. All of you. You've never loved. When you love you love everything. A man loves a woman – he loves her mind and her body. He gives her body the pleasure of his body – sight, touch, sensation. Not in the dark or under a blanket or secretly. The man makes love to the woman.'

Albert glanced round the transport café which had become strangely silent; lorry drivers, their knives and forks still, were gazing steadily at their plates.

Patricia Gort said, academically shaking her tea spoon at him: 'If you have been having sexual intercourse all these years with all those women and you've never seen one naked – then you have not been making love to them, you have been making love to yourself.'

'Hm!' Albert said, his face red.

'A sort of assisted masturbation,' Patricia Gort said. 'When you see a pretty girl and say "Cor!" you are not seeing her as a person but as a kind of desirable cavity.'

'Dirty bloody bitch,' a lorry driver told his mate when Albert and Patricia Gort had been blasted out with the juke box.

His mate said, heavily: 'That's your convent school.'

Dorothy, painted and groomed and wearing a freshly-ironed shortie-nightie, was sitting in a tumble of blankets on the couch playing queens and loyal subjects with her dog when Albert and Patricia came into the office at three o'clock that afternoon.

'You're supposed to knock three times and wait to be summoned,' she told Albert. 'All right,' she told the dog, 'you may go for the present. It's supposed to walk backwards three paces,' she told Albert.

'I thought you'd gone home,' Albert said.

'How could I?' Dorothy said. 'You took it with you. You and your sister!' she added, with a modified bitterness, for she was in a good humour. 'Mrs Finbow said you haven't got a sister.'

'Oh Christ,' Albert said. 'She hasn't been here?'

'I look all right, don't I? We've been holding court, haven't we Sir Gustard? He brought me baked beans on toast –'

'Never mind that,' Albert said, 'who else has been here?'

Dorothy, regally refusing to be rushed, started repainting the silver finger-nails.

'Well go on!' Albert told her. Then to Patricia Gort: 'Init marvellous. Talk about bad publicity.'

'Oh, I know you're ashamed of me,' Dorothy said. Then, forestalling Albert's pent-up anger she said: 'If you must know we've had quite a busy day – the police –'

'The police!' Albert exclaimed.

'The inspector and a constable – quite nice, they were. Then there was a Mr Corby and a Major Simpkins and – oh, yes, very honoured we were, the Borough Surveyor, a Mr Cornwallis –'

'Oh, my God!' Albert said.

He sat down behind his desk and Patricia Gort held his shoulder. 'His wife's in welfare – she thinks I'm Treasure's sister. Brother, I mean.'

Dorothy gave him a disgusted look. 'Going round telling everybody they're your sisters. I expect you'll say that's what I am. Well you'll have a bit of a job explaining Fred.'

Albert stared at her: 'Who's Fred?'

Wordlessly and not without pride of ownership Dorothy tapped her stomach. 'I know it's a boy,' she told Patricia Gort, chattily, as one woman to another, 'I can feel him playing cricket.' She giggled. 'My aunt Dora used to say that. I take after her. She lives at Gamlingay. Her husband works in fruit canning. His name's Fred. I was bridesmaid at their wedding – I was only sixteen and he was a bit keen on me. He took me home from the reception on his bike. All the cars had gone and we were both tight as lords. I caught my foot in the front wheel, you should've seen my dress.' She stopped because they were both listening to her too intently. 'Your place has been broken into,' she told Albert. 'That's what the police wanted –'

'Well why the hell didn't you say so?' Albert exclaimed. 'I'd better get back,' he told Patricia Gort. 'I don't know – the one night I'm away.'

'Wait for me!' Dorothy said.

'You're all right where you are for now,' Albert told her.

458

'No thank you very much – I'd rather be in my own place. So would Aubrey. Come on, Aubrey. No don't bother,' she said, as Albert threw her clothes at her. 'They've got sick all over them. I'll get dressed in the car.'

'I'm taking it to get a new windscreen put in.'

'I don't mind,' Dorothy said.

She slipped her coat over her nightie and followed Albert out.

'Better see what Corby wants,' Patricia Gort called from the top of the stairs.

'He probably got it,' Albert said, allowing Dorothy to pass him on the way down.

'I should think that Major Simpkins could be terribly passionate,' Dorothy said, as Albert put her into the car. 'He wanted to come back lunchtime – he whispered it. I told him you'd be here. He's very impressive, isn't he,' she said, thoughtfully. 'Talks nice.'

'Albert!' Hetty came hurrying from the shop. 'Have you heard? There was a break-in last night – we've had the police here and the insurance and everything.'

'Here?' Albert said.

'They stole the peacocks, five hundred pounds out of the tin and no end of things – I'm getting a list out now for the insurance company. Good job I kept it up.'

'See you later, Hetty love,' Albert said.

'I told you I'd make this place pay!' Hetty called as he drove away.

She went back into the shop, gaily humming. It was better than a fire, anyway, with all that livestock. It was probably the only bit of Callendar's training which had stuck. If there's a fire or a robbery, multiply everything by ten.

'We won't get to this till five o'clock or gone,' the garage foreman told Albert. 'Perhaps later,' he added. He was looking at Dorothy who was sitting on the back seat pulling on her stockings.

Dorothy looked out at them and smiled. 'I'll be all right. I've got heaps to do. Mending to catch up on and everything.' She settled down to sorting through her cases. 'Feathers everywhere,' she grumbled. 'Have you got a brush?' she asked the foreman.

Albert said: 'Give it a lubrication while it's here, will you? Do the plugs and so on.'

Amongst the mechanics and salesmen who had gathered in groups around the big workshop at a whispered rumour about the girl in the car was Jackson from stores.

'Your wife, old man?' he called to Albert.

'A squatter,' Albert told him.

He could sense that the laughter was only partly in his favour. He didn't know what Jackson might have been saying about him.

'What's the lease like on this place?' Albert chose the smartest dressed man there, judging him to be a manager. 'Any chance of it running out? Make a nice skating rink, this would. What this town needs. A good sports centre.'

Jackson said: 'Are you thinking of starting one, old chappie?'

'Could do,' Albert said. 'Get the right site. Skating, dancing, bowling, the lot. Go like a bomb.'

'You're right, Albert,' Jackson said.

Albert warmed towards him a little. 'Tip me if there's any chance of getting the lease.'

'What would you be prepared to go to, Albert?' Jackson asked.

'Oh, I dunno. Say twenty thousand. Want a ten-year lease for that. No restrictive covenants of course,' he added, suddenly remembering something else he had picked up. 'Find out afterwards you can't do what you like with it and let the council have it for peanuts.'

Jackson said: 'What do you think the turnover might be?'

'Twenty thousand a year,' Albert said. 'And that's conservative.'

'Phew!' Jackson said. 'You've come a long way since the old days, Albert.'

460

'Well, you've got to move, haven't you?' Albert said. 'Can't let the grass grow, Jacko. Ta ta, mate.'

The laughter began before Albert had got to the door but Jackson quelled it. 'What did I tell you? See what I mean?'

The laughter grew again and Jackson rode on it with a word to the boss: 'If ever you want to sell the place, Mr Travers, eh?'

The laughter went louder and higher for the boss. Albert heard it and turned round. He saw the laughing men and beyond them he saw his car rising into the air on the service ramp, Dorothy busy doing her housework inside. Albert went on his way. Just for an awful moment he had thought they were laughing at him; that Jacko had been taking the mickey in some way.

The thought depressed him. Those serfs. Those wage slaves. Didn't know they were living. They wouldn't know an opportunity if they saw one. Jacko in his cow-gown. At least Albert was somebody. A bit of a character. A bit of a celebrity. All he needed was money. The depression remained. He made a mile detour of the town to find Sid on point duty just to get a reassuring hail.

'Up your pipe, Sid!' Albert called.

Police Constable Sid, aware that his sergeant was somewhere near, did no more than nod his head at Albert.

Half an hour later Albert wandered into the public library, he didn't know why. Alice was stamping somebody's book.

'Hello, mate,' Albert said. 'You look lovely.'

If he had fired a shot he could hardly have commanded more attention in the quiet room.

'What are you doing here, Albert?' Alice whispered, her face crimson.

'Come to see you, haven't I?' Albert said. And looking around at all the staring people: 'This is a bit of a graveyard, init?'

'Ssssh,' Alice said. Then she picked up a pile of books and

461

motioned Albert to follow her, led him through the book walls to a secluded alcove. 'Where've you been, Albert? Last night?' she asked, quietly. 'I've been terribly worried.'

Albert was staring at her, puzzled. 'What's the idea of them goggles? Are your eyes bad or something – why didn't you tell me?'

'I only wear them here –'

'And what's this?' Albert took hold of her green smock and lifted it to show her legs. 'It's about two sizes too big – you look like a bloody freak. You're letting yourself go, you are, mate – no wonder I stay out all night.'

'Please, Albert!' Alice said, wretchedly.

A man came round a book case, holding a volume. 'I found it,' he said to Alice. There was a feeling in the air that he had come to rescue her.

'Oh, good,' Alice said, brightly. 'I thought it was there.'

'Are you all right, Alice?' the man said.

Albert stood waiting, feeling on the outside.

'I'll stamp it in a minute,' Alice said.

Reluctantly the man left them.

'Alice yet?' Albert said. 'Who's he, then?'

'He comes to the literary society,' Alice said.

'What's he doing here, then? Is he out of work?' Albert laughed. 'I bet he's one of your old income tax bods. He ought to be at work, not hanging round you.'

'This is his work,' Alice said, softer still, trying to influence Albert's volume. 'Research. He's an author.' Then to get the conversation into a normal, safe channel, she went on: 'Look, there are some of his books. Over here, Albert.'

She took a book from the shelf and Albert examined it, weighed it in his hand.

'Pretty good,' he said. 'Is that his name, Horace Fenton?'

'Yes.'

'You'd think he'd change that,' Albert said. 'Never be a success with a name like that. You want something with a ring to it.' He gave her back the book.' I could write a few good books if I had the time,' he said.

'Yes,' she said. 'I'll have to go –'

'Just a minute,' Albert said. 'Is that the bod who follows you home?'

'Sssh!' she said again. Then: 'No. Yes. Well, I don't know – see you at home, Albert –'

'No, no, no,' Albert said, amused by her embarrassment and holding her back. 'Now I remember. You were always a bit gone on authors, you naughty girl!'

'Please, Albert –'

'Where was *I* last night? Where were *you* last night? Playing draughts, eh? Har har har!'

'Albert! That wasn't my idea – Mother asked him in. He didn't stay. He didn't know I was married. Please don't shout.'

'Does he know you've got a kid? Ah, I thought not. Our little secret, eh?'

Almost in tears Alice broke away from Albert and hurried back to the desk. They were the focus of all attention with nobody actually looking. A woman from the desk opposite slipped into the office and a man came out with her, staring across. Alice, stamping Horace Fenton's book, made one last appeal to Albert who was hovering, belligerently.

'Please go, Albert.'

'Come and have a cup of tea,' Albert said.

'I can't!' She was talking with her head down. 'I'll get the sack!'

'Blimey,' Albert said. 'Everybody bloody frightened of getting the sack, creeping around, whispering – come on out of here.'

'No smoking!' the librarian said, coming across.

'What?' Albert said.

'If you want to smoke you'll have to go outside,' the librarian said.

'Christ!' Albert said.

He went out.

'Who was that?' the librarian asked Alice.

'I don't know,' Alice said.

Horace Fenton touched her hand as he took his book.

'We're outnumbered, mate,' Albert told himself.

There was no room for the individual any more. Not in this town. Not in this country. To get anywhere you had to be a combine or a council or a public utility; everybody else were slaves.

'She's right,' Albert said.

He was talking about Patricia Gort and his pace quickened. What he would do was, he would cut. Simple as that. The car could stay where it was and Dorothy with it – and her dog and her embryo and her fleas. Alice was happy in the library, she wouldn't miss him. As for her mother – that would be a happy release. From now on, he thought, he would do without women altogether and settle for Patricia Gort. With his brains and her father's money they'd go off to the Bahamas.

'What about Treasure?' he said to himself.

'Well, she's had it,' he said. 'It was her choice.'

'What about the property?' he said.

'What property?' he said.

He crossed the road without noticing and caused a minor chaos.

'As for the pet shop,' he said, 'Hetty can have that – I'll settle for what's left in the tin.'

'Bloody menace,' the police sergeant said, staring after Albert.

'I bet he's got something on,' Police Constable Sid apologised. 'He's usually got something on when he's like that.'

'Albert ...'

Hetty called him into the shop as he was about to enter the side door.

'Can you spare a minute for this gentleman?' she asked.

Impatiently Albert went into the pet shop to find a man there looking round, suspiciously.

'Insurance,' Hetty explained. 'He wants you to sign the declaration of loss. I have given him the list.'

The insurance man said: 'It seems incredible to me that you could have had all that stock.'

464

Albert, looking at the list, also found it incredible. Besides eight peacocks, a dozen mink, many other animals and birds and reptiles which she could only have found in a zoo book, Hetty had listed such unlikely things as china and hardware, household appliances and linen, toys and transistor radios.

'I showed you the recipes, didn't I?' Hetty said.

'Let's have a look at them,' Albert asked her.

He studied a bunch of dog-eared receipts covering a wild variety of goods; old receipts from her Callendar Warehouse days which Hetty had found at home and up-dated to suit the occasion.

'I've been explaining how we was just branching out with all these side-lines,' she told Albert.

With many misgivings Albert signed the declaration. 'Have you got any clues?' he asked the insurance man, anxiously. He looked at Hetty. 'Fingerprints, for instance?'

'I don't think so,' Hetty said. 'They did start taking them till the sergeant got bitten.'

Marjorie Mason was standing outside with her 'L' plates when Albert left the shop.

'Sorry, love,' he said. 'Car's in dock.'

'Oh, Albert!' she cried. 'You *can't* do this to me – I've got the date for my test. There's only a few days left. Can't you get it? Do something, petal. If I pass Cedric's going to get a car.'

'There's nothing I can do,' Albert said.

'Little Albert will be disappointed,' she said.

Albert said: 'I wish you hadn't called him Albert.'

'It'll break his little heart, petal,' Marjorie Mason said.

Albert said: 'You pass your test and you'll soon be breaking his neck. Come on,' he added, relenting. 'Let's go and get it.'

'You are a flower,' Marjorie Mason said, gratefully. She kissed her fingers and pressed them on Albert's cheek.

Patricia Gort was looking down from the window above. 'Albert!' she called, militantly.

They looked up, Albert guilty again.

'Mr Corby's been on the phone,' Patricia Gort told him. 'It's urgent I think. You ought to see him.'

Marjorie Mason said as they walked away: 'I hope you don't let them bully you?' And a moment later, reflectively: 'I wonder who'll be testing me?'

Albert glanced at her. 'I bet you get that sewn up,' he said. She gave him a playful tap with her 'L' plates.

Dorothy was knitting in the front seat of the car which was now parked near the entrance and ready for collection, a bill under the windscreen wiper. She opened the door and smiled at Albert.

'Home then?' she said. Then she saw Marjorie sticking on the plates and pulled a face. 'Not again! We've never got the place to ourselves.' And on a bright note: 'Notice anything different?'

'Got a new windscreen,' Albert said. He got behind the wheel and unfolded the bill. 'And a bill,' he added.

'Something else,' Dorothy said. Then to the dog: 'We've had a spring clean, haven't we, Aubrey?'

Albert looked around him. 'Very nice.'

Dorothy said, proudly: 'We scrubbed it, dried it, polished it, did the windows and the chrome, shook out all your carpets, cleaned out all the cubby holes –' and looked down at her knitting. 'I found some – things –' she sniffed. 'I've hid them. We ought to have a special place.' Then she said, brightly: 'I must say I'd rather be at home than stuck in the factory all day.'

Only now did Albert realise that she had not gone to work.

'All right, petal?' Marjorie Mason said.

Albert was relegating himself to the back seat with the dog when a mechanic came up.

'Mr Argyle?'

Albert admitted it.

'I've got something to show you, Mr Argyle.'

He opened his hands and showed Albert a pile of broken glass nuggets. 'Going to surprise you, Mr Argyle.'

There was something ironic about the way he kept repeating the name and Albert suspected a joke. Then among the glass nuggets he saw the bullet and it was no longer a joke.

'On your floor with all the broken glass,' the mechanic said. 'Have you got any enemies, Mr Argyle?'

'I meant to tell you,' Dorothy said, looking up from her knitting. 'It wasn't a stone broke the front window – somebody shot at you.'

Albert said: 'So I gather.'

He picked up the bullet and examined it.

'You'd better report it to the police, eh, Mr Argyle,' the mechanic said.

'No!' Albert exclaimed.

Marjorie Mason peered curiously at the bullet. 'It's not a two-two, it it?'

'Point three-o-three,' the mechanic said. 'What they use in the army.'

'OO-er!' Dorothy exclaimed. 'John was in the army. You know, what my sister said about. Who brought me that long-player and didn't even kiss me the first time.' She found the possibility exciting from the point of view of morale. 'Perhaps he knows I'm with you. He's ever so jealous.'

'Better get on to the police then, Mr Argyle,' the mechanic said.

'No!' Albert said again, his face dark with a thousand alarming possibilities dating back from the age of eighteen.

'Did you do it, old chappie?' Jackson asked the mechanic when Albert's car had gone.

All the mechanics were together now, convulsed with laughter.

'You bugger,' Jackson said.

'That always works,' the mechanic said. 'He gave me a quid to forget it. That's the fourth this week!'

'What it is to have a conscience,' Jackson said.

'Anything for a giggle,' somebody else said.

Albert was not giggling.

'Keep your head down, petal,' Marjorie said as she peered into her rear-viewing mirror.

But Albert's head was already down.

'Here he comes,' Major Simpkins said. 'Play it cool, Reggie.'

They were standing by the window in the golf clubhouse after an evening round. Albert had left his car badly parked in his anxiety to see whether Reggie Corby was there.

'Still got that little filly with him,' said the Major. 'Wish I were six months younger, what? Damned pretty nightie she was wearing. Never had them in my day. Bloody great flannel ones.'

'You know what to say?' Reggie Corby said. 'Don't let me down, old boy. Chaps like this should never be in the property business. Gives the whole profession a bad name.'

'Don't worry, do me bit,' said Major Simpkins.

Albert came into the bar lounge, looking round. Corby turned his back and raised his glass.

'Nice round,' he said to the Major.

'Mr Corby,' Albert said, coming up. He was out of breath. 'I believe you were looking for me?'

'What?' Corby said. 'Oh yes – Argyle. Yes, of course.'

'Sorry I missed you,' Albert said. 'Been a bit pressed. You know. Business.' The remark went oddly with the sight of Dorothy who now sat mending a bra in full view of the window and all the members. She had the car door open and was allowing the dog to find a corner on the gravel.

'Something came up,' Corby said, vaguely.

'Ah, good,' Albert said. 'I'd like to complete that business. Thinking of going abroad. If the price is right, of course.' He looked at the drinks. 'Not allowed to buy, am I? Not a member yet.'

'What would you like? I say, Ernie,' Corby called.

'I'll do it, old man,' Major Simpkins said. He smiled at Albert. 'Something to celebrate, eh? Large scotch? Splendid.'

Corby said briskly: 'Not to waste time – it's not really

468

the best place for business – sure you wouldn't like to call at the office tomorrow?'

'No, I don't mind if you don't mind,' Albert said. 'Thought I'd just call in. On the offchance. Happened to be passing.'

Albert had scoured the town looking for Corby ever since discovering that somebody wanted to kill him. Kill Albert, that was. It was one of those unbelievable things that became instantly believable as soon as it happened. The marvel was, Albert had realized, that nobody had made the attempt before. He had always made a point – sort of point of honour – of going with married women. It had become a kind of creed. Whenever he had departed from it there had been trouble. He had never dreamt that anybody ever minded.

'I had a word with the brewery about your site,' Corby said. 'I put your point of view – pretty strongly, I may say. Got a bit of sense out of them.'

'That's good,' Albert said. 'Thanks.' He made the thanks do for both Corby's efforts on his behalf and the drink which the Major put into his hand at that moment. 'Down the hatch, eh?' Albert raised his glass to them and took a long drink of the scotch. It cleared his head and restored his confidence.

'I can get you two thousand for it, possibly two and a half,' Corby said. 'I don't want a commission.'

'Well that's better than nine hundred,' Albert said. 'That's what I paid for it,' he explained to Major Simpkins. And back to Corby after another quick drink: 'If they'll go to two-and-half they'll go to three, say it quick.'

Corby laughed and the Major joined in. Albert was pleased with himself.

'Shrewd chap,' Major Simpkins said. 'Perfectly true, of course.'

Corby said, disarmingly: 'I didn't want to raise your hopes too much – but yes, confidentially I think I can get you three. You won't grumble at that?'

Albert said: 'They can have it tomorrow.'

They all laughed together.

'That's that, then,' Reginald Corby said. 'Have another drink.'

'I'll take one out to your – hm – secretary, what?' said Major Simpkins.

'Just a minute, Major,' Corby said.

'Eh? What? Oh yes, of course. Hold on then.'

Corby smiled again at Albert as the Major went to the bar. 'I suppose you couldn't do me a favour?'

'What is it?' Albert asked. He had a sure feeling that Corby was going to make a suggestion about Dorothy but he was wrong.

'Not important,' Corby said. 'But I would appreciate it. That place of yours in the High Street.'

'Oh, that's a dead loss,' Albert said. 'You can't sell that with the chopper hanging over it. Some of those places have been up for sale more than a year.'

'Yes, I know,' Corby said. 'I wouldn't touch any of it.'

'All coming down,' Albert said.

'In October,' Corby said.

Albert stared at him. 'What?'

'Didn't you know?' Corby said. 'They're issuing notices.'

Major Simpkins came back with more drinks and pressed another large scotch on to Albert.

'Matter of fact the Borough Surveyor was up to see you today,' Corby said. He looked around at the chattering groups. 'I think he's here. Anybody seen Corny?'

'Mr Cornwallis?' called the bartender. 'Think he's gone, Mr Corby.'

'Well anyway, you'll be getting notice,' Corby said. 'But the point is I've got a friend wants a shop for just a few months – travel agency. He's got a place going up in Butterhall Street but it won't be ready until the Autumn. He doesn't want to miss the rest of the summer season. He'd pay you ten pounds a week rent for that place – and rates, of course.'

Albert said: 'The pet shop's bringing in a hundred a week.'

'Oh, I see,' Corby said. 'Well I couldn't expect you to lose that.'

'Sorry,' Albert said.

'How about the rooms upstairs?' Corby asked. 'He doesn't necessarily want the ground floor. Just for two or three months.'

'I'll think about it,' Albert said.

'If you're going abroad anyway,' Corby said. He added, as a friendly aside: 'You want to clinch a price with the council before you go.'

Major Simpkins said: 'Somebody taking my name in vain?'

Albert said to the Major: 'How much would I get for my place – under compulsory purchase?'

'What's the rateable value?' Major Simpkins asked.

'One hundred and twenty pounds,' Corby said. He added: 'I should think. Isn't it, Argyle?'

'On the dot,' Albert said.

'You may get five hundred,' Major Simpkins said.

Corby laughed, scornfully. 'If you're here to fight for every pound.'

The Major protested: 'It is condemned property. Damned eyesore.'

'Well anyway,' Corby said, finalising, 'you'll do well with your cottages, Argyle, even if you have to write the other place off. It happens to all of us.'

Albert said: 'He wouldn't buy it, would he? Your friend?'

Corby laughed. 'That's wishful thinking. I wouldn't do that to my worst enemy let alone my best friend. Which he's not, incidentally, but I like him. I get all my travel at a discount.'

Albert persisted: 'I mean a low price. If he wants the premises. He'd get his money back.'

'And he might lose pretty heavily,' Corby said. 'Well don't take my word for it. Go along to the health office tomorrow – or see Cornwallis better still. You'll get five hundred compensation at the very most. More likely three hundred.'

'He can have it for five hundred,' Albert said.

'I don't think I could put it to him. It's hardly a proposition after all. You see I can't recommend it. It's not entirely ethical if you can't recommend a purchase.'

'You could tell him all the facts,' Albert said. And after a moment's silence, he said : 'Four hundred, then?'

'I'll tell you what I'll do,' Corby said, generously, 'I'll mention it to him.'

'Fair do's,' Albert said. 'And what about the other?'

'With any luck I'll have a contract ready for you to-morrow. That's rushing it between brethren.'

'Ta,' Albert said.

'Meanwhile let me know if you change your mind about renting that shop,' Corby said.

'I'd rather get rid of it,' Albert said. He laughed. 'If you can get out of this town with three and a half thousand quid you're doing well.'

'How true,' said Major Simpkins.

'Very true,' said Reginald Corby.

'I may go into production on the continent,' Albert said. For a little while he felt like one of the golf-club fraternity he had always so much despised. It was not a bad feeling when you were actually standing there with them and a glass in your hand. 'Belgium, that's the place,' he said. He raised his voice to reach a nearby group which, he was pleased to see, included Solly Cowell, at the moment hobnobbing with the lady Mayor. 'You get advantages there,' Albert said. 'You get well treated,' he said, using the only language he knew, the language of the 'You Get' circulars. 'You get very favourable financial concessions in Belgium at the moment.'

'Couple of years ago and I could have done something about that, by jove,' Major Simpkins said.

He was in fact looking out at Dorothy who now had one long leg out of the car showing her thigh as high as it went to the lounge-bar windows as she twisted to attract Albert's attention.

'Have they got any pork pies?' Dorothy shouted.

472

Albert hurriedly excused himself and ran out with a promise to see Corby tomorrow.

'Fascinating!' the lady Mayor said coldly, looking out of the window.

'We've got it!' Corby muttered. 'I think we've got it!'

Solly Cowell leaned closer as if to place his drink somewhere convenient and Corby turned away.

'Call a meeting, Major,' he said, softly.

Reginald Corby went through to the men's lavatory and was joined a moment later by Major Simpkins and two other men; one a leading local solicitor called Winstone, the other Sam Wrexby, branch manager of a building society. They stood in line abreast facing the plumbing.

'I think we've got it!'

'The whole block now?'

'Good God, that's marvellous. Smart fellow, Corby.'

'What's it worth?'

'Quarter million to them. Ten thousand each for us with a little something for Cornyboy.'

Major Simpkins broke wind and said: 'Funny how you shiver when you start peeing?'

Chapter Four

Albert drove back through the town keeping an eye out for a hidden marksman. He had enjoyed the drink and he was excited at the prospect of cashing in on his liabilities – which is what his property investments amounted to in his hands – but he was not relaxed.

'Would a bullet go through your head after it had gone through the glass, actually?' Dorothy inquired in a technical way from her knitting. And then she said: 'I don't think it was John. He wouldn't have missed. Must be a madman.'

'How would you like to take yourself to the pictures and get some fish and chips afterwards?'

'There's nothing good on. Don't really feel like going out tonight.'

'I want the car,' Albert said, firmly. 'I've got to take my wife to the doctor's.'

'I like that! I haven't been to the doctor's yet myself!'

'Then it's time you went. Suppose there's nothing wrong?'

'Wouldn't make any difference, would it? Now Mum and Dad know what I thought it was. Anyway, it is. So.'

'You can't stay with me,' Albert told her. 'You know you can't.'

'I don't want to, thank you very much. Soon as I get myself a job and a room.'

'You've got a job.'

'I can't go back there. Are you kidding? They all know. They saw me knitting.'

Albert took a closer look at the knitting. It was a baby's garment, coloured blue.

'I wonder you didn't broadcast whose it was.'

'I did,' she said. 'Wasn't going to let them think I didn't know.'

'Thanks,' Albert said.

'All talking and pointing,' Dorothy said. 'Jealous, that's all.'

'I'll drop you off outside the Regal,' Albert said. 'I'll give you some money.'

'What about Aubrey?'

'I'll lock him in the garage.'

'He'll bark.'

Albert closed his eyes for a prayerful moment.

'Oh, all right,' Dorothy said. 'I'll take him with me. Who's going for a nice walkies, then?' she asked the dog. And to Albert as he stopped the car: 'What time shall I be home?'

'I'll leave the door on the latch.'

'Kiss me, then,' she said.

He kissed her goodbye and drove swiftly away.

'Alice in?' Albert asked Mrs Finbow when he came into the kitchen.

'Haven't you forgotten something?'

Albert kissed her hello and again moved swiftly away.

'I'm not going to bite you!' She was washing up.

Albert said: 'You never tell me if Alice is in!'

'Temper temper,' she said.

She never had told him if Alice was in. She had always used her daughter as a bait to keep him with her a little longer.

'Is she or isn't she? Alice!' he called.

'Up here,' Alice called down.

'She's changing!' Mrs Finbow said when Albert moved towards the door.

'That's a pity. If I can't see my own wife naked.'

'Albert!'

'You're kinky, you are,' Albert said. He tried to remember what else was involved but failed.

She took it as a compliment and dwelt on the possibility after he'd gone upstairs. 'Hm,' she said, intrigued at the thought. Then she called: 'Do you mind if she goes to the pictures? I said you wouldn't.'

Albert caught Alice dressing in the bedroom and he locked the door. She watched him, puzzled.

'Come here,' he said.

He lifted her in his arms and put her on the bed, took off what clothes she had put on, kissed her navel.

'Albert, she'll come up!'

'I want you,' Albert said.

'Here I come,' Mrs Finbow called, playfully, as she came up the stairs.

'You'll never guess what we're doing,' Albert called.

'Albert!' Alice cried. She pushed him away, sat up. 'Unlock the door!'

'All right, listen!' Albert said, urgently and softly. 'You go out as if you're going to the pictures. Give me a ring and I'll answer – say I've got a business appointment. Meet me outside the town hall, okay?'

'But I *was* going to the pictures –'

'Well now you won't have to,' Albert said.

The door rattled.

'I can hear you whispering!' Mrs Finbow called. Alice was pulling on her clothes at frantic speed.

'Somebody brought her home,' Mrs Finbow told Albert after Alice had gone out.

Albert grunted. He was reading the evening paper and waiting for the telephone to ring.

NEW SUPERMARKET TO OPEN said a headline.

I don't know where, Albert thought.

'I'm glad you're not jealous,' Mrs Finbow said.

'Hah,' Albert said, as he read.

The information was that property scouts had found a possible site for the Supermarket in the town centre and negotiations were proceeding. 'I'd like a slice of that,' Albert thought.

Mrs Finbow said: 'You don't really love her, do you? You know you don't.'

'Who?' Albert said, looking up.

She had got into something comfortable in record time and was arranging drinks on a table at his side.

'Pernod,' she said, 'With ice, sugar and water. You're supposed to trickle it through the sugar lumps but we haven't time for that.'

He was saved by the telephone bell.

'Sorry,' he told her. 'Business – urgent!'

'I don't believe you!' she said. 'It's more of those tarts of yours. You don't have any urgent business except with them.'

'Very funny!' Albert said. He threw the paper at her. 'Take a look at that, then! That supermarket – they're after my site!'

Unknown to Albert, they were.

He drove Alice out of town, using the darkened side-streets.

'Why that scarf round your face, Albert?' she asked him.

'Somebody's trying to kill me,' Albert said.

She stared at him. He told her about the bullet through the windscreen.

'Oh Albert! That's awful! It might have killed you!'

'That was the idea, wasn't it?'

'I don't suppose so. I don't suppose they knew it was you. Who it was, I mean. Some kids. Young thugs. I read about it before. Air guns and things.'

'It was a bullet,' he said. 'They were after me.'

'Who are?'

'Dunno, do I?'

'You haven't been up to anything? I mean it's not to do with business?'

Now Albert looked at his wife. 'What sort of business do you think I run?'

'You never tell me anything about it.'

'Nothing to tell,' Albert said, truthfully.

'You didn't tell me your shop had been broken into,' she said.

477

'Who told you that?'

She said: 'It was in the paper.'

'Oh blimey,' Albert said.

Alice said, quietly: "I hear everything about you second-hand. Makes me feel silly, sometimes. Other people tell me first. You don't talk to me.'

'Where, for instance?' Albert asked. 'In the bathroom?'

'I know,' she said, miserably.

'We should've thought about this before,' Albert said.

They cleared the last residential roads of the town and climbed a steep country lane. Albert slid his arm around her.

'You must report it to the police,' Alice said.

He had parked the car in a gateway to a field and they were looking down at the lights of the town far below.

'Remember this place, Alice?' Albert said, sentimentally. Then he said: 'It was you, wasn't it?' And then he said: 'Oh I shouldn't have said that. Sorry.'

He went to kiss her but she moved her face and it didn't quite land. She started talking to cover the moment.

'The police might find out who it was. If you've got the bullet.'

'I wouldn't want that,' Albert said. 'Court case and everything. Bad publicity.'

'I don't see why. You didn't do the shooting.'

'People taking pot-shots at me,' Albert said. 'Doesn't make me look very popular, does it? I mean you never know what excuses they might dream up.'

Alice glanced at him as though she began to understand.

'What I mean is, well – I've got this big property deal going through.'

She remained silent.

'Don't you want to know what it is?'

'There've been so many, Albert.'

'This one's finalized,' he said. 'I was up the golf club to-night with the lady Mayor, the Borough Surveyor, Corby, Major Simpkins – they'd been looking for me all day.'

'Where were you?' Alice said.

Albert expressed his irritation. 'Women always miss the bloody point.'

'Don't swear, Albert.'

'Don't swear, don't smoke, don't raise your voice – what the hell's the matter with you, Janice? Alice? You've got your priorities wrong.' Then, after a short dark silence: 'Five thousand quid, that's what I've got to come.'

'Honestly?' Alice was looking at him again.

'Cross my heart. Signing the contracts tomorrow.'

'Perhaps that's why somebody shot at you?'

'What?' Albert said.

'To stop you singing.'

'Oh, gawd. Pictures and books, that's you. Oh yes, they're a lot of crooks, you're right there. Still, wouldn't do them much good if I was dead. They'd have to come to you.'

'I wouldn't know what to do,' Alice said.

Albert thought about this for several minutes, smoked a cigarette before feeling bitter. 'I like that,' he said at last. 'The way you said that. Never mind I'm dead.'

'You know I didn't mean that.'

He wouldn't let it go; his voice hardened with self-pity: 'You wouldn't be much worse off, would you. No, you wouldn't,' he said, as she refused to answer. 'Of course,' he went on, harshly, 'if I got bumped off after I've signed you'd be worth five thousand quid.'

'What's the matter with you, Albert?'

'I don't know. I dunno. Ah ...' He gave his face a dry-wash then opened the sunshine roof to throw out his cigarette stub. 'Look at them stars, eh?' He sprawled back, his face to the clear night sky, breathed deeply.

She stared at him in concern. 'What's the matter? You don't usually notice the stars.'

Albert said: 'You don't know what I notice. Nobody does. People think they know you.'

Alice said: 'I know you, Albert.'

'No, mate.'

479

She was looking at him, anxiously, her face in shadow.

'I'm only just beginning to know myself,' Albert said.

Alice laughed, spontaneously. 'That's an improvement!'

Unknown to Albert it was too late.

He looked at her first in hurt, then glad that he had made her laugh, laughed himself. The mood went soaring. He grabbed her and pulled her along the seat. She lay looking up at him and past him at the sky through the oblong of sunroof. As he kissed her and talked he was undressing her.

'Know what we're going to do? Mrs Argyle – I'm talking to you. Mrs Harris. We're going to take that money and we're going abroad.'

'Oh, yes. I'd love a holiday.'

'Not a holiday. For good. Somewhere warm. Make a fresh start. Some business. Just the two of us. Are you cold?'

'Three of us, ALBERT,' Alice said.

'Oh fine!' Albert took his hand out of her blouse. 'Not your bloody mother no bloody fear we're bloody not –'

'I'm talking about the baby! Just the two of us you said! What about Bennet?'

'Ben's all right where he is. They understand him better than we do. He's happier there.'

'Very convenient, Albert. He happens to be my son. I won't go away and leave him.'

'Oh, shut up for Christ's sake,' Albert said. He sat up and got out his cigarettes. 'Don't fool yourself. He don't know you from the next –'

'Yes he does! He does know me.'

'He throws his bloody arms round anybody. Half-strangles old ladies in tea shops – and God help their bloody poodles.'

'He's improving, Albert. You never see him.'

'And I don't bloody want.'

'He's started talking,' Alice said.

'Gawd help us now,' Albert said. 'I've heard some of 'em talking, remember. They're not even normal lunatics – "Have you got testicles under your bottom, Albert?" right

480

in the middle of Woolworths on a Saturday – that kid we took out with Ben when he first went. Crowd of kids followed me up the street shouting it.'

'You thought it was funny at the time.' Alice was dressing herself now.

'Lots of things I thought was funny at the time,' Albert said.

'There's a shooting star,' Alice said. 'It's gone now.'

Albert said: 'I've got a position to keep up. Don't want people laughing at me. I don't like people laughing at me.' He remembered the crowd in the garage. 'I'm not a bloody comedian.'

Unknown to Albert he was a comedian; the saddest kind who is only funny off-stage.

'He says "Sunday" now. Because he knows I'm coming,' Alice said, her voice lifting.

'That's nice.'

She looked at him. 'You have plenty of patience with some invalids. If they've got a pretty wife.'

Albert's voice cracked a protest: 'That's a rotten thing to say. I used to go to the kids' home –'

'It's not a home! There's only three places like it in the country. We're very lucky.'

'Two or three times a week,' Albert said. 'I was always taking him out for rides.'

'And Miss Potter,' Alice said.

'Who?'

'Oh, never mind.'

'No, come on, out with it. If we're not going to make love we might as well have a bloody good row – we won't get out again for another five years. Who's Miss Potter?'

'I forgot you're bad on names,' Alice said. 'She was the first one to look after Ben. The pretty one, you remember now? She got into trouble for stealing those pills and nearly killed herself with them and got the sack?'

'No!' Albert said.

'Oh, Albert,' Alice said, tiredly.

Albert stared at her in amazement. 'You don't think –

oh, come off it, Alice. A psychiatric assistant looking after
my own kid? With him with us all the time?'

Alice said: 'That's why Doctor Strong asked you to stop
taking him out. It put him back six months.'

'What the hell are you talking about?'

'I don't want to talk about it.'

'I want to know. What put him back six months? I like
to know what people are saying about me. Fair do's, eh?
What put him back six months?'

'Doctor Strong didn't say. Not in so many words. He just
said one day – after Ben had been out with you – and her
– well, they called it a traumatic experience.'

'Oh?' Albert thought about it with interest, trying to remember.

'Anyway he's progressing again now. I couldn't leave him.
Not for one week. He knows Sundays now.'

'They're doing well,' Albert said. 'He's one up on the rest
of the country.'

Alice suddenly laughed. 'That's more like the old Albert.'

Laughter had always bridged the gap to love for Albert
and he seized upon it again, holding her in his arms.

'I'm a rotten sod,' he said, 'but at least I know it.'

'I don't know why you thought it was such a secret,' Alice
said.

Albert laughed and bit her and kissed her and began to
undress her again. 'Other way round,' he said.

'You've made love on this seat before.'

'Never,' Albert told her, emphatically. 'I only have to
rough it with my wife.'

Alice laughed and then stopped him. 'I don't want any
more children. I don't want another child as long as I
live.'

'I'll drink to that,' Albert said.

He felt round to the cubby hole, opened the flap, put his
hand inside and swore. The only packet was cigarettes.

'What's the matter?'

'Nothing,' Albert said. 'I'll be careful.'

'No, Albert.'

Albert sat up and started another cigarette. 'Was your journey really necessary,' he said, bitterly.

It was a wartime travel-economy slogan that she was not old enough to remember. She started dressing again.

He dropped Alice by a late-night bus queue in the town.

'I'll give you time to get home and follow you in,' he said.

Alice said: 'I'll switch the hall light on and off if Mother's in bed.'

It was an arrangement that rang a bell with Albert. It was what her mother used to do when they were first married if Alice was in bed.

Albert cut his engine and watched the house. The hall light went on and off again, twice. He got out, crossed to open the garage doors.

'Hello, darling,' Dorothy said. 'You're late but I don't mind.'

She was sitting comfortably on a broken-down sofa which he had last seen in the jumble room upstairs. There was an old oil stove burning warmly with coffee steaming on top.

'Fancy doing all this and not telling me!' Dorothy said. 'Say thank you to Albert,' she told the dog.

'Thought it would be a surprise,' Albert said. It was a surprise to him.

'What are the onions for?' Dorothy said.

There were two strings of onions hanging on a nail in the wall.

'Bit of atmosphere,' Albert told her.

Either Alice knew even more than she appeared to know about his affairs or else her mother had made herself a love nest. It didn't matter much which.

'Fancy thinking of a hot-water bottle,' she said. She laughed and showed him: 'I've got it inside my nightie.'

He now saw that under her coat she was wearing a red brushed-nylon nightie with fur mules on her feet, ready for bed.

'Another two rows,' she said, busily knitting, 'and I think I'll turn in.'

She had put up a line across one end of the garage and on it were suspended her clothes. Albert brought the car in, closed the main doors and went across to the side door.

'See you tomorrow?'

Dorothy looked at him, disappointed. 'Aren't you going to stay a little while?'

'They're waiting for me.'

'I *don't* think! That chap's been waiting outside in his car for hours.'

'What chap?'

'Your wife's chap. Well don't pretend she hasn't got one. He's only just gone.'

'My turn now, then,' Albert said.

Dorothy put her face down and went on knitting.

'Only kidding,' Albert said.

'Kiss me good night, then.'

Albert did as he was told. Dorothy made the most of it. In some miraculous way she appeared to be bathed and scented.

'I used the Regal cloakroom,' she explained. 'Had a strip-down wash. Woman didn't half stare when I come out. Why don't you come to bed a little while? Have a rest,' she added, to take off the baldness.

'You're in enough trouble, ducks.'

'Don't matter then, does it? No good closing the gate after the cow's gone. Well, you know what I mean.'

There was the sound of a door opening somewhere, the rattle of milk bottles. Albert left her, quickly.

'See you tomorrow.'

Dorothy shaped a kiss for him and smiled.

'Stand guard, you two,' she told Sir Justin and Sir Gustard when Albert had gone.

'That's Argyle,' Reginald Corby said.

His chief clerk smiled and sang: 'You don't have to tell me, I know!'

They were looking out of the estate office window on to the busy corner of High Street and Bute Street. Albert was parking his car in the only available space.

'He's got fatter,' the chief clerk said. 'Pity his suits haven't. Always a bit too sharp. I told him they'd date – tapered trousers with no turn-ups, turnback cuffs on his sleeves, Italian jacket.'

'You know what to do?'

'Sure sure sure.'

Corby went into his private office and closed the door. The chief clerk opened his door and called to a girl:

'There's a property magnate just coming in, bring him straight in to me and don't disturb us. Mr Corby is out – okay?'

Albert entered the chief clerk's office and stopped in amazement. 'Oh no!' he exclaimed. He turned round and went out, comically. The chief clerk dragged him back, laughing.

'Oh yes!' he said.

'Max!' Albert exclaimed. 'I thought you were still inside!'

'Not so loud!' said Max.

They laughed and clasped each other as brothers, turning it into a mutual appraisal of each other's suits.

'Nice!' Albert said.

'Very nice!' said Max. 'Sit down. I'll give you a drink. How would you like a nice lemonade? Where have you been you old bastard? My goodness, this is nice. Ever see any of the old crowd?'

'Not if I can help it.'

They laughed together over the desk.

'Well I don't have to ask you what you've been doing!' Max said. He tapped a document which lay in his basket. 'When I saw your name on the contract I said: "If there's any property fiddling going on I bet it's Albert!" You shrewd old bugger – offloading this junk!'

'You've got to do something,' Albert said, modestly. 'Is that my contract?'

'And a cheque,' Max said. 'I told the boy – that's Corby – if it's Albert he'll want his money no messing about.'

'Thanks, Max – let's have a look.'

'Ha ha – careful as always, eh?' Max said. He spread out

485

the contract with an expert display so that a dotted line showed on each page; the pen was already in Albert's hand. 'Sign there, there, and there – initials on the first three, full signature over the stamp. Okay?'

'Balls,' Albert said.

Max laughed again and Albert settled down to read the contract. 'Forgive me for trying,' Max said.

'This is not the one,' Albert said. 'This is the shop.'

'That's right – the other one's not quite finalized. Matter of fact Mr Corby's up with the brewery's solicitor now – should be back any minute –'

'Two hundred and fifty quid!' Albert exclaimed, staring at another clause in the contract. 'I said four hundred!'

'Ah, that's right,' Max said. 'In fact you will get four hundred. Corby's up-priced your other property to three thousand one hundred fifty – swings and roundabouts, you know. It means his pal won't risk so much on the shop. The Council won't guarantee more than two-fifty on demolition.'

'I don't like that,' Albert said.

'Wait till he's back with the other contract, then,' Max said. 'You'll feel safer and it suits me.'

Albert said: 'He's not on the fiddle, is he, Max?'

Max laughed. 'Of course he is. Who isn't? But not about this. I've given this a good vetting for you, Albert. It's a straight deal. You're doing well. Here, have a drink.'

Max splashed whisky into two glasses and in order to do so moved some papers so that a cheque appeared from underneath. It was made out to Albert in the sum of two hundred and fifty pounds.

'Give me half an hour,' Max said. 'The bank doesn't close till half-past eleven and you can still cash this.'

Albert shared a toast with the drink, then said: 'Think I'll let my solicitor handle this, Max, if you don't mind.'

'Of course, old boy, of course. Very wise. I'll send him the contract and withhold the cheque until I hear from him – who is it?'

'Winstone,' Albert said.

'Ah yes,' Max said. 'Heard of him.' He started writing.

'How do you spell it? What's the address?' He'd got it down before Albert had finished telling him. He now picked up the cheque and slipped it into a drawer. 'How about a get-together some time, Albert? Tonight, for instance? The George? Say – nine o'clock? I've got a friend if you haven't though I'm sure you have?'

'Good idea,' Albert said. He was still looking at the drawer with the cheque in it. 'How does he know the brewery will come up with three thousand one-fifty?'

'I got a verbal confirmation myself,' Max said. He laughed. 'I'm the real power behind the throne in this place.'

Albert said: 'Why doesn't that give me more confidence, I wonder?'

They laughed together and Max poured more whisky.

'All right,' Albert said. 'I'll take it.'

'What?' Max said. 'Oh, the cheque? Well, if you're not perfectly happy?'

'Who's perfectly happy these days?' Albert said.

He signed the contract and Max gave him the cheque.

'Bird in the hand, eh?' Max said.

'Don't be filthy,' Albert said.

'Tonight, then, nine o'clock, the George?' Max said. 'If you like I'll bring that other contract with me, okay?'

'I might get back before you close,' Albert said.

'That's right – see you, then, Albert.'

'Ta ta, mate,' Albert said. 'Thanks for the noggin.'

When Albert had gone and not before Reginald Corby emerged from his office. They watched Albert drive away.

'Like a lamb,' Max said.

'Has he signed the conveyance?'

'He's signed everything. Old Albert would sign the Magna Carta to get a bit of ready cash in his pocket.'

Corby said: 'See that Winstone sends me the deeds before Argyle gets my letter.' The telephone rang and Corby took it from Max. 'Hello, yes? I wondered if you'd heard, Mr Wheatley. Yes, I'm afraid it's true – your road has already been designated. One-way traffic, no parking. . . . It hits

487

everybody. . . . Well it's bound to topple values, it always does. . . .'

'You can rely on it,' Max said into his hand.

Aside from his conversation Corby said to Max: 'Get Simpkins to call a traffic committee meeting – full house, if possible, we want all the support we can get.' Then continuing his commiserating conversation: 'You have to take the broad view – after all it is for the good of the community.'

'Amen,' said Max, rubbing his hands.

On fine Sundays while Alice took a bus to visit her child at the psychiatric home, Albert took Treasure and Charles for a ride in the country. It had become an habitual good deed. Apart from short trips in the wheelchair, which Charles hated as a symbol of resignation, it was the only way he ever saw the world.

On this particular Sunday Albert left Dorothy and her dog by the lake, the town's claim to a lido, where she could sunbathe and watch the boating, then after picking up Treasure and Charles, followed Treasure's mysterious directions to a new destination.

'Turn right along here,' she told Albert from the rear seat, ' then head towards Kinsley Woods.'

'Kahslah Wah, Ahbah,' Charles repeated.

Albert was one of the very few people with whom he could still pretend to be articulate.

'You're not going courting, are you?' Albert said.

Charles laughed.

'Rah!' Charles said.

Albert turned sharply right on to the Kinsley Road.

'Yah cah Stahs, Ahbah,' Charles remarked.

'What Charles?' Treasure asked.

Albert said: 'He said the car stinks.'

'Charles!'

'No, he's right,' Albert said. 'Cross between a bedroom a lavatory and a dog kennel.'

Charles laughed again.

Albert met Treasure's eye in his mirror: 'I've got a problem I haven't told you anything about.'

'Have you tried taking anything?' Treasure said.

They all laughed together. It was like one happy family. Mother, father and the gurgling baby.

'It's like summer,' Albert said.

'It is summer,' Treasure informed him. 'It's the best summer since 1959. Haven't you noticed?'

Albert noticed now. He drove through man-high bracken crowned with clouds of flies; great soft lakes of blue heather with the heat shimmering above; grass brown-green with summer and clumps of gorse and broom and hawthorn which presently gave way to a cool, temple-quiet forest of oak and ash with the shiny leaves of sweet chestnut and rhododendron interspersed. A strange rural district far removed from all Albert's urban worries.

'This road forking left,' Treasure said.

Albert said: 'It says private.'

'It's all right,' Treasure assured him.

'Ahs ah rah, Ahbah,' Charles assured him.

Charles, sprawled on the front seat with Albert, had been staring up through the sunroof into the sky. Now he looked ahead as though about to see something that might be important to him.

'Stop here,' Treasure told Albert.

They stopped in front of white railings. Beyond was a country mansion. On a post by the entrance to the drive and lawns was written:

COUNTY HOSPITAL HOME

'There it is, Charles,' Treasure said.

Charles was staring with his pale eyes at the mansion, the sunlit lawns, the nurses, the people in wheelchairs on the terraces.

'Gah awah,' Charles said.

Albert looked at Treasure who motioned him out of the car. Together they walked away into the woods leaving Charles to his own thoughts and feelings.

They lost themselves, purposely, amongst the under-growth, as town people do in a wood.

'How did he find out?' Albert asked her.

'He heard me talking to you the other night.'

'Oh gawd!'

'He had to know sooner or later.'

'You sound hard-hearted, Tres.'

'Yes. I often feel it. I can't tell you – I can't tell anybody how I feel about Charles now. It gets harder and harder to remember him as he was. I'm losing my loyalty to that person. I didn't know him very long. I didn't know him as long as I've known you, Albert.'

'I know.'

'This – invalid – I just feel terribly sorry for him.'

Albert took her hand as they walked.

'But I'm sorry for me, too, Albert,' she blurted out. She was crying. 'He's got some sort of – mechanism – that makes it not too bad. I mean, simple, childish – accepting things. I haven't got that.'

'I know, mate.'

'I mean, if I felt the same about him – as I did – well, I never loved him but you know. If I felt the same I couldn't even think of letting him come here, could I? All alone? With strangers. For the rest of his life. But I can, Albert!'

She stood by a tree, sobbing. Albert put an arm around her.

'Did he ever know about us?' Albert asked her.

'Yes. Everything. I told him.'

'Christ. I would never have kept coming.'

'That's why I didn't tell you,' Treasure said. 'He told me not to tell you. He said I needed you. I do, Albert.'

'You've got me,' Albert said.

She looked up at him, wiping her eyes. 'No, I haven't, Albert. Too many people have got you. You don't belong to me. You don't even belong to yourself anymore.'

'What made you tell him? What the hell made you tell him?'

'Well it was a long – well he said. You know when they

490

told him. When that bloody doctor told him. That it was incurable. When they told him what he'd got. For his own good. When they told him. When he knew.' Albert waited. She took a deep breath. 'Sorry. So he could get adjusted, they said. I still can't get over that. I don't care what anybody says. They should never have told him that it was hopeless. That there's nothing else to live for. Should they, Albert? What do you think? Really?'

'What did he say? What made you tell him, then?'

'He. Well, he apologized. One night. In bed. Well I mean – that went first of all. He used to cry. He said he was sorry for what he'd done to me. I just told him I was sorry for what I'd done to him. You and me.'

'Yeah.'

'If it wasn't for us – well it was my fault more than yours – he could have had a child.'

'Would that have been better as things have turned out, Tres?'

'He's got nothing to show, Albert. It would have been something. Nobody ever knows you've been on this earth if you don't have children.'

'Sorry.'

Albert turned away, ashamed of what he'd done to her. She pulled him back and managed a smile.

'That wasn't fair. You've been wonderful. I don't know what I'd do if – if ever you weren't here.'

He was going to tell her about getting the money and his plans for going away but he didn't.

'I'll always be here.'

She smiled at him, tearfully, nodded. They linked arms and walked back through the wood.

'Trahsay!'

The call came while they were still surrounded by low-hanging branches, out of sight of the car. Albert quickened his pace but Treasure held him back.

'No, stay here, Albert. I know what it is.'

'You'll want some help –'

'Trahsay!'

She left Albert, went a few paces, then came back, embarrassed: 'Albert – I don't like asking. Have you got any paper?'

Albert was angry with himself for not understanding her for a moment and prolonging her agony. 'Oh sure – here. Here you are.' He gave her some paper from his inside pocket. 'Is that enough?'

She nodded, too pent-up to speak, walked away a few paces and stopped. 'I can't!' she shouted.

Albert got to her in a bound, scratching his face on branches.

'Take him inside!' she shouted at Albert, her eyes bright, her mouth twisted with pain, her face a stranger's. 'Take him inside. I don't want to see him again! He's filthy!'

Albert slapped her face, shook her, let her cry in his arms.

'I'm not the right sort of woman,' she said, when she could talk. 'Some people can do it. I'll be all right now.'

'Trahsah!'

'Wipe your face.'

'I'm sorry, Albert. I'm all right now. Wait here, dear. Smoke a cigarette or something.'

He watched her walk away again. She should have been his wife. He sat down in the grass, his back to a tree, his tie undone, his only concession to summer. With his eyes closed he could have been anywhere; Fiji, Jamaica, Tobago. He heard the birds singing and he heard the car door slam. Poor bitch, he thought. Poor sod. Charles, he meant. And most of all poor Albert, he thought. She was right, he didn't even belong to himself. You were born free, but by the time you had blundered into half-a-dozen other blundering people you were trapped for life. You weren't free any more, you weren't alone any more till you went to the grave.

'Give me a cigarette, Albert.'

Treasure came back through the bushes and sat down at his side while he lit cigarettes for both. He was getting through sixty a day now, cancer or no cancer. He had decided that he would smoke until he had straightened his life out and then he would give it up.

'He doesn't want to go there,' she said.

'Do you blame him?'

'He wants to strike a bargain,' she said.

She was sitting with her head back against the tree, talking to the sunlight that filtered down.

'If I keep him at home,' she said, in a flat voice, 'I can live a natural life.'

Albert looked at her, not understanding.

Now she met his eyes. 'With you, Albert.'

'Charles said that?'

'You wouldn't think he understood as much as that, would you? He does. He knows I'm under a strain. He thinks if we have an affair – if we're lovers again – I shall be able to stand it. He's been sitting watching that house and those people and working it out.'

'He must be desperate,' Albert said.

She was still looking at him for an answer. 'Could you, Albert?'

'Not if Charles knew,' Albert said.

'I could,' she said. 'I need loving.'

Albert cuddled her close but kept his hands away from her body. 'We ought to get back,' he said.

She looked into his eyes, searching for something they used to have. They both knew that the most essential part of it was that it had been without a permit.

'Ben. Ben! No, Ben!' Alice dived on the boy before he could embrace the woman sitting by the paddling pool.

'He's all right, bless him,' the woman said.

Alice smiled at her but Benny was not all right. He looked all right but he wasn't all right. He looked sturdy and normal and bright-eyed and extremely happy. Held by his mother and thus frustrated, he went off into clouds of delighted laughter and looked around for something else to do. He was equally delighted with his ideas whether he carried them out or was stopped. The game was whether she could predict what he was going to do next and baffling her if he could.

493

For the first three years Alice thought she had got a very strong-willed child and that was all. He objected to practically everything she wanted to do – wash, dress, feed, take out, bring in, sit, stand. Whatever it was caused a fight and left him sulking and rocking himself as if for comfort. During that time Alice got the reputation for being a hopeless mother. Nobody knew how these fights left her.

Later she began to suspect that something was wrong with Bennet. He always sat in the same place and rocked.

'That's his security spot,' Albert used to say. 'I wish I had one.'

Left alone in his cot he would scream with laughter at secret jokes but stop, irritated, if somebody came in and wait for them to go and shut the door before laughing again.

'Well, he's happy,' Albert used to say.

At the age of three he killed Mrs Finbow's kitten by tearing its jaws apart to look down its throat.

'He's mentally deficient like your father,' Mrs Finbow told her daughter.

'He might be mentally deficient or he might not be,' the doctor told Alice.

Alice told the doctor that her father had committed suicide.

'He did it because he was perfectly sane,' the doctor told Alice.

The night Ben went into the psychiatric home to be sorted out Albert told Alice anecdotes about his own grandfather who had been a lay preacher until he died of anthrax caught, it was believed, from a toothbrush. He tried to share the blame in other ways and made her laugh but she never told him that she knew about him and her mother and where he was sleeping while she was in hospital having the baby. Alice never told Albert the things she had told the psychiatrist and which helped to explain Benny and gave them a chance to work on him.

'Wait for me!' Alice said when he wanted to go into the water. She sat down to take off her shoes.

'It's not deep,' said another mother. 'It's perfectly safe for them.'

It was not perfectly safe. Swift as an arrow Ben went ahead with his newest idea which was to hold a baby's head under the water until it drowned. It had taken Alice only seconds to slip off her shoes and roll off her stockings but by that time she had heard the child's cry from the crowded pool, the hysterical scream of the mother. She went plunging into the water with half-a-dozen other women. A nightmare panic of action destroyed the hot summer afternoon and Alice found herself the hated focus of a crowd of angry women while the child was being dried off and comforted.

'I'm sorry!' Alice said.

Ben stood at her side, screaming with triumphant laughter. Alice struck him and he laughed louder; she hit him again and again and the harder she hit him the harder he laughed for it was a measure of his success.

'Say you're sorry!' a woman said. 'Make him say he's sorry!'

'Sun-day,' Ben said, happily.

Alice decided to kill herself and her child.

Meanwhile, up in the woods, an almost equally dramatic thing had happened to Albert. It was not something you could see. It had happened inside Albert where it didn't show.

'We've got crab salad for tea,' Treasure told Albert as he drove them home. 'You know that Mr Granger at the Yo-Yo – who sells Charles's baskets and won't take a commission? – he gave me a whole crab.' She always said 'that Mr Granger' or 'that Mr' anybody when she knew they were interested in her and she didn't want anyone to suspect, not even herself.

'Can't stay to tea, love,' Albert said. 'Not today. Sorry. Got to pick somebody up.' Dorothy at last was useful.

'Cah bah tahnah, Ahbah,' Charles said.

Albert chose to misunderstand him. 'About Thursday,' Albert said.

That was the awful thing. 'Come back tonight,' Charles had said. And he had taken the back seat in the car allowing Treasure to sit next to Albert. He had had a long look at the County Hospital Home and he had made a decision.

Treasure's face was scarlet and she stared straight ahead.

'Cah bah tahnah, Ahbah,' Charles said again from behind them.

'Shut up, Charles!' Treasure said. 'He smokes too much,' she explained to Albert.

Albert handed a packet of cigarettes back to Charles and daren't meet his eyes. Charles groped a cigarette from the packet, his pale eyes confused and frightened as though his only remaining communication had failed him.

'You've got no respect for other people's marriages,' Treasure had once told Albert. 'You'd have no respect for your own.'

And now she was the one who, quite suddenly, on a hot rural afternoon, had given him respect for marriage. He wore it like a ghastly internal injury.

'You don't give a damn what you're doing to my wife!' Albert told Dorothy when she got into the car with her dog and a big ice-cream which they were sharing.

'Whatever's the matter with you!' Dorothy exclaimed. 'Albert's in one of his moods,' she told the dog.

But it was more than a mood. By offering Albert something which he had been helping himself to all his adult life Charles had shown Albert the enormity of his crimes. The crime of making love to another man's wife. If he had thought about it before Albert had dismissed it as something the other chap wouldn't know about or wouldn't mind if he did. Never as a violation of something sacred, precious, exclusive. Never as the tearing down of something built to last a lifetime. Never as the destruction of the human dignity of marriage with a quick half-hour on the bed. Never had Albert's sexual desires seemed so mean and small and unimportant as when Charles said: 'Cah bah tahnah, Ahbah. ...'

Driving home Albert thought of Grace and trusting Fred

and Marjorie and trusting Cedric and Coral and Gloria and Joyce and –

And now, having built up within himself a great spear of hatred of people like himself – the way he used to be, this morning – he all at once thought of Alice. Thought of any man putting a hand in a private, intimate Albert-owned place on her body and she agreeing.

'My God!' Albert said.

'Whatever's got into you?' Dorothy said.

And now of course the bullet through his windscreen became completely understandable.

At the Butterhall Street traffic signals he stopped his car in a line full of home-coming, sun-seeking families; he was surrounded by an army of urban district marriages all coming back to their married homes and married teas and married beds to get ready for the married Monday and the rest of the married week.

Albert turned up his collar and sank low behind the wheel.

As Albert had an inevitability phobia about the Agricultural Tractor Factory, so Alice Finbow had an inevitability phobia about suicide. She was a shy girl, and aesthetically the idea of suicide had always revolted her as being too spectacular. Yet it was often shy people who went in for it because they could not unburden themselves to others. Her father had been a shy man yet finally he had driven off Beachy Head in his four-square Aerial motorcycle combination singing at the top of his voice.

'He must have been drinking,' Mrs Finbow had said at the inquest.

Alice sat Ben in the cat basket which was the only place where he would stay put; having created the vacancy himself he had commandeered it in the months before he had gone away and now it was kept for him on those rare occasions Alice brought him home for tea. She put three triangular jam sandwiches on a plate and poured him a glass of milk, hoping it would be enough to keep him busy until the gas took effect. She put a folk-weave covered cushion on the threshold of the gas oven and the white nylon-fur rug on the floor and curled up as she had done before when drying her hair after a shampoo. Only this time she did not light the gas.

While the kitchen filled with the smell of gas Alice lay with her eyes open, thinking about her mother and about Albert. She saw her mother just coming back from Little-hampton Beach to join the coach for the return trip with her language class friends. She saw Albert having tea with Treasure and her paralysed husband. She saw Albert and her mother in bed together once the grief was over. Two shallow people concerned only with themselves and their appetites.

She saved Horace Fenton to think about last because she loved him.

'Sun-day,' Ben said.

'Sun-day,' Alice said.

He went on eating and she watched him. When he started blurring in her vision she reached out and took hold of his sandal to make sure he was there.

'I'll give you a choice,' Albert said, fairly, when he had driven Dorothy and the dog into the garage. 'I'll drive you home now with all your stuff, or you can go home on the bus and I'll drop your stuff round at your place tomorrow.'

'I can't go home,' Dorothy said.

'I don't care where you go, dear,' Albert told her. 'You're not going to mess up my marriage.' Having seen the light he was ready to illuminate the world. He now felt that he was probably the only person who knew something about the sanctity of marriage. None of his friends had ever mentioned it.

Dorothy cried. 'Just when I'd got everything comfortable. We could be happy together. Breaking up the home.'

Albert said, sternly: 'You'll never have a home if you go on like this. You've got no morals. I wouldn't be married to you. First door-to-door salesman that comes round and you'd

pop into bed with him – I know your sort,' he added, truthfully.

'Not unless I was in love with him,' Dorothy said.

'Come on,' Albert said, 'what's it going to be? I want to
go and meet my wife.'

'Could I just have a cup of tea?' Dorothy said. 'I'm
parched. Look, you go and meet Alice and I'll make a nice
cup of tea –'

'No you won't – that can go on forever, that can. One
more cup of tea. Finish up getting confined on my back seat.'

'I'm dying for a cup of tea,' she said. 'Aren't you? Besides,
I want to go somewhere. Is anybody home?'

'Not yet but they soon will be.'

'Would you have time to make a cup of tea while I go to
the bathroom?'

'And then you go home?'

'I'm not going home. My dad would kill me coming home
on a Sunday in front of the neighbours.'

'Where'll you go, then?'

'Doesn't matter to you, does it?' Dorothy said, with a
martyred air. Then, seeing the picture: 'I'll just walk away.
Out of your life,' she added.

'Good,' Albert said.

'After I've spent a penny and had a cup of tea,' she reminded him.

Albert led the way into the house to make sure the coast
was clear. The sickly smell of gas was everywhere.

'That feather-headed bint has left the bloody gas on somewhere,' Albert said, when Dorothy joined him in the hall.

'You shouldn't talk about her like that,' Dorothy said.
She thought he meant Alice. 'I expect she does her best.'
She had the home-breaker's sure instinct when to damn
with faint praise and give an impression of fairness and
tolerance; when to support his inner attitudes rather than
his thoughtless statement.

'Strike a match and we'd all go up,' Albert said. It would
never occur to him that somebody in his family would want
to gas themselves; if they had Albert they had everything

to live for. 'Wait a minute,' he told her; 'let's take a dekko upstairs.' He called down: 'All right.'

'Nice place, isn't it?' Dorothy was taking stock of the house as she went upstairs to join him. 'Mind you the greens clash, don't they – curtains and stair-carpet?' And when to show that she was a woman of taste. 'Oh dear,' she said, on the landing: 'That lampshade is hideous – whoever chose that? I know you didn't. It could be made lovely, this house.' And when to show that she was the right woman for him.

'I'll go and put the kettle on,' he told her. 'Hurry up –'

'Whose bedroom's this, then?' Dorothy had opened a door.

'The old woman's –'

'I thought you slept together?'

'We do –' Albert checked himself. 'I mean my mother-in-law's. Come on, hurry up if you want the bathroom – that gas must be full on somewhere –'

'Is this your room?' Dorothy had now opened another door.

'Yes,' he said. And then impatiently as she inspected it minutely from the doorway: '*Do* you mind!'

'You can't be in love if you've got twin beds.' And when to be symbolic.

'We only use one,' Albert said. The other bed had to be roughed up every morning. It meant alternating every night to keep the linen used.

'What about this room?' Dorothy said, opening another door. And when to change the subject.

'That's the spare – come on, you only want to spend a penny, not buy a lease.'

Dorothy now had the door of the spare bedroom open and was looking around at the junk. 'Make a nice bed-sitter,' she said. And when to plant an idea.

'Not for you!' Albert said. He pulled her away from the room and shut the door.

Dorothy went into the bathroom. And when to give up. For the time being.

Albert ran down to the kitchen and found the door

locked. For the first time he thought something might be wrong; for a hopeful second, swiftly banished, he thought Mrs Finbow had gassed herself. He was rattling the door now.

'Mrs F! Topsy!' He rattled the door some more, put pressure on it. Then, looking round, he saw Alice's suedette coat and woollen scarf on the hall stand with a child's mac hanging over it. 'Janice!' he shouted, renewing his banging at the kitchen door.

'Who?' Dorothy called as she clattered down the stairs.

'Alice!' Albert shouted. Then, to the alarmed Dorothy: 'Stand back!'

Albert braced himself against the stair wall and crashed his foot against the kitchen door; it broke straight through a panel and stuck. He and Dorothy pulled it out, leaving his shoe inside. They looked through the hole and saw Alice lying by the gas stove.

'Oh Christ!' Albert said. He felt too faint to do anything. 'Go next door. Telephone. Get a doctor – ambulance. Hurry up!'

'Which side?' Dorothy said.

Albert drew back his other foot with the shoe on it and kicked the door open. A piece of the cast-iron latch fell on the floor as he ran into the kitchen.

'Alice!'

He pulled her away from the gas oven and lifted her head and shoulders, looked at her face and remembered the dead Joyce Corby who had fallen from a window. Alice opened her eyes and stared at him, then looked horrified.

'Ben!' she said.

Albert looked round. The child was standing in the sink which was filled with water up to his knees, floating the washing-up; the kitchen window was wide open with a breeze coming in. There was as much gas in the garden as in the kitchen. Ben's hand was still on the open window as he looked at Albert.

'You're not barmy,' Albert said.

He picked Alice up and carried her out of the back door

on to the gravelled path as Dorothy came running through the kitchen, following him out.

'They won't answer!' she said. 'They've got "Z Cars" on!' And when to give fate a helping hand.

Alice started being sick. Albert supported her diaphragm with one hand, her forehead with the other. Ben at the open kitchen window watched the vomit with a fascinated eye.

'Turn the gas off,' Albert told Dorothy whom he could sense standing behind him, 'open all the doors and windows in the house and when it's cleared make a pot of tea.'

'Yes, dear,' Dorothy said. And when to be efficient.

She bustled through the house as though she had come at last to take charge and not before time. In the garage the dog started barking. Ben lost interest in the dwindling vomit and climbed out of the sink of water with a better idea.

'Then what happened?'

'They rescued this kid and Alice brought him home.'

'What happened then?'

'He locked himself in the kitchen and turned on all the taps.'

'What happened after that?'

'I had to bash the door down to get to him.'

'What happened?'

'He was paddling in the sink and I got him out.'

'Then what happened?'

'Alice was a nervous wreck so I brought him back here.'

'What happened then?'

Albert looked round. 'Nothing. He's sitting there drinking his tea, isn't he?'

The girl looked up from her notes. 'Oh yes, of course. What exactly was wrong with your wife?'

'She was upset, naturally. He's a bit of a handful. Never know what he's going to do next.'

'Ben is creative,' she said. 'We've discovered that.'

'He takes after me,' Albert said. She gave him a hard look and he added, quickly: 'It's the only thing, mind you.'

'What happened to your wife?'

'I told you.'

'You said she was a nervous wreck. Do you mean she got hysterical?'

'Not exactly.'

'Was she upset?'

'Oh yes.'

'Were there any physical symptoms? Pains? Headache? Sickness?'

'Who?'

'Your wife.'

'Oh. She was sick.'

'Any diarrhoea?'

'I don't know!' Albert exclaimed.

'Are you quick tempered, Mr Harris?'

'I dunno, do I?'

'Do you get into fights?'

Albert laughed. 'No! Not since school.'

'I see. What happened?'

'When?'

'At school. ...'

'Strip right off, Challice,' Mrs Frazer said.

'Can't I just keep my panties on?'

'No. If a job's worth doing it's worth doing well. Now the flimsiest housecoat you can find – that one will do. Is that yours, Mason? Challice can borrow it. Now go in to take Ben to bed and ask Mr Harris to go with you. Take him in your own bedroom afterwards to get something for Ben. Make it very natural and watch points – remember what happened to Potter.'

'It's jolly cold,' Challice said. 'Shall I give Ben a hot-water bottle?'

'Never mind Ben,' Mrs Frazer said, 'it's the parents we've got to watch.'

Later they watched Albert drive away, Mrs Frazer and the Sunday staff standing in the staff-room window.

'He said this is a disgusting way to go around in front of a married man,' Challice said.

'Not *quite* normal,' said Mrs Frazer. 'Not as nice as he was.'

'Oh blast!' said the other girl, consulting her notes. 'I forgot to ask him about the dog bite.'

'I expect Ben tried to kill one,' Mrs Frazer said.

'I wonder what happened then?' the girl said.

Albert did not drive straight home. He went into a confectioner's in the High Street and bought a one-pound box of Continental chocolates, then toured the town searching for flowers. The man who ran a flower and fruit stall outside the hospital gates for Sunday visitors was just packing up.

'I've got a few carnations, Albert.'

'I want some red roses,' Albert said.

'I haven't got any red roses. I've got some nice – here, I tell you what I have got, I've got some nice gladioli left. Put 'em in half price.'

'What else have you got?'

'I got some pyrethrums – they're nice in a big bunch. I got some – d'you want me to get them out? They're all in the van.'

'Haven't you got any red roses?' Albert asked him.

'No. Nothing in 'em for me. Well, they're in season, you see, boy. The gardens are full of 'em. November, December, January, now – that's the time to make money on red roses. How about asters? Those big shaggy ones – or dahlias, plenty of dahlias. Who're they for? Relation? Is she ill? I bet she'd like gladioli. Plenty of yellow in 'em. Cheers 'em up.'

'I really want red roses,' Albert said.

'You won't get any thanks for red roses now – she'll think you got 'em for nothing.'

'Ah well,' Albert said.

Come to that, he remembered, he could get 'em for nothing.

He drove out to a suburban district of pebble-dashed semi-detacheds standing in grass-verged tree-lined avenues, straight as furrows. An old, middle-aged man was working

504

in one of the front gardens, engrossed in a splendour of flowers. He wore khaki shorts and an open-necked cricket shirt, his brown bare feet in sandals and an old straw hat on his head against the last of the sun.

His face lit up as Albert got out of his car. 'Albert!' he called. Then it shadowed as he remembered something. 'Hello, Albert,' he said, with modified delight. He called into the open front bow-window. 'Marjorie! You've got a visitor.'

Albert came into the front garden, jumped the border on to the lawn. 'Came to see you, Cedric.'

'Hello, Albert,' Marjorie Mason called. She stood in the window, holding her son on the ledge to look out. 'It's Uncle Albert, Albert,' she told him.

'Hello, Uncle Albert,' the boy said.

'Hello, mate,' Albert said.

'Go inside, Albert,' Cedric said. 'You'll have some tea, won't you?'

'Can't stop,' Albert said.

'That's the story of your life, petal,' Marjorie Mason told him.

Albert laughed but briefly to come to the point. 'I'm looking for a few flowers for my missis, Cedric.'

'Well!' Cedric exclaimed, proudly: 'You've come to the right place. Take your pick, Albert, and welcome.'

'Have you any red roses, Cedric?' Albert asked.

Marjorie laughed but her husband frowned.

'Are you sure they're for your wife, Albert? Not for anybody else's?'

'Cedric!' Marjorie Mason exclaimed.

'I was only joking, Albert,' Cedric said. Then, unhappily: 'Come inside, there's a good chap.'

In the sitting room, with Albert, at thirty-three, sitting on the edge of a chair, Cedric Mason gave him the kind of talk he used to give him in the fifth form at Butterhall School.

'They were talking in the common room,' Cedric said. 'I couldn't help overhearing. Well, they meant me to of course. About you and other women, Albert.'

'About me!' Albert exclaimed, his voice cracking.

Marjorie said: 'I told Cedric it was a load of old rubbish, petal.' She now had their son on her lap. Hers and Albert's.

'Well they know the boy's named after you –'

'That was *your* idea, Cedric,' Marjorie said.

'Was it? I think it was. Anyway, it doesn't matter. But they know you're giving her driving lessons – Marjorie, I mean. You know how people put two and two together Albert and get inflated answers. In a town like this. "When Jesus saw the city he wept."'

'What?' Albert said.

'Oh, don't worry, I told them what you're like. Gave it to them pretty strong. You know Gabel – History? No, I don't think you do. His wife's in one of the welfare organizations – apparently they're saying you've been carrying on with some invalid's wife. Passing yourself off as her brother.'

'It's a dirty lie,' Albert said.

'I told him, petal.'

'You didn't have to tell me, Marjorie,' Cedric said. 'I know what they're like.' He grinned at Albert and shook his hand, reassuringly. 'And I know what my old boys are like – and my old scouts, eh, Albert? I felt I had to tell you, though. Warn you. Be on your guard, Albert. Get Marjorie through her test on Thursday, then I shouldn't be seen together for a little while. They'll soon find something else to talk about.'

'You're right,' Albert said.

'It doesn't do you any good,' Cedric told him, sympathetically. 'You can't afford to have people talking about you when you're in business.'

'You're dead right, Cedric.'

'A properly run business depends on goodwill,' Cedric told him. 'The most valuable thing any man has – more important than capital – is personal integrity.'

'You can't buy it,' Albert said.

'That's what I tell my senior boys.'

Marjorie said: 'I don't know what sort of people they'll turn out when you retire, flower.'

506

'You, retire?' Albert said.

'Five more years, that's all,' Cedric said. 'Nonsense, isn't it? With the country short of teachers? They're planning everything except education, Albert. And surely that's the most important thing of all?'

'Don't keep Albert if he's got to go, petal.'

Albert stood up and Cedric led the way out into the garden. 'Good chap, Cedric,' Albert thought. Fancy having a wife like that. He would like to do something for Cedric.

'See you tomorrow,' Marjorie told Albert.

Albert nodded, unhappily. 'That bitch,' he thought.

'Got some lovely deep red roses – Etoile de Holland,' Cedric was saying. 'Hope she's not ill?'

'Oh no, it's her birthday,' Albert was saying.

'Really? Give her my compliments – what *is* the date?'

'Eh?' Albert said.

This distant conversation came to Marjorie partly through the door, partly through the open window. She sighed and looked to heaven; Albert was not the man he was.

'I didn't know you could cook, Albert,' Alice said.

'I had to, didn't I? In my little room.'

Alice smiled. 'I remember your little room.'

'Don't be nasty,' he said, pleasantly. 'Eat up.'

She sat up in bed, white but bright, bathed, fresh yet tired in polka-dot pink pyjamas. She had brushed her yellow hair for half-an-hour while Albert had been out just because she felt like living again. He was making a fuss of her. Had given her the chocolates and the red roses – stuck in a jug but never mind – and now a tray of quite lightly-scrambled eggs with lots of toast.

'Cooking is a knack,' he said. 'My mum could never cook. I used to show her. Take them eggs – taste nice, don't they?'

'Mmm!'

'I'll tell you what you've got in there – butter, vinegar, mustard, pepper, salt, sugar, juice out of a tin of tomatoes and the top of the milk.'

'Marvellous. And I can never do toast like this. All buttery and scrunchy.'

'You have to bash it with a hot milk bottle,' Albert told her.

He sat on the edge of the bed, watching her and loving her.

'Aren't you having anything?' she asked him.

'Not yet. Have a fry-up later on.' He had actually cooked enough for the two of them but had forgotten Dorothy who arrived back from the vet's starving hungry. Ben had set out to break the dog in half but had only dislocated one leg. He and his queen were eating their tea in the garage at this moment.

'Who was it you were talking to?' Alice had asked Albert when she had stopped being sick.

'Don't know who it was. Came in to help.'

'It was very kind of them,' Alice said.

Now, as she chased a piece of egg with a piece of toast, she said: 'You're not going to tell mother, are you?'

'I'm not going to tell anybody,' Albert said. 'Doesn't look very nice for me, does it?'

'Sorry, Albert.'

'He drove her to it, that's what they'd say. That's what they said about Corby. Only it happened to be true, of course.'

Alice said, quietly: 'I'll never do it again. I think it had to happen sometime but I'd never do it again.'

Albert stroked her, gently. 'You've got plenty to live for you have. I've got it all planned. Soon as I get this money – this week it'll be. We'll go out house-hunting. Somewhere you can visit Ben easily. I thought about one of the new towns – Stevenage, say. There'll be enough for a deposit on a house and a few thousand in the bank.'

'Stevenage?' Alice said. 'I didn't think those new towns were very nice.'

'You'd be surprised,' Albert said. 'They're properly planned. No half-and-half larks like this crummy old place – face-lifts at the front and rats running out the back.'

In an odd sort of way the description seemed more

508

suited to Albert's way of life than the streamlined ratless environs of a new town.

'Whatever would you do in a place like Stevenage, Albert?'

Albert smiled a big surprise at her. 'Shall I tell you? What you'll do, anyway. Run a bookshop!'

Alice laughed at him. 'You don't mean it?'

'Yes, I do. Why not? You'd like that.'

'Oh, yes. Of course, we'd have to have some sidelines – stationery, boutique things, perhaps. You know, arty.' And dwelling on it because now it affected her, she said: 'Are you really getting this money?'

'Contract's already drawn up. I've sold the shop you know.'

'You haven't!'

'Yes, I have. Finalized the deal yesterday.'

'Well!' Alice cried. 'You might have said!'

'Haven't had a chance, have I?'

'How much?' Alice asked.

'I get three thousand one hundred and fifty for the lot – shop and the cottages. Not bad considering the cottage has still got a tenant.'

'It's very good,' Alice said.

'You might've missed all that,' Albert told her.

'I'll never do it again,' Alice said.

'And I'm getting out of property,' Albert said.

It was a mutual confession and a banishing of old defects.

'Taste me,' Mrs Finbow said to Albert. 'Go on, taste me.' She said: 'Lick me,' she said.

Albert was watching the Sunday night play.

'Now you taste that,' she said, giving him her arm. She had just come in and taken off her clothes – not just her hat and coat, everything except panties and bra, as she always did, reaching for her Geisha-girl shortie silk robe.

Albert obediently put his tongue on her arm without taking his eyes from the screen.

'Where've I been?'

'Littlehampton.'

509

'In the sea!' she cried, taking back her arm and tasting it herself. 'Can't you taste the salt? Marvellous great big briny waves that sweep you up and ravish you all the way back to the beach! I can swim two groynes and float for ten minutes – would that be enough to save my life?'

'I'm afraid so.'

'You miserable thing,' she said, 'stuck in front of that. Young people! A good swim in the ocean would do you good – where's Alice?'

'In bed.'

'Is she asleep?'

'Yes.'

'Oh, good – coming to bed, mon cherie?'

'No.'

She trilled a gay laugh: 'I love to tease you. You young people are so miserable. You don't know how to enjoy life.'

'I'm thirty-three and I'm watching television – do you mind? Thank gawd when we've got our own place.'

'That'll never be,' Mrs Finbow told him.

'Next week,' Albert said.

'What?'

Albert decided not to go into it but she turned down the volume and placed herself in front of the screen, bending down to his eyeline as if she was in the play.

'Now I'm watching you,' she said. 'Turn up your volume. What's your programme? How's your vertical hold?' She laughed delightedly. 'I think that's funny. Oh, what didums say darlings?'

'We're leaving here next week – got a new house in Stevenage. Alice is going to run a bookshop for me.'

She stared at him incredulously for a moment, decided to say something but then that she would be wasting her time; she continued with her play-acting, which she was rather pleased with; left him, stopped, thought, came back, re-adjusted the television for him, went out of the room and up the stairs as if on serious business.

'Wake up, Alice!' he heard her say from upstairs. 'Oh,

you are awake. Good. What's this I hear? You're not going away? Not with *him*. . . .'

The door closed and he heard only the rise and fall of her voice. 'Not with *him*?' he thought. Unknown to Albert there was an alternative.

'You haven't touched me for goodness knows how long,' Dorothy told Albert when he took her a cup of late-night cocoa. 'It used to be all you ever thought about. You haven't gone impotent have you?' Then she said: 'Sssh!' when he went to close the car door. 'He's just dropping off at last.' She was talking about the dog wrapped in the blanket on the back seat. 'How's she?' she added, lumping the two casualties as if equally important. 'I suppose she found out about me.'

'See you in the morning,' Albert said.

'Monday tomorrow,' Dorothy said. 'I hate Mondays.'

It meant that life was getting comfortably tedious again.

'I'm putting the milk bottles outside,' she called. 'I hope that's all right?' Then she said: 'Oh, sorry Aubrey, did I wake you up? How is it now, then? Nasty rough boy.'

'Leave the light on,' Alice said. 'Think I'll read a little. Will you pass me a book?'

That was one fundamental difference between them, he thought as he undressed; between him and the rest of the world probably. He would never let somebody pass him anything – a book, a glass of beer, the matches, the salt and pepper.

'Just leave the bloody stuff where it is,' he used to tell his mother. 'I hate people giving me things.'

In his Callendar Warehouse days he would make a dozen journeys with appliances and accessories, his arms full, rather than allow anybody else to carry anything for him to the car. If a waiter waited for him to take something he would get furious.

'All right, put it down,' he would say.

He didn't know why. He would get out of a warm bed

to shut a door even if somebody was standing right next to it. Things he wanted he wanted to get himself; things he wanted done he wanted to do himself. It was something to do with complete independence. It was something to do with style. Albert knew that he was stylish. He never inhaled smoke from a cigarette without diluting it with an equal quantity of air carefully taken simultaneously through the nostrils. Nobody would ever know what he was doing, to watch him smoke. People often didn't know that Albert was stylish. There was a way of picking up a salt-cellar. If somebody passed him one he would put it down and pick it up again.

'You don't read, do you, Albert?' Alice said from the pages of her book. 'I've never seen you pick up a book.'

There are times in any marriage when the partners take secret looks at each other.

'You can never take flight if you don't read books,' Alice said. And a moment later, unbidden: 'You never leave your perch, you never see over the roofs. The person who doesn't read has no horizons except the one under his nose.'

Now *she's* started, Albert thought. He sat up in the other bed, brooding with his chin on his knees. Now Alice has joined the club, he thought, after all this time.

'In the street of life you can't see over the kerb,' Elaine Townend had told him.

'You'll never do any more than talk about getting on,' Grace had told him.

'You're a tally boy,' Treasure had told him; 'it's not just a job, it's a state of mind.'

'You're living on the sickness of the times, Albert,' Cedric had told him.

People had always been telling Albert where he was going wrong. In his time he had been blamed for everything except the bomb – and some of them weren't too sure about that.

Albert leaned over and took a book from the overfilled oak book case which covered one entire wall of their bedroom. He turned it in his hands, curiously. Flipped through some pages, read a few words. They were meaningless. They didn't tell you anything. They weren't selling anything. There was nothing urgent or necessary about books. They had nothing to do with life. If Albert wanted things made up he'd make them up himself. There was no point in books that he could see. Yes, a television or a cinema passed an hour, but you didn't have to read. Albert would have to read a page two or three times to know what was being said and even then it didn't mean anything.

'What's this then?' He had picked up another book.

Alice looked across. 'That's Horace's "Vale of Tears" – the one you saw in the library. The one I showed you.'

'You didn't show me this,' Albert said. He held up the preliminary pages: 'It's got your name in it!' He read out: 'For Alice and a happier future.' He stared at her: 'Is that you?'

Alice was blushing. 'Yes.'

'You didn't tell me!'

'I didn't think you'd like it, Albert.'

'I don't like it!' Albert said. 'Too bloody true! How many people in this town are going to see this – what does it make me look like? A happier future! What's wrong with your present – and what the hell does he know about it –' Albert broke off, got out of bed on her side and stared angrily down into her eyes: 'Just a minute! Just a bloody minute! Just what's been going on between you two? Have you been having it off together?'

'Albert!'

Albert grabbed the front of her pyjamas and yanked her towards him until their eyes were inches apart:

'Has he touched you?'

'No!'

'Has he ever kissed you?'

'I do believe you're jealous at last!'

For a time Alice enjoyed Albert's new interest in her past, but after several hours she grew bored and finally hated him.

'... and what about before that in the tax office? Did any of them ever touch you?'

'I keep telling you!'

'You let me – why not them?'

'I don't know but I didn't.'

'You can do a lot of things without doing that. What did *you* do?'

'Please, Albert!'

By four o'clock his furiously jealous brain newly barbed with the sanctity of marriage had pried into every corner of her private life, not forgetting the toilet arrangements at the public library.

'What a bloody fool I've been!' Albert said.

'Are you going to quarrel all night?' came Mrs Finbow's voice from the next room. She sounded eager and hopeful.

'This bloody chap for instance!' Albert said, pointing to a uniform edition of Arnold Bennett. 'You named the boy after him! I'm so bloody blind!'

'What *are* you talking about?'

He didn't even know what he was talking about. Albert never had known. His next question proved this to her and put an end to their marriage.

'What exactly went on between you and Arnold Bennett?'

Alice could never explain to anybody why, after he'd said that, marriage was impossible. Nothing he could say afterwards would ever put it right even if he'd lived fifty years instead of barely twenty hours.

'All right, I'm sorry, so I'm wrong.' He had gathered this mostly from her despairing silence by the time the dawn was coming into the room. He went into her bed with the husband's usual generous intention to restore the wife's privileges after a night of torture, but Alice put her knees up and turned the other way but then quickly put them down again and screwed herself into a ball remembering that their delights were often only the greater for being encountered unfamiliarly and Alice had finished with him. Alice had started being faithful to Horace Fenton, the author.

Chapter Five

Summer hit the town on Monday morning with the rotting odour of old dustbins in side-alleys and the sinus-tickling memory-pricking headachy smell of hot wet dust left by the corporation water cart whose rotating brush had wet-marked a track around the outlines of gone vehicles almost the entire length of the High Street. The water-cart driver's ambition to reach the kerb had dwindled to one small patch near the pet shop when Albert's car slid in and frustrated him.

'Albert!' Hetty called from the shop doorway. She was holding a rabbit by the ears.

'Not now, duck, eh?' Albert said as he ran from his car into the side door and up the stairs, taking them two at a time.

Hetty was glad of the delay. She did not want to meet the worry head-on, what with everything in the shop giving birth suddenly and so much to do. The insurance man and the police had not accepted the robbery as casually as she had. Did Albert know where the money was kept, for instance? If he had known it would not have been there. Anyway, what would he do with peacocks? Unknown to Hetty a family of mice knew where the balance of the five hundred pounds had been put; right on top of their most recent picnic in the chaff box. Unknown to Hetty Albert's rain-check of more than four hundred pounds was being devoured and digested or made into little bits of mouse nest.

'Everybody making a fuss about battery hens,' Albert told Patricia Gort, up in the office where she was reading the morning paper. 'What do they think *they* are? They're *all* battery hens, incarcerated pigs, hobbled calves, all being fattened for the money gods. Not me,' he said, ripping open his mail. 'I'm a free-range chicken. I lay my eggs in the grass.'

'You haven't noticed, have you? No, I might've known you wouldn't notice.' She had spent the weekend painting the office cream, had laid new lino out of her own pocket, put up pretty folk-weave curtains, set flowers all around, polished the desk, hung a big white globe of a lampshade in the middle and had sat for an hour waiting for him to come in and exclaim in wonder and delight.

'I don't understand this,' Albert said, putting his feet up on the desk as he lounged back in his chair. 'I don't bloody understand this. What's Corby playing at? What the hell's Corby playing at?'

'Let me look.' And a moment later she said, 'Well isn't that lovely! After all the trouble I've gone to.' Patricia Gort was also out of her siren suit and was dressed to suit the summer in gay green and yellow gingham, long glass nylons and white high heels, her hair high and soft and red with only shreds of green paint in it. 'After all I've put into it,' she said. 'You not only haven't noticed anything, you've sold the place lock stock and barrel over my head with vacant possession – charming!'

Albert punched the desk, swung his feet off it, his eyes probing into Corby's letter, into the fog of Corby's double-dealing. 'That's not the point. That's not the bloody point. He says it's fallen through – the brewery deal. It can't fall through. I only let him have this place as a favour – it's not worth anything to anybody. It's coming down. It's all coming down. This was just a side-issue. Three thousand one hundred and fifty pounds he's getting me for the cottages.'

'Oh, Albert!' Patricia Gort said. 'How much did he give you for this place?'

'Two hundred and fifty,' Albert said.

Patricia Gort sighed. 'You certainly lay eggs,' she said, unkindly.

'Give me that 'phone!'

Patricia Gort gave him the telephone and started heating

up the coffee on the gas ring. 'I thought we'd start a proper business here,' she said. 'I was going to convert the other room into reception and telephone with a few nice bits of furniture and a map of the district on the wall – all property people have them. I've been drafting out some advertisements and I've even called up some people who are advertising their houses for sale privately. Inventing offers, just so we get the hang of talking about property.' She laughed. 'I nearly bought a detached double-fronted bungalow, three beds, bath, lounge, store room, garage, pleasant garden with fruiting trees.'

'Is Corby there?' Albert said to the telephone. 'What about Max? Where the hell are they?'

'Albert!' Patricia Gort said. 'That's not the way to talk!'

'Fucking crooks,' Albert said. 'No, not you, dear,' he told the 'phone and hung up.

'I won't have that sort of language,' Patricia Gort said. 'And stop looking up my legs.' She was squatting by the gas ring and now closed her knees. 'You're not very gentlemanly.'

Albert's appraisal was only habitual. 'The buggers,' he said.

'What happened exactly?' she asked.

Albert told her about the deal.

'But you might have known they were really after this place!' Patricia Gort said.

'But they didn't even ask me to sell it. They wanted to rent it – one of Corby's chums. I made 'em buy it.'

'They made you make 'em buy it.'

Albert dwelt on this. She was right. He had done the same thing himself many times. 'I'm losing my grip,' he said.

It was what Callendar had said the first time Albert outsmarted him. And look what had happened to Cally. As if to remind him he now noticed a registered letter still unopened.

'It might be money,' Patricia Gort said, encouragingly.

But it ..asn't. It was a small blown-up map of the town streets with a heavy cross marked over Solly Cowell's stores.

'Silly old sod,' Albert said. This was the lion he had left rampaging through the jungle. He tore up the map and let the pieces drift down into the wicker-work waste-paper basket which Charles had made him.

Dorothy meanwhile was hanging out her washing in the heat of the sun on Albert's hot car.

'Nice now,' Hetty called, from the pet shop. She was chalking a set of newly-born bargains on the window.

'Nice for drying,' Dorothy said.

'I did all mine before I came out this morning,' Hetty said.

'It's the rinsing that's difficult,' Dorothy said. 'You can never get enough water in these toilets.'

'No, I know. You got to rinse them properly with these detergents.'

'Though, mind you, some are all right,' Dorothy said. She gave a skirt an extra squeeze in the gutter hanging it on a 'Twenty Minute Waiting' sign. 'Now you take the Regal – lovely toilet, that is. Carpet, curtains, all gold mirrors and hot water pipes. The White Hart I wouldn't give a thank you for – no facilities.'

'No, I know.'

'As for the George – phew! The smell knocks you backwards. I won't go in there.'

'It can't be healthy,' Hetty agreed.

'Of course, the Odeon's nice,' Dorothy said, 'but they don't open till one o'clock – you miss all the best drying hours. The water's lovely and soft for your hair, though. You feel Aubrey's coat – I gave him a bath in the hand-basin. Just a minute, my back door's open.' Dorothy closed the back door of the car, pushing the dog's nose inside.

'Well, must get on,' Hetty said.

They went back to their chores.

'I'll have three hotels in Park Lane,' Albert said.

'Have you got enough capital?' Patricia Gort asked him.

'Just about,' Albert said. 'Here you are – five thousand, five thousand, five thousand. . . .'

518

They were playing Monopoly in the absence of any other kind of urgent business. It seemed as close as Albert would ever get to the kind of life he wanted.

'Can't you move the office into the cottage next to the old lady,' Patricia Gort suggested. 'You have to operate from somewhere.'

'I'll have some rent from you,' Albert said. And as she paid him he said: 'No, I've tried that. No dice. There's a restrictive covenant in the lease – can't be used for business purposes. You're tied up all ways in this town unless you've got a finger in. I've been too busy getting my finger out to get one in –' he laughed '– that's original, by the way.'

'I'll have one house in Mayfair,' Patricia Gort said.

'One house? Don't be chicken. You've got to think big in the property business.'

'I think that's all you've ever done, Albert,' Patricia Gort told him. 'Think big.'

Albert shrugged, unoffended. 'You've got to have luck. I'm on a bad streak at the moment, that's all. I'll sell these hotels and have three houses over here,' he added.

'Why don't you get out?' she said. 'You're not really in business at all – only in the brass plate business. Sell that Bute Place property and cut your losses. Put what you've got into a little shop or something – the pet shop, for instance, that's making money. Get Hetty new premises – rent some.'

'I don't want to finish up a bloody shop-keeper, do I?'

'What about the book shop in Stevenage?'

'Haven't got the capital now, have I? Anyway, Alice has turned funny. Tried to kill herself yesterday – what a thing to do on a Sunday.'

Patricia Gort stared at him: 'You didn't mention that?' She used the word 'mention' sarcastically.

'Slipped my mind. Thinking about this deal with Corby.'

'You're not doing anybody any good, Albert. That girl outside ought to be at home.'

'She is at home – ART 5679, High Street. Every time I try to kick her out she does something nice.'

'What are you going to do, Albert?'

'I'll have three more hotels over here,' Albert said.

'What's the matter with Alice?'

'I think she's got a boy friend.'

'A pity they all haven't. You might get down to some work.'

'I'll murder him if I catch him,' Albert brooded.

The girl gave him a long hard stare. 'You're not going to get jealous on top of everything else?'

'I had a funny feeling yesterday,' Albert said.

'I want fifty pounds from you.'

'I mean a wife is different. I wouldn't want anybody to touch Alice. A woman is a mother, isn't she? I mean a wife? I mean marriage is different.'

'Well congratulations,' Patricia Gort said. 'But you're a bit late with your funny feelings. Is that my influence?'

'No. I dunno. It's old Charles. He wants me to start sleeping with Treasure. Makes me sick.'

'Poor chap.'

'Yeah.'

Albert threw the die and moved his piece and found her hand on his arm.

'You're not a bad chap,' Patricia Gort told him.

It was their most affectionate moment and Albert had to swallow his emotion.

'I said you'd get better,' Patricia Gort told him.

Albert looked at her. 'Is this what you call better? I was a bloody sight better off when I was a bastard. Everybody loved me then. They don't now. Somebody after me with a gun. Old Cedric lecturing me about his missis – I haven't touched her for years. I haven't touched anybody. I have to get my own wife to sneak up the woods with me – then she won't. I tell you. I'm not better, duck. I'm worse. I'm sick, I am. I must be. Letting Corby put one over on me. I bet he'll get a hundred thousand for this place. I bet it's this Supermarket deal. I want my bloody head examined.' He looked at his imitation money. 'Give me two more hotels. I've been waiting years for this, I have, then I muck it up.'

520

Later in the game old Mrs Judd come slowly up the stairs and entered the office, holding the rat in her hand.

'I wondered if you could find a home for Sydney in your pet shop?' she said. 'I don't like parting with him but I'm going to live with my son. You're not allowed pets in council houses.'

Albert's spirits lightened. 'You don't mean you're leaving the cottage and giving me a chance to make a bit of money?'

'Yes. I want to give a week's notice. If that's all right.'

'That's lovely,' Albert said. 'Consider yourself evicted, Mrs Judd.' To Patricia Gort he said: 'I think we're in business. Get ready to draft out an advertisement – this valuable site!'

'I couldn't stay there without the supplementary,' Mrs Judd explained.

'Of course you couldn't. What supplementary?'

'I've been getting a supplementary pension from the welfare because of the living conditions. Three pounds a week extra as long as I stayed there. I got a letter this morning – they've stopped it.'

Albert sat down again to think about this. 'That figures,' he said.

Patricia Gort was looking at him, her optimism waning. 'What is it?'

'Who organized that pension, Mrs Judd?' Albert asked. 'Mrs Cornwallis?'

'Yes. I can't grumble really. It's been very useful.'

'You can say that again,' Albert said. Then, reproachfully: 'You didn't tell me about it.'

'They told me not to tell anyone. Else everybody would want it.'

'Very clever,' Albert said. 'I spend the best years of my life and gawd knows how much money trying to get her out and Corby and his pals pay her a pension to keep her there. I wonder how many more sitting tenants they're subsidising till it suits them?'

'It's disgusting,' Patricia Gort said. 'Still, you've got it now.'

'Because Corby's got what he wants out of me – this place.'

'But you've got vacant possession on the cottages, that's something.'

'There must be a catch,' Albert said.

As if in reply, Mrs Judd said: 'It's all coming down.'

'They're going to turn Bute Place into a public car park,' Mrs Judd told him.

Albert gave his face a dry-wash. 'See yourself out, can you, Mrs Judd? Leave Sydney with Hetty in the shop.'

When the old lady had gone Patricia Gort gave Albert a respectful few minutes. 'Now see if you can give me an intelligent break-down,' she said. 'Information-wise.'

'You let 'em shit on you,' Albert told her, 'and then if you sit here long enough they rub it in.'

'Can you make it not quite so technical?'

Albert elaborated: 'Corby's conned me out of this place for the Supermarket, the brewery's got their car-park free of charge out of public funds and I'll be lucky if I get a hundred quid compensation.'

'Oh dear,' she said.

'I'm finished,' Albert said.

'Do you want to go bankrupt?'

'Might as well. Get a bit of free publicity, anyway.'

'I mean in the game,' she said.

'No, I got five thousand quid left,' Albert said.

'In the bank?'

'No, in the game,' he said. He threw the money down, dispiritedly. 'Might as well pack it in.'

Patricia Gort was deep in thought as she packed away the game of Monopoly. 'Have you ever thought of joining them?' she asked. 'I mean, if you can't fight them.'

'How d'you mean?'

'Have you ever thought of trying to get on the council?'

'You're joking! You must be. I can't even get elected to the golf club.'

She left him with it for a moment, knowing that the idea was appealing to him.

'Mind you,' he said, 'there was a time. I mean I used to be pretty well known in this town – I told you. When I was a crook.'

'You could be again,' Patricia Gort urged. 'You don't lose a thing like that. If it's in the blood.'

'That's what my mum used to say. She believed in me. You'll finish up getting hanged, she used to say.'

They both laughed.

'Am I being funny?' Albert said. 'Blimey! That's a start!'

'You've got a good personality,' Patricia Gort encouraged him. 'You can talk. You're engaging. You get on with people. Why don't you think about it? There must be lots of things you could aim at improving in a town like this. That's the way to get votes. Associate yourself with one or two good causes.'

'I wouldn't know how to start, would I?' Albert said. For a moment he had seen himself standing in the golf club bar, making the lady Mayor laugh with a few witty jokes.

'Daddy was on Marylebone Council,' Patricia Gort said. 'I helped him a lot at election times. It's just a matter of getting yourself nominated. Find out which wards are short of candidates.'

'What's a ward?' Albert said.

'I see what you mean,' Patricia Gort said. She gave him a short lecture on local government. 'Of course you can't do it in two minutes. You'll have to build yourself up, get yourself noticed. If you've got money it's easy, you can endow hospital beds and park seats and things like that. If you haven't then you must take a voice in local affairs. Join a debating society, a local residents' association, trade groups, make a nuisance of yourself in the paper with letters about this and that –'

'I used to do that,' Albert said, enthusiastically. In some strange way this girl was raising all kinds of ghosts of the old Albert; was showing him how to be what he had already

523

been. 'I got half the population chucking stones through the town hall window once,' he said. 'That was to sell trading stamps, though.'

'This is a much worthier cause,' Patricia Gort said. 'You might do some real good in the town.'

'What, like burn it down?'

'If you like – there's nothing wrong with anarchism as long as it's intelligently harnessed. Look at Russia.'

'I'll start a salt mine and put the tractor factory out of business, eh?'

'Be serious, Albert. We've got this nice office. All we want is a few ideas. Imaginative ones.'

'To start with, how to get another office,' Albert said. 'Then how to live five years while I create my brand image.'

Patricia Gort was hardly listening to him. 'For instance – yes, this is a good idea – you could give away those cottages.'

'Give them away?' Albert said.

'Give them away,' the girl said, firmly. 'What are they worth to you? Nothing. But nobody knows that yet. Give them away before anybody finds out. It looks like a magnificent gesture. Put you on the front page straight away.'

'Put me in the nut house,' Albert said. 'Give away two houses? Who to?'

'Anybody,' she said, impatiently. 'What does it matter? Find somebody who wants one badly – a couple of hard-up families, young people getting married. That would capture a lot of sympathy. Just imagine –'

'Hold it!' Albert exclaimed. He started snapping his fingers. He got up from the desk and began pacing the room, snapping his fingers.

'What is it?'

'No, keep quiet,' he said. He snapped his fingers some more, walked to and fro. 'This is an event, this is! You'll never believe it – I've got an idea!'

'What is it?'

'Never mind what it is – I've got one! I've got an idea!' He began to knock his forehead with his knuckles. 'Christ –

it's a strange feeling. I haven't had an idea in years. Have to look after it. What's the time? Never mind. Give me a bit of paper.'

He sat down but this time in a sprung and poised and ready-to-go position, started scribbling on a square of paper.

'My photograph in the middle – there!' he said, roughing out a visual. 'Right across the top – win a house of your own for five shillings!' He looked up at her, triumphantly. 'How about that? I'll raffle them! Twenty thousand tickets at five bob each – five thousand quid plus all the publicity!'

'You can't do that!' Patricia Gort told him.

'Of course I can do it!'

'It's illegal!' she exclaimed. 'Surely you know that? It comes under the lottery act.'

'Don't be daft,' Albert said. 'I've raffled things before. I'd like as many Sunday dinners. Vacuum cleaners, washing machines, refrigerators – used to double the profit sometimes. Only way I could balance my books.'

'That was done privately amongst people you knew,' Patricia Gort told him. 'A public raffle on this scale has to be in aid of some club or charity or something. You'd have to find out about it.'

'I'll find a way,' Albert promised.

'Besides, that's no way to conduct a business. It's cheapjack. You'd get laughed out of town – it's exactly what you don't want. Give it to a charity if you like and let them raffle it. It's status and publicity you want Albert, not money.'

'I'll get both,' Albert said. 'You leave it to me. I don't know why I haven't thought about this before.'

'No, I don't know why you haven't,' Patricia Gort said, sadly. 'Estate agent raffling houses with five-shilling tickets. It's just about your level of business, Albert.'

'Nobody else has ever thought of it, that's why,' Albert told her, confidently. 'Everybody wants to win a house. It's imaginative. It'll get enough to buy two more houses and do it again. People like a gamble. Look at your football pools. That's the dream, you see. You get stuck in a factory or an office or shop and see if you're not looking for a dream – it's all they've got to live for.'

'And two tumble-down cottages in Bute Place, both condemned, is a dream?' she asked.

'I won't mention them,' Albert said. 'Desirable property, that's the line. Perhaps get a picture of a period cottage on the downs. What? You could sell twenty thousand tickets a week. Keep quiet about this.'

'I wouldn't dream of mentioning it,' Patricia Gort told him, fervently. 'I might get roped in for complicity.'

'You just stand back and watch,' Albert told her. 'How to make friends and influence people.' He clicked his fingers again. 'Think of the name of a good charity. . . .'

Patricia Gort closed her eyes and uttered a small prayer for him.

What Albert was inclined to forget was that not everybody stayed still. Some people, like Jackson, went down, some people, like Jack Moore, went up.

'You've got a nice place here, Jack.'

'Glad you like it.'

'Better than the old Church Hall, eh?'

And some people preferred not to be reminded of humble beginnings.

'Is there something I can do for you, then?' Jack Moore said. 'I'm afraid I've only got a moment.'

'That's lucky,' Albert said, 'so have I.'

'Just a moment, Mr Argyle – Harris – Albert.' Jack Moore pressed a button on a comprehensive inter-com panel on his desk. 'Miss Palmer – if Top Rank come through tell them I'll be over there at quarter-to-five. In person.'

'Yes, Mr Moore,' came the filtered voice.

'And take this down if you would be so good.' He pressed another button putting the forthcoming interview on to magnetic tape. Unknown to Albert.

'I've got a big deal on,' Albert said.

'Ah,' said Jack Moore.

'Get the old presses turning over again like I used to,'

Albert said. 'Keep you stripped to the waist. I'm talking about a three-colour job, twenty thousand off – and that's only a start.'

'Before we go on,' Jack Moore told him, 'there is an outstanding account, you know. I haven't pressed you. I know how things have been.'

'I'll take care of it,' Albert said. He took out cheque book and ball-point. 'You should've said.' Now he remembered why he had changed his printer.

'Miss Palmer,' Jack Moore said to the inter-com, 'will you give me the outstanding total on Mr Argyle's account – you'll find it in the old ledger. ...'

Jack Moore had printed visiting cards, handbills and splurges for Albert during his most imaginative period. On this same site in the old disused Church Hall, long before this skyscraper of printing works and offices had arisen out of the debris of side-streets like an enormous pile of filing trays, Jack Moore had followed Albert's hopes and dreams and ambitions with blind faith on a hand-turned printing press.

'And what about this new commercial radio station they've just opened?' Jack Moore was saying while they waited for the details of Albert's account. 'Have you got anything to do with that? I remember you were talking of starting one – I did the announcements when you were looking for shareholders.'

'No, I turned that in,' Albert said.

'Well, you were doing rather well with your cabaret work at the time, I remember.'

'Eh?' Albert said.

'Do you know, I never did manage to hear that television programme you organized. You remember you mentioned it on those washing-machine handouts?'

'That's right,' Albert said. 'I remember.'

'You certainly knew how to keep your name to the front in those days,' Jack Moore said. 'Some of the best direct-mail printing I ever handled.'

'Thanks,' Albert said.

'Expensive, though,' Jack Moore said. And then: 'Yes, Miss Palmer?'

Albert had grown increasingly apprehensive with this brief recap on the expensive glories of the past.

'Two hundred and forty-three pounds I make it, Mr Moore – could that be right?'

'Oh yes. Thank you, Miss Palmer.'

Albert laughed; an empty sound in the box-like office. 'Bit of old bomb damage there, eh?'

'You don't have to clear it all at once, Albert – though I'd prefer to close that account before opening another. It's not me, personally – it's the bank, my directors. You know.'

'Yes, of course,' Albert said. 'I insist on the same thing. Well, you've got to.' And after a miserable analysis of the state of his bank account and what such a sum would do to vitiate the two hundred and fifty from Corby, he started writing a cheque. 'Two hundred and forty-three – there we are.' In the end you had to pay for everything; even your old dreams which had come to nothing.

'I shall want priority on this new stuff,' Albert said.

'I think we can manage that, Albert.' The tone was distinctly friendlier now. 'What exactly do you want?'

'Raffle tickets,' Albert said. 'Super-duper ones. I'm raffling a couple of houses.'

'Houses?' Jack Moore said, blankly. He was now short-sighted, stooped and fifty; things like Albert were harder to take.

'Well, it's a lark,' Albert said. 'Somebody's got to do something for the Widows and Orphans.'

'It's for the Widows and Orphans?' Jack Moore said.

'Well, that's my story,' Albert said. 'We'll stick some charity down or other. Do it in little print with your name, eh?'

Jack Moore thought about this for a moment, then said, directing his voice towards the microphone: 'I must get this perfectly clear, Mr Argyle – Albert; this raffle is for a bona-fide purpose? A charity? Because if it's not it makes both you and my firm liable for swindle and fraud.'

Albert laughed his disdain. 'Oh, my goodness – I wouldn't let you in for anything like that. Oh no – this is for the local scouts. You know – Cedric Mason's lot. We're trying to get them a new assembly hall. Gymnasium, roller-skating rink, and the lot – real youth community centre.'

Jack Moore stared at Albert in some surprise. 'I didn't know anything about that?'

Albert smiled. 'Well your scouting days are over, Jack – so are mine, come to that. Except for the odd bit of wood-craft, eh?' Albert could see that his old friend no longer laughed at the same things. Will success spoil J. K. Moore, he thought.

'I wonder my boy hasn't mentioned it,' Jack Moore said. 'He's in that troop.'

'Oh, is he?' Albert said. Funny how people he thought he'd known all his life suddenly had wives and families.

'We could have done something long ago,' Jack Moore said. 'The Mayor's son – Christopher – he's in the same troop.'

'We haven't told them anything about it yet,' Albert said. 'Don't want to raise their hopes till we've raised the money.'

'I see. Any idea about the site?'

'What site? Oh, the new building? Well, yes – keep it under your hat, of course. You know I'm in the property business these days?'

'I'd heard you were,' Jack Moore said. It sounded like an admission which he'd rather not discuss further.

'I've got my eye on Carter's garage. Make a lovely con-version, that would – it's got the floor space, the frontage, cantilever roof with double-insulated treadpiles all acoustic-ally drained for air conditioning outside – a cinch for con-version, that place.'

'I thought all of Butterhall Street was scheduled by the ministry?'

Albert laughed. 'By who? You know who does the schedul-ing in this town? There's going to be a few changes round here. No more of the local villains lining their pockets at the expense of the community.'

'You shouldn't say that.'

'Ah, come off it, Jack, you know it's true. This bloody town's being run at a profit and who's paying? You and me. I've been rooked, I know. I tell you who's got it buttoned up – Councillor Corby, Councillor Major Simpkins, Corn-bloody-Wallis and his wife in welfare – I tell you they've even got the incurables doing slave labour but never mind that –'

'Oh, come now,' Jack Moore said.

But Albert had at last – disastrously as it so happened but never mind that – got into his stride.

'If you want the centre of government in this town don't look in the Council Chamber, Jack, look in the bloody golf club on a Sunday morning. That's where you'll find the power maniacs and the confidence tricksters and the crooks warming their bloody arses deciding what's good for the community.'

Jack Moore bristled a little and fell silent.

'I'm going to stop all that, Jack.'

Every time Albert said 'Jack' Jack Moore hated him a little more. J. K. Moore Ltd, was no longer the 'Jack' kind of firm. Jack was the past. Jack was the average man, the man in the street, the man who suffered, the man who couldn't do anything about anything.

Albert said, confidentially: 'They've asked me to stand as a candidate at the next election.'

'Parliament?' Jack Moore said, accustomed to the size of Albert's dreams.

'The council first,' Albert said, having collected another idea. 'The public has seen the red light. They want people like us, Jack, and not before time. You know this is a scheduled town, a city of the future, one of the new capitals of the country. A million population, that's what's coming here, Jack. They'll all want houses – bigger population, bigger profits for the villains.'

'The government are introducing legislation to stop profiteering in scheduled areas,' Jack Moore said. 'We've just printed a pamphlet about it.'

530

'That's eyewash and pig's piddle,' Albert said, dipping into Patricia Gort's lecture on local government but avoiding her language. 'What about the unscheduled areas? The fringe areas? The outlying districts? That bloody green belt's going to take a belting. Look what we've got left over from the thirties – ribbon developments, roundabout towns, shanty villages on the by-pass. It'll be the same thing only worse.'

Albert's parrot aptitude for a sales spiel learned from people like Cally Callendar and Solly Cowell now mingled with the social consciences of the people like Cedric Mason who had tried to save him and produced something fiery and splendid which he could even now, as he spoke to Jack Moore in his printing office, see himself delivering to screams of approbation and applause on some electioneering platform.

'Ribbon development?' Albert said. 'We haven't seen it in this country yet – you go stateside and see what they've got.' Albert's familiarity with the social problems, with Tammany Hall graft, with everything American, had come from people like Albert who had been selling the United States to the world for years. 'Ribbon Development?' Albert said again. 'In ten years time a map of this urban district will look like a bloody maypole. This country's going to be all one urban district, Jack. And I'm a man that loves the urban district. Fresh air makes me feel faint. My native air comes out of the gasworks and out of the tractor factory chimneys. But I do like a day out sometimes – everybody does – and where are they going to go? Kinsley Woods? They won't be there. That's the first bit of rural district where the local millionaires will stake their claims – ten thousand pound chalet villas with delightful woodland gardens.'

'The ministry would never allow it,' Jack Moore said. And he said: 'Could you give me a few details for this raffle ticket?'

'The ministry my arse,' Albert said. 'The government always delegate the power to the local bigwigs – that means Corby, Simpkins, Cornwallis, three or four solicitors, one or two bank-managers. Well, you know them Jack.'

531

Unknown to Albert, Jack Moore did know them. Personally.

'I could name a score,' Albert said. 'They'll clean up in the town before the new legislation comes through and you know how long that takes – you know their methods, Jack. De-value this street with one-way traffic and no parking, up-value this square with a nice big free car-park for the community, a compulsory purchase order on something they want, a bit of road-widening if they don't like your face. If they do like your face of course you're in. I mean you know who's in charge of personnel at the new town hall – Miss Alcott! She's been supplying them with call girls for years now they've made it official.'

'You shouldn't say things like that, you know,' Jack Moore told him.

'Somebody's got to say them,' Albert said, 'and that's why I'm going to get myself elected. Somebody's got to stop the rot. So I have to give away a couple of houses to start the ball rolling? It'll pay off, don't you worry. They need people like me and you on the council, Jack. Bridge the gap between the rich and the poor. They're always doing things for the good of the community, it's time the poor bloody community did a bit of good for themselves. The rich are getting richer and the poor are getting poorer. There's more millionaires every year, there's more crime every year – work it out for yourself, Jack.'

'I'm afraid I've got to go,' Jack Moore said.

They both stood up.

'I've got a rough here of what I want,' Albert said. He put some papers on the desk.

Jack Moore said: 'I think I know the kind of thing – green Bodoni on gold paper, perhaps?'

'That's a bit flamboyant,' Albert said. 'Let's have black on pale green. I'll let you have a new photograph.'

'I've still got some of your blocks.'

'I've changed a bit since then,' Albert said. Then, in direct contradiction, he added a friendly word: 'Vote for me Jack and I'll see you're all right – give you all the print-

532

ing you can handle once I get on the council. Tell your friends.'

When Albert had gone Jack Moore switched off the tape recorder and picked up the telephone to tell his friends.

That was a good speech, Albert thought. Have to try to get that down on tape. He stood outside the J. K. Moore block and surveyed the busy town. He could see posters everywhere. On buildings, in windows, on windscreens, carried on banners, stuck on public address loud-speaker cars:

VOTE FOR ALBERT ARGYLE AND STOP THE ROT

YOU LIVE IN BOOMTOWN – VOTE FOR ARGYLE

AND GET YOUR FINGER IN

The more he thought about it, the more he imagined it, the more feasible it all became. There were thousands of old customers from his tally-selling days would be ready to give him a vote.

STAKE YOUR CLAIM TO PROSPERITY WITH ALBERT ARGYLE ran a fluorescent orange banner on the top of a double-decker bus. Albert followed it round the corner with his eyes alight.

'Would you excuse us a minute, darling?' Dorothy said when Albert got back to the car.

A strange young man sat behind the wheel in Albert's seat, talking to Dorothy. He was wearing a dirty-white polo-necked sweater and faded jeans, his hair was a mop of greasy black which hung over his eyes.

'Is this your dad?' he said to Dorothy, after giving Albert a disdainful glance. And: 'Oppit a minute, dad,' he said to Albert.

Dorothy laughed. 'Take no notice, Albert, it's his sense of humour. Oh, by the way, this is John – you know, who I told you about who give me that long-player – here,' she broke off to say to John, 'isn't it amazing they got their silver disc – Marge said they would. Jimmy thought they would. You didn't think so, did you? Or weren't you sure?'

'I thought they would but not with that disc,' John said. 'I thought they would with the other one.'

'Marge thought they would with this one. But I didn't.'

Albert stood by his car listening to this for a moment. Was there something other than a youth centre he could aim at providing? The youth of today didn't look worth bothering about now he came to take a good look. Shaggy, dirty, untidy, empty-headed, ambitionless, going round and round with a jumble of gramophone records all sounding alike as though the singers were all sitting on lavatories straining their guts out while somebody twanged the chain.

'You want to come down and listen to the group,' John was saying.

'I'd love to but it's hard to get out,' Dorothy said, 'till we find somebody to baby-sit Aubrey. It's ages since I had a good shake. How's Jimmy getting on with the Trojans?'

'Fabulous, man! Second prize at Watford Town Hall. Recording session next week – they're learning music. Money? They're printing it! Jimmy's got purple hearts with his own initials on 'em. . . .'

'Oh my gawd!' thought Albert. It was a far cry from his own teenage and the Edwardian decorum of the early post-war years.

'Ta ta, then, eh?' John was saying as he relinquished Albert's seat. And as a parting jollity to Dorothy: 'Still getting plenty, are you?' He laughed at Albert as he went: 'You've got a real goer there, man!'

Dorothy put her face down to her knitting as Albert got behind the wheel and stared at her as if he was just getting her into focus.

'That's nice, isn't it?' he said.

'I have no idea what he was talking about,' Dorothy said.

'I have, though,' Albert said. 'Here, give me those bits of paper –' He took a bundle of pieces of paper from her glove compartment, all covered with Dorothy's scribbles. 'Let me do a bit of calculating, eh?'

'What are you insinuating?' Dorothy said.

'When did you say you missed your first period?' Albert

asked, as he scanned the scribbles. 'Let's count back, shall we? I'm not even sure I was with you – ah, you see? One, two – yes, seven weeks, that takes us to –'

'You've got the wrong bit,' Dorothy said. 'They're all out of date – this is the current one.' She gave him a scrap of paper from her pocket. 'There, you see? Beginning of June – we was up in your office nearly every night that week.'

'What about the nights we weren't?'

'What were you doing then I might as well say?'

'That don't improve anything –'

'Albert,' said Police Constable Sid, walking up with a smile of relief. 'Sorry about this.' He took a ticket off the windscreen which Albert had not yet noticed.

'What's the idea of that, then?' Albert said.

'Sorry, mate, it's not me it's the sergeant. This is your fourth obstruction today. I keep telling him you're busy but he made me book you this time –'

'I meant to tell you,' Dorothy said.

'Hello Dorothy,' P.C. Sid said, as to an old friend. 'Do you know you left your bra on the "No Waiting" sign in the High Street? I've given it to Hetty.'

'Ta,' Dorothy said. Then she added: 'Was it dry?'

'Just right for ironing,' the policeman said. He looked at Albert: 'Have to see your licence, Albert.'

'You know I haven't got a bloody licence.'

'Try and get one, Albert – they're tightening up now. All new people. What about your tax? I see that's last year's –' he frowned '– I don't remember you getting one last year? Anyway, you'll have to renew it now – how's the insurance or shouldn't I ask?'

'I'll call in the station,' Albert said.

'Don't forget, will you, or you'll get me into trouble. They're bringing in chaps from the London area – nosey lot of so-and-so's. The force isn't what it was, Albert. Get everything straight and I'll fix the date to make it right – okay?'

'Okay mate,' Albert said. 'Ta ta, Sid.'

'Ta ta, Albert. Getting plenty, are you?'

Albert waved his acknowledgment as he drove away. Dorothy was looking at him, accusingly.

'Dirty old lot,' Albert said.

Dorothy said, understandingly: 'The trouble is people don't know when you've settled down. Not unless you put an engagement notice in the paper.' And a moment later she said: 'Albert. Would you mind if I wore this ring on my third finger?'

'Which ring?'

Dorothy had taken a ring from one of her fingers. 'This one. Haven't you noticed it before? You're not very observant. It's an engagement ring, really. Jimmy give it to me. We were only engaged for two days – that was when he took me to the jazz festival at Beaulieu. Well anyway, if I could just wear it on my third finger again? I feel awkward when we have visitors – with all those blankets and things in the back room. On the back seat.'

'That's why they keep asking us if we're getting plenty,' Albert said. 'Doesn't look very nice, does it?'

'I've been thinking about that room,' Dorothy said.

'I've been thinking about a divorce,' Albert said.

Dorothy looked at him, happily: 'Honestly? From Alice?'

'No, from you,' Albert told her. 'I'm going into local politics. Got my name to think about.'

'What about mine!'

'We all know what sort of name you've got, don't we?'

'You can drop me here,' Dorothy said, in a tight voice.

'What?'

'Here. Outside the Town Hall – with the dog and all my luggage. I've had enough insults. Stop the car.'

'Whenever you want to be dropped it's somewhere where I can't. I'm taking you home tonight.'

'All right, then.'

'I suppose you'll kill yourself and get me a lot of bad publicity?'

'One thing, I wouldn't pretend to just to make you love me, like she did. Isn't that true?'

536

'Shut up,' Albert explained.

The status quo was restored between them; the dog started scratching again. Going past the Post Office Dorothy said:

'Don't forget your tax. We don't want to get turned out.'

The first thing he would do when he got on the council was give Dorothy a council house and forget where it was.

'Anyway,' she said, later, as they arrived back outside the pet shop, 'he was talking about the car.'

'Who was talking about what car?'

'When he said – you know, that. He meant the car. He'd already mentioned it. He meant the car was a good goer.'

Albert had just stopped the car. Now he stared at her like a deadpan god.

'Well he did, didn't he?'

Until that moment Albert had not thought he meant anything else but the car.

'They always call them good goers. Well, don't keep staring at me like that. Of course he did.'

'By their own utterances shall ye know them,' Albert said.

'What?'

'When Jesus saw the city he wept,' Albert said, getting out.

'Well, he did,' Dorothy said. 'Anyway. Didn't he, Aubrey?' she said to the dog. 'Of course he did. Ask Sir Justin. Ask Sir Gustard. Ask the serf and Saviour the gypsy. Ask anybody. It's a well-known saying, good goer. It's only your dirty mind. I know what he meant if you don't. Can I have my calculations back, please? If you don't mind. I haven't forgotten your insinuation. You'll be sorry one day.'

She had been talking to herself for quite some time for Albert was already in his office.

'Well, at least we've had someone to talk to,' she said then.

Quite often now Albert would use the car as if there was nobody else in it; coming out, driving, parking, leaving it without a word. Not in anger but in forgetfulness. They had settled down to their separate lives in the car and only occasionally noticed each other. For Albert the car was something to get about in; for Dorothy it was home and the garage a sort of convenient backyard or annexe. They got used to each other to the point of being almost oblivious of each other; in those few desperate days before Albert's death there were occasions when Dorothy would chat to passing friends and old neighbours, wherever she happened to have been left parked; occasions when she saw her father driving a bus and waved to him and got a cheery wave back – people so took it for granted that other people were living a normal life; occasions when Albert picked up old girl-friends and gave them a lift, chatting them up, with Dorothy getting on with her knitting or doing a 'Crozzle' or talking to her courtiers on the back seat and politely ignoring what was going on next door in the front seat.

'Can I come in the front now?' she would say.

'Eh?' Albert would turn and see her, glad sometimes that she was still around for habits became increasingly necessary to the chronically insecure. 'Sure, come in.' And when she was settled again and he was driving: 'How you getting on, then?'

'All right, thank you,' she would say. 'Aren't we, Aubrey?'

'That's good,' Albert would say.

She made less and less demands on him. She had made the most of the facilities he had put at her disposal; she had learned the habits of the household, when she could nip in and use the kitchen or the bathroom; she had got used to Albert's usual parking places and got to know the environs; she knew every lavatory and powder room in the town like a connoisseur. She had soup, tea, coffee all organized in vacuum flasks with a separate larder for the dog.

'I'm your car-wife,' she would sometimes tell Albert.

This would be when he brought a drink out to her and they sat smoking and drinking in a public house car-park. Then they would laugh at the situation and appreciate it. But there was death in their laughter and this they could not understand.

Dorothy cried the first time she saw her father wave from

the bus and drive on. Albert had all the time a madness in his brain and a panic in his heart and a yearning for the way back to the old life, the old people. Unknown to both of them they had slipped into the limbo which threatens to engulf all habitual car drivers and car users who drive and drive, who watch the cat's eyes long after they are asleep, who never get home, who, claustrophobically trapped at another red light, put their heads out of the window to breathe, who race on and on past strange faces, strange places, their only eternity another traffic jam.

'I wish somebody would steal this bloody car,' Albert told her once.

'Don't say that!' Dorothy said. She had forgotten what else there was.

Albert sometimes thought that he would like one great big crash with everything stopped and he waking up in some quiet hospital ward and other people taking charge. He wanted to cut off all complications, all responsibilities but through no fault of his own so that people would go on liking him. He wanted to get back to Alice and he wanted to be somebody again.

'Drink this,' Patricia Gort said.

'What is it?'

'Hot, sweet tea.'

'I feel better now,' Albert said. He didn't look better. He was lying on the couch, propped up on one elbow, sipping the tea from a cup she was holding to his mouth. 'What did she say?'

'I told you. She wanted to talk to you.'

'What was the chap like?'

'Quite nice. Middle-aged. Intelligent type.'

'Horace Fenton,' Albert said. 'The author.'

'Oh dear,' Patricia Gort said. 'I think they both had something to say. They seemed nervous but sort of decided – as if they'd come to a decision. Screwed up their courage. They wanted to say something important, I'm sure.'

'They've been having it off,' Albert said, bitterly.

Patricia Gort said: 'I can only guess what that means and I think you're being rather revolting.'

'What about them?' Albert said. 'What about our marriage? Marriage is supposed to be sacred. How would you like your wife sleeping around with other men? Nice, isn't it? What does that make me?'

'That's all you care about – what it makes you. When you're on the sleeping end you don't care about marriage. Don't be such an awful hypocrite, Albert. Anyway I don't think they'd do anything like that. I think they want to discuss it with you. Alice probably wants a divorce and then wants to get married, properly.'

'She is married bloody properly,' Albert said. 'That's just the bloody point. She don't know how well off she is. She's the first one I ever actually married – now look at her. Get the library on the 'phone and see if she's there.'

Patricia Gort dialled the number.

'Ask for Mrs Harris – or Miss Harris. I don't know what she calls herself.'

He went on sipping his tea, filled with self-pity to the point of tears. 'And there's me trying to make a position for us in the town. Flogging my guts out for her. I sunk two hundred and fifty quid in this new house deal just now – I've got it all set up. I've already got half the town to support me in the elections. You ought to hear the speech I made this afternoon.'

'She's not there, Albert,' Patricia Gort said, replacing the receiver. 'She hasn't been in all day. She telephoned them to give in her notice – she's left.'

'The cow!'

'She's not a cow, Albert. She's had a lot to put up with. I think she's terribly nice. I must say I was surprised. Not your type at all, Albert. Quiet, shy, intelligent, bright, very old-fashioned word, but she is. A sensitive, perceptive girl.'

'You're getting me interested,' Albert said.

'Frankly, Albert – I know we haven't got as far that – but when it came to prescribing a wife for you, Alice is exactly what I would have suggested. Not for her good, mind you, but for yours. Somebody sensitive, the antithesis of your own rather roughshod personality. Of course she would have needed an extra dimension to withstand you – a sort of spiritual reinforcement. She would have to be not too much in love with you so that you couldn't hurt her too much. She would have to be objective about you as I am.'

'Are you proposing to me?' Albert asked. 'I hope not. Not another.'

'If I felt like that,' Patricia Gort told him, 'it would already be too late for you to do anything about it. You're a sitting duck for the average female.'

Albert said: 'Where've I heard that before?'

He had heard it from Elaine Townend years ago when he was helping her to fight the trading-stamp war. 'One day you'll meet somebody like me and your life will be ruined,' she had told him.

'Now I'll tell you what to do,' Patricia Gort said, as though she had finished a long and complicated diagnosis and now had the complete cure: 'If you do anything else, if you deviate by the merest fraction or hang fire by a second – then I've finished with you. For good. I mean that.'

Only now that she stated it did Albert realize that he had become dependent upon her. Dependent upon everybody.

'You'll find Alice and get her back at all costs,' Patricia Gort told him. 'You'll go on your knees if necessary and ask her forgiveness.'

'Forgiveness for what?'

'If you have to ask that then I'm wasting my time. Forgiveness for being you, you clot. Before you do that you'll chuck that girl out of your car, throw me out of this office, tell that driving pupil of yours to go climb a pole, never see Treasure again and tell her why in a nice firm letter, move away from that awful mother-in-law, get yourself a job selling cars or something, get rid of all these brass plates and visiting cards and big deals –' She tried to think of something she might have missed.

'Not get on the council?' Albert said, helpfully.

'Not do anything except work and be a good husband and

father and forsake all others – and do it now. If it's not too late.'

'Give us another drop of tea,' Albert said.

As he drank it he summoned all his reserves, fought all his weaknesses, overcame his indecisions, started a new life. He stood up.

'All right,' he said. 'Shake.'

Patricia Gort shook hands with him.

'Now pack your bags and get out,' Albert told her.

Patricia Gort immediately began to pack her bags.

Albert said: 'You and Brooke Bonds together make a wonderful pair.'

He took a screwdriver from his desk drawer which was filled with brass plates he had not even used, went briskly out of the office and down the stairs.

'Hetty!' he called at the doorway, as he went to work wrenching off his name plates.

Hetty came out holding a hamster in each hand.

'We're shutting up shop, love,' Albert told her over his shoulder as he worked.

'It's only half-past four – I haven't got them to bed yet.'

'I mean for good. Get rid of all the livestock.' And only now did Albert realize that all those animals and birds and reptiles lay in his sub-conscious like helpless, dependent relatives, helping to root him and tie him down. 'Give 'em away, drown 'em – I don't care how you do it.'

'Oh Albert! You couldn't be so cruel – I know them like my own family,' Hetty told him, fretfully.

'Take 'em home, then,' Albert said. 'Whatever's in the kitty we'll share fifty-fifty – okay?' He took off another brass plate and called across to the car: 'Dorothy! Get out of that car.'

'Do what?' Dorothy said.

'Get all your stuff out – and the dog,' Albert called.

Patricia Gort was looking down from the window above with satisfaction.

'Now, I mean,' Albert said.

542

He returned to removing the brass plates from his door-post.

Dorothy got out of the car and watched him. Hetty was watching him as well. Patricia Gort was still looking down from the window. Seeing this group with a centre of interest several people stopped in the busy High Street and watched Albert removing his various name plates.

'What are you doing?' Dorothy asked. 'What's he doing?' she said to Hetty, who shrugged her shoulders expressively and looked to heaven. 'Init hot?' Dorothy said.

A scout master with a dozen boy scouts came trotting along the High Street, two of them carrying sacks of torn-up newspaper. It was an old-fashioned sight, like seeing a hurdy-gurdy man; the scouts didn't seem to go with the new building developments; the principle of scouting seemed out of place in the changing town.

'Honour thy mother and thy father,' Albert said, when he looked up and saw them. 'Be Prepared.'

'That's right, Albert,' the scoutmaster said, stopping by for a moment. It was Cedric Mason again.

Albert said, giving the salute: 'I promise to do my best to do my duty for God and King –'

'Queen now, Albert.'

'God and Queen,' Albert said, 'to help other people at all times and to obey the Scout Law.'

'Has he been drinking?' Dorothy asked Hetty.

'That's it, Albert – good man,' Cedric said.

'Be prepared,' Albert said. Then, looking at the impatiently waiting boys: 'Which is the Mayor's son?' A boy put up his hand and Albert knocked his beret off: 'Christopher,' he said, 'give your mother the Mayor my love and tell her yes – anytime!'

'Yes, sir,' said the Mayor's son.

'What's all this then?' Cedric asked him, looking down at the brass plates with the countersunk holes in the corners where the screws had come out. 'Are you moving?'

'I'm going out of business,' Albert said. 'I can't compete any more. I'm getting rid of everything. I'm getting rid of everything, Cedric. I've got two cottages for your scouts – they're not worth much, but you can get what you can on them to help the funds.' He called up to Patricia Gort, suddenly: 'Miss Gort – see the deeds on those condemned cottages in Bute Place get transferred to the Fifth Holy Trinity Scout Troop.'

Cedric beamed at him: 'That's very nice of you, Albert!'

'Well, it's time I did something nice for you, Cedric,' Albert said. 'I was going to do a fiddle but I thought better of it.'

Hetty whispered to Dorothy, reassuringly: 'It won't last.'

'Well this *is* nice,' Cedric Mason said. 'We could have that summer camp after all.'

'That's right,' Albert said. 'You have your camp while there's still a bit of countryside left, Cedric. By the way,' he added, looking towards Hetty and the window full of pets, 'would your boys like any animals – they're going free, hamsters, rats, rabbits, mice, puppies, kittens, birds of all nations.'

The boy scouts made a concerted excited movement towards the shop, exclaiming with pleasure – Cedric put his scout staff out as a barrier, then smiled at Albert.

'They'd love them I'm sure – but not at the moment, we've got a paper chase on. Out to Kinsley Woods and back in time for a bonfire.' Then, looking at the over-stocked shop and the distraught expression on Hetty's face, his smile for Albert wavered. 'Are you quite sure about this, Albert? It's too generous, it really is. What are you going to do? I mean, what are your plans? Is everything all right? Your wife liked the flowers, did she?' He was groping for some possible catastrophe that might help to explain things.

'I'm taking a job,' Albert said. 'I'm going to be one of the yobs. A wage slave.'

'Have you got anything in mind, Albert? Keep in line, boys, run on the spot! You have to give them something to do,' he explained. 'What sort of job? I suppose you wouldn't be interested in teaching? I could get you into my school and very glad to have you – I know you're good with youngsters,'

Cedric said, casting a friendly glance at Dorothy as if for example. 'A three-year training course – possibly only two years, Albert, and you could get in. Paid while you're trained of course – I'll be happy to recommend you.'

'I think I'd like that,' Albert said. 'Finish up headmaster with me name on the door, eh?'

'Well you never know, Albert. I've been on at you before, haven't I? It's a useful job. Something worthwhile. Perhaps your wife might be interested too – you could do the course together. There's plenty of room for two good teachers at Butterhall Secondary Modern – though of course we shall be going comprehensive under the new scheme. Come round and talk about it, Albert. All right, boys – forward!' Then he said: 'Halt! Three cheers for Mr Argyle! Three cheers for Albert! Hip-pip –'

'Hooray!' chorused the boys, their eyes on the pet shop.

Albert stood on the pavement with a brass plate in his hand, his face red, his smile embarrassed, his public suddenly unimportant.

'Now what?' Dorothy said.

She stood there with the dog in her arms, all her belongings around her on the pavement; the original cases, the record player and radio, piles of wool and knitting, an incredible assortment of bits and pieces in carrier bags and newspaper parcels and heaps of half-aired clothes, flasks of half-cold tea and soup, scraps of sandwiches and partly-eaten fruit.

Albert looked at her, helpless to assist her with his own hands full of brass plates, the screwdriver and dozens of rusty screws.

'Start bringing it upstairs, love,' he said, softening towards her again, feeling a bit of a hero with the unaccustomed cheers still sounding in his memory. 'Hetty,' he called. 'Give us a hand here.'

Patricia Gort, her bags already packed and standing by the door, now sat efficiently writing at the desk when Albert, Dorothy and Hetty cluttered in with the load of old junk.

'Are you moving out or moving in?' Patricia Gort asked Albert, accusingly. 'I hope you're not backsliding?'

'I might have known it was you,' Dorothy said. 'She's the one you want to get rid of. She's running your life, she is,' she told Albert. 'You're blind, you are.'

'Sign this,' Patricia Gort said, pushing the paper across to Albert. 'It's the transfer of those cottages to the scouts – if you don't make it irrevocable you'll change your mind and then your name won't be worth twopence in this town.'

Albert took out a pen. 'Didn't you hear them cheering me? I wouldn't let them down now, would I?'

'Yes,' Patricia Gort said. She waited for him to sign, then took back the paper and folded it twice, slipped it into a prepared envelope. 'Now go and find Alice,' she said. 'Quickly!'

'Eh?' Albert stared at her. Something she'd said had clicked with something somebody else had said and something somebody else had done and he was trying to fit the pieces together.

'Go and find Alice before it's too late,' Patricia Gort told him. 'Tell her what you've done. Tell her everything's going to be different. Tell her about the teaching job – it would be the best thing in the world.'

Hetty cackled with laughter. 'Oh, my goodness – Albert a teacher? With all them young nubile girls? They'd never allow it – everybody knows Albert, don't they, Albert? And why not? One of the only bright sparks left in this place. He'll never change! You'll never change, will you, Albert?' She said it with a hint of desperation as if she badly needed the confirmation that at least something would stay the same.

'Go on, Albert,' Patricia Gort said.

'Why don't you leave him alone?' Dorothy said.

Hetty said: 'Have a lay down, Albert. You look whacked out.'

Albert, still heavy with worry, preoccupied with a growing fear, had taken a wad of papers from his inside pocket. 'What suit was I wearing on Sunday?' he asked them.

'That one,' Dorothy said.

Albert was sifting through the papers; bills, letters, a fold of various headed notepaper which had kept step with the brass plates and had seldom ever been used, visiting cards which had never been left, business reply-paid envelopes never needed; all the excuses for getting his name into print.

'What is it?' Patricia Gort said. 'What's the matter?'

He couldn't tell her. He couldn't tell anybody.

'I got to go out,' he said. 'Urgent. Be about half-hour or so.'

'What about Alice? You may be too late,' Patricia Gort told him. 'Surely it will wait, Albert? Nothing is more important than Alice.' Albert was already going and she said: 'I warn you – I shan't be here when you get back.'

'Thank gawd for small mercies,' Dorothy said, thankfully.

'You don't know Albert,' Hetty told them, in a superior way. 'He's got an idea, that's all. He always goes off like that when he's got an idea. Like a bloody rocket, Mr Jackson used to say.'

Outside in the High Street the car blasted into life and the three women went to the window to look down.

'We'll have to get that silencer fixed,' Dorothy said.

'Mind the paintwork on the window-sill,' Patricia Gort warned them.

Down in the street Marjorie Mason had arrived waving her 'L' plates, just too late to stop Albert from taking off. Albert belonged to each of the women, exclusively, in their own departments of his life.

The telephone rang and Patricia Gort picked it up.

'Mr Argyle is out on urgent business,' she said, as a matter of habit. 'Who? Mrs Bluett?'

'Tell him Treasure called. Tell him I must see him to-night.'

'Well you jolly well can't!' Patricia Gort said.

'Dear Mummy,' she composed, 'I have decided to give up my academic career and get married instead.'

Albert drove at full belt out to Kinsley Woods, passing

Cedric and the scouts on the way. They stood on the grass verge and waved.

'Hip, hip, hooray!' came their voices in the slip-stream from the sun-roof.

'Bloody little creeps,' Albert thought, keeping his foot hard down on the accelerator. Paper chase! They would pick Kinsley Woods. He had to get there before they did, he had to find what he had to find before they did. If his name wasn't going to be the number-one laugh in the town for the next three generations. Just when he was trying to establish the new academic/politico image of Albert Argyle.

He drove through the woods, parked where he had parked on Sunday, cut his engine, got out and sniffed the warm summer-evening breeze, took his cue from it, followed a track into the bracken where the rhododendrons grew thickest, minding where he was treading.

'The things I have to do,' Albert muttered as he searched.

It was true. This was not untypical. Side-issues had always distracted him from the main event. In the long undrama of his life filled with anti-heroes and anti-heroines and anti-climaxes, this final anti-crisis – unknown to Albert it was final – dropped into place at exactly the optimum moment with unerring accuracy finding him, just when his marriage and his business were disintegrating, searching in the woods for something he didn't want to tread in. Somewhere in the grass amongst the shrubbery where the fox would soon be dropping bits of paper and the hounds picking them up were sheets of cream-laid quarto emblazoned with 'Albert Argyle Enterprises' in gold Bodoni complete with the address stuck on a pile of what Charles had done on Sunday.

'It wouldn't be so bad if it was mine,' Albert grumbled.

Unknown to Albert there was a kind of poetic justice here, a reversal of everything he had done to other people, a monument and a memorial, given a dry Autumn, which was richly appropriate.

'You look for it, you can't find it. You don't look for it and you're in it up to your arm-holes,' Albert philosophized as he probed amongst the bracken.

The sound of the first gunshots through the quiet woods did not register with Albert who now had reason to believe that he was getting warm. Having walked cautiously that way he saw what he was looking for just when another and louder gunshot sent pellets rattling through the branches over his head.

'Christ!' he said, only just remembering that he was a marked man.

He flung himself off the path into the tallest, thickest clump of bracken he could see; a choice, as a matter of sentimental fact, which had also been Treasure's. Another shot which, strangely, sounded more distant and yet felt closer. The blast brought twigs and leaves drifting down on to his hiding place.

Albert crouched as still as a bird in the green forest of fern. He heard footsteps, he heard breathing and muttering, he heard the metallic noises of the gun catches, more shells going in. Terrified, he wanted to shout but couldn't think what to shout. An apology? What for? He didn't know who it was. Perhaps they were wrong. Perhaps Albert was the wrong man. He tried to think of something more likely. There was another loud bang, almost deafening; the sound of the shot blasting through the trees was distant as if the man was firing in the other direction. At least he didn't know exactly where Albert was.

Now Albert could remember being followed out from the town. Three cars were on his tail for a time. It must have been one of those. He couldn't remember if anything had followed him up through the woods. Even if they hadn't it would not have been difficult for somebody to find Albert's parked car. The crash of another shot and Albert cringed down, trying to pull the fronds of bracken to cover his head. The next shot came so close that something stung his ear. He clapped his hand to it, looked at his fingers, fearfully, expecting blood.

Alice was right. He should have reported it to the police. This bod would have been in prison now – or a lunatic asylum.

'Is it to do with your business?' she had asked.

Now all at once Albert thought perhaps it was. Perhaps he had shot off his mouth too much about what was going on in the town. Perhaps somebody was getting frightened. There was big money in these property transactions and perhaps Albert was getting in the way. The thought gave Albert a glow of righteousness. It made things very different. It was right fighting might – he could see it in the headlines:

ALBERT ARGYLE SMASHES PROPERTY RACKETS
LOCAL MAN'S REVELATIONS AFTER SHOOTING
DRAMA

If you can tense a jelly, Albert tensed himself. The situation suddenly had a tang and flavour quite different from his original predicament. He was not hiding abjectly from a jealous husband but pitting his wits against the golf club tycoons. The man with the gun was probably Major Simpkins; although the probability was that they had hired somebody to kill him. No, they wouldn't do that, on third thoughts. It would have to be explained in some unremarkable way. First the bullet through the windscreen. Had it succeeded that would have been another black mark against the high-spirited youth of the town. And if this succeeded Albert could see the alternative headline:

ACCIDENTAL DEATH IN WOODS – GAMEKEEPER'S
MISTAKE IN BAD LIGHT

This thought gave Albert the bones of a clever idea. If there was one thing Albert could do well, it was bird noises. He had driven his mother mad, perfecting them. They did not, unfortunately, include a pheasant, but he had at his fingertips, as he used to tell her, the nightingale, the rook, the owl, Winston Churchill, Bette Davis and Horace Kenny.

'The only difference between him and me,' Albert used to tell his mother when they were watching the television he bought her, 'is that he's on the Palladium and I'm here.' He had taken his name from Argyle Street, the closest he could get to the famous music hall. He was the greatest unrecognized talent in the business.

'Choick, choick, choick, choick!' Albert said now.

The gunman, who had wandered off, now came back to listen.

'It's all impersonations with you,' Treasure had criticized him more than once. Never the real thing, she had meant.

Albert's present impersonations were the most completely successful he had ever attempted. He sat in the bracken and made bird noises for his life. Had the gunman, like the man in Albert's conscience, been looking for Albert he would have gone home. As it was he was looking for birds.

'Tuwee, tuwee, tuwee,' Albert called.

Albert's check suit, shot-silk tie and striped shirt, seen through the bracken in the late red light from the setting sun combined with the bird song (positively identified by three boy scouts) to exonerate the huntsman in the Coroner's court on the following Thursday.

'He must have been drinking,' Mrs Finbow told the court for the second time in her life.

Albert's name, found embroidered on his shirt, vest and polka-dot pants, written indelibly inside his jacket collar and on the waistband of his trousers, printed on paper and cardboard in every pocket he was wearing and stuck to the heel of his shoe, made identification not only possible but unavoidable. This had helped the police considerably for, as the medical evidence showed, one side of Albert's face – what he had called 'the best side' – had been blasted away at short range.

'But what was he doing there?' the Coroner asked.

From the evidence which could not be shown it was deduced that Albert had gone into the bushes and into hiding to answer the call of nature. This ambiguous expression brought a slow, sad, nostalgic smile to the face of Police Constable Sidney Cook who knew beyond any doubt the only thing likely to take Albert into the woods, though nobody had actually come forward.

It took twelve men to fill the vacancies Albert Argyle left behind him when he died. One each for his current girl-friends, one for his wife, five for Mrs Finbow.

On one of those wet, miserable Saturday afternoons which Albert had so hated, the town busy with weddings, football matches, haircuts, a funeral procession of a hearse and two cars stopped outside the Reverend Thoday's church where Albert and Treasure were married to different people at different times.

'Ahbah,' Charles Bluett said.

He was sitting in the rear seat of 'that Mr Granger's' car which happened, at Treasure's contrivance, to be passing at the time.

'Now what's he say?' Mr Granger asked Treasure.

'Albert,' Treasure said. She was looking round at the long box passing through the lych-gate into the churchyard. She thought it seemed bigger than the standard size. 'He was a friend of ours.'

That Mr Granger laid a sympathetic hand on her knee. Treasure didn't mind. If it couldn't be Albert then it didn't matter who it was.

THE TROUBLE WITH HARRY

"Alfred Hitchcock's second favourite of his own films. . .all its humour coming straight from Jack Trevor Story's original novel about a corpse on the heath which villagers keep burying and digging up again for their own reasons" – Leslie Halliwell, *Filmgoer's Companion*

JACK TREVOR STORY

"Scabrous, pitiless, magnificently funny" – *Evening Standard*

"A style of comedy in the line of Fielding and Sterne, unlike anything being written today; it has the insight of early Orwell into the lower reaches of the middle class" – *Guardian*

"One of the funniest writers we have" – *Sunday Telegraph*

"Story is the only novelist I know since the Orwell of *Coming Up for Air* who has written with real force about the fringes of middle class life" – *New Statesman*

"The sureness of fantasy, exactness of writing and casually mortal malice remind one of the early Evelyn Waugh though the social world and the attitude of its inhabitants could hardly be further away from those Waugh knew" – *New Society*

THE WINNERS
Julio Cortázar

The winners of a mystery cruise in a special state lottery could not be more different. And not long after they have left the jubilant dockside café in Buenos Aires the tensions emerge. For, quarantined from a certain part of the ship, served by a silent and forbidding crew, and treated more like prisoners than winners, they split into two groups; those who want to know what's really going on, and those who prefer to let sleeping dogs lie. . . .

With this brilliant and entertaining novel – part surreal thriller, part political fable – the acclaimed Argentinian writer, Julio Cortázar (1916–84), made his international reputation.

"Anyone who doesn't read Cortázar is doomed. Not to read him is a grave invisible disease which in time can have terrible consequences. Something similar to a man who has never tasted peaches. He would quietly become sadder, noticeably paler, and probably, little by little, he would lose his hair" – **Pablo Neruda**

"No less than García Marquéz, Cortázar writes out of a cornucopia of imagery, an outpouring and a richness of language that has become the signature of Latin American fiction" – *New York Times Book Review*

"Cortázar's ability to present common objects from strange perspectives, as if he had just invented them, makes him a writer whose work stimulates a rare sense of expectation" – *Time Magazine*

"One of the century's most gifted writers" – *The New York Review of Books*

THE CARRETA
B. Traven

A twelve-year-old peon named Andrés is sent by his landlord to work in a nearby town where his new master loses him to a haulage contractor in a game of cards. So the boy becomes a carretero, driving the ox-carts which carry trade along the precipitous sierra roads and through bandit-ridden passes.

This is the story, vivid and gripping, of Andrés's broadening experience and of his adventures on the road. It presents an unrivalled picture of Mexico before the eruption of revolution in 1910, when corruption was rife and the peasants were beginning to sense that life could be different if they were prepared to throw off the yoke and fight.

"In the era of the cynically exploitative bestseller it is refreshing to be reminded that genuinely popular fiction and radical politics can go together" – *New Statesman*

"While most writers who deal with the developing countries feel obliged to come up with prolonged descriptions of suffering and tirades against tyranny, Traven uses a mixture of humour and irony that is ultimately more devastating in its effects . . . a funny, sad and deeply compassionate novel" – *The Times Literary Supplement*

THE DISENCHANTED
Budd Schulberg

The Disenchanted is a great American novel which captures both the dazzling spirit and the bitter disappointment of the pre-war decades.

It is the story of Manley Halliday, a fabulously successful writer of the 1920s, a golden figure in a golden age. Halliday had everything – physical beauty, artistic brilliance, success and wealth, and the love of a strikingly beautiful wife. But he squandered his strength and his talent in folly and extravagance, in perpetual parties and perpetual drinking, riding the crest of the golden wave until it crashed, leaving him a diabetic and an alcoholic, cast up on the inhospitable shores of Hollywood.

"*The Disenchanted* is based, not too closely, on what happened to the author of *The Great Gatsby* and *The Last Tycoon* . . . Schulberg has not yet told us about the last days of Scott Fitzgerald as seen from his own youthful angle, and it is doubtful if he ever will need to. The fictional end of Manley Halliday in *The Disenchanted* is too fine a myth to be unscrambled into what is known as historical truth . . . Halliday is a three-dimensional creation who will haunt the imagination of all who have the good fortune to be coming, for the first time, to this remarkable novel" – **Anthony Burgess**

THREE LONDON NOVELS
Colin MacInnes
Absolute Beginners, City of Spades and Mr Love and Justice

"London is the real hero of these books with its capacity to nurture and absorb all species of humanity, from bent coppers to bus conductors, delinquents to debs, bigots to libertines. None of MacInnes' characters, often comically drawn, could have existed elsewhere; and it's London that shapes (and as often as not thwarts) each of their schemes, large and small" – *New Musical Express*

"Insofar that they lift the lid from aspects of London that had hitherto been unobserved or undiscovered, they can stand comparison with Dickens or Zola. . . . Brilliantly written, eminently readable" – *Times Educational Supplement*

"Although written in the late '50s/ early '60s, all three books have quite enough charm and energy to leap the decades unaided by nostalgia" – *Time Out*

"Brilliant social documentation" – *The Times*

"Strongly individual novels" – *Sunday Times*

Colin MacInnes's three London Novels are available as individual volumes or together in *The Colin MacInnes Omnibus*

THE PIER
Rayner Heppenstall

The Pier is the last major novel by "the master eccentric of English letters" – **C. P. Snow**

It is a murder story – unusual and literary – told by an elderly writer who lives in a small English seaside town where his private peace of mind is shattered by the arrival of new and noisy neighbours. As he drafts his latest book and nurses his aching teeth, he begins to formulate the plan for a new novel about someone much like himself who sets out to murder his neighbours. And as the noise mounts next door, and his fantasy plot begins to look better and better, so it becomes more and more appealing to turn his fiction into fact. . . .

Rayner Heppenstall died in 1981. He "made a notable contribution to the history of the modern novel in England" – *The Times*. He "is a writer who has given us so much that is beautiful, so much that is funny, so much that is true" – *Observer*. He "is as inquisitive as Anthony Powell, as odd as Firbank, as minute as Sterne" – *Times Literary Supplement*. He "has an eye so sharp that it dazzles and almost hurts" – *Guardian*.

THE KATHARINE MOORE OMNIBUS

Katharine Moore's first novel, *Summer at the Haven*, was published on her 85th birthday and won the Authors' Club award for the most promising first novel of the year. She followed that remarkable debut with two more novels, *The Lotus House* and *Moving House*. They have earned her an enviable reputation with the critics and have been warmly welcomed by a wide range of readers – and are here collected together in one volume.

SUMMER AT THE HAVEN

"Mrs Gaskell wrote *Cranford* in her early forties. Without in any way imitating that shrewd and gentle minor classic, Katharine Moore has, at the surprising age of 85, published a first novel which can stand comparison" – *The Observer*

THE LOTUS HOUSE

"Poignant writing and perceptive insights into human nature abound in this heartwarming book. Its bittersweet, wholly credible conclusion will haunt readers" – *Los Angeles Times Book Review*

MOVING HOUSE

"*Moving House* presents a lyrical rather than elegiac portrait of English country life throughout the century" – *The Times*